ETHAN PARK

Peter P. Parrie

ETHAN PARK

A Legacy

Ethan Park
Copyright © 2022 Peter P. Parrie
ISBN 978-1-938796-91-3 paperback

Library of Congress Control Number: 2022916898

Clovercroft Publishing

Content Editor: Connie Rinehold
Copy Editor: Fran Lowe
Interior and Cover Designs: Helen Ounjian

Ethan Park, his family, friends, and co-workers are complete figments of the author's imagination. Any resemblance to actual persons, living or dead, is purely coincidental. All references to historical persons, events, or things were researched by the author and any deviation with actual history is due to the needs of the plot or error solely on his part.

Printed in the United States of America

Those who surrender

Before facing dragons

Drape themselves

In a cloak of tragedy

E.P.

Contents

Prologue

*S*ay what you are going to do. Then do it!

The axiom that guided his grandfather's life flowed through Ethan's thoughts like a monk's chant, luring him down a directed path. Ethan expelled a deep breath as he sat at the antique desk, staring at a handcrafted wooden box. He pulled his gaze away and focused on the next to the last item on his To Do list. He'd just checked it off.

The golden letters "WP" glistened brightly on the top of the box, drawing him back to what must be done. The decision had already been made years ago, and only the final step remained. The chant echoed more loudly.

Say what you are going to do. Then do it!

Say what you are going to do. Then do it!

As he extended his hand to grasp the small brass latch on the front of the box, Ethan's focus shifted to the framed picture of his grandfather and grandmother situated on the desktop directly behind the box. It was Ethan's favorite photograph of Grandy, the man who had given him so much, including this box.

He opened the latch and raised the lid. Inside lay Grandy's Colt 1911A, cradled in a bed of royal blue velvet. With trembling hands, Ethan removed the gun from the box, inserted the fully loaded clip, and chambered a round.

Though it had taken years, he had now fulfilled every one of the items on his grandfather's list. Ethan had finally fulfilled every item on his *own* list as well, with the exception of one. The time for that one had arrived. Ethan looked again at the photograph on top of the desk. He fixed his gaze onto his grandfather's eyes. He lifted the gun . . . .

BIRTH

TO

SIX YEARS OLD

E.P.

Chapter 1
ETHAN'S BIRTH

Ethan Park's delivery into this world required skill, persistence, and a bit of serendipity. The skill was on the part of the medical team of Highland Hospital. The persistence was credited to his mother, Constance. And the serendipity, depending upon one's point of view, was that Ethan came into this world sixty years to the day after his paternal grandfather, William Park I.

Ethan's birth had been complicated by eighteen hours of labor with him in a breech position. The Park family men were known to jump into projects, issues, and recreation with their feet first, though no one in the clan could ever recall a Park coming into the world in this manner. Assisted by the talented medical staff, Ethan entered the world more conventionally, with Constance bearing the brunt of the toil. She had been persistent in her desire to wait for Ethan to enter the world on his own terms rather than be taken via scalpel.

Constance's OB-GYN, Dr. Gremillion, said that Ethan and Constance had some work to do prior to Ethan's arrival into the world. The doctor believed this work would best be accomplished without spectators, particularly those with a propensity to queasiness. Constance readily agreed with her doctor.

Never one to be comfortable with hospitals, especially when it involved his family, Bill felt both relief and guilt, believing he should be present in the room during the birth of his second son and readily available to support Constance. The guilt did not outweigh his discomfort with the medical situation, however, so Bill did not throw around his family's substantial monetary weight and insist that he remain by his wife's side.

Margaret felt similar pangs of relief and guilt. Her job, as she saw it, was to support her only son, Bill, through the labor process. This certainly was not as difficult a task as Constance was currently undertaking, but it could run a close second in the difficulty category.

Upon their entry into the family room, Bill realized that the room was conspicuously empty. Bill turned toward Margaret. "Where's Dad?" he asked.

Margaret, already searching for the most comfortable chair in the room, looked at him over her glasses. "Bill, you know your father. He's not one to break tradition. It's Saturday morning. The arrival of Trip's brother is no reason for him to upset his routine!"

"I know, Mom, but this is his grandson that's being born. He might be the second grandson but no less important than Trip. Can't tradition wait? I jumped through hoops to get Ashley to change her schedule so she'd be available to babysit."

"Your dad is *not* going to have Trip's relationship with Ethan begin on a negative note," Margaret reasoned. "You know how much Trip looks forward to his Saturday morning seashell hunts with your father!"

"But—" Bill flinched at his mother's gentle rebuke. She had a point. How did he miss these things?

Margaret continued as if Bill had not started to speak. "Your father called Ashley this morning and canceled. He told her that he would pay her for the entire time that you would have needed her to watch Trip."

"The Maestro could have told me," Bill retorted. "Ashley and I spent quite a bit of time juggling schedules."

Margaret settled into her spot and started the next chapter in her journal—actually, the Park Family Journal, of which she believed herself to be the sole custodian. Margaret had been serious about journaling since fifth grade when Mrs. Abadie insisted each student journal at least three times a week. During high school, Margaret had stepped that up to five days a week. Over the years she accumulated several bookshelves of journals chronicling her life from fifth grade through high school and college, as well as dating William Park, experiencing the early years of their marriage, and sharing in the growth of their family. As far as Margaret was concerned, every significant event and accomplishment of the Park family was contained in these journals.

Bill noticed his mother's pen and notebook. "Mom, Ethan's not even here yet. Can't it wait?" he asked, knowing he was being unreasonable but too annoyed and frustrated to do anything about it. Margaret, ignoring her son, uncapped her golden fountain pen and began writing.

✳ ✳ ✳ ✳

Trip Park (aka William Park III) wrapped his three-year-old hands around the exposed top of the conch shell and pulled with all his might, but the shell wouldn't budge. Trip stood up and kicked the shell as hard as he could. Again, the shell didn't budge. Trip searched for and found a stick. He tried to pry the shell from the packed beach sand. The shell still didn't budge.

William Park watched with amusement and pride as his grandson struggled to get the beach to release its prize. William liked the creativity that his grandson was displaying at such an early age. It was this kind of determination and inventiveness, to William's way of thinking, which would take Trip far in this world. It was this kind of determination and critical *thinking* that would make the Park family proud.

Trip turned to his grandfather. "Grandy, the sand won't let go!"

William decided that Trip, even at the tender age of three, could do with a teaching moment.

"Trip, let's watch the water for a bit," he instructed.

Trip was not going to be easily distracted. "But Grandy, we need to get this shell. I want to show it to my new brother!"

"Trip, the water will help us get the shell. See how the water is moving the sand? Maybe we can use water to move the sand more so the beach will let go of your shell. What do you think?"

William led Trip to the breaking waves to see the movement of the sand in the water. "See, we can use the water to make the job of getting the shell easier," he explained matter-of-factly.

※ ※ ※ ※

With the shell securely stowed in Trip's "Shell Bag," grandfather and grandson walked hand in hand up the beach to their four-wheeled bike built for two. "Trip, it's time to check on your mother and brother! He should be arriving sometime soon," William said.

With a huge smile, Trip sat up straight and waited for his grandfather to pump the pedals to take him to his brother. "I'm going to play with Ethan. I can show him my shells!" Trip declared.

※ ※ ※ ※

William entered the family room at Highland Hospital to find Bill dozing in one of those uncomfortable chairs typically supplied by medical facilities. Margaret had decided it was time for fresh air and was taking advantage of Highland Hospital's luscious arboretum.

Trip immediately ran to Bill. "Daddy, can I play with my new brother now?"

Bill's eyes snapped open and squinted at his son, then toward his father. "Dad, what time is it? How long have you been here?" He glanced around the room. "Where's Mom?"

William looked at his son. "I believe the more important question is, how are Constance and Ethan? Any news?"

Bill, fully awake now, straightened in the chair and rubbed the back of his neck. "I haven't been allowed into the labor room since early this morning. There are some minor complications, but there's no need to worry. The nurse is periodically giving me updates."

Exasperated, William looked at Trip and commanded him to stay with his father. Turning toward Bill, William added, "I'm going to get some information on how things are going. We should be getting status reports regularly. This is my daughter-in-law and grandson we're talking about!"

"Dad, I would rather the hospital staff concentrate on the task at hand. I'm sure if there's information we need, they'll tell us. Otherwise, I assume everything is okay!" Bill said.

William shook his head. "This family didn't get to where it is and become successful by *assuming* anything!"

With that, William left the family room in search of information. Bill looked at Trip sitting on the floor lining up the seashells from his bag. "Your Grandy . . . always one to take control!"

Trip, unfazed by the remark, continued his sorting. "Daddy, when can I show Ethan my shells?"

✳ ✳ ✳ ✳

As William stormed down the corridor toward the nurses' station, Margaret emerged from the elevator doors to his right.

"Has Ethan made his appearance?"

"No," replied William. "I'm on an information mission to get his ETA. Bill and Trip are in the family room. I'll let you know what I find."

Margaret sensed that her husband was agitated. "William, how about taking a walk through the arboretum with me? The nurses will call us when something changes."

"This is no time for taking a stroll. I need to find out what's going on with my grandson!"

"William, we've waited this long with there being no trouble, so we can wait a little longer. The staff at this hospital is more than competent to deliver our grandson *and* take care of our daughter-in-law."

"Margaret, my dear—"

His wife tapped her lips with her index finger, indicating for William to shush. She took him by the hand and led him toward the arboretum. William acquiesced as he reluctantly left the hospital building with Margaret, the only person in his world with the ability to redirect him when he was on a mission. He knew better than to argue with his wife when she was determined to change his mood or his course.

As William and Margaret strolled the path through the arboretum, William's mood softened. He began reminiscing about the birth of his own son and his walk through this very garden during that anxious time.

William observed that just as he had aged, so had the arboretum. It had matured and changed with the times. The saplings he and Margaret planted in honor of Bill's birth were now full grown. When their son was born, there was no question whether future fathers were allowed in the delivery room—they were not. This botanical garden had been William's refuge then.

Margaret stopped near a beautiful mimosa tree. The limbs of the tree created a comforting canopy over the walking path. The landscape designer had skillfully used light, plants, and imagination to create

9

a magical mood. Margaret turned and met her husband's gaze with a winsome smile. "William, it's happening—your dream, *our* dream—a large family that will carry on our name and traditions!"

William added, "And grandchildren to keep the family business viable and growing."

Margaret looked sternly at her husband. "William, this is family time, not business time. This is about the bonds of our love being passed onto future generations. Our love has done that!"

"Yes, it does all start with family. But there must be financial stability to help the family stay together," he rationalized, not for the first time in their marriage.

"Oh, William, you are impossible! However, I love you more and more each and every day that I know you."

"Margaret, you're an amazing woman." He stroked her cheek with the back of his hand. "You are the glue that keeps this family together, and I am the engine that keeps it moving in a forward direction. Together we're a great team!" William drew Margaret closer and kissed her with a passion that had not waned in their forty years of marriage.

※ ※ ※ ※

Constance gazed into her newborn's deep blue eyes. Although she had just endured long labor with many complications and was physically exhausted, her mind was emotionally charged. *Ethan has arrived. Ethan is healthy. Ethan is amazing!* her thoughts sang. In this moment, her love for Ethan, her family, and life knew no bounds.

With Ethan being her second-born child, Constance knew that these first moments alone with him were precious. She savored these moments, stored them in her heart, and planned to hold them in her memory forever. Once Ethan met the family, she would have to share her son. Constance knew that Ethan would always be hers, just as Trip had remained hers. She also knew she would have to share Ethan and his experiences with the world. That was the point after all—for Ethan to grow and learn to love, think, be a man, and raise a family.

The young nurse who had been with Constance during her entire labor came into the room. Though she flashed a large smile, Constance could see the weariness both in her walk and her eyes. Lori, a close family friend who was also a dedicated nurse with a notable bedside manner, had been ecstatic to be a part of Ethan's birth. She didn't want to miss one second of the delivery, and she hadn't.

"How are you and the newest member of the Park family?" asked Lori.

Filled with love and enthusiasm, Constance gushed, "We're doing great! Thank you for all you've done."

Lori responded, "Constance, you know it's not called 'labor' for nothing. And we both know, *you* labored!"

"Yes, but that seems insignificant now," replied Constance. "Isn't he just perfect?"

"How could he not be, Constance? He has beautiful parents and grandparents. This kid has got it made!"

"Thank you, Lori. You're very sweet, and we're very lucky to have had you with us."

The young nurse, seeing herself as more of a coach or spectator during the birth of children, blushed and accepted the compliment.

11

Turning to her more practical side, Lori asked, "Should I go get the family so they can meet Ethan?"

"Yes, yes, but give me a couple more minutes alone with my baby. Then, will you go speak to Bill directly and tell him that he's needed? Don't let on that Ethan has arrived," Constance instructed. "I want Bill to have the same few moments alone with Ethan that I've had."

Lori winked as she walked out of the room. "I understand."

※ ※ ※ ※

The door to the family room swung open and the Park family perked up as Lori entered with her beautiful smile, even though she looked as if she was halfway through running a marathon. The family stood in unison, expecting to hear the news that Ethan had arrived.

As Lori approached the Parks, William couldn't find it in himself to keep his excitement contained and asked, "Is Ethan here? Can we see him now?"

Lori, feeling a bit uncomfortable since she had known all the Parks her entire life, dreaded the thought of misleading anyone in the family, most of all William. Tactfully, and keeping her conscience clear, she looked directly at Bill. "Constance has asked for you to come to the labor room," she announced.

William, alarmed, jumped in. "Is everything all right? Is Ethan okay? Constance?"

Lori looked at William and Margaret. "Everything is fine. Miss Constance just needs to see Bill," she said reassuringly. Before anyone could respond, Lori deftly pulled Bill by his arm toward the door.

Prior to making it through the door, Lori turned to an addled William to again assure him that both baby and mom were doing well and were healthy. Lori believed she had navigated her way through this dilemma without compromising her ethics. She deeply loved the Park family, but sometimes their dynamics were quite interesting.

"Are Constance and Ethan really all right? Do I need to be prepared for something?" Bill asked as they approached Constance's labor room.

Lori grinned up at Bill. "Yes, you do. You need to be prepared to meet your son, Ethan." Lori pushed open the door to Room 2112 and Bill entered.

As he set foot inside the room, it seemed to Bill that one of Hollywood's best directors could have set the scene. Bathed in a pool of amber light, Constance sat up in bed with Ethan cradled in her arms, her face aglow.

Tears welled up in Bill's eyes, and his heart burst with joy. Without a word being said, he intuitively knew why Lori had pulled him away from the family. He also knew the architect of this moment was Constance. She always knew . . . .

Bill stood in awe at the sight of his beautiful wife and infant son. "You are stunning, my love. You have brought so much joy to my heart. . . and worked so hard."

"Bill, I didn't do this alone. This is *our* son. Meet Ethan!" Constance held Ethan out to Bill.

Being a veteran father, Bill didn't hesitate as he did when he first held Trip. He had been petrified that he would drop or mishandle his first-born child. It was different this time. Bill now knew that he could hold Ethan, love Ethan, and nurture Ethan. He savored the moment, for he knew it wouldn't last.

⁂ ⁂ ⁂ ⁂

Bill closed the rear door of the brand-new Tesla Model X, a gift from his parents to celebrate the arrival of their newest grandson, Ethan. William insisted that his grandchildren be transported from any Point A to any Point B in one of the safest vehicles on the planet. Bill shook his head with a smirk as he walked around the car to the driver's side. Though his Porsche Cayenne was also rated as one of the safest vehicles on the road, his dad obviously believed the Model X was just a notch better than his Cayenne. *Typical Dad, always has to have the very best*, Bill thought as he folded into the driver's seat. He closed the door and fastened his seat belt.

Glowing with excitement, Constance looked over at her husband. "Bill, you have made me so happy. I'm the luckiest woman in the world."

Bill smiled at his wife. "My love, I am the luckiest *man* in the world. You and our sons are my life. Let's get home and raise our family." Bill pressed the accelerator. The dual motors whirred to life, and the Model X began to *safely* transport the Park family to their home.

⁂ ⁂ ⁂ ⁂

As Bill made the turn into their driveway, he noticed that William's car was already parked in "William's spot." This spot was located closest to the side door that led into the kitchen. William didn't outright insist that this particular location be designated as his, but he made it well known with not-so-subtle hints when others had taken the liberty to park there. William insisted he park there for Margaret's sake so she wouldn't have to negotiate the slippery slated drive during inclement weather. No one pointed out—within William's hearing—that William always had dibs on this spot, regardless of the weather.

Bill looked at Constance. "Sweetheart, I know you're probably ready for some rest in your own bed, but you know Park family tradition—"

With a sparkle in her eyes, Constance cut Bill off mid-sentence, "Every Park baby comes home to the whole family. Are you kidding? I'm famished. Hospital food for two days is torture. I'm ready for a 'Grandy Steak' and some of your mom's potato salad."

Bill grinned, "I guess there's one thing that can be said—you will never be alone or go hungry in the Park family. Let's eat."

As Constance and Bill approached the kitchen door, Bill cradled Ethan in his arms. Trip, wearing a grilling apron with his name embroidered across the top, flung open the door and announced Ethan's arrival, "My brother's here!"

Margaret cooed at Ethan in Bill's arms. "May I hold the newest member of the Park family?" Bill gently placed Ethan into Margaret's waiting arms. No grandmother could have been happier than Margaret at this moment.

Constance looked down at Trip and asked, "Are you helping Grandy with the grill? How are the steaks coming along?"

15

Chagrined, Trip looked up at his mother and replied, "Mom, I'm cooking. Grandy is helping *me.*"

As Trip was proclaiming his tenure as head grilling chef, a beaming William, wearing a matching apron embroidered with 'Grandy,' rounded the corner into the kitchen. "Welcome home, Constance. Welcome home, Ethan."

William had the traditional cigar already planted in his mouth and held another out to Bill. "Let's us men go on the deck and enjoy our celebratory cigars." As the men moved toward the door to the back deck, William reached into his shirt pocket and, much to Trip's delight, produced a blue bubblegum cigar.

"Yes, let's us men . . ." Trip paused and cocked his head. "What are these, Grandy?"

Margaret teased William, "You're already teaching Trip your bad habits? How about teaching him how to *not* burn our steaks?"

William opened the back door and chuckled. "Come on, gents. Let's get outside before I get into any more trouble with Granny!"

Margaret, holding a cooing Ethan, gave an exasperated sigh and then smiled wistfully at Constance. "I remember bringing Bill home from the hospital. What an absolutely wonderful feeling. William was giddy, what with all his plans for the future. And now he has the CEO and CFO to run Park Enterprises. Life is certainly good."

Constance raised an eyebrow. "Margaret, you know how Bill feels about the family and business. The two should never cross. Let's leave it up to Trip and Ethan as to their career aspirations. Plus, I think we can hold off on those conversations for a few years."

Margaret shook her head. "I know, dear, but William hasn't been this excited about anything since Trip was born, not even the closing of the Esplanade deal."

Constance opened the refrigerator and pulled out a large bowl of potato salad. "Well, let's just hope it all works out and everyone gets along," she said brightly.

Margaret, not one to dampen the mood, replied, "I agree. Let's make sure we steer the men away from anything remotely close to business."

Trip bounded into the house and raced through the kitchen. "Mom, Granny . . . . Grandy says to get ready for steak." Trip kept running right to the stairs.

"Slow down," Constance called. "Where are you going in such a hurry?"

"Gotta get the shells to show Ethan," Trip called as he slowed his pace. For a little over three years old, he was already displaying the Park family athleticism. With that, the newly enlarged Park family was off and running.

Chapter 2
BIRTHDAY BASH

The rest of the Park family continued to move through the higher achievement percentiles in all things academic and athletic, and Ethan was not to be left out.

On an unusually warm February afternoon, Constance and Margaret were enjoying a respite from the winter cold while watching William play with Trip and Ethan in the yard. William considered himself as fit as any person half his sixty-one years. He awoke every morning at five a.m. for his three-mile run and insisted on cranking out a total of a hundred push-ups throughout the course of the day. Today's workout consisted of chasing and being chased by an almost four-year old Trip. Giggling with pure delight, Trip pursued Grandy around his baby brother Ethan's outdoor playpen.

Constance sighed in sheer contentment as she poured Margaret a glass of iced tea. "It's so wonderful that William finds such joy in the kids."

"Actually, it's quite astonishing." Margaret took a sip of her tea. "Who would have thought that he could take his mind off work long enough? But then, as he always says, 'We work for our family, and we have a family for our work.'"

Placing her glass of iced tea on the table, Constance smiled, "Family *is* everything."

Ethan focused on Grandy and Trip as they circled his enclosure. He grew restless and displayed unhappiness by pulling on the side of the playpen while doggedly standing on his wobbly legs. As with the entire Park family, being confined physically or intellectually was not amenable to his nature.

Seeing this, William let Trip catch him, and then William made a big show of falling to the ground. Trip quickly climbed on top of Grandy. William tickled Trip, who squealed and ran laughing to his mother. William feigned chasing after Trip, calling out, "The tickle fingers are coming to get you." Trip let out a huge laugh as he jumped into the safety of his mother's lap.

William crawled on all fours to the playpen and began playing peek-a-boo through the mesh with Ethan. Ethan brightened up and giggled. William reached over and lifted Ethan out to enjoy the freedom of the yard.

Looking back toward the patio, William exclaimed, "Constance, your days of leisure are about to end. Today, you will have two walking toddlers. Ethan is going to walk today. I can just *feel* it."

Constance laughed. "Life of leisure. Surely, you jest."

William took Ethan by the hands and held him up in the standing position. Ethan frowned as he rocked on unsteady legs and immediately fixed his gaze on Grandy. Grandfather and grandson were totally focused on each other and the moment. William's heart swelled with pride at his grandson's intent look of determination.

As Ethan pulled his little hands away from Grandy's to give a joyful clap, he fell flat on his diaper-padded bottom, landing on the thick St. Augustine grass. Ethan's hands immediately reached out so he could be lifted to his feet once again. William complied. Ethan pulled his hands back to clap—the result being the same in that he landed on his rear end, this time with a high-pitched giggle. Ethan's hands went up. William lifted him to his feet. Ethan had a sly look on his face as he pulled his hands away from his grandfather's. This time, Ethan's rear end didn't meet with the grass. Ethan stood on his own two feet.

William called out to the ladies, "Look at that. He's standing on his own."

To the astonishment of everyone watching, Ethan managed to move his right foot forward, thus moving his entire person in William's direction. Ethan had taken his first step! Then, to everyone's amazement, he took his second and third steps toward his grandfather.

The cheers of encouragement and praise from William, Constance, Margaret—and Ethan's laughter—reached the side of the house where Bill had just exited his car. Not a fan of missing the fun, Bill detoured to the backyard, following the sounds of the cheers. He spotted his dad on his knees, hugging Ethan.

"What's all the cheering about?" Bill asked as he rounded the corner to the backyard.

Constance continued to clap as she grinned at him, "Bill, Ethan just took his first steps with an assist from Grandy."

As if on cue, Ethan reached out to his grandfather. William lifted Ethan once again to a standing position. Looking directly at his dad as if to say *Watch this*, Ethan took his hands away from his grandfather and moved forward two steps. He promptly plopped down and clapped and giggled. Everyone clapped, including Trip, who started running around the backyard shouting, "Look at me. I can walk, too."

Bill smiled and asked if anyone needed anything from the house as he opened the door to go inside to change into his play duds. He shut the kitchen door and slammed his briefcase down on the counter. "One red light and I miss a milestone."

※ ※ ※ ※

Planning a birthday party for a two-year-old can be a tricky task. Whom to invite? What activities should be provided for the children? For the adults? What kind of food to serve for both groups of people? Are there party favors? If so, what are they? And many more details that parents, grandparents, aunts, and uncles fret over in an effort to ensure that the guest of honor has a good time.

In accordance with Park family tradition, Ethan's second birthday would be acknowledged with a party in his honor. But the logical, pragmatic side of Constance realized that this party was more about the guests than about the guest of honor, who had no real knowledge of what a party was or that it was being thrown in his honor. Of course, Constance did desire that Ethan have fun, open presents, blow out candles, and enjoy some birthday cake.

With that in mind, Constance began planning for Ethan's party. It would be held on the second Saturday of the month. So technically, it was not exactly on Ethan's birthday. That special day fell on a Monday this year—not a prime day for a family party. That would be an excellent time for a late adult dinner to celebrate William's sixty-second birthday. Again, pragmatism won out over tradition and the party in Ethan's honor was set for the weekend.

Constance dialed her mother-in-law. "Hi, Margaret! How are you this morning?"

A definite morning person, Margaret cheerily replied, "I'm doing well, dear. How are you? How are plans for the big birthday bash coming along?"

"Things are moving along nicely," said Constance. "What would you think about an idea that is a bit non-traditional?"

Margaret inquired, "What's the idea? Is it something that we need to order? If so, we need to decide soon since we're only two weeks out."

"Oh, no, it's nothing we need to order," answered Constance. "Well, actually it is. It would be a second birthday cake."

Puzzled, Margaret waited for Constance to continue.

"You see, there is the cake to eat, and then there is another cake called a Smash Cake," she explained.

"What's a Smash Cake? I don't believe I've seen a recipe for one of those."

"It's not a cake that you eat. It's a cake that we'll put in front of Ethan and let him smash it, play with it, throw it—what not—with his

23

hands. A chance for him to have fun. It makes for some very funny pictures," said Constance.

"Can we get one for the adults, too? I can just see a Park family food fight."

Constance laughed. "Exactly. Imagine William throwing a piece of birthday cake. . . ."

✳ ✳ ✳ ✳

Trip and William held hands as they walked along the beach on their usual Saturday morning quest for seashells. Trip looked up at his grandfather. "Grandy, are you coming to Ethan's birthday smash today?"

"Trip, it's simply called a birthday party. You know that. And yes, I wouldn't miss it for the world."

"Momma said we're having a birthday smash, not a party," declared Trip.

William chuckled. "Well then, I guess we'll just have to see what your mother has in mind."

At that moment, Trip noticed an iridescent shell at the edge of the surf. "Grandy, look at that shell. I could give it to Ethan for his birthday."

"That would be the perfect birthday present for your little brother."

✳ ✳ ✳ ✳

Constance decided that in honor of Ethan's second birthday, the day would be "brought to you by the number 2," a la *Sesame Street.* The entire day would be themed around this idea. When someone asked for a cookie, they would get two. If someone wanted a hamburger, they would get two, etc. Constance created smaller half-sized portions of all the food. This was done in an effort to not overly expand the waistlines of the guests in a negative fashion.

Large, stuffed renditions of Bert and Ernie from *Sesame Street* greeted the guests as they approached the side door. Two-foot-tall cutouts of Thing One and Thing Two from Dr. Seuss fame welcomed guests onto the deck in the backyard. Large blow-up floats of Dory and Nemo were awaiting playmates in the pool.

And there were two birthday cakes on the table under the cabana—the cake for eating and a smash cake.

As Constance was putting the finishing touches on one of the charcuterie boards she was assembling, Bill returned from a visit to the family butcher with burgers, hot dogs, and a few steaks. Roscoe wasn't the *official* family butcher, but he just happened to be the butcher from whom William had been obtaining the finest cuts of meat for as long as anyone could remember. Just as Oliver, Roscoe's father, provided meats for William's family when William was a young boy, Roscoe now supplied the Park family with provisions of the highest quality. When it came to purchasing meats for the Park family, everyone in the family insisted that the meats had to come from Roscoe.

"Hey, honey," Bill called. "I picked up all of the meat. Roscoe, as usual, has outdone himself and already set the steaks and hamburgers to marinate. All we have to do now is get a fire going, pour a nice cool beverage, and tend to the grill."

Constance looked up from her work. "That's awesome, Bill. Let's make sure we add a little something extra to Roscoe's Christmas bonus this year. He takes such good care of us."

"Have Dad and Trip returned?"

"Actually, I asked your father to make the beach outing with Trip a little longer this morning. That way Trip wouldn't be underfoot while we're getting ready."

Bill changed the course of the conversation. "I need to talk to Dad about Trip starting flag football later this summer."

"Why's that?"

"Well, looks like game days will be on Saturday mornings. Also, I've been asked to help coach," replied Bill.

Constance chuckled. "Wait, they've asked you to coach? You've never played football in your life."

"I know," said Bill, "but at this age it's not so much about football as it is about sportsmanship, teamwork, and having fun. I think I can manage that."

Constance affirmed, "Plus, it will give you an activity that you and Trip are doing together . . . father-son time. I think that would be good for both of you."

"Yes, it will be. We, rather I, need to break the news to Dad that Saturday morning shell hunting will have to be rescheduled."

As Constance was putting a cover over the charcuterie board, she looked at Bill with concern. "You know how your father is about his commitments and traditions."

"Yes, I know quite well," said Bill. "But this wouldn't be Dad missing a commitment. This is just change. He'll get over it."

Closing the refrigerator door, Constance frowned at Bill before starting on her way to check the decorations on the deck. "At any rate, Bill, this is not a topic that should be discussed at the party. It could create too much tension. No one wants that."

✳ ✳ ✳ ✳

Parties at the Park family residence were always a festive occasion. Attendees enjoyed the great company and delicious food. Moreover, they could always count on a show of some sort displaying the family dynamics, which shouldn't be construed as purely negative, however. In fact, on several occasions these dynamics proved themselves quite humorous. Today though, during two-year-old Ethan's birthday party, the dynamics, if one was paying attention, could indicate the rumbling of a volcano.

Jerry Wallace walked with his wife, Beth, and their two boys, Mark and Roger, down the neighborhood street toward the Park residence, anticipating a great time, though there was the possibility of seeing just a few sparks fly. The idea of Trip playing flag football was apt to create tension between the elder Park men. While it was rare for the Park family to publicly exhibit family discord, this was a small gathering with just the Parks and Wallaces. In a smaller setting, such as today's party, the potential for fireworks would be great, depending on how and when the subject was broached.

"Can you hold Roger for a second?" Jerry asked Beth. "The strap on my guitar backpack is cutting into my shoulder."

"I'm not sure why you feel the need to bring a guitar to a birthday party for a two-year old," replied Beth.

Jerry looked at his wife. "Bill asked that I bring a guitar so we could jam a bit while the kids are playing in the pool."

Beth glanced at Jerry and winked. "How about you boys pay attention to the eye candy at the pool? Namely, your wives."

"Beth, you know you're always the apple of my eye, but I can play guitar and admire your beauty at the same time," chuckled Jerry.

"Yeah, right. Just remember this is Ethan's party, not a gig for you and Bill . . . . and you know William will be here, and he's not overly fond of the band thing!"

"I know, I know. We'll be cool."

After a moment, Jerry added, "I'm more concerned about how William has taken the news that Bill signed Trip up for flag football on Saturdays."

"Oh, I thought William liked football," said Beth.

"He loves football," Jerry said as he took Roger back. "But Bill seems to think he may have some *issue* with the whole deal."

"I'm sure it won't be a big deal, and they'll figure it out," Beth said, ever positive. "They are the Parks, after all."

"We'll see."

"It's Ethan's birthday party. Let's go into this with *fun* in mind!"

As the Wallaces neared the Park residence, William positioned his Tesla Model X just so in his unofficial parking space. Fortunately for William and Margaret, or maybe by William's design, this spot not only had the advantage of being near the side door to enter the kitchen, but it was also under the shade of a stately oak tree. The stylish transportation of the elder Parks would not be too warm when they were ready to leave. The car had the ability to maintain its interior temperature to suit William's liking, but why take chances?

Jerry, Beth, and the boys walked up the drive as William and Margaret exited their car. Mark ran up to William. "Mr. Grandy, are you going to play squirt guns with me and Trip in the pool?"

William chuckled. "Well, hello to you too, Mr. Mark."

"Mr. Grandy—"

"It's Grandy, Mark. There is no Mister."

"Um . . . okay, mister . . . I mean, Grandy, look at this water gun. Let's go play," Mark said.

"Mark, there will be plenty of time for Grandy, the water guns, and the pool," Beth chided. "Let's be polite. Say hello to everyone first."

"Yes, ma'am," Mark said glumly.

William greeted Beth with a hug and shook hands with Jerry. "Are you coming from playing somewhere?" he asked. "Do you want to store that in my car? I keep the AC running."

"No, that's okay. Bill asked that I bring a guitar so we can play a little later."

"I see," replied a vexed William.

Margaret embraced Beth and Mark, then turned toward William. "Oh, it'll be fun. Live music is wonderful."

Music seemed to be on everyone's minds. Constance opened the kitchen door to greet her guests and let them in the house. As the door opened, Raffi could be heard on the stereo system exhorting everyone to "shake their sillies out!"

Constance smiled warmly. "Hi, everyone. Timed arrival, I like it. Bill is in the backyard with the boys. Come in. Can I get anyone something to drink?" she offered.

Raffi was continuing his exhortations to everyone in the backyard as Jerry and William headed toward the cabana where Bill was firing up the grill. By the standards of the National BBQ Association, Bill was no pit master, but he could hold his own among his contemporaries in the neighborhood with his state-of-the-art natural gas grill.

"Let the grilling begin!" Jerry said.

Bill smiled. "Just fired her up. She should be ready for action in about fifteen minutes. Can I get you anything to drink? Dad?"

Simultaneously, William and Jerry responded, "Water."

"Okay, two waters coming up," announced Bill. "I guess that's in keeping with the theme of twos."

Bill noticed that William was holding a small paper bag. "What's that, Dad? Did you get Ethan a school lunch for his birthday?"

William had almost forgotten that he was holding a bag of hickory chips. "I brought these to put in your grill so the meat would have a hickory flavor, as if it were cooked on a real wood- burning grill."

"Ah c'mon, Dad. You know I would've had to be out here an hour ago babysitting a wood-burning grill. Who has time for that in today's world?"

William retorted, "Only those who cherish tradition and hickory grills."

Jerry jumped in. "Come on, guys, you are *both* awesome working your grills to their fullest. You'll never hear me turn down an invitation to a grilling event from either of you."

※ ※ ※ ※

As far as parties for a two-year-old go, Ethan Park's party was a hit. The kids played in the guitar-shaped pool, which had been designed by Bill to further exhibit his love of music. Grandy jumped in on the water gun fights. Ethan smashed his smash cake with aplomb. All managed to get the hang of receiving two of whatever treat or drink they requested.

The weather appeared to have been delivered by the local chamber of commerce. Ethan opened his presents, or rather, Constance opened presents for Ethan. He clapped and cheered for presents that he didn't really know how to use.

Late in the afternoon the little ones—yes, even the guest of honor—had had enough and were ready for some down time. Roger Wallace had taken naps many times at the Park residence. Thus, it didn't require much effort to send both Roger and Ethan off to dreamland in record time. The older boys, Mark and Trip, were engrossed with Trip's earthworm farm, while the adults relaxed in the late afternoon sun on the pool deck with their first mai tais of the summer.

"Constance, you did it again. What a wonderful party!" Margaret held up her glass as a toast.

"I definitely agree," Beth chimed in. "The 'two' theme was genius."

"Wait until Ethan turns five," Bill exclaimed. "Then we'll all be as big as a house eating five of everything."

Everyone chuckled. Then Margaret turned to William. "Are you water-logged? I believe you spent more hours in the pool than all of us put together."

William laughed. "I believe I may not get in the water again until next year's party."

"Shall we try out a few tunes for you folks?" Bill asked eagerly.

Margaret, Beth, and Constance nodded while William stood up to refresh his drink, giving Margaret a sideways glance as he walked toward the bar.

※ ※ ※ ※

The melody section of the B-sides—the melody section being Jerry and Bill—completed their repertoire of songs. The assembled audience—the assembled audience being William, Margaret, Beth, and Constance—clapped enthusiastically. Well, almost everyone did. William's response would have to be considered more of a golf clap.

It wasn't that William didn't enjoy music. In fact, William had a passion for music from all eras and genres. William's issue with the *B-Sides* was that it took Bill away from his family. There were usually band practices once a week, and twice a week prior to the B-Sides playing an actual paying gig. Then there were the gigs themselves, which also took Bill away from Constance and the boys. Many times he would miss the day after a gig while catching up on sleep because the gig ran until after midnight and he didn't make it home until almost sunrise. For William, there were very few things worthy of taking time away from one's family.

Actually, only one reason would be considered acceptable for taking time away from one's family, and that was anything to do with the family business. Ultimately, the family business was for the family, was part of the family, and helped the family reach its goals.

✳ ✳ ✳ ✳

The sun was sinking lazily into the horizon, as was the adults' energy. It had been a lovely day, but also a long day.

Jerry looked toward Beth and inconspicuously pulled on his left earlobe. While Carol Burnett had used the pulling of her left earlobe as a way to say hi to her grandmother, the Wallaces used it as a signal to each other that it was time to leave.

Jerry wasn't as inconspicuous as he thought because Bill broke into song, accompanied by Constance, singing, "I'm so glad we had this time together . . . ."

Jerry, Beth, Bill, and Constance all started laughing at each other and themselves. Constance set down her glass and rose from her chair. "I can't think of a better group of people to help celebrate Ethan's birthday. Thank you all for making it so special."

✳ ✳ ✳ ✳

The Wallaces collected their boys, along with their toys, said their goodbyes, gave hugs all around, and then headed a couple of hundred yards down the street to their home. The adults of the Park family immediately began their ritual of dividing leftovers for the refrigerator and for William and Margaret to take home. The clean-up of a Park family party could be a party in itself. They reminisced over events that happened a few hours ago, talked about the next party, and discussed who would play host.

While Bill was putting some of Margaret's famous potato salad into a container, he looked at his father and said, "Dad, I want to let you know that we signed Trip up to play in a flag football league this summer."

William continued to gather up dishes. "That's awesome. There's nothing like athletics to reinforce the value of commitment, adherence to rules, and being a champion."

"Dad, this is a league for five- and six-year-olds. I think if we can just get them all running in the same direction, that will be an accomplishment in itself."

"Yep, I guess you're right to a point. But you can never start too early teaching those values," opined William.

"Dad, it's about fun," Bill countered.

Constance jumped in. "I can hardly wait to go to the practices and games."

Margaret nodded in agreement. "And seeing all of those fresh little faces full of determination and anticipation." Bill felt the mood was as good as it was going to get and added what he knew would be the one fly in the ointment. "It will be a lot of fun and great family time. A wonderful way to spend Saturday mornings—game days—together."

Taken aback, William put the glasses he held down on the table. "Wait, what? Saturday morning is when they play the games?"

"Yes, Dad," said Bill. "Every Saturday morning for six weeks."

William quickly responded, "Well, what about our shell-hunting adventures? We can't just cast those aside."

"Dad, it's only for a few weeks. You and Trip will be able to continue once the season is over."

William would not be put off. "I don't think this is a good idea. Family should come first. Trip and I have been going to the beach every Saturday morning since before he could walk. We can't just—"

Margaret, trying to calm things down, interjected, "William, it will still be a family outing, but this time with the whole family."

"You mean like Bill is still in the family but not part of the family business?" William retorted. "What is this teaching the kids?"

Adept at quelling disagreements between the two Park men, Margaret spoke up before Bill could respond. "William, let's say our goodbyes and call it a night."

William gave his wife a reluctant nod and regarded his son with a frown. "Okay, Bill, think about this, and then let's come up with an alternative."

Bill shook his head. "Dad, there's nothing to think about. I've made the decision. Trip is playing football on Saturdays."

✳ ✳ ✳ ✳

"I'm sorry, Constance. I didn't mean to end the evening on a down note," Bill said, breaking the silence left by his father. "I just felt that I needed to let him know that this is going to happen. I knew he wouldn't like it."

Constance rubbed Bill's shoulders. "I know. He's stubborn in his ways and doesn't like his traditions or schedules altered."

"I'm not going to budge on this one," Bill shot back quickly. "This is *our* family. Yes, we are still part of the Park family, but we have to forge our own way because we have our own traditions, too."

Constance gently took her husband's hand in hers. "Bill, I have always supported you and will continue to support you in what you believe to be right."

"It's not *your* support I'm worried about. I know you and I are together on this." Bill checked the lock on the back door. "It's my dad."

Chapter 3
GRANDPARENTS STEP IN

Constance nostalgically paused at the framed family photographs lining the upstairs hall on her way to wake Trip and Ethan. A new school year always seemed to bring anticipation, hope, and challenge to both parents and students.

Her heart smiled as her eyes landed on the time-worn pictures of Bill in his school uniform. In one particular photograph he was holding a book bag that looked like it weighed more than he did. Staring into Bill's five-year-old eyes, Constance wondered what his anticipation, hopes, and challenges had been way back then. Had Bill been excited by the anticipation of a new school year? Had he hoped it would go by fast? That he would get good grades? Make new friends? That school would be academically challenging? Socially challenging? Knowing her husband as she did, Constance imagined that Bill would have enjoyed the social aspects of his education far more than he would have the academic ones. Of course, on his first day of school, just like on Ethan's, these thoughts would not have acutely coalesced like that.

The mind of a five-year-old, no matter how intelligent the parents believe their child to be, rarely thinks farther ahead than a day—two at the most. With these thoughts in mind, Constance opened the door to Ethan's room.

"Wake up, Ethan," she said in a soft but cheery voice. "Today is your first day of school."

Ethan roused and rubbed his small hands over his eyes. "Mom, is Grandy going to take me and Trip to school today?"

Before Constance could reply, Trip popped his head through the door. "C'mon, Ethan, you ready for school?"

"We're getting there, Trip." Constance looked back at Ethan. "Yes, dear, Grandy *and* Granny are taking you boys to school this morning."

"Is Grandy going to sit in a desk next to me?"

Constance laughed. "Oh, no, Ethan. Grandy is only taking you to school. He can't stay. He's already finished kindergarten. But you'll make new friends who will sit near you." She folded back his blanket. "Let's get dressed and then go downstairs for some breakfast."

※ ※ ※ ※

William and Margaret entered through the side door as Constance ushered Trip and Ethan into the kitchen for breakfast.

"Grandy! Granny!" Trip and Ethan shouted in unison as they ran forward.

William dropped to one knee to be hugged and tackled by the boys. "Good morning. You guys ready for the first day of school?"

Trip declared, "Grandy, I'm going to learn *everything* this year. I'm going to be as smart as you."

"Grandy, can they teach me everything, too?" Ethan piped up.

William hugged his grandsons. "It sounds like you boys have the right attitude. I sure hope those teachers are ready."

Constance placed plates of scrambled eggs and grits on the breakfast table. "Okay, boys. Give your grandfather a little breathing room, and sit down for breakfast."

She turned toward William and Margaret. Constance hugged her mother-in-law. "Margaret, thank you so much for taking the kids to school. I'll be off to the airport shortly. Bill will be waiting for me at baggage claim by the time I get there."

William straightened up. "Our pleasure, Constance."

"Would anyone like coffee?" Constance picked up the coffee pot.

William nodded. "Of course. Nothing like a little joe to get the day going."

Comments about the weather and a few reminiscences died down as the boys finished their special first-day breakfast. Constance looked at the clock. "Okay, it's time to go. But before we leave, let's get the traditional First Day of School picture for the family wall."

The boys, dressed in their school uniform of khaki shorts and a short-sleeved blue polo shirt with blue tennis shoes, were ceremoniously posed on the front steps of the house. Trip was placed at the newel post on the left with Ethan standing immediately to his right. Trip had stood in this exact position for his three previous First Day pictures and, God willing, all future First Day pictures of the boys would be taken in this

39

same spot. This tradition would allow family and friends to follow the boys' growth through their school years.

As soon as both boys were safely buckled into their car seats, William pressed the button to engage the closing mechanism on the Tesla Model X's falcon-wing doors. "Okay, guys, we're off to learn everything we can so that we can conquer the world."

Margaret patted Constance's arm. "It's a shame that Bill couldn't arrange his flight so he could be here this morning."

William seated his wife in the car. "Okay, we should roll. There should only be one person in the Park family late today."

Margaret shook her head. "Oh, honey, give Bill a break. You know he would be here if he could."

Constance peeked her head into the backseat. "Have a wonderful first day. Ethan, Trip, Mommy will pick you up this afternoon."

After pulling out onto the street heading in the direction of the elementary school, William glanced at the boys through the rear view mirror. "You young men sure look handsome with your fresh haircuts," he commented.

"Mr. Ronnie gave us each a lollipop because we sat still for him," Trip proudly announced.

"What color lollipop did you choose?" William asked. "When your dad was a boy, his favorite was purple."

"I picked purple, just like my dad!" Trip exclaimed.

"Red!" Ethan called out.

"Purple and red," William echoed. "Great choices."

Margaret looked back at Trip and Ethan. "Are you excited to meet your teachers and make new friends?"

Trip nodded and bounced within the confines of his seat belt. "Granny, I'm going to take Ethan around school and show him where the bathrooms are, too."

"That's good, Trip," she responded. "You're the big brother. You need to take care of Ethan."

"I *am* the big brother," Trip replied with pride.

✳ ✳ ✳ ✳

After delivering Trip and Ethan to their classrooms, William and Margaret were sentimental and teary-eyed on the drive home. The realization hit them both that a chapter of their lives was closing. The grandsons were no longer babies—*their* babies. These young, precious boys would go to school, learn new things, make new friends, and begin having lives outside of the Park family enclave.

William realized, though, that as one chapter was closing, another chapter was opening. Their grandsons were on the way to realizing their future destiny. Brushing a tear away from his eye, he glanced at his wife. "Those two young boys are the future of our family."

Margaret nodded in agreement. "Yes, they are the future. However, William, they are little boys still. Let them live in the present."

✳ ✳ ✳ ✳

41

Rarely in life do events fall neatly into place as do the pieces of a jigsaw puzzle. Many people crave a life of this type of orderliness, as did Constance. Unfortunately, though, life doesn't always hear nor care about what is preferred. Life decides, sometimes seemingly on a whim, when the time is right. Time for anything, or time for nothing. Or, time for a baby . . . .

Claire Park decided to make her appearance on the very evening that Ethan was on stage for his first-grade class's rendition of Jan Brett's book, *The Mitten*. Ethan had been chosen to be the one to lose the mitten. In true Park fashion, he was leading the way.

To help Constance and Bill with the overlapping puzzle pieces of life, Margaret and William attended *The Mitten*. They sat on the front row with Trip positioned between them. Margaret leaned toward William and remarked, "I wonder if little Claire is going to make her grand entrance at the same time Ethan makes his."

William smiled at Margaret. "Claire, like all of the Parks, will make her entrance when she's good and ready."

At that moment the lights in the theater dimmed, and the opening music started playing over the auditorium's sound system. The curtains opened and the play began.

※ ※ ※ ※

Once again in one of the labor rooms at Highland Hospital, Constance and Bill awaited the arrival of another child. This time, much to Constance's relief, Bill would not be asked to vacate the labor room. Claire appeared to be making the transition into the world in a much more conventional manner than her older brother Ethan. Bill's presence had a calming effect on Constance. He was always able to supply her with the confidence that together they could accomplish anything.

On the other hand, Bill wasn't feeling that confident. Hospitals, in fact, anything medical or having to do with blood, were not his thing. Bill was often heard saying, "I get queasy just driving past a hospital, much less actually having to go inside." However, to support Constance and be a "Park Man," he knew that he had to conquer this queasiness so he wouldn't end up on a gurney next to his wife.

＊ ＊ ＊ ＊

Margaret, William, and Trip all enthusiastically clapped as the curtain reopened and the cast of *The Mitten* took their curtain call. The applause increased as each student took two steps forward to take a personal bow. Because he had the leading role, Ethan was the last to take his bow. As he stepped forward, the auditorium erupted in thunderous applause. Yet no one was clapping louder or with more enthusiasm than his older brother Trip.

Filled with pride, William smiled at Margaret. "I sure hope he gets used to this. He will bowl people over his entire life!"

"Do you think he'll be an actor?" Margaret asked.

William replied, "No, indeed not. He will be wowing the business world when he takes over Park Enterprises."

"Oh, William, let him enjoy his youth. You never know, though. Maybe he'll go into the performance world like his father."

William's smile disappeared. "Let's hope not," he retorted. "We need both Trip and Ethan to carry Park Enterprises into the future."

＊ ＊ ＊ ＊

At about the same moment as the curtain dropped on *The Mitten*, Claire Noelle Park made her debut into the world. Mom, Dad, and daughter were all exhausted from the experience but in good health. Claire was snuggled against her mother's chest, sleeping soundly. Bill, the proud father, looked lovingly at both his wife and brand-new baby girl.

Although physically drained, Constance smiled radiantly back at Bill. "Isn't she just perfect?"

"Yes, she is. We have a beautiful family," Bill tenderly replied. "The pieces are all in place . . . ."

EIGHT

TO

TWELVE YEARS OLD

E.P.

Chapter 4
PARENTING ETHAN

Traditions, and especially those on Saturday mornings, were a big deal to William. In fact, Saturday morning traditions with family were considered *sacred* to William.

Throughout the weekdays and into a lot of weeknights, William worked hard at Park Enterprises. Building large commercial edifices was an extremely competitive and complex business. The projects contracted to Park Enterprises made erecting a five-thousand-square-foot home look like child's play.

The scope of a Park Enterprises design required multiple engineers, architects, contractors, and even a team of attorneys. The contracts often extended for several years, requiring detailed project plans, extreme accuracy, and extensive record keeping.

The weekends, for William, were meant for relaxation. Over the course of their almost forty-five-year marriage, Margaret could count on one hand the number of times William sacrificed a weekend of syrup cookies and ice-cold milk. She thought it quaint that after a week of building large, complex structures, her husband would choose to spend a part of his weekend in his woodshop. Over the past several years, he and

Ethan had spent Saturday mornings building birdhouses, chairs, end tables, board games, and just about any other household item that could be hewn out of a piece of wood.

"Hey, guys," called Margaret from the front door of the shop, "I have some syrup cookies, piping hot out of the oven, and ice-cold milk, if you're ready for a break."

William removed his safety glasses. "Ethan, I believe it's time for a break. We can't let those syrup cookies get cold—"

Ethan jumped in with his part, "Or the milk get warm!"

Break time had become part of the weekly ritual of woodworking that eight-year-old Ethan especially liked. Learning how to build things and spending time with Grandy was great. Granny bringing treats to them in the woodshop was an added bonus.

Margaret asked Ethan, "Is your Grandy spending more time teaching you about woodworking, or quizzing you on your multiplication tables?"

"Mathematics," William interjected, "is extremely important for building anything from a birdhouse to a skyscraper, and it appears Ethan is well on his way to being able to do both."

"Yes," an enthusiastic Ethan replied. "I have all the way to the eight times tables down pat. Isn't that right, Grandy?"

William beamed. "You could put Einstein to shame!"

✳ ✳ ✳ ✳

After Margaret had made her weekly delivery of baked goods to the woodshop, William sensed a slight shift in Ethan's demeanor. Ethan usually possessed and maintained an even keel. He was not a child who displayed drastic fits of rage or despair. Conversely, his highs were high but always a bit reserved.

That's not to say, though, that Ethan didn't have the "terrible two" tantrums as a toddler, because he did. Like most toddlers, he learned early how to leverage a tantrum to his advantage. As he passed through the tantrum stage of being two years old, however, his demeanor and moods stabilized.

Over the past five years of William's Saturday mornings with Ethan, reading his grandson's mood had become second nature. Hence, he quickly picked up on this change in Ethan's emotional state.

William decided to probe Ethan. "Which do you like better, Granny's syrup cookies or her oatmeal raisin cookies?"

A smile brightened Ethan's face because he loved Granny and especially loved eating the cookies she baked. "Oh, I don't know, Grandy," replied Ethan. "They are both so good. But I really like the syrup cookies."

Grandy responded, "Yep, I like them, too. They make me feel happy when I eat them."

"I get a happy feeling in my tummy."

"Do you have a happy feeling in your tummy now?"

"I guess . . ." Ethan mumbled.

"Is something bothering you, Ethan?" William asked.

Ethan pouted as he stared down at his cookie. His expression settled into a pensive frown. "Grandy, my dad makes me feel sad sometimes."

Unaware that the conversation would take this turn, William was careful not to betray his surprise. "Well, you know us adults. We can be moody at times."

Ethan looked up at his grandfather with a doleful expression. "But Grandy, it's not like that. When Trip comes home with a trophy from football, Dad gets all excited and makes a big deal about it. He puts it up on the trophy shelf. When I bring home something that I made for him, he just says, 'That's nice, Ethan,' and puts it in his closet."

"I'm sure your dad is just as proud of you as he is of Trip. Maybe you just haven't made the right thing for him yet. We need to think of something super special we can make here at the woodshop for your father. What do you think?"

Ethan perked up. "Do you really think that's it? What could we make?"

William put on his biggest grin. "Let's think really hard about what he likes to do and make something that will help him do that."

With a stoic look, Ethan said, "He likes to coach Trip's football team and play music."

Enthusiastically, William replied, "Well, then, we'll come up with an idea for one of those."

Grandfather and grandson went back to work sanding the parts for their version of the twelfth-century European game of Shut the Box. William's hands were deftly working the sander and the wood, but his thoughts were far from the task in front of him. His mind was racing and slightly raging about his conversation with Ethan. *The poor boy is feeling slighted because he chose not to play football. This warrants a serious discussion with Bill.*

✳ ✳ ✳ ✳

Trip had been playing football in various leagues since he was five years old. At eleven years of age he had now become one of the more proficient players to take the field. Trip had spent many Saturday mornings between his fifth and eleventh birthdays on the gridiron. During those years, Bill had coached Trip and his teammates, teaching them the fundamentals of the game, but also instilling within them the importance of teamwork and dedication.

The old saying that the apple doesn't fall far from the tree has much truth to it. Siblings often tend to be similar in many ways, yet not in all ways. In the case of Trip and Ethan, the apples didn't land side by side, but they did land very close. Both boys were eager to attack challenges, though not always of the same nature. Ethan had not exhibited a desire to play football as Trip had. His interests and challenges lay elsewhere. Yet the decision not to play football couldn't be called a decision, as no verbal declaration had been made. It was more influenced by his grandfather than by any lack of sporting preference.

Woodworking on Saturday mornings in Grandy's workshop presented a perfect activity for Ethan and had become his favorite part of the week. Unbeknownst to Ethan, however, Saturday mornings had become a point of contention between his grandfather and father. If asked, members of the Park family asserted that discussions arose rather than all-out arguments. An outside observer might suggest differently as these "discussions" often resulted in raised voices, bulging temporal veins, and elevated blood pressure for all involved, most specifically William and Bill.

The topic of the argument tended to broaden and bring into play festering resentments or points of contention. William would dig deep into the time machine and remind Bill that he had abandoned the family by not following in his father's footsteps to take a leadership role at Park Enterprises. Bill would counter with William's obsession over the family business and how he appeared to care more about the business than he did his own son.

These arguments would go round and round, sometimes spanning several days. The adults always made sure the arguments took place away from the presence of the youngsters. While there was discord at the upper levels of the Park family, there was, and always had been, unspoken rules of engagement to Park family disagreements. These were similar in many ways to John Graham Chambers' famous Marquess of Queensberry Rules, which insisted upon a certain decorum in the boxing ring.

As allowed in the Queensberry Rules, each participant would have a "second," in this case, *not* to tend to physical injury, give tactical advice, or encourage or incite a participant to carry on. Rather, Margaret and Constance would put their efforts as "seconds" into trying to quell the match, get their respective participant to "drop his gloves," and employ reason in lieu of emotion.

Knowing that fighting a battle on two fronts could result in defeat on those two, both participants would drop their metaphorical gloves to keep the peace with their wives. But letting go of their resentment didn't always follow. This specific argument had been in the making for some time. How Ethan spent his Saturday mornings wasn't the reason but the catalyst.

✳ ✳ ✳ ✳

Father-son talks had been a long-standing tradition in the Park family. These talks weren't always of a serious nature. The topic of conversation typically wasn't the point of the talks. The fact that the two men were communicating and spending time together was of the utmost importance. If topics and issues were discussed, mulled over, and potential solutions found, then that was considered lagniappe.

When Bill was a young boy of about twelve years old, no more than seven to ten days would pass before William and Bill would have a talk. They would walk the park, visit the beach, or go out for a slice of pizza to spend time alone chatting. These talks continued in earnest over the years, though the time between talks widened naturally when Bill went off to college. After Bill and Constance married and started their own family, the talks between Bill and William grew even more infrequent. This decrease in frequency crushed William.

The diminishment of the talks was also a result of Bill's burgeoning career, specifically a career *not* at Park Enterprises. From the launch of Park Enterprises, William had planned for the company to be passed down only within the family. Bill's decision to start his own company in a completely different industry upset William's plans. He was not shy in letting Bill know of his disappointment and displeasure. If there were a crack in the Park family veneer, this was it.

✳ ✳ ✳ ✳

Late Sunday evening, William called Bill and mentioned that they hadn't spent any significant quality time together in quite a while. William suggested a beach walk. Bill agreed that time together would be good so they could catch up with each other. They decided that Monday after work would be ideal.

The beach seemed to have a calming effect on both Park men. The sound of the waves crashing ashore, the beautiful light as the sun reached "magic hour," and the oneness with nature all worked together to create a tranquil backdrop. These elements had the power to keep a difficult discussion between father and son civil, or so William hoped.

The two men walked for several minutes, sticking mainly to small talk—the news, weather, and other mundane topics. This was one of the rare father-son talks that had a set agenda. Bill was not aware there would be an agenda when William had called him.

Stopping to face the crashing waves, William folded his arms. "There is something specific that I'd like to talk about with you."

Bill jammed his hands into his front pockets and turned toward the ocean as well. "Yes, what is it?"

Watching a late-evening windsurfer harnessing the wind and traversing the waves, William launched into the discussion. "This past weekend Ethan and I had a talk. He mentioned, in not so many words, that he doesn't feel that you are proud of him. He thinks you're prouder of Trip."

Bill grimaced. "Really? What exactly did you say to him to bring that about?"

William turned and faced his son head-on. "Bill, it doesn't matter what exact words were said. The point is, Ethan feels that you make a bigger deal over Trip's accomplishments than his. That's devastating for a young boy."

Bill gave a short, derisive laugh. "Yeah, Dad, it's devastating for a grown man as well."

"This is *not* about you. This is about Ethan," snapped William.

"Dad, I treat both boys the same." Bill crossed his arms. "There is no difference. It's not my fault that Ethan would rather do woodworking than play football. I'm a football coach, not a woodworker."

William began to reply when Bill cut him off. "Dad, you do the same thing to me. You have been disappointed in me since I made the decision to not be a part of Park Enterprises. You show your disdain over that decision in many ways. How do you think that makes me feel?"

William looked back out at the windsurfer. "Bill, you should know I'm proud of you. But I will *never* agree with your career choice. I can't help it if you don't feel I support you in something that I don't believe is helping our family."

Bill frowned and straightened his arms at his sides, fists closed. "Dad—"

"Again, Bill, this isn't about you. This is about Ethan and what's best for him."

"You're wrong, Dad. This *is* about me. It concerns my son and how he views me."

"Bill, you know what I mean. We have to see after Ethan. You and I can hash out our differences at another time."

Bill glared at William, exasperated by his father's refusal to see how one issue revolved around the other. "Okay, Dad, what's your grand plan?"

William took a deep breath. "Bill, just get a little excited about his accomplishments. He's come up with the idea that he's going to make something special for you. When he does, and no matter what it happens to be or how good it is, make a big deal over it. Let him see that you're proud of him." William turned, facing Bill directly. "There it is. You know what to do."

Understanding quite well that this was his father's way of closing out an uncomfortable conversation, Bill stooped down to break loose a shell. Then rearing back, he hurled the shell into the surf.

* * * *

Constance walked into Bill's music studio after tucking Claire in and making sure the boys were in their beds reading a book prior to falling asleep. She immediately noticed that Bill was in a mood.

Fortunately, when Bill and Constance designed their home, specifically the music studio, sound proofing was almost as high on the list of priorities as acoustic integrity. Bill wanted to be able to work in the studio and not disturb anyone else in the house, or for that matter, in the neighborhood. Mission accomplished.

When she entered the studio, she was met by a "wall of sound," to put it in the terms of Phil Spector, the music producer responsible for developing this technique. "Shredding his axe," as Bill would put it, was a clear sign that he was letting out pent-up frustration about something.

Bill was immensely proud of his guitar collection, which ranged from a rare vintage cigar box guitar to one of his newest acquisitions, a Gibson Les Paul Custom. Constance knew that the only thing Bill treasured more than these guitars was his family.

Upon seeing Constance enter the control room, Bill played one of her favorite guitar pieces he had written especially for her. As he was nearing the end of the riff, he snapped the G string on the guitar. He abruptly turned the volume on the guitar down to zero and set the guitar in its stand in an uncharacteristically rough manner.

There was no doubt in Constance's mind that something was bothering Bill. She gently shut the door to contain the sound. "Honey, you don't normally break a string when you play that piece, especially the G. What has you so wound up?"

Bill sighed and led her to a chair. He and Constance had been married long enough and knew each other well enough that it would do no good for him to feign ignorance. It would be a waste of time at the least, and insulting at the most.

"You know my dad and I had a father-son walk earlier this evening."

Constance met his gaze with a half-smile of commiseration. "You really should make the effort at having those talks more often—communication is the key to harmony."

"What would be the point?" Bill said as he flopped into another chair, then spun it to face her. "Talking to my dad is like talking to a brick wall. You know how bull-headed he can be. And this talk was anything but harmonious."

"Is everything all right?" Constance asked, clasping her hands together, her elbows on the arms of her chair. "What's going on? Is there anything I can do?"

Since the earliest days of their relationship, Bill found love, comfort, and confidence in Constance. When he felt he needed support in one of those areas, he looked to his wife. At times he felt he was being nestled and comforted by her very soul. This was one of those times.

He reached over, peered into her eyes, and found what he knew was there. "It's complicated. I'm hurt, mad, frustrated. All of the above . . . and more!"

When designing the music studio in their home, Constance and Bill attacked the job like they did most things in their marriage—as a team. Bill handled all the technical aspects of the spaces while Constance focused on the aesthetics. Constance diligently researched recording studios and control rooms and toured any to which she could gain access: The Muscle Shoals Sound Studio, Sun Records, Sunset Sound, Le Studio, Electric Lady Studios, and many more. No detail was too small.

Armed with thousands of photographs and notes from conversations with the owners and operators of these studios, she put together a good plan to ensure the studio would be comfortable and relaxing. Constance hadn't realized at the time that the comfort of the studio would also be beneficial for discussions of the heart. She shifted to the plush control room sofa and patted the space beside her. "Let's dig into this," she said.

Bill was quick to claim that space—and Constance's hand. She gently reassured him, "We'll figure it out together, whatever this is. You know that, right?"

Bill took a deep breath. "Ethan told my dad that he doesn't think I'm as proud of him as I am of Trip. Or something to that effect."

Constance gave Bill's hand a slight squeeze. "I can see how that would hurt you. I know you love the boys and Claire equally. In different ways, but equally."

"Of course I do," Bill said.

"Did your father say what prompted this conversation? Did something happen?"

"No, he didn't. But I think it has something to do with sports. Dad is always grumbling about Trip's football," Bill said with a frown. "It's frustrating that Ethan would . . . I could see him not wanting to say anything to me. He could have come to you, though."

Constance thought for a moment and then nodded. "Bill, I hate to admit this—but there is some validity to what your dad is saying."

Bill pulled his hand from Constance's grip and sat back in his chair, eyes wide. "What? You're taking my dad's side?"

"I'm not taking anyone's side. There are no sides. But you do spend a lot of time on football with Trip."

Bill guffawed at his wife's statement.

Constance continued, "Bill, listen. I know you love Ethan and are proud of everything he does. But from a child's perspective . . . well, I can see how Ethan might feel left out."

Bill jumped out of his chair and began pacing the perimeters of the control room. "I'm not leaving him out. I knew this whole deal with my dad monopolizing Ethan's Saturdays was going to end up being trouble."

Constance decided not to argue this point with Bill. She wanted to defuse the situation so that she and her husband could calmly and rationally discuss the issue. "Bill, I'm sorry if my initial response seemed harsh. You know I love you and want only what's best for you *and* our children."

She reached over and patted the chair that Bill had previously occupied. "Please come sit back down and let's figure this out. Yes, you're right, Ethan could have come to me. But you know he and your dad are really close. They have been that way since he was a toddler. Ethan opening up like that may not have been intentional. It may have just slipped out quite naturally—and innocently."

Bill looked at Constance and plopped back down in the chair. "Maybe. I guess you're right . . . or maybe Dad led Ethan into it. Do you really think I favor Trip over Ethan?"

Constance had managed to quell the potential eruption, but she knew she still had to be careful. "You know," she began, "it may be that Trip is playing football, which has a season. And then there's the pizza party at the end with trophies and prizes."

Bill closed his eyes and sat completely still for several minutes. Constance remained motionless while Bill collected his thoughts and feelings. "I understand what you're saying. Ethan doesn't play any sports. He doesn't get the parties, trophies, or prizes. He sees me coming home with Trip and the trophies. So he's feeling excluded."

"Exactly!" Constance squeezed his hand and smiled.

"Okay, so what do we do?" Bill asked.

Constance wanted to keep the momentum going in a positive direction. "He's really into working in the woodshop, which I know, at some level, annoys you—"

"It annoys me at many levels."

"But honey, it's something that's important to him, at least for now. So, we need to show more support for this version of *football* for him. He's

60

always bringing home the projects he makes with Grandy. How much interest have you shown in those projects?"

Bill clasped his hands behind his head and under his breath mumbled, "You must be taking notes from my dad. That's along the same lines of what he was saying." He turned to Constance, "So, I get it. I could be more enthusiastic about his woodworking?"

Constance nodded. "Yes, I can as well. But we can't pour it on too thick. Otherwise, Ethan might suspect that his Grandy narced on him or that we're patronizing him."

Bill allowed his sour mood to dissipate and then let out a slight laugh. "Do you really think he knows what 'patronizing' means?"

"You're right, he probably doesn't know the word, but I bet he knows the feeling," Constance responded with a small chuckle of her own.

A thought came to Bill. "You know, I do believe we should encourage Ethan to take up a sport. He needs the camaraderie, discipline, and dedication that comes with being part of a team."

Constance raised their hands and kissed his. "Yes, that's something we should consider. But, if we do, we should be subtle in suggesting this to Ethan."

With a twinkle in his eyes, Bill looked at Constance. "Speaking of teams, we are a world- class team. Thank you, sweetheart." With that, he leaned over and kissed her tenderly.

Pleased that she and Bill managed this situation so successfully, Constance decided to push her luck. "Bill, what would you think about thanking your dad for coming to you with this? I know you are upset that Ethan went to his grandfather instead of us. What if your dad had said nothing?"

"Wow. You really are pressing your luck."

Constance gave her husband a grin that melted his heart.

"As usual, though, you're right. As much as I didn't like the conversation or his delivery, I could let Dad know that I appreciate his effort."

Chapter 5
FAMILY BONDING

W inston Churchill mused, "We shape our buildings, and afterwards our buildings shape us." These were the thoughts of the great man in 1943 while assessing the damage to the House of Commons due to German bombs. In the time since Winston's thoughts on the topic, numerous psychologists have found evidence to support his ideas.

Churchill's words struck Bill as he walked onto the grounds of the Park Enterprises corporate offices. As a young boy he had watched his dad pore over the bubble drawings that indicated spatial relationships between functional units. Once the bubble drawings were completed to his satisfaction, his father then spent as much, if not more time, poring over the architectural and engineering plans for the complex. To Bill's young mind, his dad should just hurry up and build it.

But the elder Park knew this was a crucial step for all concerned. These plans had to be perfect. Through experience, William also knew the execution had to match the perfection of the plans.

As Bill assessed his surroundings, he wondered what Winston and the psychologists would say about these buildings. "Did the man shape the buildings? Did the buildings eventually reshape the man?" Bill imagined that the first question could be answered in the affirmative. He was not sure that the second question could be answered the same way. His father had definitive ideas about everything. Bill hadn't noticed a significant shift in his dad's goals, principles, or methods at any time during his life.

William's executive assistant, Barbara, welcomed Bill and escorted him down the elegant hallway to the executive dining room. If one observed the pictures adorning the hallway, they would see a pictorial history of Park Enterprises. The images were hung in chronological order beginning at the end of the hall closest to reception, through the hall, and then on to the entrance of the dining room.

The images nearest the reception area were pictures Bill had seen through the years. The earliest images had been shot in the dining room of a young William and Margaret Park. These photos had been shot with a small Kodak Instamatic, so they were grainy and often not clear. Yet, no matter the fuzziness of the focus in the image, one could observe the laser focus in the young William's eyes. It was little wonder to Bill that the images closest to the dining room were now professionally produced by a staff photographer. The focus in the more recent images, like William's, was laser sharp.

"How are Constance and the kids?" Barbara asked Bill.

For as long as Bill could remember, Barbara had been with Park Enterprises as William's executive assistant. She was considered part of the family. She had witnessed both the family and the company grow and thrive.

"They're doing well—growing like weeds."

Barbara chuckled. "I'm looking forward to seeing everyone at the annual company picnic."

"We are as well. It's always a lot of fun."

While he waited for his dad, Bill sat comfortably in one of the leather sofas facing a panoramic view of the city. The name, "executive dining room," seemed to Bill to be a bit of a misnomer since it felt more like an extension of his parents' home. This was not surprising in that Margaret had designed the interior of this space and selected a décor tailored to both their liking. The room was elegant, bright, and airy, yet added a certain level of coziness to it as well. It was a space where William and his top-level executives could entertain clients, business associates, politicians, and anyone else who needed a *special* experience while visiting Park Enterprises.

William insisted early on that all resources be put back into the business. Thus, the Park Enterprises offices were built prior to the Park family residence. In reality, it was William and Margaret's home that emulated the executive dining room.

William walked in and greeted Bill. "Good morning, son. I'm so glad you arranged for us to have lunch today."

"Yeah, Dad. And it's great to see you, too. I'm looking forward to a nice visit."

William took a seat in the club chair closest to Bill on the couch. "What a view! Even after all the many times I've walked into this room, I continue to appreciate this space."

"It's definitely stunning," Bill agreed.

"Yes, your mom was right once again. I'm glad she convinced me that this view belonged to the dining room and not a private office."

Bill laughed. "Mom has a way, especially with you."

William grinned at this. Over the years he had come to the realization that Margaret was not only the love of his life but also the compass that always helped him find true north.

The two men headed toward a table near the windows and took their seats. The menu at the executive dining room rivaled the cuisine at any of the local five-star restaurants. The fact that William was able to lure Chef Duke away from one of the most esteemed dining establishments in the area was a tribute to William's persuasive abilities and the reputation for high standards at Park Enterprises. Chef Duke was given free rein to experiment with the latest in culinary technique and menu options. To date, William had not been disappointed with the results.

William folded his napkin and set it beside his plate. "Now, that was a lunch to remember."

Bill smiled at his dad. "I don't know how anyone can get work done after a meal like this. I'm ready for a nap."

With the traditional cups of coffee on their way, Bill thought it was the right time to get to the point of why he asked his father to meet for lunch. "Dad, I should have bought lunch for you since I have something I want to discuss with you."

William nodded as he leaned back in his chair. "I figured you had something on your mind when you called about lunch in the middle of the week. Is everything all right?"

"Everything is fine. In fact, the reason I wanted to see you today is to thank you."

William tilted his head in question. "Thank me? For what?"

"As difficult as our conversation on the beach last week was, I really appreciate that you told me what you did," explained Bill.

William smiled inwardly, happy with his son. "Bill, you know how I feel about our family—"

"I know, Dad. And it means a lot that you and I talked about how Ethan is feeling. I know we don't always agree on how things should be done—"

"But we do agree that our family is more important than anything."

"Yes, we do," Bill affirmed.

The setting of the dining room, his turf, encouraged William to take the lead in the conversation. Bill, after all, had opened the proverbial door. "So now that you've had some time to think about it, what do you think?"

Bill, being a Park and William's son, recognized the shift in the conversation. In this instance, he was all right with William's subtle grabbing of the reins as a server brought their coffee.

"Constance and I discussed this for a bit. The love we have for the kids is unequivocal. They truly are gifts to us. They are alike in so many ways."

"Well, they say the apple doesn't fall far from the tree."

Bill chuckled. "You're right about that. The thing is, not all the apples are exactly alike. Each one needs to be cared for in their own way." Bill related his feelings about being upset that Ethan hadn't gone to either him or Constance.

"You know, Bill, that's why we have family. Think if Ethan didn't feel comfortable to talk openly with me or your mother. Who would he turn to then?"

Bill nodded in agreement. "You're right. It's just—"

"I understand. But I have an idea."

"Okay, Dad, I'm open."

"Let's come up with a project that Ethan can make in the woodshop. Something specific that you would like and use."

Bill once again nodded. "All right. I'll think of something and let you know."

"Great." William appreciated that they had found common ground.

Bill reflected on their discussion at the beach. Ethan had definitely taken to making things in the woodshop. Having Ethan craft something for him that he could use or proudly put on display was a clever idea. But he also wanted to make the point that it was time, past time, for Ethan to branch out and start participating in team sports. "Dad, I also think we need to get Ethan involved in sports. He needs structured time with other kids his age."

William hesitantly agreed as he remembered how the sports leagues had caused the demise of his shell-hunting adventures with Trip. "As long as it doesn't interfere with our woodworking on Saturdays," William proclaimed.

"Dad, just like with Trip. Ethan is *my* son. Constance and I will decide when and where Ethan goes."

"I guess my involvement with him then doesn't matter—"

Bill shook his head. "I do value the time and experiences you bring into Ethan's life, but he is my son." Attempting to soften the mood, he continued, "Besides, you have acknowledged that the values taught in sports go a long way toward the making of a good person."

William readily agreed. "Yes, they do. They prepare people for the real world—the work world."

Bill pushed his chair back from the table. "Speaking of the work world, I should get back to it. Thanks for lunch, Dad. I'm glad we could get together. I'll have you over to Park Productions next time."

※ ※ ※ ※

Standing in William's backyard, one would not have known that a major storm had brought three inches of rain to the area the previous evening. The grass displayed a vibrant green, the flowers were radiant, and the sun shone brightly. It was a great day to enjoy the fresh air by having the doors to the woodshop open.

Ethan and William had been working diligently on their project. Now it was break time. Ethan knew that Grandy believed in hard, concentrated work. He was also well aware that Grandy had a refrigerator full of soft drinks in the corner for break time. Ethan was glad Grandy insisted they take periodic rests.

Surprisingly, William enjoyed the breaks as much as he relished shaping, painting, and polishing wood into a finished product. Often Margaret would initiate the beginning of break time by arriving at the woodshop with a plate of her latest baked goods and a pitcher of ice-cold milk. This Saturday was no different in that regard. William and Ethan were enjoying the results of Margaret's wonderful baking skills and, at the same time, the opportunity to just sit and talk.

William treasured these moments with his grandson. He knew these occasions were a building time, but not just a time to build something physical requiring the use of one's hands. No, this was a time for building with one's heart. William perceived this as both the building of the relationship with his grandson along with the building of the future of the family.

Ethan set down his glass, which was now empty. "Grandy, who is Walt?"

William turned to look over his shoulder at the sign hanging above the entrance to the shed. "Walt was a woodworker known as the 'Dean of the Workshop.' He knew more about woodworking than anyone," William replied.

"Why do you have his sign?" Ethan inquired. "Did he build this woodshop?"

William laughed. "No, he didn't build this woodshop. That sign was made by my dad. He had it hung in *his* woodshop in honor of the 'Dean,' Walt Durbahn. A very long time ago Walt had a TV show called *Walt's Workshop*. As a little boy, I watched that show with my dad. Then my dad and I would go into the woodshop and try the things Walt did on the show. It was great fun."

Ethan smiled. "Does Mr. Walt still have a TV show?"

William looked thoughtful. "No, Mr. Walt has passed on. But he wrote two good books that contain a lot of his knowledge and techniques. And we can still go back and look at the TV shows."

William reached for a cookie, put it on Ethan's plate, and took another for himself. "So, we hang that sign to honor Mr. Walt's memory and my dad, your great-grandfather."

"Grandy, am I going to get to hang the sign when . . ." Ethan's voice dropped off, and he stared down at his cookie.

"Yes, Ethan," replied William. "One day when you have a woodshop, you will hang this sign over its door to keep the family tradition."

Ethan looked at the sign and then back at his grandfather. "Grandy, I don't want the sign anytime soon."

"I'm not looking to give it to you anytime soon." William poured milk into both glasses. "You know, Ethan, Walt always stressed the importance of having a well-thought-out idea that could be put into a well-thought-out plan."

Ethan, connecting the dots, replied, "Is that why you asked me so many questions about this case we're making for my dad's microphone?"

"Yes, you have to know what you're building before you can start. You should have a good idea of what you expect," William explained. "Otherwise, how do you know where to start? And how will you know if you've succeeded?"

※ ※ ※ ※

Not by design, but more by happenstance, the young Park family arrived in separate vehicles at their residence at the same time. Bill brought his SUV to a stop. With a mock bow and a flourish with his arm, he let Constance pass before turning into the drive. Constance laughed at her husband's dramatic motions and showed her appreciation by blowing Bill a delicate kiss as she turned in ahead of him.

71

By the time Constance had walked over to her husband's car to welcome Bill and Trip home, Ethan grabbed the case he had crafted for his dad and made a beeline into the house. Constance gave Bill a kiss. "How did it go?"

A wide grin stretched across Bill's face. "Coming home to a reception like this, I think we need to have a muddy win every week."

Trip rounded the back of the car and came into Constance's view. His mother gasped when she saw him. Or rather, what she thought was her oldest son. He was covered head to toe in dried mud. The only parts of his face not caked with mud were his eyes and mouth.

Seeing the harried look on his mother's face, Trip played it up. "Hi, Mom, it's me, your son. Can I give you a hug?"

Constance drew back. "I think not." Looking at Bill, she inquired, "What have you done with my beautiful son?"

"He's in there somewhere because I can still read part of the number on his jersey. That rain last night really made a mess of the field. There was a question as to whether we should let the boys play."

"Seeing this," Constance bent to kiss the top of her son's head, "I would have voted no." Swiping at a mud-caked cowlick, she laughed. "Did you play football, or just slide around in the mud?"

"C'mon, Mom," Trip answered. "We had a blast."

"Trip, now you know that the mud room isn't strictly for the dogs. Go in there, strip down, hose off, and hit the showers," Bill encouraged.

Trip called out over his shoulder to his parents. "I can't wait to tell Ethan how much fun it was to play in the mud today."

"Make sure you take that shower first," Bill barked.

Constance shook her head. "I'll never understand the thrill you guys get out of rolling around in the mud."

As Trip headed toward the mud room, Constance informed Bill that Ethan had finished his project with Grandy, and Ethan would be giving it to him tonight after dinner.

"What do you think? Did he do a good job?"

Constance was the type of person who loved both surprises and surprising people. She had read studies that showed surprises have the potential to increase a person's emotions by almost four hundred percent. Happy surprises like this one would surely meet the study's benchmark and maybe even exceed it.

"I'm not sure," she deadpanned. "I don't know what a microphone case is supposed to do or how it's supposed to look. Just make sure you don't look disappointed when you see it."

This response left Bill bewildered. Normally Constance was very upbeat about anything the kids did or made. Bill thought she would be especially so for this project. He began to worry that perhaps he was going to have to give an acting performance worthy of an Oscar nomination.

Inwardly Constance knew that Bill would be amazed when he saw the microphone case. William had spent extra time with Ethan over the past few weeks working on the design. Grandfather and grandson had spent several afternoons at the lumber mill inspecting different types of woods, stains, hinges, and latches.

William had decided early on that this project could serve multiple purposes. The primary purpose, of course, was so that Ethan would build something special for his dad that he could fawn over in appreciation.

William also took this opportunity to work with Ethan on creating a vision for the project, designing a plan for the project, properly preparing for the project, and then executing the project to its fullest.

Say what you are going to do. Then do it!

If one should ask William about his proudest moments in construction, he would list this project of Ethan's in his top five. His grandson had performed admirably, like a true Park. Ethan had helped create a masterpiece like any seasoned construction engineer. In William's mind, Walt Durbahn would also be proud.

✳ ✳ ✳ ✳

Dinner at the Park household was a family affair. Everyone who could be present was expected to be present. The Park's dinner table was situated in the alcove that looked over the backyard, the swimming pool, and the outdoor kitchen. There was no television within eyesight or earshot of this space. This wasn't due to a lack of planning. In the minds of Constance and Bill, this was due to intentional forethought.

When the Parks designed their home, they envisioned dinners as being a time to talk with the family—to hear about everyone's highs and lows. In fact, each person at the table was highly encouraged to tell about their high and low for the day. This ritual sparked great conversations. It also gave the family the opportunity to revel in each other's successes as well as show support for each other during their low periods.

After dinner Trip and Ethan were putting the last of the dishes into the dishwasher. Constance turned to Bill and suggested, "Bill, why don't you open that bottle of Cannonau di Sardegna? I'll take Claire upstairs for her bath and put her to bed."

Following Constance's lead, Bill replied, "Sounds good to me. Let's meet in the studio. C'mon, boys. Grab a couple of soft drinks. We're going to take a 'Musical Journey' tonight!"

✳ ✳ ✳ ✳

By the time Constance stepped into the studio, Bill had adjusted the lighting to a soft, welcoming level. Classic rock was playing on the studio monitors. That is how nights usually began when the family gathered in the studio. It was a relaxing time, a time for everyone to slow down their minds from the day. It was a time to share in some wholesome family fun with music and each other.

Bill had named these evenings a "Musical Journey." The evenings typically started with a selection by Bill or Constance. Next, someone else suggested a song. As the evening progressed, one song led to another. When one particular song or lyric reminded someone of a phrase, artist, or band, a new suggestion was put forth and the next leg of the journey would be underway.

Bill and Constance enjoyed these evenings. They loved time with the boys, and they loved music as well. They also saw these evenings as an opportunity to teach the boys about music. Bill emphasized to his sons, "You *play* music, you don't *work* it." These evenings were about being immersed in the art of music. In addition, Bill and Constance acquired a better understanding of the boys themselves through these fun-filled gatherings.

Trip and Ethan appreciated these evenings as well because they believed *they* were teaching their parents about music. The boys had different musical tastes than their parents. So, they used this opportunity to teach their mom and dad how to be hip by showing off their own musical prowess and knowledge of contemporary performers.

At some point in the evening, the mode usually shifted from listening to music to participating. If one could play an instrument, sing, or dance, they were required to perform. Everyone in the Park family could do at least two of the three. This led to a lively evening of singing, dancing, and laughing.

❇ ❇ ❇ ❇

As the echo of Bill's last vocals were ringing out in the studio, Constance gave the call, "Gentlemen, I believe that's a wrap. It's getting late and I'm one tired momma."

This was a part of the unwritten script for musical journeys. Constance gave the call and the boys always responded, "But Mom, one more song."

Everyone in the family knew the song. It was the swan song for all of their "Musical Journeys." The show closed the same way each time. As the boys finished their plea, the first notes of "Come On, Get Happy!" by the Partridge Family emanated from the studio monitors. The family gathered around the microphones and sang their hearts out, even taking the traditional Partridge bow to their make-believe audience. It was a wrap.

The boys rose from their bows. "Dad," Ethan exclaimed, "we should get a bus and paint it like the Partridge Family did and tour the country."

Trip seconded his brother's sentiments. "Yeah, Ethan can play guitar and I'll play bass."

Bill laughed. "We'll think about it. For now, let's strike the studio."

Just as the expectation was for everyone to participate in the journey, the expectation was also that everyone participated in the *strike*. This was a term Bill had taught the boys early on. When a band is done with a gig, you don't *pick up* the equipment—you *strike* it.

The boys were adept at striking the studio after a musical journey. They rolled the cables and put them in their proper storage places, folded the mic stands, put away the instruments, covered the piano, and returned the sound board back to "normal" before turning it off.

Ethan had decided after his mother's suggestion earlier in the day that the strike would be the perfect time to give his dad the microphone case. Everyone knew Bill was very particular about his musical equipment, especially about the microphones because the mouth of a performer often came in contact with the mic. To Bill's way of thinking, microphones were like drinking glasses—you don't normally drink out of someone else's glass. He strongly believed everyone had to have their own microphone.

Bill began putting the microphones in their designated cases. A case marked "Constance" held her mic. There were similar cases for Trip and Ethan as well as for Bill. These were the standard plastic cases that came from the manufacturer. They consisted of good, solid construction but were nothing special.

Bill purposely planned to put his microphone away last. As he closed the clasp on the last mic case, Ethan approached him.

"Dad, would you take your mic out of the case for a minute?" Ethan asked nervously. "That case looks broken."

Bill looked up. "I don't think it's broken."

From behind his back, Ethan brought forward the case he crafted. "Dad, I made a special case for your mic so that when you have a gig, your mic is safe and clean."

Constance was standing just off to the side and behind Ethan when Bill saw the case. He was stunned and overcome with emotion by the sight of his son holding what looked like a museum piece. Constance was willing to bet two things. One was that Bill would not get nominated for an Oscar because he was not acting. The second was that Bill's emotions had intensified by way more than the study's four hundred percent.

Ethan took a deep breath and handed the case to his father. "Here Dad, it's for you. I hope you like it. I made it with Grandy."

Bill smiled at his son and carefully took the case from Ethan's hands. He felt the smoothness of the finish. It was flawless. As Bill turned the case over, he looked intently at all six sides. There was not one nail hole visible on the exterior of the case. It was impressive. Turning the case face up, Bill looked at the small gold plate that was affixed to the top. It read,

Bill Park

"The B-Sides"

Bill turned the small brass clasp on the front of the case and opened the lid. In the bottom was a small cradle to hold a microphone. The interior of the case was lined with crushed velvet in Bill's favorite color, purple. Opening the box fully, Bill noticed a small frame inside the lid. In the frame was a picture of Bill, Constance, and the three kids sitting in front of the mixing board. Margaret had taken this picture a couple years ago after Bill had installed the new console.

Earlier when Ethan showed his mother the case, she was amazed. She always knew that William had a knack for woodwork, but this surpassed her expectations.

As she observed Bill seeing the case for the first time, Constance realized that this hand-crafted project and what it meant was incredibly special. Her eyes met Bill's. Though this was a gift from Ethan to Bill, they both knew this was also a gift *from* William . . . to Bill.

There was a secret about the construction of the case known only to William. It was a secret William would never divulge. Bill sensed something, but he couldn't pin down the origin of the feeling. William knew Ethan would be credited with the construction of the case. Although he had guided, coached, and instructed him, it was Ethan's hands that did the work. Or so everyone thought.

Even though Ethan managed to diligently follow instructions, at nine years old he didn't have the physical dexterity to manipulate the tools to exacting standards. Ethan's attempts and results had been admirable and of high quality, but William believed that for this case to become a family heirloom, the quality would need to be better. He knew his grandson would need a little help.

So, William devised a plan. On Saturday afternoons after Ethan had gone home, he inspected the results of their efforts from that morning. William then reworked the components of the case. In a couple of instances, he built new ones to the level of accuracy needed for the pieces to fit together properly. William had been diligent in making sure that the work he did in the afternoons would not be noticed by his grandson. He placed the newly crafted pieces in the cubby where Ethan stored his projects until he returned to work on them the following Saturday. Then he would take the faulty pieces to work for disposal.

Bill, still mesmerized by the fine workmanship, looked up at his son. "Thank you, Ethan. This is remarkable. I can't wait to show the guys in the band what you made for me."

"You're welcome, Dad. I picked out the purple because I know it's your favorite color."

"That's right, purple *is* my favorite color." Bill looked back at the case. "You built this all by yourself?"

"Well, Grandy helped a little but not that much." Ethan placed his hands on his hips and pulled back his shoulders. "He said to me, 'This is *your* baby.' So I tackled the job."

As Ethan and his father shared their enthusiasm, Constance opened the manufacturer's case containing Bill's microphone. She handed the microphone to Bill. He carefully placed it in the new case. "It fits like a glove! Ethan, you are an excellent woodcrafter."

Ethan smiled with pride and the slightest hint of relief.

Chapter 6
BILL DROPS THE BALL

Ethan pumped the pedals of his vintage Schwinn Scrambler hard as he and Roger crested the hill that led them home. As they reached their street, Roger peeled off first down his drive with his customary yell of "See you later, alligator" followed by Ethan's reply, "I hope your legs grow straighter." Ethan then continued down the street toward the Park residence.

The boys enjoyed the ride from Shadowfield Middle School to their respective homes. As each school day ended, they would traverse a couple of neighborhood streets and make their way through shade-covered park paths that offered a few jumps and twists. Then they would hit what they had come to call "The Freeway." This was a long stretch of the street through the neighborhood that had three nice-sized hills on which they could obtain maximum speed on their downward slopes. For the boys, this meant maximum fun.

Today's ride had been especially enjoyable for both boys and exceptionally quicker than usual. The adrenaline coursing through their veins encouraged their legs to push the pedals even harder. The sixth-graders at Shadowfield Middle School were going to have a "Go To Work

With Your Dad Day." The boys were eager to tell their mothers the big news.

Ethan loved going to his father's office. Actually, however, whenever Ethan went to work with his dad, they hardly spent any time at all in the office. Instead, most of their time was spent in the shop where the stages and lighting rigs were designed, fabricated, and assembled. Or, on some days, they spent their time in the back lot where the stages, lighting rigs, and setups were tested. On special days they visited one of the local venues where a stage was being set for a live show. Sometimes Ethan even had the opportunity to be on stage for a sound check.

❊ ❊ ❊ ❊

Constance was in the kitchen putting the finishing touches on today's after-school snack when Ethan entered through the side door. Two things tipped off Ethan to the fact that today's snack would be his favorite. The first was the smell of grilled cheese in the air. The second was the sight of Claire in her booster seat with a large smile on her face and a half-eaten grilled cheese sandwich in her hand.

Constance greeted Ethan, "Good afternoon, Ethan. How was your day?"

"It was good, Mom. I need to tell you about 'Go To Work With Your Dad Day.'"

Constance placed a grilled cheese sandwich beside some potato chips on a plate and set it on the table for Ethan. "How about you put away your backpack and say hello to your sister first?"

82

Ethan looked at his sister. "Hi, Claire Bear," he teased. Claire giggled at her brother's pet name for her. "Can I have a bite?"

"No!" Claire shot back as she hugged the sandwich to her chest.

The temptation of his own grilled cheese suddenly outweighed the excitement of the news he had for his mother. Ethan tore into the sandwich.

"You know, Ethan, you don't have to eat that all in one bite."

He swallowed the large chunk and washed it down with milk. "Mom, you make the *best* grilled cheese sandwiches in the world."

Constance smiled. "Why, thank you, Ethan. What's this big news you have about going to work? Aren't you going to finish school before you start working?"

Ethan smirked. "Mom, it's only for one day, and I go to work with Dad. You know, just like Trip got to do when he was in sixth grade. Then I have to write a report on it for class."

"Ethan, that should be fun. Your dad will be excited for you to spend a day with him at his job. What day are you supposed to go?"

Ethan polished off the last of his potato chips. "It's on the sheet that's in my backpack."

"Okay, we'll take a look later when you start your homework."

"I don't even have to go to school at all that day—just to Dad's work," Ethan enthused.

"I'm sure you and your father will have a great day together."

Trip ambled through the side door of the kitchen. "Hi, Mom. Where's my grilled cheese sandwich?"

Constance tilted her head and raised her eyebrows. "How about saying hello to your brother and sister?"

Trip bent down eye level with his little sister. "Gimme a bite," he teased.

Claire pulled her hand back, holding the sandwich over her shoulder. "No!"

"You boys sure do think alike. And stop picking on your sister."

He looked at his brother's sandwich. "Ethan, can I have a bite of *your* sandwich?"

Ethan feigned shock and pulled the sandwich to his chest. "No!"

Claire, Constance, and the boys laughed.

"Trip, take a seat. I have enough sandwiches for everyone."

After finishing their snack and putting their glasses and plates in the dishwasher, Trip and Ethan headed outside to play pitch-and-catch. Neither boy had played T-ball or baseball in their younger years, but they reveled in the fact that they were relatively adept at playing pitch-and-catch.

After about forty-five minutes, Constance opened the back door and called out to the boys, "All right, guys. Let's come inside so we can get to your homework."

Trip took the glove off of his left hand and commented to Ethan as they walked inside, "Look at the red mark you made on my hand!"

"Wow!" Ethan observed Trip's hand. "That must sting."

"Well, it doesn't feel great. You're throwing the ball really hard," Trip replied as he massaged his hand.

"You boys need to be careful. Don't hurt each other."

Rolling their eyes at the typical *mom* response, Trip and Ethan grabbed their backpacks from the mud room.

"Mom, I'm going to my room to study," Trip yelled over his shoulder as he headed for the stairs.

Constance watched Ethan unload what appeared to be every book in his academic arsenal. *If he needs all of those books for today's homework, we'll never eat dinner tonight.*

After arranging all his books on the table, Ethan opened his homework folder. This folder actually was more for the *parents* than for the student. Yes, the contents of the folder did list the homework assignments for a particular day, but it also contained all communication to the parents that the teacher believed were relevant.

"Any notes for me from Miss Peart today?"

"No, Mom," answered Ethan. "But here is the paper telling all about 'Go To Work With Your Dad Day.'" He pulled the paper out of the folder and handed it to his mother.

Constance scanned the sheet from Miss Peart. Ethan's teacher had planned out a rigorous day for her students. This didn't look like a day for the kids to follow their fathers around just for fun. Constance noticed a list of about twenty questions or observations that the student would have to report on to the class about their dad's occupation as well as the day spent at his place of work.

The section of information at the bottom of the page contained the logistics for the day. It was here that Constance noted the date and checked the family calendar that was kept on the desk in the kitchen. What Constance saw did not look good. There would be a conflict with Bill's schedule. She had learned over the years that it was rare for Bill to have the opportunity to leave a band during the middle of a tour. This was going to be a problem.

Constance was well aware of Ethan's excitement for this event. It was something all of the sixth-graders looked forward to experiencing. Not only would they each get a day away from the classroom, but it was also a chance to spend time with their fathers instead. To be the center of their dad's attention was special for many. In Ethan's case, he would get to see things that most of the other kids wouldn't. After all, his father worked in the entertainment business.

Constance sat down in the chair next to Ethan. "Honey, I have some bad news. It looks like your father is going to be out of town on a two-week tour. The 'Go To Work With Your Dad Day' happens right in the middle of this trip."

Ethan's shoulders sank as he dropped his pencil on the table. He really wanted to go to work with his dad. And the students who didn't go to work with their fathers had to go to school and do busy work for the entire day.

"Mom, can I go to meet Dad during the tour—just for the day?"

Constance stroked Ethan's hair. "I don't think so. The flight is four hours long. But we'll think of something."

Ethan's countenance brightened. He sat up straight. "How about if I go to work with Grandy instead? Would that count?"

86

The fact that Ethan quickly suggested a possible solution rather than wallowing in defeat and misery comforted Constance. This seemed to be a common occurrence in the Park family. When adversity hit, no matter at what level, they didn't let it get them down. The Parks would quickly devise an alternative plan.

"You know, Ethan, I think Grandy would be quite proud to bring you to his place of work. But let's check with Miss Peart."

⁂ ⁂ ⁂ ⁂

"Thank you, Miss Peart. Yes, I really appreciate your approval of Ethan going to work with his grandfather since his father will be traveling at that time," Constance said into the phone.

"Ethan is such a wonderful student," the teacher replied. "He has spoken often of his grandfather. He should have no problem being able to successfully complete the assignment."

Constance once again thanked Miss Peart. The ladies said their goodbyes.

Hanging up the phone, her mind was already working on the most challenging element of the situation. It wasn't going to be easy to tell her husband that he would have to miss "Go To Work With Your Dad Day." Three years ago, Bill had thoroughly enjoyed showing off Trip to the Park Productions staff when he was in sixth grade. At the same time, he had been proud to show off his work environment to Trip. Constance's recollection was that Bill had been as keyed up about that day as Trip.

Bill had listed his "high" for that day as time spent with Trip on "Go To Work With Your Dad Day" in spite of the fact that Bill had closed on that very same day a lucrative concert tour deal with an artist he'd been courting for several years. Bill had been pleased to close this deal, but he had been even more pleased to be with Trip. He was not shy about bragging on his oldest son and his gridiron accomplishments.

✳ ✳ ✳ ✳

Constance drove to the offices of Park Productions to meet Bill so they could enjoy lunch together.

To the uninitiated, walking into the Park Productions warehouse appeared as if one was walking into sheer chaos. The main fabrication space was large and loud, operating at a frenetic pace. If the sounds of saws, riveters, welding machines, hammers banging on a wide variety of materials, employees shouting instructions in a lingo of their own making, and various other sources of cacophony weren't enough, overlaying this soundtrack of production was music being piped out of a massive amplifier system at seemingly earsplitting volume. Bill's theory was that music created positive energy among the staff.

For Constance, there was always the sense that she was walking into the belly of the entertainment beast whenever she entered this fabrication building. As she moved through a walkway cordoned off to keep visitors safe, Constance marveled at the amount of work and people it took to stage a show. It required hundreds of staff members to design, engineer, build and transport the stage, lighting, and sound systems. The shop floor is where the dreams and visions came to life.

The creative process actually began behind the windows situated three stories above the hustle and bustle of the fabrication floor. This was Bill's office, the administrative and design offices of Park Productions. It was in these offices where Bill and his staff made sure the happenings on the main floor were more of a controlled rather than total chaos.

The elevator delivered Constance to the suite of offices on the third floor. As she walked down the corridor toward Bill's office, it was not lost on her that framed images of past sets, shows, and stages created by Park Productions adorned the walls. Just like the pictures on the walls at Park Enterprises, these photographs also displayed a journey through time. These images told the story of Park Productions from the humble beginnings of the company to its present-day status as a powerhouse in the entertainment industry.

Constance had also noted a change in atmosphere when she exited the elevator. For all the frenetic energy on the main floor, these offices exuded a more relaxed timbre. Bill held the philosophy that a tranquil, steady atmosphere enhanced creativity. He also believed this type of environment helped to keep existing as well as potential clients on track when working through the details of a design or contract.

Kelli, the Park Productions receptionist, greeted Constance, "Good afternoon, Constance. It's great to see you."

Constance smiled. "Hi, Kelli. It's nice to see you, too."

Kelli picked up the phone. "I'll find Bill and let him know you're here. Can I get you a coffee?"

"No, no, no," Constance waved her off and shook her head. "I get energized enough just walking on the fabrication floor. I definitely don't need any caffeine now." She pointed to Bill's office door. "If he's not engaged, I'll just go in."

"All clear, Constance," Kelli said with a shrug and a sweep of her hand. "Go right in and get comfortable. He'll be right up."

Constance chuckled as she "got comfortable." Kelli's shrug, she knew, was code for, "Maybe he'll be *right* up," or "Maybe it will take a little longer."

Seated in Bill's office, Constance had a bird's-eye view of the fabrication floor, minus the cacophony. From this vantage point, the work on the floor appeared more orderly and directed. Constance imagined reality lay somewhere between the two perspectives. She knew that Bill was the one leading the entire effort. If asked, his staff would say they relied on Bill for his vision and leadership as well as his ability to keep the company on the cutting edge. If Bill were asked, though, he would say he relied on his staff to help refine the vision and make the vision into something tangible. Yes, Constance reflected, Bill and his staff had created as perfect a symbiotic relationship as possible in the working world.

Bill awakened Constance out of her reverie as he entered the room. "I know. Sometimes I, too, find that large chunks of time pass while staring out the window watching all of those smart, creative people."

"It's incredible—the work they do." Constance turned to her husband. "And you have provided the optimum atmosphere to make that possible."

"It's certainly been a team effort," Bill replied. "I was thinking about a quick lunch at Frankie's Place. We can grab a bite. What do you think?"

Constance wrinkled her nose and shook her head. "Bill, you know I'm not a fan of that place. That's for you and the guys. Can we come up with something a little quieter where we can talk?"

"Well, I really had my heart set on those chili-cheese fries," Bill sighed. "But I get it."

"I know you like their burgers and fries. But I was hoping for something a little more sedate."

"How about Aldo's?" Bill suggested.

His wife was a *huge* fan of the little Italian bistro for a couple of reasons. First, Mr. Sal, the proprietor, had developed an incredible menu. But, even more so, Constance loved Mr. Sal because he catered a feast of the highest order when he hosted her engagement party with Bill almost twenty years ago. That had been the beginning of a beautiful culinary friendship. Aldo's became the spot where Bill and Constance turned when intimacy and coziness were desired along with a special dining experience.

Constance immediately jumped on the offer. "I think Aldo's is a great idea. Have you ever known me to turn down one of Mr. Sal's meals?"

※ ※ ※ ※

Upon their arrival at Aldo's, Sal appeared from the kitchen with large servings of hugs and focaccia bread. For several minutes he fawned over the Parks and asked about their children.

As Constance was seated at their favorite table, she knew their taste buds were in for a delightful adventure. In lieu of having a waiter take their order once they were seated, Sal started sending dishes of sumptuous food to their table. He must have had a sixth sense because he always seemed to fix dishes that satisfied their current mood and taste. Just as

Bill and Constance knew that entertainment productions didn't happen by magic, they appreciated the true genius of Sal.

✳ ✳ ✳ ✳

Bill put down his demitasse and remarked, "Wow! What a lunch. I don't think I need to eat for at least a week."

Constance laughed. "Sal sure knows how to hit the spot."

In spite of Bill's last remark, he picked up the last cannoli and broke it in half. He offered one half to his wife. As she shook her head no, she reached out and took the treat anyway.

Before starting in on the cannoli, she glanced up at Bill. "I want to talk to you about a school event for Ethan."

Bill's hand froze with the cannoli halfway to his mouth, and he immediately met her gaze. "Yes?"

"It's the 'Go To Work With Your Dad Day'—"

"*Yes!* It should be a blast. Trip and I had such a great day when he was in the sixth grade."

"I remember. Trip still talks about that day." Constance shifted in her chair. "Honey, I checked your travel schedule and unfortunately, for Ethan's day, you will be on tour with Thump."

Bill gaped at Constance. "What do you mean? The 'Go To Work With Your Dad Day' is planned for while I'm on the road?"

Constance toyed with her spoon. "I'm afraid so."

"Maybe I could fly in for the day . . . ."

"Do you think that would be possible? I know this is a huge tour, and usually you aren't able to leave in the middle of it."

Bill dropped the cannoli back on the plate. "You're right. I was dreaming. It's our first tour with these guys—I *have* to be there."

"It's amazing how you and Ethan think alike at times," Constance interjected as Bill trailed off. "He said that maybe he could fly *out* to be with you."

"And?" Bill wanted to know.

"It just wouldn't work," Constance responded, "for either one of you. The school scheduled it on Friday this year, giving the students the weekend to work on their reports."

"And the biggest Thump show of the tour falls on that Friday night. You know how these artists are—they'll be on pins and needles for the entire day." Bill crumpled his napkin and tossed it onto the unfinished cannoli. "I'll have to be there to make sure they feel confident things will go well."

Constance reached for Bill's hand. "I'm sorry. I know how much you really want to spend this day with Ethan."

"As much as I love my job and all that it's given us, this time away from family hurts."

Silence enveloped the table. Bill took in a deep breath, sat up straight, retrieved his napkin and folded it. "We can't have Ethan sit at school all day doing busy work while the rest of his class is at work with their fathers. So, we need a plan."

Constance was aware that what she was about to say would be adding insult to injury, but there was nothing else she could think of to do. She also knew that as disappointed and upset as Bill would be, he always chose an option that he believed was favorable for the children.

Constance sipped the last of her wine. "Ethan asked your father if he could go to work with him."

"Great," Bill huffed. "Another bullet in Dad's arsenal about how I don't put the family first."

Chapter 1

GO TO WORK WITH GRANDY

Ethan walked proudly beside his grandfather as they strode through the front door of Park Enterprises. He knew spending the day with Grandy would be a vacation from schoolwork but definitely not one from work. Grandy would expect him to be an active participant in the activities of the day. Ethan would not only have to fulfill the requirements of the assignment from Miss Peart, but he would also have to complete the tasks assigned to him by his grandfather. Though it would be an exciting walk through the workings of Park Enterprises, it would certainly be no walk in the park.

William pushed the button in the elevator that would take the two of them to his office. Turning to Ethan, he said, "All right, here we go. Get ready to learn and work."

"I'm ready, Grandy. I reviewed the assignment list you gave me last night."

"Excellent," William responded. "It's always a good idea to review the night before what you have on your plate for the following day."

As the elevator began its ascent to the top floor of Park Enterprises, Ethan sensed his grandfather's desire for his eventual ascent within Park Enterprises.

※ ※ ※ ※

Barbara made it a habit to be in the office at least half an hour prior to William's arrival, though this was not a requirement put on her by William. Her boss was not in the habit of demanding his executive staff to punch the clock. His requirements were simply that everyone be prepared and the work be accomplished on time and on budget.

For this reason Barbara always arrived before William. Though she had reviewed William's To Do list the previous afternoon, these thirty minutes gave her time to ensure the accuracy of her work and make any necessary updates. She also obtained any documentation required for him to accomplish the list, confirmed meeting requests with those who were on William's schedule, and arranged the office in a general state of readiness for the workday.

As William and Ethan entered the office, they smelled the pleasant aroma of freshly brewed coffee. Each morning Barbara placed a carafe of her boss's favorite brew on the sideboard. Knowing that Ethan would be in the office today, Barbara had added cinnamon raisin bagels to William's serving of bran bagels.

"Miss Barbara is a person who thinks, plans ahead, and executes." William poured two cups of coffee and offered Ethan a bagel. "She knew you'd be here, and she knows you like cinnamon raisin."

"It looks like Miss Barbara is always one step ahead of you, Grandy."

William chuckled. "I believe you're right. And that's a good thing. It's dedicated folks like her who have helped make Park Enterprises successful."

William took a seat behind his desk. In the center of the large desk lay his leather executive folio with the Park Enterprises logo embossed in gold. Ethan sat in the guest chair, facing William. On the side table next to Ethan's chair was an identical leather executive folio.

"Let's take a look at how Miss Barbara has arranged our day." William opened his folio. "Miss Barbara created a Park Enterprises folio for you, too."

Ethan set his cup of coffee milk on the side table. He picked up the folio and slowly ran his index finger across his name embossed in gold. He opened the folio and observed on the left side, a To Do list. On the right side he noted a schedule designed to ensure that the To Do list on the left could be accomplished within the day.

"The first thing I want to talk about with you, Ethan, is how the list in the folio is created."

Ethan picked up his pen and looked at his grandfather. "Okay, I'm ready."

"You will notice," William continued, "that there is half an hour this morning for the two of us to consult. That's what we're doing right now. I want to use this time to talk with you about the day. We will discuss what is expected and how to design a day so that at the end of that day you have accomplished what you set out to do. Very important in business . . . and in life."

Ethan, becoming overwhelmed, studied the folio contents. "This schedule looks very busy, Grandy."

"It is. And it can be achieved with focus and determination. But that's not the point. Not right now. Right now, we're going to talk about how the schedule is made."

Ethan nodded and took a sip of his coffee milk.

"Each afternoon before going home, I look at the To Do list for that day. I review what boxes can be ticked and which ones were not finished and can't be ticked. Those unticked items are the basis for the start of the To Do list for the next day."

"So, if you didn't finish an item, you put it first on the list for the next day?" Ethan asked.

"Exactly. Of course, I have to coordinate that with my calendar to make sure there are no conflicts. Sometimes unticked items get pushed to later in the day or another day. This process can take time and be frustrating when things don't sync together. But it's necessary for efficiency and effectiveness."

"I thought Miss Barbara did all of this for you," Ethan said.

"Yes, she does do a lot of it for me. But ultimately, I am responsible. Therefore, I need to make sure that I'm able to fulfill any commitments I make or that are made on my behalf," William explained.

Ethan's eyes grew wide. "That seems like a lot of work just to create a To Do list."

"To be sure. But we must set goals, commit to those goals, and then accomplish those goals."

"It's like you always tell me, Grandy, *Say what you are going to do. Then do it!*"

William smiled. "Yes. The key that most people miss in that, though, is this: It doesn't necessarily mean that you speak the goal out loud. If you say to *yourself* that you are going to do something, whether or not you told anyone else, you do it."

✳ ✳ ✳ ✳

Ethan sat next to his grandfather in the executive conference room, near the center of the large, well-polished mahogany table that had been gifted to Park Enterprises. Actually, the table had been a gift to William from one of his suppliers in Honduras.

From his vantage point, Ethan felt the table appeared to go on forever. Others seated included the Park Enterprises executives. William had insisted that Ethan have a seat at the table and not be relegated to sitting along the wall. If Ethan would truly shadow William, then he needed to be seated right alongside of him.

William opened the meeting. "Good morning. You have all met my grandson, Ethan. He will be following in my footsteps today as part of an assignment for school. Therefore, he will be sitting in on all of my meetings. As usual, please feel free to talk openly. Ethan, do you have anything you would like to add?"

Ethan hadn't expected his grandfather to ask him to speak. But he knew his grandfather well enough to know that he was being tested and there was a teaching point in here somewhere. His stomach flipped and his heart sank. This was big—really big. He couldn't mess up. He wanted to represent his grandfather and himself appropriately. He wouldn't make Grandy look bad.

99

Stalling, he gathered his thoughts. His mouth was so dry his lips were sticking to his gums. Ethan cleared his throat. He straightened his posture, squared his shoulders, and took a deep breath. "Uh . . . g-good morning. My name is Ethan Park." Once he began speaking, he gained a modicum of confidence and continued. "Thank you for allowing me to sit in on this meeting. I look forward . . ." Ethan cleared his throat again as he searched for words he believed would make sense to this intimidating group of people. " . . . to learning more about Park Enterprises, about business, and just how business works."

The group seated around the table collectively welcomed him.

Ethan looked over at William. His grandfather gave him a nod of approval. Ethan felt the pounding of his heart slow to a more moderate pace. *Oh wow, I did it!*

William took charge of the meeting. "We are here to discuss the position that we are to take due to the supply chain issues we have experienced, which led to a delay in the fabrication of the NK-59 and NK-63 trusses and their complementary supports," William stated. "Dan, would you take it from here?"

Ethan pondered, *I sure hope Mr. Dan explains what trusses and supports are and why they matter so much.*

Dan Stokes had been with Park Enterprises for his entire career. Over the years he had watched William grow the business as well as grow with the business. Dan knew this meeting, unfortunately, was necessary to discuss one of the rare occasions when a Park Enterprises goal was in danger of not being met. The necessary raw materials had not arrived on time. The probability of missing this deadline was in the "critical" category. He was well aware William considered missing a deadline a failure.

Dan began with a positive. "The remainder of the materials to fabricate NK-59, NK-63 and all of the complementary components have arrived from the supplier. These components are now in production. Rich is going to give us a quick fabrication update, and then we'll discuss the options for moving forward."

In the executive conference room of just about any other company, the production report that lay open in front of Rich Barrington would have caused him great concern, which would have been twofold. First, there was the concern that the fabrication delivery deadline would be missed. Second, in missing this deadline, Rich knew it could possibly cost him his job. But Rich wasn't in just *any* executive conference room he was in the Park Enterprises' executive conference room.

Rich began giving the report. "No need to sugarcoat any of this. The news from the fabricator isn't good. In fact, it's bad. But it's not beyond redemption." Rich took a breath to check his notes and allow everyone in the room to feel the weight of the situation.

Ethan shifted his gaze from Rich to his grandfather. *I wonder if Grandy is going to get mad at Mr. Rich.*

"There are several options available to address the issue. They range from doing nothing to putting on a full-court press to meet the deadline, or to get as close to it as possible."

Ethan braced himself as he heard his grandfather take in a large breath of air. "Rich, I appreciate the work that you and your team have done, and are doing, to address this situation," William Park I said. "Let's hear all of the options but focus on the ones that create the best situation for success."

Rich reached for a stack of papers in front of him and began handing them out. "Of course, William. You will notice in the handout the options are listed in order of the chances for success."

William took two reports from the stack as it came around the table. He kept one and opened it, then handed the other to his grandson. Ethan flipped through the report and looked at the columns of numbers, dates, and dollars signs. *No definition of what a truss is or does. I guess I'll have to ask Grandy later. At least I know my math.*

※ ※ ※ ※

Before the second ring from the phone on Barbara's desk sounded, the screensaver on a computer located immediately to her left switched to a photograph of the caller. An image of Bill Park appeared. The screen also displayed a myriad of information about the caller to aid Barbara in how she should best assist Park Enterprises' VIPs. There were only a handful of people with access to this number, every one of them a VIP.

"Good morning, Bill," Barbara said enthusiastically as she answered the phone. "Did you and Constance enjoy dinner last week with William and Margaret at Anthonie's?"

Bill chuckled, "Ah, Barbara. Are you looking at the VIP Info on your screen? Or, are you that good?"

"I'll never tell."

"Keep them guessing, huh?" Bill said. "Is Dad available?"

"Bill, William is in a meeting. You know the rule, 'No interruptions during meetings unless it is a *major* emergency.' In all the years I've been here, though, your father hasn't exactly defined what he means by *major* emergency."

"Actually, I'm really looking for the younger Park, Ethan," Bill explained. "I'd like to see how he's doing. Is he around?"

"Oh, Bill, it's so cute. Your father has him glued to his side. He even has a seat right next to your dad at the executive table. Ethan is receiving the full experience."

"That's great," Bill said with a note of forced enthusiasm. He hoped his dad wasn't pushing the boy too hard. "Can you get him for me?"

"Bill, you know I can't interrupt the meeting."

"Barbara, I'd *really* like to speak with Ethan. Please go get him for me."

Detecting a sudden tension in Bill's voice, Barbara offered, "Bill, I see a hole in William and Ethan's schedule at two o'clock. Would you be able to call back then? I'm sure Ethan would love to talk to you at that time."

"No, I can't. That's in the middle of a sound check. Thanks anyway."

Nothing had changed. It was still business first with his father. On the other side of the country, Bill grimly hung up the phone.

✳ ✳ ✳ ✳

With the morning meeting schedule complete, William and Ethan headed to the executive dining room for lunch. They were seated at a table with a great view of the city skyline. The stepped flooring, at the time of

103

construction, was costly and had given William pause. Though Margaret had never designed an executive dining room, William implicitly trusted her in all things. Therefore, he had put aside his hesitation and gave Margaret free rein with the design and budget to create the ambiance for the dining room.

William thought back on that decision as he sat with his grandson, who was soaking in the refined atmosphere. It had been one of Margaret's requirements that every table have a great sightline to the cityscape. William arrived at the same conclusion he had many times over the years—his trust in Margaret was well-founded. This vantage point would be Ethan's to enjoy when *he* held the reins of Park Enterprises.

"Grandy, are you all right?" Ethan noted a faraway look in his grandfather's eyes. "You have a strange look on your face."

The sound of Ethan's voice startled William, bringing him back to the present. "Oh, yes. I was thinking of your Granny. She created this room. And what a creation it is."

"I didn't know Granny worked for Park Enterprises."

"Everyone in the family worked for Park Enterprises back then," William proudly stated. "We had no choice if we were going to build a successful business to pass on to you kids."

"That's really cool!"

"I don't know about being cool. But Granny and I committed to making a go of it and making Park Enterprises a success." He reached across the table to take the menu from Ethan. "Chef Duke said we don't need to order. He has prepared a special lunch for us in your honor."

✳ ✳ ✳ ✳

Documentary evidence exists indicating that great leaders of the world, dating back to King Solomon, Alexander the Great, Nero, and more recently George Washington enjoyed a cold or frozen sweet treat after finishing the main meal. The treats these leaders indulged in were distant relatives to the desserts created today.

Chef Duke, aware of Ethan's sweet tooth and his love of ice cream, had dug deep into his personal archives to find the recipe for his family's prized homemade vanilla ice cream. After several trial runs, and with a staff that enjoyed the role of tasters, Chef Duke created a sweet, frozen confection that he believed would have made his grandmother proud.

Ethan finished the last spoonful of ice cream and gazed down regretfully at his empty bowl, wondering if it would be *mature* to ask for seconds. *I guess not,* he thought as the server removed the dessert bowls.

"What do you think of your first half-day of work?" William asked, breaking Ethan's focus from the disappearing bowls.

"Pretty cool, Grandy," Ethan replied as he mimicked William's action of placing his napkin on the table. "I do have a question for you about the meeting this morning, though."

"Did you hear something that you didn't understand?"

Ethan sat up a little straighter in his chair. "I thought that one of the reasons a business exists is to make money," Ethan stated. "In the meeting this morning, it seemed like you decided to do something that would probably cost Park Enterprises more money. So, now I'm confused."

William smiled. "Ah, you were paying attention. That's great. It's easy to tune out when a meeting goes long."

Ethan's eyes grew wide. "Grandy, how can someone not pay attention? That was so interesting."

"Sit in enough meetings, and sometimes the excitement dwindles," chuckled William. "At the end of Mr. Rich's report, he gave three basic options. Two of the options would mean delivering the trusses late. The other option, which we chose, delivers the trusses on time."

"I think I understand the three options," Ethan said. "What I don't understand is why the third option was selected. To me, it seems like that one would cost more money because of having to pay for people working longer hours."

"The reasoning behind this decision goes back to a basic business principle." William finished his coffee and set down his cup. "Actually, that life principle taught to me—*drilled* into me by *my* father is, *Say what you are going to do. Then do it!*"

"I've heard you say that at least a million times, Grandy."

"Yes, you have, Ethan. It's probably *the* most important thing my dad taught me," William reflected. "From the beginning of Park Enterprises, we as a company strive to live by that motto. It's important that our employees, clients, suppliers, partners—everyone that we do business with—know that we can be trusted to come through on our promises.

"In any case, your conclusion is correct, Ethan. We could have taken one of the first two options, and Park Enterprises would not lose money on the deal. However, we would lose something more valuable than money. We would lose respect. We signed a contract, meaning we promised to deliver those trusses on a specific date."

"But, Grandy, it's not your fault. Isn't the mill late delivering the steel?"

"Yes, they are, Ethan," replied William. "We could go to the client, throw our hands up in the air, and say it's not our fault. It's the steel mill's fault.

"But the bottom line is *we* committed to deliver the trusses by a certain date. Our job is to do that. Yes, we will have to pay overtime to get the job finished, but we will have stood by our commitment. Telling the client that the delay is the mill's fault ends up looking like an excuse. It also sullies the reputation of a longtime, faithful partner. I'm confident the mill has done its best but fell short on this job."

"Shouldn't the steel mill have to pay something?"

William snapped his fingers and pointed to Ethan. "You are a very astute learner. Yes, we will talk with the mill about them picking up some of the tab for the overtime. There will also be discussions with the mill about the reasons for the delay and what they'll do to make sure it doesn't happen again."

Ethan sat a little taller because of Grandy's praise. Maybe he had learned more in the meeting than he thought.

William continued, "They won't get another high-profile job from Park Enterprises until they can prove that they have solved the delivery issues. Park Enterprises will use the mill again on other smaller projects. We will watch them very carefully, though. We'll want extra measures put in place to monitor their work."

"Wow, Grandy, building buildings can be complicated, like putting together a jigsaw puzzle."

William nodded. "Yes, it can be. But always do the right thing, even if it hurts in the short term. Remember what my dad used to say—"

Ethan jumped in with, *"Say what you are going to do."* Both smiled and declared in unison, *"Then do it!"*

✳ ✳ ✳ ✳

Ethan climbed out of William's car and donned the hard hat and safety vest, both bearing the Park Enterprises' logo. Barbara had given him this equipment before he and William departed the office. Ethan's name was printed in bold type directly below the logo on the hard hat and embroidered below the corporate logo located on the left breast of the vest. Anyone seeing Ethan on the job site would identify him not as a visitor but as an actual member of the Park Enterprises staff.

Ethan proudly walked next to his grandfather as they entered the construction site of the new headquarters for the Lucas Corporation. This was his first opportunity to be on an active Park Enterprises' site. In the past, Ethan had toured many of the buildings constructed by his grandfather's company. But those tours had taken place *after* the work had been completed, so there had been no need for personal protective equipment.

The Lucas Corporation project was still in its infancy. Thus, heavy equipment and cranes were everywhere. Barbara had not only provided Ethan with his personalized hard hat and vest, but she also had given him a brand-new pair of safety boots—and in his size. Ethan felt like he really was part of the team. *Wait until I show Trip all this cool stuff. Heck, wait until I show it in class. Maybe I could just wear it all to school.*

"Good afternoon, Johnny. How are you today?" William greeted the safety officer on duty.

A safety officer is on duty at every Park Enterprises construction site during all the building processes. Johnny Anderson, a relatively new employee of Park Enterprises, was designated the chief safety officer for the Lucas project. Though he had been with Park Enterprises less than a year, he had already become a "company man." He had also, in that short amount of time, come to admire the work ethic and integrity of the CEO of Park Enterprises, along with the way William conducted himself and ran the company. In Johnny's mind, he had landed the perfect job and was working for someone who didn't believe a company should be driven only by profits.

"Good morning, sir," Johnny replied. "It's good to see you."

Ethan stepped forward, put his hand out to Johnny, and introduced himself, "Hi, Mr. Anderson. My name is Ethan Park."

"Good morning, Ethan. It's great to have you on the job site today." Johnny shook Ethan's hand. "I'm the safety officer for this project. It's my job to make sure no one gets hurt and that everyone goes home to their family in one piece."

Ethan scanned the job site. "Wow! How do you do that?"

"Well," Johnny began, "the first thing I do is greet everyone when they come onto the site. Then I make sure they are wearing the proper PPE. I see you and your grandfather have on the appropriate gear."

"What does saying hello to everyone have to do with safety?"

Johnny smiled. "Well, actually there are two reasons. First, at Park Enterprises we like to make sure everyone knows they are important to us as people and employees. That's an ideal embedded by your grandfather into the Park Enterprises' culture. Second, greeting everyone lets me get a read to see if they have the right mindset to be on a heavy construction site."

"A read?" Ethan interrupted. "What does that mean?"

"Well, it means I check to make sure they don't appear to be under the influence of any drugs or alcohol, which is not really a problem with our staff. But then I also take a close look to make sure they are not angry or upset about something that could distract them while they are on the site."

"Do you mind if I take some notes? This is for a class assignment." Before Johnny could answer, Ethan opened his Park folio and retrieved a pencil from his shirt pocket.

"Not at all," Johnny replied. "Ready? Do you want me to start over?"

"No, sir," Ethan stated as he began writing. "I'm ready."

Johnny nodded. "You know, there's a lot of activity on the site. If one is not paying attention, they could endanger themselves or someone else."

The conversation between Johnny and Ethan continued for several minutes as Johnny gave Ethan a rundown of all his responsibilities as the chief safety officer. Ethan continued taking notes and asking questions.

William stood back and observed the interaction. He was impressed by his grandson's candor and the questions he asked of Johnny. The depth of the questions showed that not only was Ethan engaged, but he was also understanding and genuinely thinking about the idea of safety on the work site. William's mind made the leap forward: *Here is the future CEO of Park Enterprises.*

Once Johnny and Ethan finished their discussion, William thanked Johnny and stepped into the conversation. "How is Julie? How are those twin boys, Sammy and Mikey? I bet you have your hands full."

Johnny laughed. "Julie is great. The boys definitely give us a workout, but we wouldn't trade it for anything."

※ ※ ※ ※

Ethan warily studied the construction elevator. It appeared shaky and, unlike every other elevator he had ridden, it was open to the air and the outside world. The openness was unsettling. Ethan put his apprehension aside and strode onto the elevator, exuding as much confidence as he could muster. He glanced at the two men standing beside him. *Johnny's here to make sure we're safe, and Grandy doesn't appear to be concerned, so the elevator must be okay.*

William leaned over and whispered in Ethan's ear, "Good job! First-time riders in a construction elevator are usually scared. You're doing quite well."

Ethan looked at Grandy and smiled. He liked how his grandfather always seemed to know what he was thinking and feeling. Ethan was grateful his grandfather had not made a big deal about his anxiety and did not embarrass him in front of the other workers on the elevator.

William turned to the elevator operator. "Good morning, Eddie. How are you this morning?"

"I'm doing well, Mr. Park."

"Eddie operates the elevator on site and makes sure it is safe." William winked at Ethan and joked, "His job certainly has its ups and downs."

Ethan grinned at his grandfather's play on words.

"Mr. Park, I want to thank you for the beautiful bouquet of flowers that you sent to Allison and me for our anniversary. The gift certificate to Athonie's was much appreciated as well."

"You're welcome, Eddie," replied William. "You and Allison are an admirable couple. Being married thirty-five years—now that's what I call standing by your commitment."

The elevator began its ascent. Unconsciously, Ethan gripped the rail.

✳ ✳ ✳ ✳

The upper floors of the Lucas Corporation project were far from complete. However, the skeleton of the building had been completed and most of the steel decking installed. A bevy of workers occupied just about every square foot of the space. To Ethan's untrained eye, it appeared the workmen were oblivious to each other's presence. To William's discerning gaze, what he saw was a well-choreographed team working in perfect unison. The team was intent on achieving two common goals—being safe and finishing the project on time.

As William guided Ethan through the skeletal maze, he explained how the final product would look and function once complete. Ethan took notes furiously as he and William toured the spaces.

Ethan learned that designing a building, such as the Lucas Corporation headquarters, was only the beginning. Once the designs had been completed, the team would work on developing the project plan.

William stopped at a table and picked up a large piece of paper illustrating the current work plan. "Just as an orchestra has four different sections of instruments to create music—strings, woodwinds, brass, and percussion—so also a construction team has sections, though many more than four, to erect a building." William pointed to the list of teams and steps to complete this phase. "All the sections must work in harmony to create the building as it has been designed. In both disciplines, timing is critical. For example, a woodwind coming in a beat too early has the potential to throw off the timing for everyone else in the orchestra and end up sounding like a kluge of noise. So, too, the timing on a construction project is ruined if the flooring team is on site before the concrete slab has been poured."

"Grandy, is there a conductor to this 'orchestra?'"

"Yes, there is. That person is called the project manager." Ethan flipped to a new page in his folio and continued to write. "His job is to coordinate with all of the different disciplines, get the status of their part of the project, and make adjustments to the schedule where necessary."

"The project manager really *is* like a conductor." Ethan smiled and waved his pencil as if directing an ensemble of musicians.

"You've got the picture." William laughed. "And just like Miss Barbara helps me create my daily To Do list, the project manager works with all of these folks to create their daily To Do lists."

William and Ethan rode the construction elevator, operated by Eddie, several more times. Ethan became more and more comfortable with each successive ride so much so that Eddie let him operate the button panel that put the elevator in either an upward or downward trajectory, depending upon the desired destination. William continued the tour on each floor. He introduced Ethan to just about every worker on site. There were so many different people that Ethan had no idea how Grandy kept all the names straight.

※ ※ ※ ※

The scent of roasted meat, potatoes, and carrots drifted through the kitchen as Constance opened the oven door to check on the status of the dinner she was preparing for William, Margaret, and the children.

Margaret breathed in deeply and savored the aroma. "Constance, you sure do know how to make a fine roast."

"I have to give all of the credit to my mom," Constance replied with a large smile. "She spent many hours teaching me the art of making meals that will please the family."

"She taught you well," Margaret said. "I love it when you call to invite us over for a roast. I'm so glad that we're getting together for dinner."

"You're welcome. Ethan's not used to going without his after-school snack. I'll bet both of them are famished from their long day together at Park Enterprises."

"I'll bet you're right," answered Margaret. "We can drill Ethan on exactly what William does all day at work."

Constance giggled. "Maybe we'll finally find out how he has become 'master' of his universe. But more than likely, he's sworn Ethan to secrecy." The kitchen door opened as both ladies laughed. In walked Ethan and William.

"What's so funny?" William asked as he walked over to kiss Margaret. Ethan headed straight for the refrigerator and grabbed the pitcher of tea.

Constance and Margaret looked at each other, shrugged, and replied in unison, "Nothing."

This brought on another round of laughter from the ladies. William turned to Ethan. "See? You work all day and come home only to be laughed at."

Constance looked at Ethan, who was proudly wearing his hard hat and safety vest. "How could we laugh at such an auspicious-looking young executive?"

"Ethan," Margaret said, "it looks like Grandy is ready to take you on full time—right now."

Ethan stood tall. "Today I went up in a construction elevator, and they even let me operate it."

"That's very neat," Constance replied. "Did you get all of the information you need to write the report for Miss Peart?"

"Yes, ma'am." Ethan handed the folio to his mom. "Look at this. Miss Barbara gave me a leather folder . . . and my name's on it . . . engraved in gold!"

"That's beautiful!" Constance gushed. "May I open it?"

"Yes, Mom. You'll see the notes I took that I can use to write my report."

Constance opened Ethan's folio to look at his notes. "Ethan, this is amazing. You took all these notes? Did Grandy give you a lunch break?"

"Ethan was definitely busy today," William said. "But Chef Duke did prepare us a wonderful lunch."

"Yes, Mom. And Chef Duke served us his special homemade vanilla ice cream for dessert."

※ ※ ※ ※

Dinner at the Park's was definitely a family affair. Trip had made his way home from football practice by the time the roast was ready to come out of the oven and all the side dishes had been prepared. Although Bill was not home to join in on the fun, the table was filled with Parks and lively conversation covering an eclectic assortment of topics. As with all Park events, everyone had the opportunity to participate. Claire, while sporting her big brother Ethan's hard hat, joined in the fun. She told everyone about her day at school and an upcoming field trip her class would be taking to the zoo.

Trip took the hard hat from Claire and placed it on his head. "I have one of these with *my* name and the Park Productions logo on it upstairs because I went to Dad's job. But today I was wearing a Frey High helmet when I made an awesome one-handed catch for a touchdown. You should've seen me!"

"Yeah, I guess you would've looked pretty funny wearing a hard hat catching a football," Ethan joked.

Trip regaled everyone with the story of his incredible catch during the day's practice. Of course, Ethan had the big news of the day since he had spent all of his with Grandy at Park Enterprises.

After William and Margaret departed and Trip and Ethan were loading dishes in the dishwasher, the phone rang.

Constance picked up the receiver. "Hello, Park residence."

In a voice disguised to fool Constance, Bill asked, "Hello Park residence. May I speak to the lady of the house?"

Constance laughed. "Bill, you can't fool me. I'd know your voice anywhere. How are you?"

Bill switched to his best fake French accent. "*Moi, en essayant de vous tromper?*" he crooned.

"Listen, mister, my husband would not appreciate you saying things like that to me."

Bill couldn't contain himself any longer and started laughing. "Well, that's the extent of my French. I can't go on anymore," he confessed.

"Bill, it's a good thing you have a day job. You would never make it as a spy."

"Speaking of days, how was yours?"

Constance leaned back against the counter. "It was good. We just finished dinner with your folks."

"That's nice to hear. How did it go for Ethan today? Earlier I called the office, but they were in a meeting, and you know how Dad feels about being disturbed. You would think that Ethan could have left—"

Constance broke in, "From the reports of Ethan and your dad, they had a great day. Let me give the phone to Ethan."

Ethan reached for the receiver. "Hi, Dad! I'm sorry I didn't get to go to work with *you* today. But I did learn a lot with Grandy."

"That's great, Ethan. I wish you'd been with me, too."

"Oh, Dad, there is so much to tell you!"

"I don't have much time," Bill replied in a hurried manner. "Thump goes on stage shortly. But I wanted to check in on you."

"I think I want to build buildings like Grandy when I get older," Ethan declared.

Bill inwardly groaned. "Well, you have some time before you have to make that decision, so you may change your mind. You know, working with me and staging concerts can be a lot of fun."

Bill winced at the realization that he sounded a lot like his father.

＊ ＊ ＊ ＊

History tells us that it was the ancient Babylonians who developed the seven-day week, based upon the idea that there were seven planets in the solar system. Seven, a special number to the Babylonians, was thought to hold mystical powers. Thus, seven seemed like a good number of days to make up a week.

It was in Britain where the first documented use of the word "weekend" appeared. This was printed in the English publication *Notes & Queries* in 1879. After many years of working completely at the factory owners' beckoning, the workforce and factory owners worked out an agreement that stated the employees would take a day and a half off and then return to work on Monday. This day and a half, the half-day being Saturday, turned into two full days sometime early in the twentieth century.

Saturdays at the Park residence were usually a time away from the hustle and bustle of work and school. However, it was not a day for lazing about or sleeping into the afternoon. As Constance would say, the house would "wake up" just as early on the weekends as it did during the week.

On this particular Saturday morning, Constance was busier than usual. The day proved to be slightly unusual in two respects. One was that Bill was currently on tour with a band whose concerts were produced by Park Productions. The other was that William wouldn't be stopping by for Ethan.

During dinner Friday evening, it had been decided Ethan would *not* spend Saturday morning in the woodshop with William. Miss Peart was expecting a report on Ethan's day spent at Park Enterprises first thing Monday morning. Thus, Constance believed it best that Ethan write his report first thing Saturday morning while his recollections of the day were still fresh in his mind. Much to everyone's surprise, William agreed with this departure from routine.

After the hustle and bustle of breakfast and coordinating of schedules, the dust had finally settled. The house was now empty, with the exception of Ethan, who was in the den immersed in the writing of his "Go To Work With Your Dad Day" report. Claire left to spend the morning with friends at the water park. Trip had gone to football practice and then would be off to ride the bike trails with Mark Wallace.

Constance usually planned her days so that she would have the luxury of enjoying a cup of coffee in quiet solitude. It was during these morning respites that she reflected on what she needed to accomplish for the day, choreograph the sequence and timing, and then get to it. She took pleasure in that her days were spent with activities that resulted in the well-being of her family, brought them happiness, and made their lives better.

Despite having a household of two adults, one teenager, one pre-teen, and one young child in grammar school, the phone at the Park residence wasn't in continuous use. The phone rarely rang. The Park family socialized often and were quite active. Yet, they didn't rely on the telephone as their main means of communication. To their way of thinking, why talk on the phone when one could drop by for conversation and a delicious cup of coffee, and maybe even a slice of homemade pie?

So, the moment the phone rang, it immediately brought Constance out of her interior planning.

"Good morning, Park residence," Constance said as she answered the phone.

"Good morning, my love."

"Oh, Bill," Constance said happily, "how are you? How did the show go?"

"It went well. Actually, it was phenomenal. The trucks should be arriving at the next venue in about an hour."

"When is your flight?"

"The plane boards in about fifteen minutes. I called to get more of your read on how Ethan's day went yesterday."

120

"Here I was thinking that the love of my life called because he felt he just couldn't make it through the day without hearing the sound of my voice," Constance quipped.

"Of course, my dear. You got me. That is the number-one reason why I called," Bill answered, playing his part.

"Right . . . but that's okay. I know where my bread is buttered," Constance giggled. She then composed herself and continued, "Ethan seemed like he had a wonderful day. Your dad, and of course, Barbara took good care of him."

"Do you think he was upset that I was out of town?"

This was a loaded question Constance would have preferred to have gone unasked. "I think he would have had a great day with you."

"That didn't really answer my question. I don't mean to put you on the spot. I guess there really isn't an answer," Bill responded, a bit dejected.

Constance consoled her husband. "Bill, we can't expect to be at every one of the kids' events. It's just not possible, especially when your job requires so much travel."

"I guess you're right," Bill mumbled.

"We are fortunate that we have your mom and dad so close and that they like to be involved. Look, Ethan could have spent the day in a classroom doing busy work," Constance countered.

"Of course. It's just one more thing—"

"Bill," Constance interjected, "everything is fine. Ethan had a meaningful day. In fact, last night before he went to bed he sat up to make a To Do list for today."

"Great," Bill said. "Now he's picking up my father's rigid habits."

"There are far worse habits he could acquire."

"Listen, they are boarding the plane. I need to run. I'll call you when I get to the hotel. I love you!"

Constance blushed. "I love you, too."

* * * *

The knock on the kitchen door was no surprise to Beth Wallace because she was expecting Ethan to come over this morning. It was unusual in that she knew Ethan's Saturday mornings were normally spent with his grandfather in the woodshop. Beth was aware that William valued his time with his grandson on Saturdays. There had been many instances over the years when she wished that Ethan could have joined Roger on a Saturday morning outing. Beth frequently asked Constance. She knew going in, though, that the answer would most likely be no.

It was amazing the pull a sixth-grade teacher could have with parents, and yes, even grandparents that they would be willing to alter their Saturday morning routines for an assignment. Constance had talked with Beth, and they both agreed that the boys had to write their reports first thing Saturday morning. Since Ethan would have the remainder of his morning free after writing his report, Beth suggested that Ethan come over to have lunch and hang out with Roger in the afternoon.

Beth opened the door to welcome him in. "Good morning, Ethan."

"Good morning, Miss Beth. How are you?"

"I'm doing well," replied Beth. "Did you finish your report for Miss Peart?"

"Yes, ma'am. It's all finished. I'm ready to see Roger's new drums."

"Okay, okay. But first, I made lunch for you boys. Roger should be down in a second."

"Mom," Roger moaned as he walked into the kitchen, "my report is almost done and ready for you to proofread. Is it all right if Ethan and I check out my drums right after lunch? I'll finish my report later this afternoon."

"Yes, dear, I think that'll be fine." Beth placed lunch on the table for the boys. "Just be sure you finish your report before dinner."

Beth believed young boys should be fed, and fed well. She also believed comfort food could be just as important as the USDA's recommended diet. A family, actually children, would be more apt to approach mealtime enthusiastically and participate in discussions if the food served was something they liked to eat. Beth recognized there were times when memories and interactions outweighed straight nutritional value. The good memories and feelings of having lunch with a best friend were priceless.

Ethan and Roger's eyes grew large and their mouths watered as they gazed upon the hot dogs, chili, and homemade french fries in front of them. Roger's mom was saving the best for last—vanilla malts for dessert.

※ ※ ※ ※

Buddy Rich began playing drums on stage at the tender age of three as "Baby Traps, the Drum Wonder." Buddy was considered by many to have been one of the best drummers to ever pick up a set of drumsticks.

Roger did not begin playing drums as early as Buddy, nor was it likely that Roger would garner the acclaim received by Buddy Rich. Roger's parents were musically inclined and had talent proven to be above average. Both Mark and Roger were more adept than most with their respective musical instruments, Mark on the bass guitar and Roger on the drums.

Ethan and Roger entered the Wallace's music studio. It wasn't a studio on par with the one at the Park house. Instead, it was simply a bedroom that had been converted. There wasn't much space or a control room. The boys understood, when making music, it isn't the studio that makes the music—it's the musicians.

It would be hard to miss Roger's newly installed twenty-piece drum kit, not simply because the breadth and depth of the kit consumed a large portion of the room, but also because the kit was a bright cherry-red in color with chrome trim everywhere. Ethan's jaw dropped as he admired the ensemble.

Roger walked behind the kit and took a seat on the drum stool. "So, what do you think?"

Before Ethan could reply, Roger performed a "round house," touching just about every drumhead and cymbal on his way around the set.

Ethan gaped. "Roger, when you told me you were getting new drums, I thought it would be something to replace your old second-hand five-piece kit. This is amazing."

"Well, it does replace the old kit." Roger added with a chuckle, "It just takes up a little more room."

"Wow!" Ethan exclaimed, still stunned.

"All right, enough. Pick up that guitar and let's see if we can make some noise."

Ethan and Roger played several songs together, their jam session lasting for almost an hour. They ran through their entire repertoire of songs a couple of times, performed ad-lib solos, and goofed off as well. The Wallace studio had the physical space to accommodate the instruments and musicians, but it wasn't designed for this type of exertion. Because Beth had spent many hours in the studio, she knew well the air conditioning could not keep up with the caloric burn of the boys.

"Hey, guys, that sounded awesome," Beth said as she walked in with a pitcher of lemonade and a couple of glasses.

"Thanks, Mom," Roger replied.

"Thank you, Miss Beth." Ethan took a long sip of the cool drink. "This lemonade is awesome, too."

"You boys should start your own band. Give the B-Sides some competition," she suggested on her way out the door.

Ethan gulped down the last of the lemonade in his glass and held it out to Roger. "Fill 'er up, please."

Roger filled Ethan's glass. "What do you think? You want to start a band?"

Ethan looked at his friend. "I don't think your mom was serious."

"Well, think about it—serious or not," Roger said. "It's a great idea. We could get Phil to play bass and Tommy to play rhythm and do vocals."

Ethan looked at Roger with skepticism. "You really think we could play music that someone would want to listen to?"

"Maybe we could just get together and jam. See what happens—"

"I don't know." Ethan hesitated. "Bands take time. Look how many hours our dads spend rehearsing, practicing . . . and we've got school."

"They have work," Roger countered.

"You're right. Let's think it over. But, speaking about work—"

"'Go To Work With Your Dad Day?'" Roger cut in. "It was a blast! You know how much fun it can be on the fabrication floor."

Ethan played a riff on the guitar. "I know. But I had a pretty good time at Park Enterprises, even though it's way different than the fabrication floor."

"Yeah." Roger tapped out a beat on the snare. "I wish you could have come to the fab floor with me. We could've had a wild time."

"It was a bit of a bummer that my dad was gone and all," Ethan said. "But I had an awesome day with Grandy, and I learned a whole lot. It really makes me think that I want to build buildings like my grandfather."

Roger looked a little disappointed. "Oh, I just thought it would be cool when we grow up if we work together at Park Productions—just like our dads."

FOURTEEN

TO

SEVENTEEN YEARS OLD

E.P.

Chapter 8
SETTING GOALS

The end of a school year is a time for celebration. For the Parks it meant three months of taking trips to the beach, camping, hosting swim parties, and watching outdoor movies late into the night.

Before experiencing all that summer vacation had to offer them, the Parks wound down the school year with a family pool party, complete with a dinner of summer fare and desserts. The evening was capped off with a special activity for the children, a late-night swim. This was planned to reward the kids for their academic successes, and for surviving another year of homework. It also served as a way to congratulate the parents for surviving another year of take-home school projects, PTA meetings, food drives, and the annual school fair.

Bill sipped a tall, cool glass of lemonade made with freshly squeezed lemons from William and Margaret's lemon tree. He set the grill burning at the optimum temperature needed to envelop the steak fillets in a velvet heat that would ensure juiciness combined with savory flavors.

William stopped as he walked out the back door onto the deck. He observed Bill taking a sip from his glass of lemonade.

"If that doesn't look like a man who has vanquished another school year in style, I'll eat my hat," William exclaimed.

Bill, looking as if he were ten years old and had been caught with his hand in the cookie jar, turned and smiled at his dad.

"Ah . . . you caught me taking a break from my duties as head chef. Can I pour you a glass? It's made with lemons from your very own tree."

"Most definitely," William said. "If the ladies come out, I'm the assistant chef."

"Deal." Bill chuckled.

"It's hard to believe that Trip is now an upperclassman. That's what they call juniors in high school, right?" William said.

"Right." Bill stared at the kids wrestling on the lawn. "It doesn't seem possible."

"Ethan is *starting* high school and Claire is going to be a big, bad fifth-grader," William said.

"It's amazing, Dad. I remember the barbecues in your backyard when I was in school. Wow. That seems like a million years ago."

William's face took on a sentimental look as he gazed at the sun setting behind the large oak trees at the back of the yard. "In some ways it does feel like a long time ago. A million years. But really, it's a million experiences all woven together to bring us here."

Bill looked at his dad with mock amazement. "Dad, are you becoming philosophical in your old age?"

"Old age? I'm just hitting my stride."

Bill smirked. "That's funny. That's exactly what I said to Trip this morning when he called *me* Old Man."

The sound of Margaret and Constance bringing more snacks, drinks, and frivolity created a conspiratorial mood for the guys. Bill elbowed his father. "Look, Dad, here come *our* old ladies," he said under his breath.

"You keep talking like that, son, and you may not make it to be an old man," William said with a laugh.

The kids had already changed into their swimsuits. Trip, Ethan, and Claire sat on the edge of the pool, dangling their feet into the cool water while eating, slurping, or drinking their Hokey Pokeys. This treat was a sugary confection made with two basic ingredients, red crème soda and condensed milk. Although it wasn't a complicated concoction, every child who visited the Park household always displayed a huge smile when they saw Miss Constance walk out with a pitcher full of Hokey-Pokeys. Constance made this frozen delight only during the summer months. Enjoying this treat after dinner was a definite signal that summer had arrived.

The adults enjoyed one of their favorite summertime staples created by Margaret, lemon meringue pie. The pie had also been made with lemons from William and Margaret's tree. Bill enjoyed his mom's lemon meringue pie with such gusto that, in his teen years, he threw tradition aside and insisted that on his birthday he not have a cake but his mom's lemon meringue pie instead. The meringue had just the right consistency to hold his birthday candles upright.

"Here we are," Constance said. "The passing of another school year and the start of another summer."

"Oh my, how time flies!" remarked Margaret.

After finishing their sweet treat, the kids jumped into the pool and began a game of Marco Polo. With eyes closed, Claire giggled as she tried to track down her evasive brothers. The boys managed to remain just out of arms' reach.

"Margaret, I'm sure you and William felt this way when Bill was a boy—that kids should stay young forever," Constance said.

"Oh, of course," Margaret said, a bittersweet smile on her face. "But then we wouldn't have these beautiful grandchildren."

"Now, what a tragedy that would be," Constance replied.

"They are definitely blessings," William agreed. "But they do have to grow up, go to work, and keep the family moving forward. That's the natural way."

Bill set his plate aside, keeping it close by for a second helping of pie. "Well, they *do* have to grow up, but from there they get to forge their own paths."

"It's our job as grandparents and parents to direct them on the correct paths," William insisted.

Bill glared at his father. "It's our job to advise them, and then support whatever decision they make."

"Dad, come play in the pool with us!" Claire shouted.

"I will, sweetheart. Let the adults finish dessert. Then we'll join you."

"Ethan's starting high school this fall," William said. "I think we should encourage him to focus on courses that will help him toward a business major."

"Would anyone like another piece of pie?" Constance asked, trying to derail what she believed could be an explosive exchange.

Margaret quickly picked up Constance's lead. "I do. Shall we bring you gentlemen each another slice?"

Both men quickly lifted their empty plates indicating they would be quite happy to have another piece of pie. Margaret and Constance walked to the house to retrieve more, hoping that their diversionary tactic would thwart a conversation that could only result in hot heads and heavy hearts.

"Dad, Ethan hasn't even started his freshman year," Bill firmly said, taking advantage of the ladies' retreat. "Can't we just let him enjoy high school before we start badgering him about how he wants to spend the next fifty years of his life?"

William watched the kids playing in the pool, and remembered how he and his two brothers had spent a good portion of every summer swinging from a rope and dropping into the local watering hole.

William, as the youngest, had looked to his older brothers for guidance in so many ways. As they approached adulthood, William watched how the relationship between his siblings and his parents deteriorated. He saw the many times where his dad would comfort his mom as she wept due to the harsh things her two older sons had said or because they were yet again in trouble. He witnessed his dad's angst and anger over the ways the two older boys created familial stress and discord.

William decided at an early age that this was not the path he would take. He loved his parents and only wanted to see their happiness. Even as a young teenager, he realized that he may not always agree with his dad, who may not always be right about things. He also realized that his parents always put the well-being of him and his brothers first. He didn't understand why his brothers couldn't see that. William vowed that he would always try to heed the advice given to him by his parents. At the very least, he would listen and consider their advice before making a contrary decision. In effect, he learned from his brothers' mistakes.

In Bill, William could see some of the rebellious nature of his brothers. His son hadn't acted with full-out defiance as William's brothers had. Instead, his rebellious acts took on a more subtle nature, but they were troublesome just the same. Bill and William's brothers would have gotten along well, thick as thieves.

"You know, Bill, I kept my mouth shut when Trip started high school." William shot back. "Now look where we are. He's going to be a junior, and he still has *no* idea where he wants to go to college, much less what his major will be."

"*We* are not anywhere. Trip is doing well in school. He's a junior in *high school.* Some kids don't declare a major until they're juniors in college."

"Damn it, Bill," William steamed. "He's a Park, not 'some kid!'"

"Dad, let Ethan enjoy high school," Bill demanded. "Let *him* decide what *he* wants to do when *he's* ready."

"Bill, it's *our* job to be his mentors, to direct him along the correct path," William said with a shake of his head.

"The problem is, Dad, you only see one path—Park Enterprises."

"Someone in the family has to run the business after me. You didn't want it."

"It's not that I didn't *want* it. I wanted something else."

"Something else?" William shook his finger at his son. "Your mom and I invested our lives into creating something for our family, something for you, and you wanted *something else?*"

"Dad . . . I don't know that you'll ever understand." Bill lowered his head, his tone just short of dejected.

"You're right about that. I will *never* understand because it makes *no* sense."

"Dad—"

"We will *not* go down that path with Ethan. It's not fair to him or to the family!"

Looking his father straight in the eyes, Bill replied forcefully, "Dad, Ethan is *my* son. I will decide how he is raised."

Margaret and Constance emerged from the kitchen with the extra slices of pie and another pitcher of Hokey-Pokeys for the kids. Both women immediately recognized that the conversation had not only continued in their absence but appeared to have escalated. The ladies made eye contact and acknowledged that it would be up to them to de-escalate the situation and bring calm back to the evening.

"Here's more pie."

"And I've brought a fresh pot of your favorite coffee," Constance said.

William looked at Bill, and then at Margaret. "I'm ready to go. We can put our pie in a container and eat it at home."

"William, stay and have some coffee with your pie," Constance said, determined to salvage the evening. "Let's plan the Fourth of July barbecue."

"We can talk about that later," William muttered as he rose to leave. "We may be out of town."

Margaret turned to Constance. "It's getting late," she said apologetically. "We should get going. Thank you for a wonderful dinner."

Constance set down the coffee tray and smiled regretfully, recognizing that it would be best to let the guys have a cooling-off period.

Trip, Ethan, and Claire immediately noticed all of the adults getting to their feet. Claire called out, "Yay! They're going to get their suits on to get in the pool."

"I'm going to be on Grandy's team," Ethan yelled.

Margaret walked to the edge of the pool. "I'm sorry. Grandy is not feeling well. We're going to be leaving now."

"Aww!" the three kids moaned in unison.

"Come up here," Constance instructed. "And give Grandy and Granny a hug and tell them 'bye."

Bill muttered under his breath, "Good going, Dad."

※ ※ ※ ※

Constance and Claire patiently waited in the car for Ethan. Each of the Park children were held responsible for completing various chores. One of Ethan's responsibilities was to make sure the trash cans were brought to the bottom of the driveway for the Saturday pickup. Trip held this same responsibility for the trash collection on Wednesday.

"Ethan, thank you for taking the cans out," Constance said as Ethan climbed into the passenger seat of the car.

"You're welcome, Mom. They were especially heavy today for some reason."

Constance looked toward Ethan, "You know, Skosh doesn't pick the trash up until late in the afternoon on Saturdays, so it could have waited until you got home."

"I know, Mom. But when Dad assigned me to Saturday trash duty, I promised to take the cans out *first* thing in the morning."

"Well, thank you again."

"You know, Mom . . . *Say what you are going to do . . .*" As Ethan started the mantra, Claire jumped in and finished it with him, ". . .*then do it!*"

Constance laughed. "Grandy sure has you both trained well."

Ethan and Claire giggled as Constance backed the car out of the driveway to begin their Saturday morning activities. Constance and Claire were meeting one of Claire's classmates and her mother for brunch and then seeing a play at the local community theater. Keeping with their routine, Ethan and William would be in the woodshop. This Saturday they would continue to work on the frame they had been making for Ethan's eighth-grade graduation certificate.

"Ethan, why do you have your Park Enterprises folio with you? Are you putting your certificate in the frame today?"

"No, Mom. The frame won't be ready until next week. This week we're applying the final finish. Grandy and I are going to talk about high school and goal setting. He thought it would be a good idea for me to bring my folio to write down any ideas we come up with together."

"That's great, Ethan. It's always good to plan ahead." Constance pulled into her in-laws' driveway and stopped the car. "Just remember, your dad wants to work on this with you. It's important to him," she reminded Ethan as he opened his door to get out of the car.

"I know, Mom," Ethan said. "But Grandy is really good at this goal setting stuff."

"Your dad isn't too shabby at it either, you know. He just takes a different approach."

Constance and Claire continued on to meet their friends for brunch. Many thoughts ran through Constance's head concerning Ethan's high school career and the expectations that both his father and grandfather had for her son.

High school is certainly quite different from grammar school. In high school, students are required to change classrooms, teachers, and desks every hour. Added to this are the academic and social changes that arise as students transition from pre-teens to teenagers, from freshmen to seniors. Constance wondered how Ethan would navigate this transition.

During the last month of summer, all incoming freshman who would be attending Frey High School for the upcoming school year are required to schedule a session with their class counselor. This session is designed to help identify and set the expectations of both the parents as well as the incoming students. The counselor explains the concept of class credits and that students in high school become more responsible for themselves. The counselor also informs the students that they have freedom in making their academic selections, such as taking elective classes that interest them and possibly align with their personal academic goals.

Ethan's academic goals were a contentious point between his father and grandfather. During the past couple of months, persistent friction developed between the two concerning this issue. It started with the heated discussion at the beginning of summer. Constance could see merit in both sides of the argument, though she leaned more toward Bill's point of view. As Ethan's father, Bill was most directly responsible for him. It was important for Ethan to set goals for high school, as William believed, but Constance didn't think it needed to be a primary focus.

High school was Ethan's last time to really be a kid, she reasoned. She did not want Ethan caught in a power struggle between his father and his grandfather

✳ ✳ ✳ ✳

In the forty-eight years William and Margaret had been married, they'd come to know each other's likes and dislikes, moods and temperaments almost as well as they knew their own. Margaret figured William would talk to Ethan this morning about his upcoming high school career. She had suggested to William that he leave this discussion where it belonged, between father and son, but he would not be dissuaded. He insisted that this subject required his input.

He recalled in his conversation with Margaret how lost he had felt when he started high school and that he didn't really *get it* until late in his sophomore year. It was then that his grandfather, observing William's struggles, pulled him aside and counseled him. From that point on, high school had a purpose for William, a defined goal. He had remained grateful to his grandfather for the advice given to him.

Because William insisted on speaking with Ethan about the matter, Margaret cautioned him, "Make sure you don't put Ethan in a position where he has to choose either your way or Bill's."

"I understand. We're going to discuss goal setting . . . that's it," William responded. "How could Bill not be on board for setting goals?"

Over the years William had used the mornings in the woodshop with Ethan to teach him not only about craftsmanship and woodworking, but also to impart some of the wisdom he had obtained from his father and grandfather, along with his own life experiences. William always strove to make sure the sessions were entertaining and that they would not feel like lectures for Ethan. William knew consistency and repetition were key to ingraining thought processes into one's mind. So, he oftentimes said the same things over and over during their weekly visits.

At the same time, he wanted to make sure that Ethan looked forward to these Saturday mornings. To this end, William created small guessing games that allowed them to take a break from the current project and have a little fun. For example, they might guess the length of a random piece of wood, estimate the number of nails in a jar, or try to collect exactly three ounces of sawdust in a paper cup. The game they both enjoyed the most was guessing the type of treat Granny might bring to the woodshop for their snack that day.

"Wow, that's good work, Ethan," William declared. "I believe this is going to be one of the best finishes you've done so far."

Ethan looked up and smiled. "It's been really hard, but also quite fun."

"You've definitely put in some elbow grease on this one. Your efforts will pay off. Let's take a break while it dries."

"Grandy, what treat do you think we're getting this morning?"

William played along. "Oatmeal raisin cookies. You?"

Ethan tapped his finger to his temple in thought. "Hmm . . . I think she's going to bring . . . brownies."

Unbeknownst to William and Ethan, Margaret heard their conversation as she was about to enter the shed. She stopped her progress to let the game continue and hear more guesses. Once Ethan had finished, Margaret entered the woodshop carrying a tray with two large slices of apple pie and two ice-cold glasses of milk.

"You're both wrong," she laughed. "Shall I return this to the kitchen?"

"Oh, I think not," William said.

"Granny, I'll eat *anything* you bake."

"I'll remember that when I bake the opossum cake next week," Margaret joked as she turned and walked out of the woodshop.

Ethan crinkled his nose and scratched his head. "Does Granny really make a cake out of opossum?"

"I wouldn't put it past her," William laughed. "I'd also be willing to bet that if Granny bakes it, it will taste good."

"I don't know . . ."

"Let's get down to the business of eating *this* pie and discussing you becoming a big freshman at Frey High School," William said. "Did you write down a couple of ideas about goals for next year?"

Ethan reached onto the shelf above the workbench to retrieve his folio. William reviewed the list of goals that Ethan had created since their phone conversation earlier in the week.

"These look good, Ethan. However, I think we can do some fine-tuning."

"Yes, sir," Ethan responded.

"It's most important that once a goal is set, you let nothing get in the way of achieving that goal," William stated. "Goals help us focus on what is important. They are a testament to our commitment."

Ethan nodded and began taking notes. "I get it."

"If you see someone not attaining a goal," William said, "it shows either a lack of commitment or focus. Maybe, in some cases, both."

"But Grandy, suppose something happens that won't let me reach my goal?"

"Ethan, I can assure you things will happen that could stop you from reaching every goal you set. That's where commitment and focus come in. You have to be committed to work your way around the obstacles. You must be focused enough on the goal to not let the obstacle become the object of your focus. Never let your goal out of your focus."

William continued, "The setting of the goal is one of the most crucial parts of the process. A goal, a *real* goal, has to be something not that you just want or would like to have. A real goal is something that you feel you *cannot live without.*

"A lot of people set goals that are not actually true goals. Things like losing fifteen pounds, running three miles a day, or reading a certain number of books in a year are not solid goals. It's the same with New Year's resolutions. They don't really mean anything. They won't alter the lives of the people setting them whether they are attained or not. That's why most people don't attain the goals that they have set—because they are trivial and not *real* goals. Understand?"

Ethan had been furiously taking notes in his folio. He looked up. "I think I do."

"So," continued William, "people train themselves to believe that not attaining their goals is acceptable. They do this by making all these nonsensical goals and then missing them. Again, real goals are something that, if attained, will change the course of your life. They are not to be taken lightly.

"The next step in the process is creating a plan to attain those goals. Because each goal will be life altering, they must mesh together and work together. The goals should never be counter to each other. The plan for one goal should enable, or at the very least, not inhibit the progress to attaining another goal."

"Okay, Grandy, I think I understand that. So, I shouldn't set one goal to be a sumo wrestler and another to be a jockey?" Ethan chuckled.

"Exactly. You've got it." William clapped his hands. "Not goals I would aspire to, but it's obvious you get the picture.

"Of course, the plan should include a timeline. It does no good to set a goal and not have a deadline to meet the goal," William said. "If there is no deadline, it will keep getting pushed off until tomorrow. Tomorrow *never* comes.

"Also, if you can't, or don't, identify a completion date, that should be an indication to you that it's not something you feel truly committed to."

Ethan and William continued discussing the process of setting goals. They talked about creating checkpoints in the plan to verify progress is being made and ways to deal with obstacles that could arise along the way.

"Ethan, remember the mantra, *Say what you are going to do . . .*" Ethan enthusiastically joined with his grandfather at this point since the mantra always seemed to either start or finish a discussion like this. " *. . . Then do it.*"

"That's right, Ethan. Once you set a goal, don't let anything get in the way of attaining that goal."

"Grandy, I'm going to rethink these goals that I've written down for high school."

"You may want to think further out than high school because what you do in high school will affect your college years *and* your career.

"I realize we spent a lot of our woodworking time today with me talking to you and you listening to me. But setting goals is incredibly important."

※ ※ ※ ※

The architects of Frey High School had nestled the school in a rolling valley with wide-open fields surrounding it. There was ample space for the main school building, classroom buildings, athletic facilities, stadium, and track. The cohesiveness of the campus suggested that the team operating the facility was serious about education.

The administration building was situated in the center of the valley. A large circular stone drive led visitors from the street onto the campus. The area contained within the circular drive was filled with lush emerald-green grass, an array of picnic tables, and an assortment of seats and benches so students could read, socialize, and take in the fresh air that consistently swept through the valley.

Bill guided his car into a parking space near the top of the drive. He rubbed his hands together with excitement. "Well, Ethan," Bill said. "This is the beginning of your high school years."

Constance glanced at Ethan over her shoulder. "It seems like just yesterday we were bringing you home from the hospital."

"Mom!" Ethan rolled his eyes.

"I had some of the best times of my life during high school," Bill said, "You need to make sure you squeeze out all the fun you can."

"Dad, I thought I was coming here to learn and get ready for college."

Constance turned in her seat to face Ethan more fully. "You are. But it's also a time for having fun and growing as a young man. You can learn and have fun, too."

✳ ✳ ✳ ✳

"I'm Sarah Olson. Please, take a seat," Miss Olson said as she invited the Parks into her office. "I will be Ethan's guidance counselor while he is here at Frey High School."

"Thank you," Bill replied as he, Constance, and Ethan sat across from the counselor.

"You will notice that my office doesn't look like a typical one," Miss Olson said. "There are no desks, file cabinets, or other office-type furnishings. I want the students to feel relaxed while in here."

145

Constance glanced around the room. "You've done a beautiful job. This looks as comfortable as our den at home."

Miss Olson smiled. "Ethan, I'm here to help you navigate through high school. Not just academically. Athletically, if you decide to participate in sports. Also, socially. High school is a big change from grammar and middle school. Sometimes students come to me for help with figuring out the changes in the social dynamics. If you are wondering about anything—school, social issues, whatever—you can come to me. Do you have any questions? Mom? Dad?"

"Yes, is this the meeting where I choose the classes I'm going to take while in high school?" Ethan asked.

"I'm glad to see you're ready to get to work." Miss Olson smiled in approval. "A lot of our new students first want to know what food is served in the cafeteria. To answer your question, yes and no. Today we will select the classes for your freshman year."

Ethan had brought with him his Park Enterprises folio and the course selection guide he had received in the mail from the school a couple of weeks earlier. He opened the folio. "I really want to concentrate on—"

Miss Olson stopped him. "Ethan, you sure are eager. Before we discuss specific classes, let me ask you a few questions. Have you thought about what you would like to accomplish in your time here at Frey? Academically? With student government? Athletically? Toward college . . . goals along those lines?"

"Actually," Ethan replied, "I have. I'm going to be the valedictorian of my graduating class."

"Ethan," Bill said, letting out a nervous laugh, "let's slow down and figure out your freshman year, son."

Miss Olson's gazed skimmed from father to son. "Ethan, that's an admirable goal. Your father's right, though. Let's discuss *this* year."

"I understand what you're saying, Miss Olson," Ethan replied. "But my ultimate goal is to be valedictorian when I graduate. It's my understanding that grades from *all* four years go toward determining who is named valedictorian."

"Ethan, please listen to Miss Olson," Bill instructed.

Constance felt the tension emanating from Bill. During the summer she and Margaret had managed to keep a degree of peace between Bill and his father where Ethan's high school career was concerned. She hadn't expected that the talks between William and Ethan would have had such a definitive effect on Ethan, though.

Constance reached over and put her hand on Bill's arm. "Honey, you're right. This is *Ethan's* freshman year." She turned to her son. "Let's concentrate on this year's schedule and make it a great first year of high school."

Miss Olson had enough experience as a high school counselor to realize the situation was deeper and contained more facets than were appearing before her today. She also realized that defusing the situation would be in everyone's best interest.

"You are correct, Mrs. Park," Miss Olson said. "We are only going to set a schedule for this year. We'll monitor how it goes. Next summer we'll get together and set the schedule for Ethan's sophomore year."

Turning to Ethan, she said, "Let's talk about the specific classes you've selected for your first year of high school."

Ethan removed three sheets of paper from his folio, handing one to each of his parents and one to Miss Olson. "At the top of the page you'll see the classes that I would like to take my freshman year . . . ."

※ ※ ※ ※

"You know, Ethan," Constance began as she turned to face him in the back seat of the car, "when your dad and I went to high school, we didn't get to pick the classes we would take. They were assigned to us."

"Right! They handed us a schedule and told us where and when to be there," Bill said with mock indignation.

"I know, I know. And you had to walk uphill in the snow, both ways," Ethan joked.

Bill snorted. "Maybe a little walk in the snow would be good for this generation."

"Oh, Bill, you know if we could have picked our classes, we would have," Constance said. "And I know you would have selected every class to be with me," she added with a smile.

"Are we still dropping you off at Roger's?" Bill asked as they approached the Wallace's driveway.

"Yes, Dad. We're going to compare schedules and see if we have any classes together, and then work on a few new songs for Available Light."

Bill and Constance watched as Beth opened the front door, waved to them, and welcomed Ethan into the house.

"Wow," Bill exclaimed as soon as he'd backed onto the street, "I can't believe he did that."

Constance knew Bill would be upset, but she was taken aback at the amount of stress in his voice. "Who did what?"

"My dad. He knew I didn't want him filling Ethan's head with grand ideas. But he went ahead and did it anyway."

Constance believed it best to let Bill vent and then discuss the situation once he had released some pressure.

"It's typical of him trying to orchestrate everything. He tried to do that when I was young. He's still mad because I didn't choose to work at Park Enterprises."

Bill turned the car into the driveway. "Did you see those notes in Ethan's book? It looked like notes from a corporate strategy meeting. Can't he just let Ethan enjoy his four years of high school before he starts in on all of this?

"Valedictorian. I have no doubt Ethan could be valedictorian, but I don't think he should be set up to go in with such aspirations. He could get to the last test of his senior year and lose out on being valedictorian by missing one question on that last test. Who's going to pick up those pieces?"

"Bill, I get it," Constance said. "I understand how frustrating this is for you."

"I know you do." Bill parked the car in the garage and gave her a half-smile.

"There are two things we are sure of in this situation. One is that we, including your father, all want what's best for Ethan. Second, we know when it comes to the kids, especially with Ethan, your dad can't help himself."

Bill grunted. "That's an understatement."

"Okay, let's go with that," Constance said. "If we know that, we should expect that and figure out how to deal with it. You looked totally taken aback when Ethan opened his folio."

"Did you see—"

Constance cut him off. "I did. But I wasn't shocked. I knew your father would talk with Ethan about this. They spend a lot of time together on Saturday mornings."

"You're right," Bill said as he disabled the alarm and opened the side door. "That's been the perfect time for my father to indoctrinate Ethan to his way of thinking."

"That's a little strong." Constance stepped into the house. "I don't think your dad is trying to *indoctrinate* Ethan. I think he's just trying to teach him what he thinks is the right way to go."

"But we're the parents." Bill followed her inside and closed the door. "That's *our* job."

"I agree," said Constance. "And we can't keep Ethan, or any of the kids, away from your dad. That wouldn't be right because he's their grandfather and, besides, he has so many great qualities to offer to them. Not to mention, they love him to death."

"So . . ."

"So," Constance continued as she walked through to the kitchen, "what we should have done was gotten together with Ethan prior to his scheduling session."

"Hmm," Bill said thoughtfully, "at least that way we wouldn't have been caught off guard."

"Bill, your father loves our children. And he loves *you*. He just wants what he thinks is best."

"That's just it, what *he* thinks is best."

"Maybe you and your dad need to pick up the pace on your walk-and-talks," Constance suggested, pouring two glasses of sweet tea. "It may be helpful for you and your dad to communicate more regularly."

"That's a good point, Constance. In fact, because Ethan's now in high school and will be presented with situations that he's never seen, he's going to need guidance. It's probably time Ethan and I start having our own walk-and-talks as well to make sure we're on the same page."

He accepted a glass of tea and stared out the window, envisioning walks on the beach with his son where differing viewpoints would be respected.

✳ ✳ ✳ ✳

Dinner at the Park's was not always fancy. It was rarely gourmet in style or taste, but always appetizing and filling. It didn't matter whether it was Bill or Constance who created the menu or prepared the meal, no one walked away from the dinner table wanting more.

151

For the last "official" dinner of summer, Constance decided that Sloppy Joes with homemade french fries served out on the back deck would be a great way to celebrate the end of another three months of freedom from schoolwork and super-busy schedules.

"Who wants the last fry?" Trip asked with an expectant look.

Bill laughed. "Hmm . . . I would say that if you're asking, it means *you* want that last fry."

"Go ahead," Constance said. "It's all yours. But that also means you get to take the empty plate into the kitchen."

"Well, that signals summer's end," Bill exclaimed. "Trip eating The Last Fry of Summer."

Constance and the children laughed. Trip snatched up the last fry and popped it into his mouth, savoring the salty taste as he swallowed.

"A new family tradition—who gets to eat The Last Fry of Summer," Ethan announced. "An honor fit for a king!"

"All right, your Royal Highness, King Trip, you get it this year since you called it first." Constance teased. "Let's get these dishes into the kitchen."

Bill picked up the serving platters. "Ethan, Claire, as royal subjects we get to help as well."

Constance and Ethan led the way carrying dishes and silverware to the kitchen. Bill, Trip, and Claire brought up the rear with the other various accoutrements of the outdoor meal.

"Trip and Claire," Constance began, "if you will help your dad bring in the cushions and tidy up the deck, Ethan and I will take care of the dishes and everything in the kitchen."

Ethan was busy organizing and placing the various condiments in the refrigerator when Constance began, "Ethan, thank you for helping."

"You're welcome, Mom."

"How do you feel about tomorrow being your first day of high school? Are you excited? Nervous?"

"I'm excited, Mom! I have all of my things in my backpack, so I'm ready to forge ahead."

Constance smiled. Throughout his youth, Ethan had always demonstrated a desire to be ready when asked and obediently follow rules. Constance observed Ethan to be a pleaser, someone who wants to do what is expected of him. He had always been dutiful and respectful as a young child. She wondered where life would lead him as a young man and then into adulthood. At times, she worried that Ethan tried too hard and put too much stress on himself to please.

"That's great," Constance replied. "Just remember, high school is not only about academics, though that's a big part. In fact, it's the main part. But it's also about becoming a young adult. You will build some of your fondest memories during these next four years."

"I know, Mom."

"It's just . . . I know how you are about . . ." Constance started. "Well, you have put a lot of pressure on yourself declaring that you *will* be valedictorian."

153

"Mom, we have to set goals." Ethan shut the refrigerator door. "And that's my goal for high school."

"Are you sure you want to take that on?" Constance asked. "The challenge to be valedictorian can be extremely competitive. You never know what can happen in the future. Anything could prevent you from reaching your goal."

"I know. But it's like what the 'Great One' said, 'You miss 100 percent of the shots you don't take.'"

"The 'Great One?'" Constance asked with a quizzical look.

"Wayne Gretzky, the hockey player," Ethan explained. "He scored more points than any other hockey player in history—2,857 points."

Constance placed the last of the dishes into the dishwasher. "That's quite impressive. Just be careful you don't set yourself up for a disappointment not of your own making."

"Mom, this is my goal. I'm going to take a shot at it." Ethan added with a slight chuckle, "If I don't, there's a 100 percent chance that I *won't* make it."

Chapter 9
CHANGES IN GRANDY

The setting sun, along with tall pine trees lining the path, created long shadows across The Crescent Trace. The trace had been a joint project between the state and local municipalities to convert unused railroad passageways into paved hiking trails. It was given the moniker, The Crescent Trace, by locals because it traced its way across the state linking several communities. Over the years the Parks had enjoyed many walks, bike rides, and runs on the trace. Even though Bill thoroughly enjoyed spending time at the beach, he discovered that when he needed to tackle deep thinking, he preferred to walk among these large pine trees.

Ethan's first year of high school was quickly coming to a close. He experienced academic success during this first year and also had successfully maneuvered through the social aspects. Yet, Bill was concerned about the upcoming event Ethan would be attending. It would be his son's first high school dance.

"This sure is one beautiful place to walk," Bill said to Ethan.

Ethan gazed up at the tall trees. "I wonder what it was like three hundred years ago. Do you think people once walked exactly where we are right now?"

"I'm sure someone did," Bill reflected. "I'll bet they could've never imagined the world that we live in today."

"It seems that life must have been a lot simpler back then," Ethan speculated.

"In some ways it probably was," Bill stated. "But I'm sure they had worries, fears, and dangers as well—only different from ours."

"Like disease? Starvation?"

"Oh, you can bet they had to deal with those things. But parents also worried about their children, just as parents do today."

"What do you mean?" Ethan asked.

With that question, Ethan opened the door for the type of discussion Bill hoped to have with his son during this walk-and-talk session. Bill slowly moved farther down the path, collecting his thoughts. "When a child is a toddler, the parents are in total control—well, as much as anyone is in control of all the things in a child's world. Pretty much nothing happens in a toddler's world the parents don't at least know about."

Bill paused briefly, thought for a moment, and continued, "As the child gets older, the boundaries widen. The child starts doing things away from the parents. The parents are no longer always in the same room with the child. This can be both a blessing and a curse. The child develops independence, which is good, but there are dangers.

"Suppose the child climbs on a bookshelf and falls? Or finds something in the room that could hurt them? Potentially, the parent may not see these things, resulting in injury to the child.

"The reality is that independence is part of the maturing process. It comes in different levels. First, it's about a young child old enough to play in their room without the parent present. Eventually, it involves a spring high school dance where the teenager definitely doesn't want their parents present."

"Okay, Dad, I get your point." Ethan added with a sideways glance, "Pretty crafty weaving the settlers' lifestyle three hundred years ago into a lecture . . . . I mean, a father-son talk."

"All right, I've been caught," Bill said laughingly. "But do you *truly* understand what I'm saying?"

"Yes, Dad, I do. And I know Mom will stay up sitting in the den waiting for me."

"You realize that she'll do that not because she thinks you'll get into trouble. It's because someone else might, and it could affect you.

"What do you mean?"

"Ethan, your mother and I know you're a good kid. You have never given us any reason to believe otherwise. We also know that some kids out there like to play dangerously. In high school, there is a massive amount of peer pressure and the desire to fit in."

"Dad, I've seen a lot of that just in my freshman year. I'm not sure why some kids pretend to be something they're not. It's crazy."

"It's good to hear you say that, Ethan. Usually those kids have low self-esteem and want to be part of the crowd."

"I've noticed some guys have done totally stupid stuff just to belong," Ethan said.

"Remember, Ethan, be true to yourself, and when you are tempted to try and fit in, that whatever you do when you are out, you should be able to come home and tell your mom and me all about your adventures in great detail—and not be ashamed."

"You mean like when I was in grammar school and would come home to tell about our games of tag?" Ethan baited his dad with a smirk.

"Exactly," Bill said, giving Ethan a fatherly slap on the shoulder. "You're a fine young man. Have a great time at the spring dance. You know the difference between right and wrong. I'm confident you'll always choose wisely."

✳ ✳ ✳ ✳

Henry Ford did not obtain his first driver's license until he was fifty-six years old. In modern America, most citizens obtain their license to drive well before their twentieth birthday. It seems there is no greater sign of independence for a teenager than a driver's license. This credit card-sized bit of plastic is another sign of growth toward adulthood and a teen's ticket to adventure.

Applicants must meet certain chronological, academic, and skill requirements before being issued a license to drive. In all states, the most stringent of these requirements is placed upon teenagers.

To date, Ethan had met one of the three requirements. The week before, Constance had taken Ethan to sit for the driver's written exam. Despite several ambiguously worded questions that thoroughly tested his understanding and knowledge of the motor traffic laws, he passed the test with a perfect score. Ethan had been rewarded for his efforts with his state-issued learner's permit.

There would be nothing Ethan could do to satisfy the chronological requirement for driving except marking off the days on the calendar until his sixteenth birthday. He could, however, since obtaining his learner's permit, work on the third and final requirement. For this, he would have to demonstrate skillful prowess behind the wheel.

Ethan sat in the driver's seat of his grandfather's car with William seated on the passenger side. William had backed the car into his usual parking spot so that Ethan would not need to back down the lengthy driveway and out onto the street. Rather, Ethan simply had to pull forward and be on his way.

"Okay, Ethan," William instructed, "we're all buckled in and ready to go. Make sure you don't ever start the car until everyone in the car has fastened their seat belt. At the end of the driveway, take a right turn."

Ethan sat rigidly in his seat. "Grandy, are you sure it's okay that I drive?"

"Of course it is. Why wouldn't it be? You have your learners permit, right?"

"Yes." Ethan dropped his hands from the steering wheel and stared through the windshield. "Dad says he only wants me practicing with him as I clock in enough driving hours to get my full license."

"Who do you think taught your dad how to drive?"

"You," Ethan mumbled.

"That's right. So let's go."

Ethan shook his head, took hold of the gear shift, and attempted to put the car in drive. He pulled on the shifter a couple of times, but it wouldn't move. He looked toward his grandfather with a perplexed expression.

"Grandy, why won't it go into drive?"

William smiled. "You have to put your foot on the brake first, then you can shift the car into drive."

Ethan knew this. He rolled his eyes, frustrated that he'd forgotten. Then he put his foot on the brake, took hold of the gear shift once more, and placed the car in drive.

"Success," Ethan exclaimed.

William gave a nod of approval. Ethan released the brake and lightly pressed on the accelerator, causing the car to move forward. At the end of the driveway, Ethan stopped the car. He then activated the turn signal, looked down the street in both directions, and executed a right-hand turn onto the street.

"Where are we going, Grandy?"

"I thought we would drive for a while to let you get your feet wet in my car and then stop at Melba's Kitchen for an ice cream sundae," William replied. "No reason we should be all work and no play."

William, recalling the days when he first got behind the wheel, remembered how stressful it could be for a novice. Learning to drive was a daunting task. There were three mirrors, two side and one rear view. Other cars seemed to be everywhere. The traffic lights changed too quickly. The turns were too sharp. Everyone drove too fast. The other cars followed too closely. Keeping this in mind, William decided before Ethan even got behind the wheel a visit to Melba's Kitchen would take place after about thirty minutes of driving time.

Melba's Kitchen wasn't really a kitchen, but a drive-in reminiscent of motoring days gone by. The parking lot at Melba's appeared to have been designed with young drivers in mind. All one needed to do was navigate their vehicle close enough to the speaker to place the order.

After a half hour of driving, Ethan was relieved that a stop at Melba's was part of his grandfather's plan. They each ordered an ice cream sundae, cherry for Ethan and blueberry for William.

"Well, Ethan, what do you think about navigating the roads in a car instead of on your bicycle?"

Ethan had just put a large spoonful of cherry sundae in his mouth. Out of excitement and in an effort to quickly answer his grandfather, he swallowed as fast as he could. The rapid intake of ice cream hitting the roof of Ethan's mouth triggered a phenomenon commonly known as brain freeze. Ethan experienced it in what felt like, to him, the most severe way possible.

"Take your time," his grandfather said with a laugh. "I've had my share of brain freezes, too."

After several moments, Ethan's trigeminal nerve relaxed and the blood vessels in his head opened to their normal size. The pain subsided. "I'm loving it, Grandy!" Ethan finally answered. "Though there is *so* much to keep track of all the time. How do people do it and make it look so easy?"

"Ethan, think back to the time when you were learning to play tennis," William began. "Remember telling yourself, 'Bring the racket back, put my weight on my front foot'? Plus, you had to remind yourself about the other myriad things you needed to do to hit a good shot. You don't do that now that you're an accomplished player, right?"

"You're right, Grandy. Now, I just hit the ball."

161

"Driving will be like that for you—eventually. You have to take it slowly, though . . . train your reflexes . . . develop muscle memory. Remember, you have to learn to crawl before you can walk—"

"—and walk before you can run."

"Right," said William. "Are you finished with your sundae? I'll bring the cups in and visit the boys' room."

William returned to the car and closed his door. "Okay, James," William said. "Homeward."

"James?" asked a perplexed Ethan.

"Oh, yes," William laughed. "It's an old saying. Chauffeurs in all of the old movies seemed to be named James."

Ethan looked at his grandfather as if he were waiting for something.

"What are you waiting on? Start the car and let's go . . . James."

Ethan peered at William again with a look of expectation.

"Well?" William asked with a slight tinge of annoyance.

"Grandy," Ethan said, "you told me not to start the car until everyone has buckled their seat belt." Ethan gestured to his own belt that was already fastened.

William, a bit confused, looked down and noticed he had not buckled his seat belt when he returned from the restroom. He quickly grabbed the belt, drew it across his waist, and engaged the buckle.

"Ah . . . I was just testing you, Ethan," William hesitantly pronounced with a faint chuckle.

On the way to Melba's, William had given Ethan turn-by-turn directions at every decision point, even while on the streets in Ethan's neighborhood. William had done this knowing that Ethan's mind would be fully occupied with the details of mirrors, other cars, blinkers, etc. William repeated this guidance for the journey home.

"Grandy?" Ethan asked while stopped at a red light. "I thought we were going home."

"We are," replied William.

"But this can't be the way home."

Looking perplexed, William queried more to himself than Ethan, "Where are we?"

"I don't know, Grandy," Ethan replied. "I don't think we came this way, though. None of it looks familiar."

"I wasn't asking you," William snapped. "I was asking myself."

Ethan, taken aback by his grandfather's abrupt response, wondered what he had done to cause such a reaction. "Sorry," he said, unsure how to respond.

"Take a right turn here." William threw his hands up in frustration. "I'll direct us home since you aren't capable!"

Ethan frowned as he made the turn, suddenly feeling uneasy over his grandfather's odd behavior.

What's going on with Grandy?

✳ ✳ ✳ ✳

Society, it would appear, rewarded the famous or popular. For example, the office of the President of the United States had only been held by five individuals who had not previously been elected to a public office. The same held true at the state level and continued down through the different social circles all the way to the high school level.

In the average high school setting, the popular students are most often involved in athletics or student government, or both. Typically, the varsity quarterback dates the head cheerleader, but this trend had been disrupted at Frey High School. The varsity quarterback was not the one dating the head cheerleader. That honor and privilege, in Ethan's own words, went to Ethan Park.

Not only was Ethan *not* the varsity quarterback of the Frey Eagles, but he wasn't even on the team. Ethan hadn't tried out for football. His interest in attending the Eagles' games hadn't blossomed because of his penchant for the sport. No, his consistent attendance at the Friday night games was due to his fondness for the head cheerleader.

Ethan had noticed Lauren Summers in third period Algebra II of his sophomore year. He found that once his eyes and heart had fallen for Lauren, it was much harder to pay attention to Mr. Richard's explanation on solving quadratic equations. Ethan and Roger quickly became regular fixtures under the Friday night lights, always finding seats positioned with a clear view of the cheering squad.

Midway through the summer between his sophomore and junior years of high school, Ethan built up the courage to let Lauren know about his affection for her. What Ethan hadn't realized in all those days in Mr. Richard's Algebra II class, throughout the hallways of Frey, or during the many football games he had attended with Roger was that Lauren had also noticed him.

Their high school romance blossomed. The parents of the young couple would say that Ethan and Lauren were not only infatuated with their relationship, but they were also infatuated with each other.

Ethan and Lauren would counter this comment by saying they had a "controlled" infatuation. It was true that they spent most of their free time together. The two teenagers completed a great deal of their homework assignments either at the Park's or the Summers' dinner table. It was also true that Ethan hadn't missed a home football game in which Lauren had cheered. In turn, when Ethan's rock band, Available Light, performed, Lauren was always seated in the front row.

But cheerleading practice for Lauren, band practice for Ethan, and family obligations for each of them reduced the amount of time the two could be together. It did not dampen their affection for one another, however, nor their desire to be in each other's presence as often as possible.

Neither one of them had invited each other to the Senior Ring Dance. They simply knew they would attend this dance together, a rite of passage commemorating their successful transition to their senior year. Their relationship had grown such that it was a given, not only for Ethan and Lauren but all who were acquainted with them, that they would attend the dance as a couple.

Prior to the event, the young pair had an obligation to fulfill. A dinner had been planned by their families to celebrate the accomplishment of Ethan and Lauren reaching their senior year of high school. Though the two of them were eager to spend the evening together at the dance and celebrate the marking of this passage, they did not view the dinner at the

Park residence as an onerous obligation. They were just as excited about dinner with both families as they were about attending the dance.

This would be the first dinner where the two families would come together for a celebration. During the weeks preceding the senior ring festivities, Lauren's mother, Janet, and Constance had planned the dinner together. It was being held at the Park residence in the middle of the afternoon. This would allow time for the young couple to return to their respective homes to primp, preen, and don their selected formal wear before heading to the dance. With their mothers' assistance, Ethan had chosen a stylish double-breasted tuxedo and Lauren decided on a pale green flowing formal gown.

The sound of the Westminster chimes echoed through the Park house. The occurrence of the ringing chimes signified not only that someone rang the bell at the front door, but also that it would be this visitor's first time at the Park's residence. Friends and family learned over repeated visits that the family entrance was located at the less formal location of the kitchen door. Lauren, as a frequent visitor, quickly learned this, but Lauren was not with her parents right now. She and Ethan had met with some friends immediately following the class ring ceremony. So Drew and Janet Summers were flying solo on their first visit to the Park home.

"Hello," Constance said as she opened the front door. "We're so glad to be sharing this momentous occasion with you."

"Hi, Constance!" Janet exclaimed. "Wasn't that a beautiful ceremony at the school?"

Constance flushed. "I hate to admit it, but I had to take out a tissue."

"It's hard to believe our little babies are all grown up," Janet replied.

"I know."

"This is Lauren's father, Drew." Janet put her arm around her husband.

"Hi, Constance," Drew said. "We've really enjoyed having Ethan around the house. You've raised a fine young man."

"Thank you," a beaming Constance replied. "It's been a family effort. We feel the same about Lauren. Please come in."

Constance ushered Drew and Janet into the den. Bill entered the room from the kitchen, introduced himself, and offered to make drinks for the Summers.

Drew inquired, "I hear that Ethan's grandparents are also joining us for dinner? From what Ethan has told us, your father is one amazing fellow."

Bill took a sip of his drink and placed it on the side table. "Yes, he has done some remarkable things in his life and has been very influential with the kids, especially with Ethan."

"That's what I hear," Drew replied. "Sounds like he and Ethan spend quite a bit of time together. That's great. I never had the opportunity to meet either of my grandfathers."

"Oh, I'm sorry," Bill responded.

"They both passed away before I was born. So, I don't have any idea what it must be like to get that kind of mentoring."

"I can tell you this," Bill said, "Ethan and his grandfather are exceptionally close." *Too close for my comfort.*

Ethan noticed as he and Lauren pulled into the Park driveway that his grandfather had arrived moments before and was opening Granny's door.

William, Margaret, Ethan, and Lauren all walked through the kitchen door together. They found both sets of parents, as well as Ethan's brother and sister, in the kitchen laughing and telling stories. Introductions were made all around.

"Wow," William stated. "The party starts all at once."

"Yes, you all arrived together. Synchronicity," Constance commented.

"Kismet," William declared. "Just like when Ethan was born. It was exactly sixty years to the day I was born."

"Really?" Janet inquired. "Did it really happen that way? Was it planned?"

"That's pretty cool," Drew commented. "No wonder you guys are so close."

Constance picked up a serving bowl and headed to the dining room. "No, if I had been given the ability to plan it, he would have been born two months earlier," she said over her shoulder.

"And if *I* had been given the ability to plan it, he would have been born two months earlier," declared Bill.

"Okay, okay . . . enough. Ethan is here and is now a senior in high school," Constance said. "Let's have dinner and celebrate so these two can get to the dance on time."

Due to the number of people and the milestone the occasion represented, this meal would be enjoyed in the rarely used Park dining room. Constance had covered her grandmother's antique table with a lace tablecloth tatted by her mother. But that's where the formality of the occasion ended. Constance and Janet had decided that even though the dinner would be held in the dining room, the fare would be less formal. This would, after all, still be a family meal. No need to put on airs.

Claire scooted in to grab one of the seats next to Lauren. She leaned in toward her. "What color is your dress?"

Lauren glanced in Ethan's direction, and then whispered, "It's pale green and goes all the way to the floor."

Claire's eyes got big. "That's my favorite color. I wish I could see it. I bet it's beautiful."

"I hope Ethan likes it." Lauren smiled. "I'll make sure you get one of the pictures."

The atmosphere around the table was lively yet relaxed. The conversation and rapport between the Parks and the Summers dovetailed together as neatly and finely as the corners on the microphone case Ethan made for his dad several years earlier. A comfortable ease filled the room that afternoon.

Just as Constance was about to offer Margaret's contribution to the afternoon, lemon meringue and apple pies, William abruptly rose from the table, knocking his chair over and against the wall. He quickly made his way around the table and began closing the blinds on the four windows that looked out onto the front yard.

Ethan reached over to right his grandfather's chair. Bill asked, "Dad, what is it?"

With a bewildered look, William replied, "Shhh . . . if we keep the blinds closed, the zebras won't know we're in here. Quiet, everyone."

Bill, thinking his dad was playing, inquired, "Should I get my buffalo rifle?"

William glared at Bill. He walked to his chair and sat down. William noticed everyone looking at him expectantly. "Yes? What is it?"

"Grandy, what about the zebras?"

"Zebras?" William asked with a puzzled frown. "What zebras? Ethan, what are you talking about?"

"Grandy, you shut all of the blinds and told us to be quiet so the zebras wouldn't find us," Ethan stated while shooting his dad a look of alarm.

"I have no idea what *you* are talking about," William retorted. "Are you feeling all right? Are you trying to make me look like a fool? Maybe you need to go lie down."

The silence at the table during this exchange was palpable. Claire shrank back in her chair and looked at her mother. A definite sense of unease now permeated the room. Something had happened, or was still happening, but no one could tell who it was really happening to, or what it was.

"Come on, Grandy," Ethan pressed. "You were just talking about zebras."

"Damn it, Ethan," William snapped. "I am not amused. Nor, I wager, is anyone else."

Trip caught Ethan's eye, put a single finger to his lips, and gave a slight shake of his head.

The exchange between William and Ethan caused the jaws of everyone in the room to drop, with the exception of Ethan's. He was crestfallen. He could feel his eyes beginning to water. Over the course of Ethan's life, his grandfather had rarely reprimanded him. The few times

William did reprimand Ethan had never occurred in front of anyone, and his grandfather certainly had never cursed at him.

Margaret took action. "William," she said definitively, "it's time for us to go."

William reacted petulantly, "But I didn't get my pie."

"We'll take some home with us," she said in a soothing tone. "Dinner has run long, and the kids have to get ready for their dance."

Margaret made apologies and quickly said her goodbyes. She then ushered William to their car, putting him in the passenger seat.

"Why are you driving?" William asked.

"Your face looks flushed. I should drive. Just to be safe."

William's temperament took a one-hundred-eighty degree turn from where it had been only minutes earlier. "Okay. Better to be safe than sorry. That's what Sammy the Safety Squirrel says," he stated with childlike enthusiasm.

Margaret looked over her shoulder and backed out of the driveway, feeling an urgent need to get William settled in his own home.

Among the others remaining around the table, the occasion wound down as quickly as tact and decorum allowed. Lauren's parents ushered her to the door, claiming it was time for her to get ready for the dance because Ethan and Lauren certainly wouldn't want to be late. Lauren gave Ethan's arm a comforting squeeze and followed her parents out the door.

Ethan waved halfheartedly and had the odd feeling that it might already be too late, though for what he didn't know . . . .

171

✳ ✳ ✳ ✳

Bill looked around the table at his children and wife. "Okay, we all need to take a deep breath. I don't know what got into your grandfather. But obviously, something's not right."

Claire moved to sit in the chair next to Constance and reached for her mother's hand. "I'm scared, Mom."

"I understand, sweetheart. It's going to be okay. Your grandfather just isn't feeling well."

"Trip, help me clear the table." Bill exchanged a look with Constance and began stacking plates.

Trip broke the mindless gaze he had directed to his plate. "Sure, Dad."

"Ethan, why don't you start getting ready for the dance?" Bill suggested.

"Yes, sir," a dejected Ethan replied. Somehow, the thought of a celebratory dance had lost its appeal.

✳ ✳ ✳ ✳

Ethan finished brushing his teeth and returned his toothbrush to the holder on the counter. He stood with a thousand-yard stare into and through the mirror. His mind was racing, jumbled with thoughts of the scene that had just occurred and how he would make it through the night.

Water swirling in the sink and down the drain was the only sound in the room until Ethan heard a sharp knock on the door.

"Yes?"

"It's me, Ethan. Can I come in?" Trip asked. "I thought I'd make sure you'd tie your tie properly—and maybe talk a little."

Ethan turned the handle on the faucet to stop the water. "Sure."

Trip entered the bathroom that straddled their bedrooms. He leaned against the door. "That was kinda crazy, yeah?"

"Kinda crazy? That was off the charts," Ethan shot back.

Unfazed by his younger brother's gruff response, Trip picked up the tie laid out on the counter. "But you can't let it ruin your whole night."

Ethan took the tie held out to him. Trip watched as his brother placed the tie around his neck and fumbled with the intricacies of tying a St. Andrew knot.

Ethan looked down on the counter at the piece of paper illustrating the steps to tying a successful knot. "It just doesn't make sense—"

"I agree. I've noticed subtle changes in Grandy whenever I come home from school," Trip said as he turned to face the mirror while Ethan pulled the longest portion of the tie through the knot. Trip fine-tuned his brother's work. "I just figured maybe he was getting cranky and forgetful in his old age."

"This was more than cranky and forgetful."

"It was, bro." Trip retrieved the suit coat from the hanger on the door and held it so his brother could put it on.

173

"I don't know, Trip." Ethan straightened his arms in the jacket. "How am I supposed to have a good time at the dance after this? Not only was I humiliated, but I'm also worried about *why* Grandy acted the way he did."

Ethan faced the mirror to assess the look of his tuxedo. Trip stood just behind him and brushed his shoulders, smoothing out any wrinkles.

The brothers' eyes met in the mirror.

"You need to try to put this out of your mind for the next few hours," Trip said. "This is not only a special night for you but for Lauren as well."

"I'll give it my best shot."

Trip gently squeezed his brother's shoulder. "You can do it."

※ ※ ※ ※

Saturday mornings in the Park kitchen could be just as active as weekday mornings. The kids didn't view Saturday as a day to sleep late. Trip had roused early to get back to campus to work on a paper due Monday. Bill and Claire pulled out of the driveway behind Trip so Claire could attend the first day of rehearsals for the upcoming fall play. Ethan would be the last to leave today, so before going to spend time with his grandfather at the woodshop, he would have a few minutes alone with his mother.

If there was a morning that Ethan needed to spend time alone with his mom, this was it. He'd awakened with bittersweet remnants of yesterday mixed with an anxious need to get to Grandy's woodshop. He really, really needed to see if his grandfather was okay. *Surely he was. Or their day together would have been canceled . . . right? Right!*

174

He was still worrying over his grandfather's alarming display during dinner the previous afternoon. Fortunately, later that evening at the ring dance, Lauren had helped Ethan temporarily forget about the dinner incident with his grandfather. But the darkness returned first thing this morning.

"Yes, that will work. Let's get together later this morning," Constance spoke into the phone. She listened for a few seconds, then ended the call.

Ethan entered the kitchen as Constance put the receiver back into its cradle. "Good morning, Mom," Ethan said, taking a seat on one of the stools at the breakfast bar.

"Good morning," Constance brightly responded. "I thought it was tradition that seniors didn't wake before ten o'clock on the morning after their ring dance."

"I'm used to getting up early on Saturdays to do woodworking with Grandy . . . though —"

"That was Granny on the phone," Constance broke in.

Dread knotted in his throat.

"I think you and I should talk about a couple of things before you go to your grandfather's this morning," she continued.

The knot seemed to drop into his stomach. "You mean how Grandy acted crazy and jumped on me in front of Lauren and her parents?" Ethan asked with a tinge of sarcasm. "That was beyond embarrassing, more like humiliating." He dropped his head, lowering his voice. "And it was scary."

Constance winced. "Yes, we need to discuss that. But first, tell me about the dance. Did you and Lauren have a good time?"

"Mom, I don't feel like talking about the dance. I didn't even want to go after . . . everything."

Constance could see the anguish in her son's face and knew that his harsh statement covered a deeper worry and not a little hurt. "I'm sure the entire evening wasn't horrible. After all, no one at the dance knew what happened at dinner except for you and Lauren."

"Yes, you're right, Mom," Ethan said, "and Lauren knew I was still upset, but she said I shouldn't let that ruin our night. She kept me on the dance floor most of the time."

Constance laughed. "Good for her. I'd guess she's a keeper."

"I don't know, Mom." Ethan managed a smile. "I don't think I'll be able to walk normally for a week."

"I thought she was a good dancer."

"She's a *great* dancer," Ethan exclaimed. "I'm sure we looked pretty funny to everyone, with Lauren being so smooth and me with my two left feet."

Constance leaned across the kitchen island and patted his arm. "But you have terrific rhythm. I'm sure you looked quite smooth yourself. So overall, it was worth all those years of studying to make it to the Senior Ring Dance?"

"Yes, it was," Ethan said, "but Mom, I can't get yesterday's dinner out of my head. Why did Grandy act like that?"

Constance walked around the island and sat next to Ethan. She paused for a moment, then looked at her son. "Ethan, I think something may be wrong with your grandfather. Granny and I spoke this morning. She has been noticing some things. She's coming—"

"I've noticed some things, too. Like how he humiliated me. Something's definitely wrong."

"Ethan! Is that all you're worried about—the blow to your pride?"

Ethan flinched and gave a heavy sigh. "No Mom, it's not. I'm . . . scared for Grandy. This wasn't the first time . . . ." His voice trailed off.

Constance composed herself, knowing she needed to calm Ethan's fears. "Ethan, we're not sure what is going on. As I was saying, Granny is coming over this morning while you are with Grandy."

"I don't un-understand," Ethan stammered.

"Ethan, I can tell you this," Constance began. "Granny talked with Grandy when they got home last night and again this morning. He has no recollection of what happened at your dinner yesterday."

"He doesn't remember talking about zebras? How can that be?"

"We're not sure," Constance softly replied. "We don't want to assume anything. That's why your dad and I are getting together with Granny this morning."

"And then what?"

"We don't know," Constance replied, attempting to contain her emotions. "But I do know this—your grandfather loves you very much and would never purposely do anything to hurt you."

"I don't understand any of this." Ethan shook his head and blew out a breath. "It makes no sense."

"Ethan, I'm going to be direct with you," Constance said, knowing her son deserved more than platitudes. "Granny is concerned that Grandy could be showing some early signs of dementia."

"What?" Ethan whipped his head around, his brows drawn together. "Dementia? Not Grandy!"

"Now, Ethan," Constance cautioned. "We don't know that for sure. It's just a guess. He hasn't seen a doctor about this yet."

"This is crazy." Ethan swept his gaze around the kitchen as if he were searching for answers. He'd read about dementia in one of his science books from school—and he'd seen stuff on TV.

Constance, feeling Ethan's angst and sensing his emotions beginning to crack, tried to comfort him. "Ethan, we don't yet know what to think. I do know what we should do until we find some answers. We behave normally. Grandy *is* expecting you to spend time with him at the woodshop—just like always."

"Really?" Ethan asked. "And I'm supposed to act like nothing happened?"

Constance smoothed her hand over his hair, taming an errant strand. "Remember, he has no recollection of what happened yesterday. He thinks things are normal. Tell him about the fun you and Lauren had at the dance. Just stay away from mentioning the dinner altogether. If you sense something's not right, just be calm and try to act normal. This may help prevent the situation from escalating. As soon as you can, let me, your dad, or Granny know what has happened."

"Mom, I don't know . . . ."

"Ethan," Constance said reassuringly, "what happened yesterday was not your grandfather."

"But Mom, he treated me like a two-year-old in front of Lauren and her parents."

Constance reached over and gave Ethan a hug. "I know that embarrassed you and hurt your feelings, Ethan. I believe everyone in the room knew that Grandy was not himself. Something came over your grandfather. I know this is hard. Just remember, Grandy always wants the best for you. We will get this figured out."

"Okay, Mom," Ethan quietly replied. "I'll be fine."

He only hoped Grandy would be the same.

✳ ✳ ✳ ✳

Constance was preparing a fresh pot of coffee when she heard Margaret's car door closing. She quickly put the carafe under the drip spout on the coffee maker and turned toward the kitchen door to welcome her mother-in-law. Margaret entered the kitchen and immediately fell into Constance's arms. The Park ladies stood in the kitchen, hugging for several moments.

"How is William?" Constance asked as she felt Margaret loosening their embrace.

"How is Ethan? Bill? And Trip and Claire? And you? How are you? I'm sure everyone is confused," Margaret countered.

Constance headed to the cupboard next to the coffee maker, retrieved two coffee cups, and began pouring. "Bill and I talked last night after Ethan left for the dance. He's concerned. He wants to appear strong in front of the kids. He's dropping Claire at school and will be back in a bit."

"That's good. I'd like the three of us to talk."

179

Constance nodded. "Trip is emulating his father. Claire is frightened. Naturally, she was very clingy with me last night. But I think I was able to soothe her enough that she got a decent night's rest. I insisted that she go to rehearsal and Trip get back to school to work on his research paper. It was good of him to race down to be here for Ethan's dinner." Constance cleared her throat and looked down into her coffee. "I'm concerned about Ethan. He's upset . . . shaken."

"That dear boy," Margaret said. "I felt *so* bad for him. I know he was crushed. I could see it in his face."

"Yes, to tell the truth, he is taking yesterday afternoon pretty hard," Constance agreed. "We talked a bit this morning. He's confused, as we all are, but he's strong. I reassured him that Grandy loves him."

Margaret took a seat at the dinner table. "There's no doubt about *that*."

Constance brought the two cups of coffee to the table and sat next to Margaret. "How about William? Is he all right?" she inquired again.

Margaret took a sip of coffee. "As I mentioned earlier, what you saw yesterday afternoon was not the first occurrence. I mean, yesterday was bad—definitely the worst, but not the first."

"Ethan hinted that he'd witnessed other incidents." Constance angled her head. "You mentioned dementia earlier. How long has this been happening? Yesterday seemed to come out of the blue."

Margaret sat more erect in her chair. "There have been several events over the past few years that individually didn't appear to be anything. But, if I link them together and think about them as a whole, I see a pattern forming.

"William has become what one might call 'forgetful.' You know, he's getting older, as we all are, and we start to forget certain things."

Constance smiled faintly. "Life gets busy. We all have too much going on."

"I think this may be more than that, Constance. Not only has he been forgetting small things, but he's starting to forget the big ones as well."

Margaret closed her eyes briefly and began to speak very fast, as if she had to get it out before she changed her mind. "A few weeks ago Barbara called at ten in the morning asking for William. He'd left for work at his normal time. He hadn't mentioned any off-site meetings.

"He hadn't shown up at the office yet. Barbara was calling because he had a ten o'clock meeting scheduled with a client to sign a contract. He wasn't there. No one knew where he was. At about ten thirty he walked in the house with a milkshake from Melba's."

"That's odd," Constance interjected.

"I know. When I asked him about the meeting and why he hadn't gone to work, he looked shocked. He said he thought he'd surprise me with a milkshake before going to his meeting and he'd just lost track of time. Then, he quickly set down the milkshake and raced out of the house. I suppose I'd been courting denial until then. He has never lied to me about anything, big or small."

Constance listened without comment.

"Not only has the forgetfulness increased," Margaret continued, her voice hitching, "but his behavior has become . . . so . . . unWilliam-like. And he is becoming edgier and more aggressive. You know he's never been afraid to state his position or make a point, but normally he likes to make his point for the point's sake, not to upset people. That doesn't always seem to be the case now."

Margaret paused and took a deep breath. "There have been instances where he's been just plain belligerent, almost wanting to pick a fight."

Constance nodded. "Is something going on at work? Is he under heavier than normal pressure? I have seen a few instances recently where he and Bill have gotten into it. But I figured that's just the method of communicating they've developed over the years when they disagree."

"There's nothing at work that I believe would be causing this," Margaret said. "It just appears William is now finding more to disagree on . . . and with everyone. He's done a good job of masking it, but I think it's beginning to get the better of him.

"For example, last week we were at Roscoe's. William stormed out in a rage insisting that Roscoe had the order wrong. Constance, I heard William on the phone earlier when he ordered the meat. Roscoe prepared exactly what William had requested."

Constance kept silent, letting Margaret get it all out, not knowing what to say.

"Then later, when we were pulling in the driveway just after leaving Roscoe's and running a couple of other errands, William turned to me and said, 'We forgot to stop at Roscoe's to pick up the meat.' Constance, he had no recollection." Margaret let out a deep sigh. "It's disconcerting."

"Margaret, have you consulted with a doctor about his forgetfulness and moodiness?"

The door to the kitchen opened. Bill walked in and went straight to his mother, giving her a hug. Margaret buried her face in her son's shoulder.

"Mom, are you okay? How's Dad?"

Margaret took a step back, grasping her son's hands in hers. "He appears to be okay this morning—as if nothing happened." She returned to her seat next to Constance as Bill filled his coffee mug. "I was describing to Constance some of his other behaviors that have been troubling me."

The coffee caught in Bill's throat, and he swallowed hard. "Have there been a lot of strange behaviors? Do we need to take him to see a doctor?"

"Yes, I believe it's time for him to see a doctor," Margaret nodded. "But he got so defensive when I suggested it a while back. Your father said he would handle it, but he's been so busy. Neither of us has broached the subject since."

She sighed. "And I just haven't wanted to see him upset any further. I confess I've been trying to ignore it myself." She shook her head and bit back a harsh laugh. "I've never felt so . . . unnerved." Margaret's voice broke.

Constance turned and reached for the tissue box on the sideboard behind her, then slid it over to Margaret. "You mentioned dementia over the phone. Do you really think that's what's going on?"

"Honestly, I'm just not sure what to think," said Margaret looking sad and shaking her head as she accepted a tissue. "I've recently done some research and it appears he could be showing signs of Alzheimer's, though I would hate to jump to that conclusion."

"Oh my," Constance said with a sigh. She should have been more surprised, but she'd had a similar thought earlier. Constance looked toward Bill as he shook his head in disbelief.

"There have been quite a few things," Margaret went on. "I've found his car keys in the freezer more than once. He goes outside to get the paper and then forgets why he's out there. It's strange because he's usually so on top of everything."

Constance pondered aloud, "I wonder how much of this behavior the kids have seen. And he and Ethan . . . they spend so much time together."

Margaret sniffled, "I don't know. But because Ethan and his grandfather are so close, this could end up being quite confusing for him."

"Bill, what do you think?" Constance asked. "I know you and your dad have had your differences, but this must make you feel uneasy as well."

Bill paced the length of the kitchen, his brow furrowed.

Constance went to her husband and took his hand. Bill looked at his wife and touched her cheek. "I'll be okay . . . it's the kids." He looked over at his mother. "As Mom said, especially Ethan. He's the one that hangs on his grandfather's every word."

※ ※ ※ ※

1964

America was experiencing an invasion it had never seen before this. Not an invasion of troops landing on a nation's shores equipped with heavy weapons and the intent to militarily conquer. No, this had been a cultural invasion embraced by most of the nation's populace. At the very least, it had been embraced by the younger segment of society. It was known as the British Invasion.

As a part of this younger demographic, Margaret took a liking to the music that had made its way across the Atlantic Ocean and onto U.S. shores and airwaves. Her husband noticed this and made plans to surprise her. William took Margaret to New York City under the guise of a weekend away, wrapped around a series of meetings for the fledgling Park Enterprises. William had obtained two very-hard-to-get tickets to see the Beatles.

There had been an additional component to the trip that William had kept hidden from Margaret as well. While the Beatles were introducing New York and the nation's youth to the British version of rock 'n' roll, the rest of the city was preparing for the opening of the World's Fair two months after the Beatles invasion. During this World's Fair, Ford Motor Company would unveil its answer to the Chevrolet Corvette with its very first public viewing of the 1964 Ford Mustang.

A fact of which the public had been unaware was that this latest innovation in the Ford Motor Company stable, the Mustang, had arrived in New York City simultaneously with the Beatles. William had arranged to get a sneak preview of the car while he and Margaret were in the Big Apple.

One could view this added dimension to the Park's journey to New York through two different lenses. It could be viewed in a positive light since they were some of the first non-Ford people to get up close to this innovative vehicle. Or, it could be viewed in a negative hue because it was something that ended up costing William money that he and Margaret didn't really possess. Alas, Margaret had fallen in love with the 1964 Ford Mustang.

※ ※ ※ ※

The Present

With the top down and "Love Me Do," sung by the Beatles, blasting through the speakers, Ethan pulled into his grandfather's driveway in the very same poppy red Mustang that William had bought for Margaret after that trip to New York City not long after they were married.

He had to laugh. *Grandy was a romantic. Who knew?*

There were many reasons Ethan loved driving this Mustang. First and foremost, it had been a gift from his grandparents once he had fulfilled all the requirements to obtain his driver's license. Second, he loved this Mustang because he knew it was a treasured family heirloom that one day would be passed down to one of his own children. He also had fond memories of many joyous top-down rides to the beach with his grandparents, not to mention this beauty of a car stood out from the everyday vehicles that most of his contemporaries drove. Ethan had been ecstatic when Trip had turned sixteen and asked his grandparents for a newer tech-enhanced vehicle, leaving this beautiful classic available for him on his sixteenth birthday.

On this particular morning, even with the upbeat music of the Beatles reverberating from the stereo, Ethan was in a pensive state of mind. He still wasn't able to shake the sadness he felt regarding the way his grandfather behaved at dinner the previous afternoon and the manner in which William spoke to him in front of Lauren and her parents. Adding to his grim mood was the conversation he had with his mother this morning. How could Grandy *not* remember anything about the zebras?

✳ ✳ ✳ ✳

186

Ethan paused in the doorway to the woodshop, wary for the first time in his life of what he might find inside. Grandy was poring over the plans for their next project. The plans, such as they were, were not complicated. Dominoes—in one form or another—had been around since China's Song dynasty during the thirteenth century. The dominoes made in those ancient times were carved from ivory. The dominoes William and Ethan were making would be hewn out of red oak. Each of these tiles would bear the traditional game-playing pips on one side, and the opposite side would be adorned with a gold-leafed capital "P." Grandy, being Grandy, would leave nothing to chance. This set of dominoes would be perfect!

Ethan watched Grandy for a few minutes, searching for signs that all was not well, and found none. With tension dissipating, he forced a smile and entered the shop. "Good morning, Grandy."

William looked up from the plans. "Good morning, Ethan."

"Grandy, I did some research and think I understand a little more about dominoes."

"That's wonderful," William answered. "But wow, you're all business this morning. Aren't you going to fill me in on how the dance went last night?"

This was a topic Ethan didn't want to broach. He didn't believe he would be able to maintain his composure through a lengthy discussion. But he also knew he couldn't ignore his grandfather's question and had to appear, as his mother had intimated, "normal."

"Ah . . . um . . . we had a good time."

"A good time?" an aghast William inquired. "All that hoopla . . . for . . . 'a good time'?"

187

Ethan dug deep and spoke with resolve, trying to sell his contained enthusiasm to his grandfather. "We had a great time. Lauren is awesome and so much fun to be with."

"All right," William smiled, "that's more like it. You need to grab life and embrace the memories."

Ethan decided this may be a good time to move to safer emotional ground, so he quickly changed the subject. "Which set are we making?" he inquired. "A double six or a double nine?"

William chuckled. "You really have done your homework. I figured we wouldn't bite off more than we can chew, so we're making a double six. Thus, twenty-eight tiles."

The familiar feeling of working together on a wood project as they had done since Ethan was a little boy immediately pushed his gloomy feelings to the back of his mind. For the time being, he focused on the task at hand and enjoyed the company of his grandfather as they embarked on a new woodworking endeavor.

"The fifty-five tiles of a double nine overwhelms you?" Ethan teased.

"Perhaps. Remember our discussions about goals? They have to be . . ." Grandy paused and gave his grandson an expectant look.

"Realistic and attainable," Ethan answered.

"Ready? Let's get started. So Ethan, yesterday lived up to your expectations?"

Ethan averted his gaze and stifled a sigh. "Yes, yesterday was a day I will probably never forget."

EIGHTEEN YEARS OLD

E.P.

Chapter 10
STAGE FRIGHT

Over the course of the next several months, the elder Parks continued to monitor William's behavior. They pored through articles and discussed how best to move forward. Dr. Stevens, the family physician, was brought up to speed. He offered his suggestions on possible causes. But, as Margaret, Bill, and Constance had already surmised, the most logical cause of these illogical episodes was the early onset of dementia. As they quickly learned, dementia touches everyone within love's reach of the affected.

After dinner one Friday evening, Bill gazed at his family with pleasure . . . and trepidation because this would be the time he and Constance talked with their children about Grandy. Trip was home from college and had no plans for the evening. Ethan had completed his final exams and was now waiting for the results. He, too, had no plans. Claire was studying for her finals. "Since we're all together, for once, I think we should gather on the deck for dessert and catch up on family happenings."

Bill and Constance thought it best that the discussion with the children about their grandfather's condition should be in a comfortable location where happy memories lived. They wanted the kids to be in a setting where they could talk openly, ask questions, and, more importantly, feel safe expressing the emotions they might experience during a discussion of this nature.

"All right, let's get these dishes cleared." Constance rose and began stacking plates. "Then everyone head out to the deck for dessert."

"Yes, ma'am!" Trip, Ethan, and Claire replied, nearly in unison.

"Get ready for a double special treat," Bill added. "Not only are we going to have dessert out on the deck, but it's going to be—"

Before Bill could finish, Claire jumped in. "Hummingbird cake! It smells delish."

"That's right," Constance declared. "I guess I can't get anything past your nose."

With the table cleared and everyone gathered on the deck, Constance handed Bill a slice of the much-loved hummingbird cake. Trip, Ethan, and Claire were already washing down their first bites with sips of ice-cold milk.

"Mom," Trip joked, "just how many hummingbirds does it take to make a cake?"

Constance laughed as Claire moaned, "There aren't really any hummingbirds in hummingbird cake."

"Then, if there are no hummingbirds in the recipe, why is it called a hummingbird cake?" Trip countered.

"The traditional story," Ethan intoned as he stood, adopting an officious posture, "is that the recipe originated in Jamaica. The national bird of Jamaica is the hummingbird. Whoever came up with the recipe decided to name it after their national bird. But that's just a theory. No one really knows." He abruptly sat and rubbed his hands together. "Let's eat."

Trip laughed and applauded. "Thank you for the lesson, Mr. History."

The banter between siblings and parents continued for some time. The conversation covered many disparate topics: academics, music, the latest movies, and plans for summer vacation. As with many Park family evenings, the atmosphere was light and relaxing. Everyone was at ease sharing their thoughts, views, and feelings.

Little did the Park children realize that both the evening and mood were about to change. The time had arrived for the difficult discussion about their grandfather. A dissonant silence fell upon the gathering. Bill and Constance exchanged strained looks.

The glances between his parents caught Ethan's eye. He set his fork down carefully and exchanged serious looks with Trip and Claire. "Okay, what's up, Dad? Mom?"

Bill frowned. "Why would you think something's up?"

"The sudden, deafening silence," Trip said in a monotone.

"The not-so-subtle looks back and forth between you and Mom," Ethan said.

"It's either good news, or bad news," Claire offered with a solemn nod.

Trip grumbled, "I'm betting on bad news."

"Now, now. I'm proud of you kids," Bill began. "You're loving, intelligent, and a joy to spend time with—and you are each too discerning for your own good."

"Aw, shucks, Dad," Ethan replied with mock humility as he shot an alarmed glance at his siblings. Since none of them had done anything out of the ordinary, Dad's high praise could only mean one thing. Something was going on . . . .

"Seriously, Ethan," Bill continued, "you guys are all doing well. Trip, you've had a successful start to your college career. Ethan, in spite of my misgivings about biting off more than you could chew, you are excelling in school, and you just may achieve your goal of being valedictorian."

Ethan gave a dramatic shake of his head. "Dad, I *will* be valedictorian. I set that goal, created a plan, and have only a few weeks of execution left before completing that goal."

"Yes, you are doing well," Bill acknowledged. "Claire, you are an amazing young lady academically, socially, and always with such a positive outlook."

"What's the rub, Dad?" Trip inquired. "Sounds like you're about to ask to borrow money from us."

Taking on a more somber disposition, Bill shook his head. "No, I wish that were the case."

"This is something more serious that money can't fix," Constance said.

"Your mom is right."

"It's *not* good news," Claire said sadly.

"It's about Grandy, isn't it?" Ethan sat forward in his chair.

194

Bill also sat forward and then rested his forearms on his knees. "We—your mom, Granny, and I—believe that Grandy is showing signs of dementia. I'm sure you have noticed some of his unusual behavior over the past several months."

"It may be easy to think that Grandy is in a bad mood or just being forgetful," Constance explained. "But if you realize it could be due to illness, you may see it from a different perspective. When these instances become more frequent, it leads one to believe . . ." Her voice thickened with emotion, and she had to stop.

Bill reached for Constance's hand and picked up where she left off. "There have been many instances recently, most of which you haven't seen—and it seems to be getting worse." He took a small sip of milk. "Grandy hasn't been diagnosed by a doctor yet."

"Well, why hasn't he been to a doctor?" Trip asked.

"It's tricky," Bill said. "Your grandfather is a proud man. He always likes to be in control. It's hard for someone, anyone, to admit—" He shook his head and swallowed. "He has to be willing to see the doctor. We can't force him."

"Wow!" Ethan said in shock. "It's hard to believe this is really happening to Grandy."

"Yes, Ethan," Bill replied, "but, as unbelievable as it may seem, it is reality."

"We as a family need to do everything we can to support Grandy and Granny during this confusing time," Constance said.

"Well, we need to get him to a doctor." Trip stood up and began to pace alongside the pool.

"Yes," Bill replied. "We will get him to a doctor, as soon as possible. Your mom, Granny, and I are working on a way to get him there." He ran his hand across the back of his neck. "He *is* stubborn, but we *will* be very patient with him. We will *not* take his outbursts personally because he doesn't even know he's having an outburst most of the time."

"Listen," Constance said as she sat forward in her chair, "Grandy loves each of you very much. He will *always* love you! Although the episodes he's having are becoming more frequent, and he can seem mean at times, he is his usual self—most of the time, for right now."

"What's the plan? Is there something I can do?" asked Ethan.

"The best thing you can do, that each of us can do, is to love Grandy like we always have," Constance answered. "Spend time with him. Savor that time for your sakes as well as his. Continue to make good memories with your grandfather."

"But realize," Bill cautioned, "there may be times when he's forgetful. Or, he may say or do something that seems weird or odd. Play along, but don't patronize him or let him put himself or you in any danger."

Claire began to cry. "Dad, all of this is scaring me."

Constance put her arm around Claire. "It's okay, baby. It is frightening. But . . . we love Grandy, and if we stick together, we can get through this."

"I didn't mean to scare you," Bill gently explained. "I just need each of you to know what is happening. It would be easy for any one of us to think that Grandy is becoming a grumpy old man. But that's not what it is. He may have a disease."

"We don't actually know that for sure," Ethan said defensively, fighting both reason and emotion.

196

"You're right," Bill countered. "We don't. When we get him to a doctor, we will find out for sure. But the research, and his behavior, all point—"

"I can't see Grandy letting this stuff you're talking about get the best of him," Ethan challenged.

Bill rubbed his forehead. "Grandy can't control this."

"Ethan, this isn't something someone chooses," Constance said.

Ethan mumbled under his breath, "Grandy still has a lot on his To Do list . . . ."

※ ※ ※ ※

For as long as Ethan could remember, he had been spending his Saturday mornings with his grandfather. There were very few things that had arisen over the years to cause Ethan or William to miss this time together. Ethan had made it crystal clear to Roger and his other bandmates in Available Light that time with his grandfather trumped all band commitments. He also didn't commit to any sports or clubs that might cause a Saturday morning conflict.

Ethan had the top down on the Mustang, enjoying the fresh air of late spring and listening to his favorite band playing loudly on the stereo as he drove to his grandparents' house early Saturday morning. The sun had just risen over the horizon and was shining brightly, causing the poppy red paint on his car to appear even more vibrant. Ethan was bursting with pride and joy.

There had been another family meeting last night. Miss Olson had called Ethan into her office the day before to inform him that it was official. The last of the exams had been graded and the results tabulated. Ethan had been named valedictorian of his graduating class at Frey High School.

Despite the great news, the fresh air, the loud music, and the frenetic freedom he felt while driving with the wind whipping through his hair, Ethan was apprehensive. His grandfather's behavior continued to become more unpredictable as each day passed. This had been one of the most distressing and frustrating aspects of his grandfather's condition—one never knew how truly present he would be at any given moment.

Ever since he found out about Grandy's situation, Ethan followed the advice of the family counselor and his parents. He continued to treat his grandfather with the same amount of respect and dignity he had always shown him. Ethan made sure to steer clear of any topics or discussions that the family had learned would upset Grandy, most specifically discussing his condition. William had always confronted problems head-on. But, like many others with William's affliction, he was using denial as a defense mechanism.

Over the years Ethan had observed that his grandfather thrived in a well-ordered environment. Ethan learned from the family counselor and his own research that organization and set routines can help those who struggle with forgetfulness to feel secure and more in control.

William looked up from sweeping the floor to see Ethan enter the woodshop. "Good morning, Ethan."

Ethan breathed a small sigh of relief. It appeared, at least for now, that Grandy was *here*.

"Good morning, Grandy."

William looked up at the clock. "On time, actually a little early. As always. That's a very valuable habit to have. It will serve you well."

Ethan smiled broadly. "It already has."

"Why do you look like the cat that just ate the canary?"

"Well, Grandy, I didn't exactly eat a canary. But I do have some pretty big news."

"Okay, come on. Out with it."

"Grandy, I said I would be valedictorian, and Miss Olson informed me yesterday that I *am* the valedictorian," Ethan said proudly. "I did it!"

"Oh my!" William said as he reached for one of the stools he and Ethan built last year. "I need to sit down. That's wonderful news."

"It sure is," Ethan said. "It was a tight competition. There were three of us that were in contention, but overall I ended up with the highest GPA."

"That's great, Ethan. See? A goal. A plan. Hard work. Determination. Works every time."

"See it?" Ethan continued, "I not only saw it. I lived it."

"Remarkable news." William folded his arms across his chest and nodded. "What an accomplishment."

"I couldn't have done it without you."

"Ethan, you did this on your own. You did this because you set a goal, created a plan, and did not let anything distract you from your goal.

"Remember," William continued, "remember this feeling of success, this feeling of completion. You said what you were going to do, and you did it."

"To Do lists really do work," Ethan avowed.

"To Do lists keep us focused," William instructed. "They help us to keep on track. Don't let anyone or anything ever deter you from your To Do list . . . your goals."

"You got it, Grandy. In fact, I need to add something to my To Do list right now."

"What's that?"

"That I need to write my valedictory speech. I want you and Granny sitting in the front row with Mom, Dad, Trip, and Claire as I deliver that speech."

"I wouldn't miss it for the world, Ethan."

※ ※ ※ ※

Throughout human history, there have been many orators who have reached their audiences at the deepest of intellectual and emotional levels. These orators have spoken with such eloquence and power as to move their audiences to action, introspection, adulation, and even to the offering of their very lives.

Over two thousand years ago, the Athenian orator, Pericles, was inspiring and persuading his audiences with enough fervor for them to create hundreds of temples and even the Pantheon. The sixteenth President of the United States, Abraham Lincoln, took inspiration from Pericles to compose his well-known and highly regarded Gettysburg Address.

Ethan prescribed himself to follow the examples set by Pericles, Lincoln, and many other gifted speakers. He noted that these great leaders rarely spoke without giving careful thought, planning, and practice to their words. The greatest speakers of history didn't ad lib; rather, they preferred to prepare their speeches to ensure the message transmitted the desired impact to their audiences.

※ ※ ※ ※

The spotlight shone brightly on Ethan as he stood at the podium. It was so bright he had trouble seeing the audience. This was disturbing to him because great orators like to "read" the audience as they deliver their words. Still, Ethan was confident that his words would have the inspirational impact he desired. So, he stood tall as he delivered the closing remarks of his valedictory speech. The audience erupted in enthusiastic applause.

The audience, such as it was, consisted of Bill, Constance, Trip, and Claire. This was another dry run. Leading up to graduation day, Ethan had enlisted his family to be the audience, and critics, as he rehearsed over and over again.

"That was your best delivery yet," Constance said.

"That was awesome," Claire said proudly. "Not even boring . . ."

Trip rolled his eyes and nudged his little sister with his shoulder. "You should have quit at 'awesome.'"

"Thanks," Ethan said. "You really think it's good?"

"Yes," replied Constance, "you hit all of the right notes."

"Absolutely," Bill agreed. "The content is good, and your delivery is great."

"I just hope that I don't get too nervous," Ethan said pensively. "Talking in front of you is one thing, but speaking in front of an auditorium full of people . . ."

"You'll be phenomenal," Bill said, with an encouraging clap on Ethan's back.

"I really want to make sure I do well," Ethan said, "especially since Grandy and Granny will also be there."

※ ※ ※ ※

The sun forced its way through the blinds and onto the wall in Ethan's room. On a normal day this would not wake Ethan. But today was no normal day. Today was Graduation Day! He thought it pointless to remain horizontal. The anticipation of being a high school graduate and the pride in reaching the goal of becoming valedictorian had been too exciting for Ethan to attain a deep sleep. He shot out of bed and decided to read over his speech one final time. He positioned himself at the desk where he'd spent countless hours reading and studying. Initially the antique desk chair that had been William's when he was in high school had not been comfortable to Ethan. Now, several years and many study sessions later, the contours of the chair enveloped Ethan in a comforting embrace.

The Park folio, given to Ethan by Barbara when he was in sixth grade, lay on the top of his desk. The sight of this folio brought back fond memories from the "Go To Work With Your Dad Day." This day stood out to Ethan as the day when he first consciously thought about his future. It was the experience at Park Enterprises that fomented the thought that he would follow in his grandfather's footsteps, both professionally and on a personal level.

Ethan admired the philosophy by which his grandfather lived. He found stability and comfort when he thought about the direction and consistency that creating a To Do list had brought to his days.

He opened the folio. Though his speech was in the pocket on the right-hand side of the folio, Ethan's eyes immediately looked to the left-hand pocket where his ongoing To Do list had resided since sixth grade. Over the years Ethan read this list with an obsession. He did this to reinforce his commitment to these goals and be reminded of the direction in which he wanted to travel.

As Ethan accomplished items on the list, he checked them off. Monthly he would recreate the list, moving the To Dos yet to be completed to the upper echelons of the list. There it was, boldly stated in his own handwriting, "Graduate from high school as valedictorian."

Thinking back to Grandy's mantra, Ethan had said what he was going to do and then he did it. Technically, he hadn't yet. There were two items remaining to see this goal to completion. He had to deliver his speech and then receive his diploma from Mr. Miller, the principal of Frey High School.

The box would remain unchecked until he returned from the graduation ceremony.

Ethan's introspection was broken by a light tap on the door followed by his mother's voice. "Ethan, are you awake?"

"Yes, come in," Ethan replied. "How did you know I was up?"

Constance opened the door and entered. "It's mother's intuition. And I know this is a big day for you."

Her glance skimmed from Ethan to his open folio. "You're still tweaking your speech?"

Ethan looked down at the folio and then back at his mother. "Actually, I was going to. Then I started thinking about my To Do list and the goal I had set to be valedictorian . . . ."

"I know, Ethan," Constance began, "that's quite an achievement. You have done well."

"Grandy really gets a lot of the credit. As do you and Dad."

"Thank you," Constance said. "But you did all of the *hard* work."

"Mom," Ethan began with a forlorn look on his face, "I just wish Grandy was more like himself. It's been so hard . . . . I just never know . . . . He's been so unpredictable."

"Ethan, of everyone, you are the closest to Grandy. So, you have felt the brunt of his mood swings and weathered more 'storms' than either Trip or Claire have."

Constance walked over to the suit hanging on the closet door and smoothed the fabric. "In spite of that, you have managed to keep your relationship with Grandy positive and uplifting. Even when he's not *here*, I know he can feel the love and respect you have for him. You have helped him maintain his dignity. That's been important toward helping your grandfather."

"Thank you, Mom."

"All right," Constance said brightly, "enough of this heaviness. Come downstairs in about twenty minutes. A special graduation muffin is on the counter for you."

"I can't wait for Grandy to see me on stage tonight delivering my speech."

※ ※ ※ ※

The last of the water trickled down the drain in the bathroom sink. Ethan patted his face with a hand towel and viewed his image in the mirror. At this stage in his life, Ethan didn't have a large amount of facial hair. He did have enough, though, that it required a session with the razor and shaving cream before walking on the stage to represent his graduating class.

His gaze slowly moved from the inspection of his chin up to the hair on the top of his head and then down to his eyes. He contemplated the direction he would take now that he had completed the first major milestone of his life.

His parents, of course, played a major role. They had been supportive, though, at times, Ethan felt that his father believed his goal to be fraught with the potential for disappointment. It hadn't been that Bill didn't believe in Ethan's abilities, but that Bill also believed in the abilities of Ethan's classmates, and in fate. Of course, he *wanted* Ethan to be successful. What he didn't want was Ethan to set a goal that could be missed due to the vagaries of life, thus creating long-lasting regret.

His grandfather had been the one individual who had been unwavering in his support of both Ethan and his goals. Grandy had been the inspiration and driving force for the setting of this most important of goals.

Ethan's reflection smiled back at him as he thought about all the conversations he had with Grandy as they celebrated the incremental victories along this path to success. He recalled the times Grandy comforted and offered advice if the plan appeared to be coming undone. Ethan wondered how many more times he would be able to look into Grandy's deep blue eyes and find counsel.

Ethan's internal sense of timing broke him away from these thoughts. He needed to finish getting dressed so that he could drive to Frey High School for his last time as a student. He picked up the tie he and his dad decided would be most appropriate for the ceremony, a red and blue striped "power tie," as his Dad called it. Ethan donned the tie with a Classic Windsor knot to exude confidence and add a touch of elegance.

One more mirror—Ethan, fully dressed in his dark blue suit, inspected himself as he stood in front of the full-length mirror located in the corner of his bedroom.

One more image—Ethan again thought about the journey he had traveled to get to this point, and he was pleased. Grabbing his folio from the desk, Ethan headed toward the stairs to make his descent to the kitchen.

He paused on the first step with a weird mixture of uncertainty and anticipation. For a moment it weighed on him, and in the next, it carried him down to the kitchen and to the rest of his life.

"Wow!" exclaimed Claire as Ethan walked toward the counter. "You look like a movie star."

Ethan blushed at his sister's flattery. "It's still just me, Claire-bear."

"Ethan, I do have to say," Trip chimed in, "you clean up pretty well."

Ethan gave Trip a once-over. "Maybe you should try it sometime, big brother."

Constance watched with pride as her three children bantered with each other. She knew they weren't perfect, but they had been perfect for each other. She and Bill together had managed to create an environment conducive to encouragement, good natured teasing, and loving support among the siblings.

"Hi, Mom," Ethan said with a slow pivot, "how do *you* think I look?"

"Dashing."

"You're not just saying that because I'm your son, are you?" Ethan teased.

"Why, certainly not!" Constance replied with a mock affronted look as she handed Ethan a small bag. "Here's your blueberry muffin to go."

"Thanks, Mom. Do you have all of the tickets?" Ethan asked. "Do Grandy and Granny have theirs?"

"Yes," Constance reassured Ethan.

"Great! I'll see everybody there then."

✳ ✳ ✳ ✳

The same sun that forced its way into Ethan's room this morning also made its presence known at his grandparents' house. The sun created an array of shadows as light streamed through the ferns hanging from the eaves of the house.

William and Margaret basked not only in the sunlight filtering through the windows, but also in the pride that came from knowing that their grandson had attained a goal. His big moment of recognition would be later today at the graduation ceremony. That would be *public* recognition. William swelled with pride in the knowledge that although Ethan welcomed the public recognition, he didn't need it for validation. The recognition important to Ethan came from his inner self, knowing that he had set out to accomplish a task and successfully completed it.

"You look like you just won the lottery," Margaret joked with William.

"Why wouldn't I? Our grandson has successfully attained the first major goal of his life."

"Valedictorian," Margaret grinned. "He has been incredibly determined to get this far. Kind of reminds me of someone—"

"Ha!" William retorted. "I *had* to be determined, or who knows where we would be today."

"I admire your determination." Margaret rose from her seat. "But right now we need to determine ourselves upstairs to get ready—"

William began vigorously shaking his head from side to side. He grimaced as he put his hands over his ears.

"Honey, what is it? Are you all right?"

William stared blankly at Margaret and continued to cover his ears and shake his head. A pained look crossed his face. He hit the side of his head with the heel of his hand, similar to the method used by swimmers to get water out of the inner ear.

"William!" Margaret hurried to his side. "What is it?"

"Lady, you need to help me! Someone has put BBs in my ears. I feel them rattling around. It hurts! Help me!"

"William," Margaret said, forcing calm steadiness into her voice, "it's me, Margaret."

Frustrated, he said, "I don't know you, lady! But please help me. These BBs are painful!"

Margaret was now fully aware that her husband was in the throes of an episode. She had to remain calm and attempt to settle him down as much as possible.

"Can I take a look inside your ears to see the BBs?" Margaret asked.

"Yes, yes! Please hurry!" William frantically replied.

"Okay, I'll look. Let me get a flashlight." Margaret quickly retrieved the flashlight kept on the kitchen counter and returned to her husband's aid as he continued shaking his head from side to side and moaning pitifully.

William removed his right hand that was covering the side of his head. Margaret turned on the flashlight and peered into his ear. She took several seconds to search for foreign objects—just to be sure.

"William, I don't see—"

"They're in there! I can feel them!"

"I don't have any way to see down deep," Margaret calmly explained. "How about we take a ride to see the doctor?"

William became petulant. "I don't want to see a doctor. Just get them out of my ears!"

Margaret felt the scene escalating. Up until this point, she had managed to work through these episodes on her own. This situation had intensified faster and harder than previous ones. She felt her husband was heading toward hysteria. Action needed to be taken quickly.

※ ※ ※ ※

Parents, grandparents, siblings, and friends of the graduating class of Frey High School were being treated to a sound and light show highlighting each of the graduates and their accomplishments over the previous four years as they awaited the actual ceremony. Large screens displayed various images of the graduates as they studied, played, ate, and made their way through high school. The images were complemented with songs from the graduates' favorite bands as well as sound clips of the graduates, faculty, and staff.

The Frey High School Alma Mater smoothly replaced the soundtrack from the slide show. On cue, the screens dissolved to images of the school's crest. Red, white, and Columbian blue lights—the school colors— bathed the walls of the auditorium as well as the stage. As the rear doors of the auditorium opened, a series of spotlights illuminated the center aisle. The graduating class of Frey High School filed into the auditorium in two columns. As students reached the front of the stage, one column turned right, and the other turned left. The students stepped up onto the stage and took their assigned seats.

Bringing up the rear of the columns were the salutatorian and Ethan, the valedictorian. Immediately behind Ethan and his cohort were the principal and faculty. Ethan discovered during graduation ceremony rehearsals that his side of the line would be on the right, and his parents and grandparents would be seated on the left. He was disappointed that he would not have the opportunity to acknowledge his loved ones prior to him reaching the stage.

As Ethan took his seat on the stage, he eagerly looked out to where he knew his family would be seated. The light show, which had been designed by his father and installed by Park Productions, limited his ability to see past the front edge of the stage. Ethan hoped that when he stood at the podium to give his speech, they would come into view. The words and details of the speeches given by Mr. Miller and other esteemed members of the Frey High School faculty washed over Ethan as he waited his turn.

Ethan's palms were sweating. His time was near. He focused his attention on the podium and Mr. Miller's words of introduction. ". . . Not much more can be said about this impressive young man. Ethan, you are an inspiration to all of us. I remember Miss Olson telling me about your first counseling session as an incoming freshman. You made the declaration that you would be the valedictorian. As you displayed throughout your entire time at Frey High School, you are a man of your word. Congratulations!"

He took a step to the side and turned toward Ethan. "Ladies and gentlemen, I present to you the valedictorian of Frey High School, Ethan Park."

The auditorium exploded with applause, the loudest coming from behind Ethan. Over the past four years, Ethan had been more than just a classmate. He had become a friend to many in his graduating class. He had earned their friendship and respect largely because he returned the same to each of his classmates, but also because they knew him to be honest and reliable.

With his Park Enterprises folio firmly in hand, Ethan stood and proudly walked to the podium. Mr. Miller offered his hand and leaned in, speaking into Ethan's ear. "Son, you have done it. Enjoy this moment, and know that I am proud to say that I was able to have a small role in your success."

"Thank you, sir." Ethan looked at Mr. Miller and nodded with a subtle smile. "Your leadership inspired me to consistently work hard."

He placed his folio on the podium and paused to assess his audience. Ethan recalled Grandy's words as he looked out over the crowd: "Take a moment before you speak. It's called a pregnant pause. Let the anticipation build in your audience. By doing this, your opening words will carry more impact."

Ethan scanned the audience. Most of the lighting was directed toward the stage, so he was still unable to distinguish faces, especially in the farther reaches of the auditorium.

He resisted temptation and did not look toward the area he knew his family would occupy until last. A little bit of light leaked from the front of the stage onto the first row where his family was seated. His gaze fell first on his dad, proudly holding his mom's hand. As usual, Claire was sitting beside her mother. When Ethan's gaze fell on his sister, she enthusiastically waved. Next to Claire sat Trip. His older brother gave him a thumbs-up and a wink.

Ethan continued scanning the front row. The next two seats . . . were empty. Grandy and Granny weren't there! Ethan's eyes darted back toward his dad. Bill made a slight, shrugging gesture that Ethan interpreted as, "I don't know."

The pause turned into an uncomfortable silence. Ethan was shaken to his core. A lump began to form in his throat, and his eyes began to sting. His mind raced with a progression of thoughts. *Grandy promised. He has never broken his word . . . ever. Something's wrong.*

Mr. Miller approached the podium. "Ethan, are you all right? Do you need some water?"

Ethan looked at Mr. Miller. "No, sir. It's . . . just such a big day."

"I understand," replied Mr. Miller.

Ethan knew Mr. Miller didn't really understand. He also knew his fellow graduates and their families didn't understand. Ethan himself didn't understand. However, he knew that he couldn't ruin the graduation ceremony for his fellow graduates. He had said that he would give the valedictory address—and give it he would.

What happened? He refused to contemplate the possibilities and opened his folio. Clearing his mind and his throat, Ethan began to deliver his well-rehearsed speech.

"Classmates, family, friends, and faculty of Frey High School, I am proud . . . ."

❋ ❋ ❋ ❋

213

The former students, now graduates, congregated backstage. Each of the four hundred thirty-two students had proudly walked across the stage, shook hands with faculty members, and then received their diploma from Mr. Miller. With the ceremony concluded, it was time to bask in the glory of a job well done and revel in the anticipation of what the future would offer.

Smiles and laughter multiplied as the graduates and their families congratulated each other. Camera flashes abounded as families strove to document the joyous event. Amid the frivolity, tears were also in abundance—tears of joy as well as tears of sadness. Many of these now former classmates grasped that a chapter in their lives had ended, meaning they may be separated from each other by choice of college, job, geography—or fate.

In typical Park fashion, Ethan maintained a good front despite his disappointment. He smiled, shook hands, and graciously posed for pictures with his classmates. He was cordial and respectful when his teachers and the parents of his classmates came by to offer their congratulations.

Constance and Bill made their way backstage as quickly as possible. They jostled through the proud families and elated graduates. Constance spotted Ethan and rushed toward him. Ethan's ability to mask his tears of sadness as tears of joy evaporated when he made eye contact with his mother. He hugged her tightly.

"Ethan—" Constance began.

"Mom," Ethan interrupted, "where are they?"

Constance looked at her son. "We don't know right now."

Catching up with his wife, Bill interjected, "Your mom and I are going to their house to check on them."

"I'm going, too."

"No," Bill said firmly, "it would be best for you, Trip, and Claire just to go straight home."

"Right, if something has happened, we don't want to have all of us trooping over there. We'll call you as soon as we find out something."

"But, Mom—"

Bill placed his hand on Ethan's shoulder. "Ethan, give your brother and sister a ride home."

Constance stepped in to kiss her son's cheek. "I know you're concerned. Your dad and I will call as soon as we can. Go home. Most likely, everything is fine. Grandy or Granny may have just been feeling under the weather."

"No, it's got to be something more serious," Ethan insisted. "Grandy told me he wouldn't miss this for the world."

Chapter 11
ETHAN MAKES DO

Bill and Constance had made the drive to Highland Hospital several times over the years. These trips were mainly happy occasions, such as the welcoming of a new member to the Park family. At no time had the trip seemed to take as long as it did on the drive this late afternoon.

Constance was mentally urging Bill to drive faster. He was driving with what he termed "controlled aggression." Constance thought it best not to distract him with conversation. And, they didn't have any facts. Small talk seemed inappropriate. Bill needed to focus.

At last Bill drove into Highland Hospital's emergency room parking lot. He spotted Margaret's car and pulled into a nearby empty slot. Stopping the car, he turned off the ignition. As Bill opened his door, Constance grasped his arm just as he turned to get out of the car. Bill looked back at his wife. Their eyes met.

"I'm sure everything is fine," Constance reassured her husband.

"Hope so," Bill responded hastily.

"Maybe your dad had one of those bad migraine headaches he sometimes gets."

Unconvinced, Bill shook his head. "It could be. Let's go find out."

They exited the car and quickly walked toward the emergency room entrance. As they neared the door, Constance clasped Bill's hand in hers and gave it a squeeze. The doors whooshed open, and they walked in together.

✻ ✻ ✻ ✻

Bill opened the door to William's room. His mother was sitting in a chair she had pulled close to the bed. She was tenderly holding his father's hand in hers. He appeared to be resting, and at best, sleeping. William was connected to the usual array of wires linking him to the hospital's telemetry systems.

Fortunately, there didn't appear to be a massive number of tubes. In Bill's mind, this was a positive sign. One lone tube wended its way from an IV into William's non-dominant left hand. The steady, consistent, soft beeping of these systems eased some of Bill's anxiety.

He immediately went to his mother's side and gave her a hug. Constance also embraced Margaret. For several moments the three of them remained silent as they looked at William. Bill broke the silence as he moved the only other visitor's chair in the room next to Margaret's. He then gently indicated for his wife to take a seat.

Finally, Bill spoke. "How are you, Mom?"

"I'm all right," she responded, holding back tears. "I'm so sorry that we had to miss Ethan's graduation."

Constance patted Margaret's shoulder. "Margaret, Ethan would be the first to agree that William's well-being is more important. What happened?"

"I don't really know," Margaret replied. "We were in the sunroom enjoying the morning. Everything seemed fine. We were talking about the graduation. Then . . . um . . . ah . . . the doctor is keeping him overnight for observation." Margaret's voice grew weak.

"It's okay," said Constance. "Let's just sit for a bit."

A pall fell upon the room as the beep of the monitors kept pace with William's heartbeat. As Bill looked at his father lying in the bed, he observed that in this state his dad no longer looked like the huge force behind the Park family and Park Enterprises.

Margaret broke Bill's train of thought. "They gave him a sedative. He's going to sleep for a while. Let's go for a walk so we can talk."

The three Parks made their way to the arboretum. They walked the path that had been constructed and paid for by the man they had just left. Husband. Father. Father-in-law. Grandfather. William Park. Margaret stopped at the stand of trees that she and William had planted to commemorate Bill's birth.

Margaret turned to her son. "I think your dad must've handed out an entire box of cigars during the planting ceremony for these trees."

Bill smiled. "I'm sure he did."

Margaret stopped and sat on one of the benches neatly tucked in an alcove off the path. Bill and Constance perched themselves on the bench across from Margaret and waited for her to apprise them of the situation.

Margaret smoothed her skirt and sighed. "I didn't really want to talk in front of William. I know he's asleep. But I've read that even though a patient isn't conscious, his brain still picks up on the sounds and feelings of those around him. He may not be able to recall the words or the conversations, but it's still somewhere in his subconscious."

"Yes, Mom, I've read that as well." Bill said with forced patience, "Can you explain to us what happened? How bad is it?"

"Bill," Margaret replied, "as I mentioned in the note I left for you on the kitchen door, it's not life-threatening at present. But it is threatening his life in the sense that I believe we are losing him. He's slowly vanishing. The life we've had, the man we know and love . . . is . . . "

Constance walked over and sat beside her mother-in-law. "Margaret, I'm so sorry."

"Mom, please tell me exactly what happened and what's going on."

"Take your time, Margaret." Constance gently added, "We're here for *you* as well as for William."

Margaret took a deep breath. "As you know," she began, "he's been having these episodes of . . . well, mental lapses. He's also had some instances when he sees or hears things that aren't there. It's similar to what happened at the dinner for Ethan's ring dance. But they've become worse, more frequent, and he ends up more panicked.

"This morning we were in the sunroom enjoying the day and discussing the ceremony. All of a sudden, he started shaking his head from side to side."

Bill and Constance listened intently as Margaret recounted the events of the day. Margaret's telling of William's episode not only provided them with the details of the event, but it also provided Margaret with a mechanism to share—and ease—her burden. She wouldn't be in this alone.

"Mom, how often has this occurred?"

Margaret thought for a few moments and then responded, "I would say he has one or two very minor things, several times a week. You know . . . lost keys . . . misplacing something, even a memory . . . the things we all do when we're overly busy. Of course, now I've become hyper-sensitive to these behaviors."

She plucked at her skirt, raising little tents in the fabric. "Something like today I've not seen before. It feels like the pace and intensity of the episodes are increasing. I've started keeping a journal of these events so that I can know for sure. I feel bad about that. It seems like I'm spying or going behind his back."

"Margaret," Constance said, "you're not doing anything subversive. It's for his own health and safety. Yours as well."

"I know," Margaret answered. "It's—"

"What does Dad say about . . . all of this?" Bill asked.

"He doesn't say anything," Margaret answered. "He doesn't usually remember them, and he doesn't want me to discuss them, either. I think he's in denial, which is common for those dealing with dementia."

Wordlessly, Bill stared at the tops of his shoes.

"You know," Margaret continued, "he's been in charge, or in control, for so long. He's a proud man. The thought that things may be slipping from his grasp . . . I guess . . . he's just having trouble dealing with it."

Bill blinked rapidly and stuck his hands in his pockets. "I wonder how Dad's going to reconcile in his mind that he missed the ceremony today."

✳ ✳ ✳ ✳

The sedatives prescribed by William's physician had been effective. William was still resting peacefully when Margaret, Bill, and Constance returned to the room. The beeping from the telemetry units continued their steady cadence. Bill believed Margaret's assessment of William "vanishing" from the family was accurate not only from the mental standpoint but also the physical—William appeared small and weak lying in the hospital bed.

Bill suggested, "Mom, why don't you let Constance take you home so you can get something to eat and then freshen up? I'll stay with Dad."

"That's a great idea," Constance said.

Margaret nodded wearily and allowed Constance to escort her from the hospital room. Bill watched as his mother and his wife walked away, Constance's arm around Margaret. He sank into the chair his mother had vacated and lowered his head into his hands.

✳ ✳ ✳ ✳

The sun continued its journey toward the horizon as Ethan pulled into the parking lot at Highland Hospital. The array of overhead lights began to flicker to life as he drove down the second row of parked cars.

He found Granny's car holding vigil and parked next to it, facing the entrance to the hospital.

Ethan switched the ignition on his 1964 Mustang to the off position. His heart was beating as ferociously as the 210 horses under the hood had been just moments ago. Ethan paused before removing the key from the ignition. He stared ahead at the entrance to the hospital, fearing what he would find inside Grandy's room. He turned toward his grandmother sitting in the passenger seat.

Before he could speak, Margaret, her eyes filled with tears, lightly rested her hand on her grandson's arm. "I'm so proud of you! We are so proud of you! You know you didn't have to come here, today of all "

"Granny, I know," Ethan interrupted. "You needed a ride back here. And anyway, this is where I want to be. You and Grandy have helped me so much over the years. I need to be here, for both of you."

"Ethan, I understand," Margaret softly admonished, "but this is your graduation night. You should be out celebrating with your friends."

"No, this is where I belong," Ethan insisted. "Family *always* comes first."

※ ※ ※ ※

Bill sat with his eyes closed and let the rhythmic tone of the heart monitor lull him into a trance-like state. As he allowed his mind to drift about, memories of his childhood and adolescence floated to the forefront. Thoughts of the many vacations, walk-and-talks, holidays,

223

birthdays, and various other occasions he had enjoyed over the years with his parents flooded to the surface.

Bits and pieces of conversations and sounds of laughter merged with images of family, friends, and festive events. Both his mind and heart re-conceptualized the plenitude of love he had received from his father as he grew from child to adult—

"Where am I? Is Margaret all right? What happened?"

Awareness was sudden, realization startling as Bill heard his father's voice. He rose from his chair and placed his hands on his father's shoulders, gently urging him to lie back.

"Whoa, Dad! Slow down," Bill said, instinctively speaking in a calm, soft voice. "We're at Highland Hospital. Mom is fine."

Bewildered, William continued to struggle. "Why are we here? What happened?"

"Dad—" Bill urged his father to lie still. "You blacked out. Mom thought it best to bring you to the hospital to get things checked out."

"No, I couldn't have." He looked up at Bill, his gaze darting around the room. "Blacked out? Where's Margaret? What about Ethan's graduation? We have to go. I promised Ethan I would be there."

The door swung open, and Margaret and Ethan entered the room. Bill glanced up at his mother and then quickly back to his father. "As I said, Dad, you blacked out, and the doctors want to keep you overnight for observation."

"Overnight?" William said, alarmed. He fought to sit up. "You need to get ready for your graduation."

Margaret gave Ethan a slight nod.

"Grandy, it's late in the evening right now. The ceremony already happened."

The realization that he had missed the graduation brought a distressed look to William's face. "I told you I would be there!" William replied, disappointed.

"Grandy," Ethan started, "your health is more important to me than any ceremony."

"Yes, but—" William looked down toward his hands. "I said . . ."

Ethan continued, "Grandy, I brought my speech with me. You and I can re-enact everything right here."

"It's not the same," William protested.

"You're right, Dad, it's not," said Bill. "But that's okay. We have to work from where we are."

"Once I'm finished with the speech, I'll tell you all about the event," Ethan offered. "It will be just as if you were there."

Margaret stepped forward. "William, the doctor is keeping you overnight for observation. Ethan has offered to stay with you."

"Stay with me? I don't need anyone to stay the night with me." William swept an affronted glance over his visitors. "Besides," he turned and looked at Ethan, "you deserve to be out celebrating with friends!"

Ethan took a wide stance and placed his arms across his chest. William's mouth opened and closed, as if he had searched for words to argue and found none. He exhaled and sank down into the bed, oddly relieved that for once, a decision had been made for him.

✳ ✳ ✳ ✳

Hospitals are not known to be the epicenters of culinary delight, and Highland Hospital was no exception. The evidence of this was plain on the tray a candy striper brought to William thirty minutes ago.

Despite William's hunger, he managed in that span of time only to rearrange the food on the overly thick plastic tray. An extraordinarily small amount of the hospital's offering ended up in William's stomach.

"Dad, you really should try and eat something."

"Really?" William said mockingly. "Are you trying to kill me? This is . . . I don't know what this is, but it isn't anything I'm going to eat."

"Do you want us to go get something for you?" Margaret asked.

"No, that's okay," William gave his wife a reassuring smile. "I don't feel like eating anyway. You and Bill go home and get some rest. Ethan, you should go as well. I'll be fine by myself."

Ethan shook his head. "Nope, Grandy. I'm here to stay."

William adjusted his hospital bed into an upright, sitting position. He hugged Bill and kissed Margaret goodbye. Margaret looked at her husband. "I love you!"

William smiled. "I know you do. I love you, too!"

Margaret pledged, "I'll see you first thing in the morning."

Ethan hugged his grandmother and father. He then commandeered the rolling hospital tray and placed it at the foot of William's bed. He set his Park Enterprises folio on the tray and opened it to his speech.

As Bill walked out the door, he looked back and saw Ethan standing tall behind the hospital table just the way he had stood at the graduation ceremony only hours earlier. Just before the room door closed completely, he heard Ethan begin, "Classmates, family, friends, and faculty of Frey High School. I am proud . . ." Bill smiled to himself with slight amusement and a lot of pride.

✳ ✳ ✳ ✳

William wiped tears from his eyes as Ethan reached the conclusion of his valedictory address. Ethan closed the folio, paused for a moment, and then looked up to gauge his grandfather's reaction.

"What did you think, Grandy?" Ethan inquired. "Was it really that bad?"

"No, not at all," William said. "Actually, it was *that* good."

"Thank you. I wrote, revised, practiced, revised, and practiced . . . just like you said."

"It's obvious that you did what you said you would do. That was a great speech—*and* delivery." William shifted in the bed. "I should've been there. I didn't do what I said I would do. I let you down."

"Grandy, it wasn't your fault."

William looked at his grandson with pride. "Come over here. I have something to tell you."

Ethan hesitantly walked over and sat on the edge of the bed. Grandy reached up and placed his hand on his grandson's shoulder.

227

"Ethan," William began, "you have done a tremendous job. I think you know that. I am incredibly proud of you. Keep doing what you're doing. You are a fine young man with a bright future. You bring honor and distinction to the Park name."

Ethan swallowed, blinked, and stared down at his hands as Grandy said the words he most wanted to hear. He knew his grandfather loved him, but Grandy being proud of him . . . that had to be earned.

"You have truly embraced the ideals I believe necessary for success and happiness. So, I owe you honesty. I think there might be something wrong with me. This isn't the first time I've blacked out. I'm not even sure what's happening to me."

Tears filled Ethan's eyes. "Grandy—"

"Wait," William interrupted, "I don't know that I'm going to be able to do all of the things that I've said I would do. I'm just not sure . . . ."

"But, Grandy," Ethan said, "you can get better. There's always a way. There's always a Plan B. There must be a cure."

William observed the pain in his grandson's eyes and shook his head slowly. "No, I don't think there is."

Tears now spilled from Ethan's eyes. "Grandy, what about all of our plans? Park Enterprises? The things on our To Do lists?"

Chapter 12
TAKEN TO THE EDGE

Constance looked at the calendar hanging on the wall next to the refrigerator. It indicated that more than half of the year had passed. For that matter, half of the summer had passed. She realized that in a few short weeks another one of her children, Ethan, would be leaving home for college. Then two of her loved ones, Trip *and* Ethan, would no longer rest their heads nightly on pillows under her roof.

Always one to look for the positive in any situation, Constance reveled in the fact she had *all* her children home at the present moment. She knew, at any moment, those children would be bounding down the stairs for breakfast and lively conversation as they had been doing since they were toddlers.

Constance especially enjoyed breakfast time in the summer. Claire, still in grammar school, filled her days hanging out with friends or spending time with her mother. Each of the boys worked summer jobs, Trip at Park Productions with his father and Ethan at Park Enterprises with his grandfather. No one needed to rush off to school. Constance appreciated that there was time for a leisurely breakfast shared together by the three siblings.

"The grits will be ready in about five minutes," Constance pointed out as Ethan entered the kitchen with hard hat and safety vest in hand.

"You're awesome, Mom," Ethan declared.

"Good morning to you, too. But that's not going to get you out of pouring the drinks for everyone."

Claire bounced into the kitchen. "Mom, I don't want a big breakfast today. Alexa's parents are taking several of us to the beach this morning. Remember?"

"Yes, I do," Constance replied. "But you *do* have to get something into your tummy before you go."

Trip walked into the room. "I'll take whatever Claire doesn't eat."

"Working on the Fabrication Floor burns the calories, huh?" Constance queried.

"Mom, just thinking about work on the Fab Floor burns calories," Trip chuckled.

The Park children knew the routine and today was no different. Ethan poured the drinks, Claire set the silverware, and Trip placed the plates of breakfast food as his mom finished cooking. Once the table was completely set, the food and drinks prepared and served, everyone sat down together. The sumptuous dishes of grits, bacon, eggs, and toast made their journey around the table. With plates full, everyone dug in.

"Mom, when does Dad return from his trip out west?" Ethan inquired.

Constance put a pat of butter on her grits. "His flight lands next Friday. So, in a little over a week."

"That means I'm in charge at Park Productions!" Trip gloated.

"Oh no!" Claire teased. "There goes the company."

"Funny, Claire-bear," Trip said. "Don't worry. I'm not really in charge of the whole place. But I am in charge of the lighting design team for the Busted Bolts show."

Ethan's eyes lit up. "That's neat. I really like those guys."

"They are pretty cool and *quite* creative. I'm learning a ton from them," Trip said between bites.

Constance passed the plate of bacon to Claire. "How are things at the other Park endeavor, Ethan?"

"It's going well, Mom. I've learned an incredible amount about construction in these past six weeks with Grandy."

"I'm glad you're really getting into it." Constance took a sip of juice. "Are you going to a site today? I see you have your hard hat and vest."

"Yes, Grandy wants to take a look at the roofing substrate application on the TCD building." Ethan reached for the toast.

Trip glanced at Ethan, drawing his brows together. "Is it a good idea for Grandy to be going on the roof of a building? I mean . . ."

"He's fine. He's *fine*." Ethan rushed through the rest of his breakfast. He didn't want to answer any more questions.

Grandy had suffered a few more episodes . . . but . . . those could be considered minor. The medication his doctor had prescribed appeared to be doing the trick, and Grandy, for the most part, was back to his usual self.

For the most part . . .

＊ ＊ ＊ ＊

On the cusp of his college career, Ethan, as a summer intern at Park Enterprises, did not spend the past six weeks exclusively at the side of his grandfather as he had when he was in sixth grade. William had assigned Ethan real tasks and responsibilities that required him to work on his own as well as interact with many of the staff.

On occasion, William did arrange for Ethan to work with him as closely as they had on that day so many years ago. For though William periodically polled the staff on Ethan's job performance, William also liked to see things for himself.

Ethan knew he and his performance during this summer job were being judged by his grandfather and coworkers. The proverbial ruler was being placed at his side to see just how well he measured up.

＊ ＊ ＊ ＊

Johnny Anderson peered through the window of the construction trailer, which had been his office for the past three months. The blustery clouds had been collecting and rumbling over the job site all morning. As the safety officer for the TCD Industries job site, it was his responsibility to ensure the site and weather conditions were conducive for a safe work environment.

He didn't like what he saw, or what the weather reports indicated. Johnny understood that if these conditions persisted, he would have to shut down the site. The safety of the construction team was by far more important than any and all deadlines. Johnny reviewed the project Gantt charts daily. The TCD project schedule looked good, and he had ten unused rain days as a cushion. If he was going to use a rain day, today might be the day.

✳ ✳ ✳ ✳

The same system of clouds that had given Johnny cause for concern had also spent the morning gathering above the Park Enterprises headquarters. William and Ethan had been unaware of the activity in the atmosphere, though. Their focus had been on reviewing their schedules for the day and attending the morning update meeting.

With the morning activities completed, Ethan and William left the headquarters building on their way to the TCD Industries job site to evaluate the second-layer roof membrane installed earlier in the week. As the two walked to the car, Ethan observed the dark clouds scudding across the sky. "Grandy, there are some ominous clouds above. I hope it's not like this at the TCD site."

William looked up. "It does look nasty, but the site is forty minutes away. We should be okay."

Ethan zipped up his safety vest. "I'm sure Mr. Johnny is watching conditions closely."

"Yes, I'm sure he is. He's pretty good at gauging these things. We'll see what he thinks when we get there."

✳ ✳ ✳ ✳

Johnny's concern over the weather increased. The clouds continued to display nasty inclinations, which confirmed the forecast from the weather service. Johnny made the call to shut down the site until the storm system passed through the area. He spoke with each of the crew chiefs individually to ensure the site had been cleared.

His next task was to document his decision. Johnny knew William would never question his decision to secure a job site, but William would want validated documentation for the client.

As Johnny sat down to work on the report, he looked out the back window of the trailer and noticed William's truck parked next to his. Barbara had notified Johnny late yesterday afternoon that William and Ethan would be out to evaluate the installation of the roof membrane. He now thought it odd he hadn't found William and Ethan waiting for him in the trailer. But then, with the site shut down, William may have stopped to talk to one of the crew chiefs.

❋ ❋ ❋ ❋

Earlier, Ethan had stood outside Johnny's trailer as William emerged. "He's not here. He must be on the site. Let's head to the back of the building. The freight elevator is much faster to the roof."

"Don't you think we should locate him to get his assessment on this weather?" Ethan suggested.

William powered on to the back of the job site toward the freight elevator, talking with Ethan over his shoulder. "We'll see Eddie Fomby, or one of his operators. They'll know where to find Johnny."

"Okay," Ethan said as his gaze swept over the area. "But the site looks pretty empty."

Looking at his watch, William laughed. "Could be a union break."

Park Enterprises standard operating procedure required that all job site construction elevators have a designated and trained operator. These operators were trained by Eddie Fomby and reported directly to him, who reported to Johnny Anderson. As Ethan and William approached the large freight elevator attached to the superstructure of the TCD Industries building, Ethan noticed there was no elevator operator in sight.

"Grandy, where's the operator?"

William walked onto the elevator, and in an exasperated tone responded, "Union break. Didn't we discuss this? Let's go."

"Shouldn't we find Mr. Eddie or Mr. Johnny?" Ethan inquired nervously. "Mr. Johnny may have already secured the site."

"Ethan," William barked. "Let's go, or we're going to get caught in the rain."

"But—"

"I've been around job sites and bad weather all my life," William said. "Let's get a move on."

In spite of his misgivings, Ethan complied and followed his grandfather onto the elevator. Ethan grasped the handle on the safety door, pulled it shut, and secured the retaining latch. William turned the key to energize the four slip-ring induction motors, then pressed and held the "up" button. The elevator began its ascent toward the roof.

As the elevator passed through the superstructure of the building, Ethan saw that all the levels were eerily silent, with no noticeable activity. This didn't appear to be a union break, as his grandfather had sarcastically called it. There were no workers snacking, drinking coffee, or huddled in groups talking. No workers were present anywhere.

The wind increased the higher the elevator took them. The air was chilly. Ethan turned to his grandfather. "Grandy, it looks like Mr. Johnny has shut down the site."

William darted his gaze around the site, then looked at Ethan in confusion. "What?"

Ethan stepped closer to his grandfather and angled toward him, raising his voice to compete with the rising wind. "I believe Mr. Johnny has shut down the job site because of the weather. We should go back."

"We're almost to the top now," William insisted. "It'll take only a minute."

Ethan shook his head. "I think we should leave right now."

The elevator reached the peak of its ascent and came to a halt. William unfastened the retaining latch and slid the door open. "We're here. We may as well do what we came for. It won't take long."

William and Ethan started walking across the roof. Ethan glanced at the angry clouds above, which appeared to be getting angrier. The wind ruffled and grabbed at the folder in Ethan's hand. Bits of paper and other small debris swirled around their feet. Large drops of rain slammed into their hardhats and onto the roof of the building. The sudden drop in temperature, and what it meant, was not lost on Ethan.

"Grandy," Ethan yelled over the howl of the wind. "We need to leave *now*."

Lightning flashed, ripping open the sky. Thunder crashed, drowning out Ethan's voice. Hail fell, bouncing off the tops of their hardhats and the roof's surface.

William's face suddenly tightened with strain. His skin paled, eerie in the charged air.

Ethan grasped his grandfather's arm. "We need to find cover. Let's get to that overhang...it's closer than the elevator."

William pulled his arm from Ethan's hold and shielded his eyes as he glanced up at the sky. "Yes, it's getting mighty nasty out here."

"C'mon, Grandy, let's go."

"I'm right behind you."

Ethan ran to the overhang and gasped to catch his breath. He glanced over his shoulder. Grandy wasn't there!

He looked around the wall and saw his grandfather still standing in the middle of the roof, seemingly oblivious to the events surrounding him as he was pelted by the wind, rain, and hail.

Ethan could barely see through his foggy safety glasses and the driving rain. He forged out, not thinking about his own safety. Adrenaline coursed through his body, urging him forward. He fought to keep his balance on the slippery roof membrane.

He reached out to his grandfather and grabbed his arm. Grandy's face was blank, unaware.

"Grandy—" Ethan shook his grandfather, wrapped his arm around Grandy's shoulders, and leaned close to his ear. "Are you all right? You don't look so good."

Bewilderment replaced blankness. "What? Who? Why are you in my backyard?" In that moment, he didn't seem to recognize his own grandson.

Ethan forcibly pulled Grandy to the overhang. The storm's ferocity increased. The way was wet, slick with hail. The wind pushed back. Thunder cracked and boomed. Lightning strobed the sky. Grandy resisted his efforts.

With the strength of youth, Ethan pushed Grandy ahead of him and beneath the shelter of the overhang.

"Grandy," Ethan began, "do you—"

A loud clap of thunder drowned out the last part of Ethan's question and caused a piercing ring in his ears. A bolt of lightning struck the freight elevator. The elevator flashed, shook, and looked like it had just been hit by a grenade. It was clear to Ethan that this twisted, steaming steel could not be their path to safety.

William gaped at the smoldering remains. Frightened, he darted from under the shelter of the overhang.

Ethan's blood ran cold. "Grandy!"

William moved as if in a trance, straight for the nearest edge of the roof. Ethan ran after his grandfather, fighting the wind, ignoring everything else. William advanced toward the edge of the roof.

Ethan slipped and fell. His left hand landed on the roof and quickly was surrounded by a pool of red water. A three-inch piece of slag stuck out of his left palm. Mindlessly, Ethan pulled the slag out of his hand. The blood flowed more freely. Pain followed full force. Ethan felt faint but braced himself.

I have to get to Grandy. Intuitively, he removed his safety vest and wrapped it tightly around his hand as he struggled to his feet.

William was only ten or eleven steps from the edge of the roof. Ethan ran as he had never run before. He lunged, and tackled his grandfather. They both landed on the roof's membrane with a powerful thud. Ethan's mind raced as Grandy struggled beneath him.

✳ ✳ ✳ ✳

Ethan sat up as best he could manage on the emergency room gurney. His hand throbbed. Impatience pulsed as he waited for details about Grandy's condition.

The curtain was pulled back to reveal the haggard but smiling face of Johnny Anderson.

"Hey, my man," Johnny said. "How are you doing?"

"I've been better." Ethan grimaced. "How's my grandfather? The nurse wouldn't say more than he's fine."

"He was disoriented and agitated but is resting now," Johnny said. "You guys had us really worried!"

"How did you know we were up there?"

"I noticed William's truck," Johnny replied, "but I hadn't seen William. I thought maybe he had stopped to talk to one of the crew chiefs. When the storm hit and there still was no sign of him, I began calling the other trailers."

"He checked your trailer when we first got there," Ethan said. "You were out. He wanted to go on the roof, so we went to the freight elevator."

"Yeah, eventually I figured that out," Johnny said with a look of relief. "When the lightning struck the elevator and I saw that the car wasn't on the ground floor, I got real concerned. You know the drill—on a secured site, all elevators are set on the ground floor." Johnny rubbed his forehead. "I knew I had to send a rescue team up . . . I was hoping . . . Well, I just played for the worst and prayed for the best."

"I tried to stop him—"

"It wasn't your fault." Johnny paced in front of the bed. "It was just a bad situation. It was dangerous for the crew, but they're well trained. You guys were found face down on the roof. You had lost a decent amount of blood. Your grandfather was very unsettled, to say the least. You both are lucky something worse didn't happen."

"He *insisted* on going up." Ethan's head sank back onto the pillow.

"Not to speak out of school, but sometimes he can be hard-headed."

Sadness thickened in Ethan's throat. "I don't think this was one of those times."

※ ※ ※ ※

The sun's descent seemed to pick up speed as it neared its final resting place on the other side of the horizon. The high temperatures of the day followed the sun as the cooler temperatures took their place in the Park's backyard. The automatic accent lights placed around the yard flickered to life, creating a relaxing atmosphere.

Ethan reclined in the chaise lounge chair as best he could. Though his right hand was dominant, he realized the purpose of a left hand was not simply to finish out the set. He relied heavily on his left hand for many things, situating himself in a chaise lounge being one of them. The sling, supplied by the emergency room doctor to keep the hand immobilized, inhibited his ability to adjust the back of the chair.

"Here, let me help you with that," Constance offered as she put down the pitcher of iced tea.

"Thanks, Mom."

"Does it still hurt a lot?"

Ethan frowned down at his heavily bandaged hand. "It's not a consistent pain, but it wakes up now and then and hits hard, like a jackhammer." He sat forward to allow his mother to adjust the back of the chair. "Not to mention, it's a pain not being able to adjust a chair— among other things that I can't do for myself right now."

"It's only been one day." Constance slid a pillow under his arm. "I'm sure it will get better in no time."

"Yeah, I guess eventually it will. But it means that I'm out for all of Available Light's remaining summer gigs. I can't play guitar with just one hand."

"I'm sorry," Constance consoled her son. "I know you were so looking forward to the last summer playing local clubs with the band before college." She looked up at the sound of the back door opening.

Bill walked onto the deck, carrying a large tray and bearing a wide smile.

"I bet your dad has fixed something that should make the inconvenience a little more bearable."

"Here we go." Bill lowered the tray to show its contents. "Nachos with homemade salsa." He swept the tray up again out of reach. "But you have to share."

"Your favorite," Constance said.

As Bill set the tray down on the table, Ethan grinned. "I'd clap . . . but what's the sound of one hand clapping?"

"Well," Bill said, "at least you still have a sense of humor."

Constance poured iced tea for herself, Bill, and Ethan while Bill put a healthy helping of nachos and salsa on everyone's plates. The three took a respite from conversation to enjoy their evening snack. Made with tomatoes, onions, and various other vegetables from their garden, the salsa was a delightful treat.

Each of the Parks savored the flavor and were appreciative of the moment. This was an unannounced sigh-of-relief celebration because Ethan and William made it through the harrowing experience on the roof. The three Parks were also a bit nostalgic, recognizing that Ethan would soon be leaving for college. These evening get-togethers would become less spontaneous. Ethan's school schedule and distance from home would require pre-planning for any future events.

Bill took a long sip of his iced tea and placed the glass on the table. He looked at Constance and then to Ethan. "You and your grandfather gave us a huge scare yesterday."

"Believe me—" Ethan said as he scooped up salsa on a nacho and took a bite, "there was no one more scared than I was."

242

"I'll bet," Constance said. "I'm so sorry . . . ."

"The worst part wasn't that storm or being caught on the roof." Ethan reached for his glass of iced tea. "No, the scariest part for me was realizing that Grandy was in the middle of one of those episodes. Mom, Dad, I didn't know what to do for Grandy—or the situation. It was terrifying. Grandy had *no* idea where he was, who he was, or who *I* was. That's when I *knew* we were in real trouble."

"It seemed the medication that Dr. Lebeau prescribed in June was working quite well," Constance commented.

"His last episode was graduation day, right?" Bill picked up the pitcher and refilled their glasses. "That was, what? Six, maybe seven weeks ago."

"I really feared he was going to walk right off the edge of that roof. Then, when I fell and gouged my hand . . ." Ethan shuddered as the scene on the roof flashed through his mind. "I really thought I was going to see my grandfather fall to his death."

"Thankfully," Bill said, "you were quick-thinking and used a great tackling technique."

"I've watched Trip play enough football to know that it would give me the best chance to stop Grandy."

The conversation trailed off as each of the Parks contemplated the events of the previous day. Thoughts and discussions moved from the specifics of the ordeal to how close they had been to losing one, or both, of their loved ones. This discourse led naturally to the cause of the ordeal and its long-term ramifications for the business and family.

"This is a serious situation," Bill said.

243

"Yes, it is," Constance agreed. "It was a traumatic event."

"What I mean," Bill explained, "is that this happened on a job site. Reports will have to be filed with the authorities."

"Dad's got a point here, Mom. We entered a closed site. There could be some legal issues."

"Oh." Constance frowned. "I hadn't thought of that."

"As much as I'm not looking forward to it, it's probably time I get with Dad and have a talk with him about all of this." Sitting upright, Bill rested his arms on his thighs and clasped his hands. "I can guarantee he's not going to like it."

Chapter 13
IMAGE OF THE MAN

Every fall, millions of new college freshmen undertake a rite of passage known as leaving the comfort and protection of their parents' home to step into their future. It's an uncertain future, to be sure, though most parents are hard pressed to convince their offspring of that. Many of these youth feel they are immortal. They have just conquered the academics and rites of high school. Filled with huge amounts of optimism, they believe there is nothing that can stop them from attaining their dreams.

Parents, too, are traveling through a transitional period. It is the first time the little bundle of joy they brought home from the hospital just eighteen short years ago will no longer live under their roof. Their baby has grown up and is now moving into adulthood and gaining greater independence.

Ethan had spent the previous evening packing the things he believed necessary for his passage into a hope-filled future. The approximate 8.5 cubic-foot trunk capacity of his 1964 Mustang would influence his decisions in this matter. He planned on also taking advantage of the space the back and passenger seats offered. Still, he knew that not everything he would like to have with him could fit in his car.

As he often did, he remembered the talks about ways to prioritize that he and his grandfather had during the many Saturday mornings they spent together in the woodshop. As a result, Ethan used a good portion of the previous evening *not* packing but rather making lists and prioritizing. Once his lists had been finished to his satisfaction, then the packing began.

Ethan reflected upon how Saturday mornings with his grandfather would now be a thing of the past. This was one of the many parts of the bitter in the bittersweet equation of going off to college.

He leaned into the backseat of the Mustang and positioned a box of books on the floorboard behind the passenger seat when he heard his mother approach.

"Here is another one to fit in there somehow. Your dad is bringing the last box that you had placed in the 'To Go' pile."

"Thanks, Mom. Too bad Grandy didn't buy Granny a moving van instead of a Mustang."

Constance giggled. "Yes, I'm sure you would have looked really cool going to the prom in a moving van."

Bill walked up, carrying the last box that would make the journey with Ethan into his future. "It doesn't look like you have room for a guitar unless you strap it to the trunk."

Ethan chuckled at the image of his guitar hanging on the back of his car like a bicycle. "Probably not the best thing for a Martin."

"No," Bill mused. "I wouldn't recommend it either."

"Besides," Ethan flexed his fingers, "my hand still isn't limber enough where that slag got me. It may be a while before I can play again."

"Are you still doing your physical therapy with the rubber ball?" Constance asked.

Ethan smiled as he pulled the ball from his pocket. "I never leave home without it."

"Speaking of leaving home, the day is slipping away." Bill advised, "You should get moving so it won't be real late when you make it to campus."

"You're right. It's time for me to turn some miles," Ethan said, emotion creeping into his voice.

Constance walked over to her son and embraced him firmly. She whispered into his ear, "You're such an amazing young man. I love you."

She kissed him on the cheek and then took a step back. Bill and Ethan looked at each other, smiled, and then hugged. "You are the *best* dad anyone could have," Ethan said, his eyes moist with tears. Glancing toward his mother, he added, "You are the best *parents* anyone could have. Thank you both for everything."

Ethan bent down and gave his mother one last kiss on the cheek. He then turned to his car, opened the door, got in, and started the engine. His parents stood arm in arm as they watched their son crank the window down. "I'll call when I get there. I love you."

※ ※ ※ ※

Ethan and his father had carefully mapped out the most efficient route for him to get to the campus. They selected places along the route where he would make stops based upon gas mileage estimates and the amount of time before Ethan would need a break from driving. The route wasn't overly long, but at just under two hundred miles, it would be the longest solo drive Ethan had made to this point.

Almost as soon as Ethan left his parents' driveway, he made the decision to deviate from the planned route he and his father had created. Minutes later he pulled into his grandparents' driveway. Margaret saw the poppy red Mustang and smiled. She greeted her grandson at the kitchen door.

"Ethan, you came to see us before you left." She beamed. "You are so sweet."

"Hi, Granny." Ethan gave his grandmother a hug.

"Your grandfather is in his office. It's amazing how he has embraced this idea of working from home since the . . . well, you know . . ."

"That's great." Ethan and Granny walked into the house arm-in-arm. "So, he's okay not being so hands-on anymore?"

"I wouldn't go *that* far." Margaret gave Ethan a half-smile. "But he realizes he has limitations now. The incident on the roof affected him."

"Granny, I have never been so scared in my life."

Margaret's eyes moistened. "I know, Ethan. And your grandfather knows it, too. He realizes the danger that he put you . . . and the crew in. It's made him see that he has to finally face this issue and deal with it."

Ethan shook his head and turned, looking around the kitchen, searching for some sense to it all.

"Ethan, this is a good thing. He's the one who decided it was time to face this, and with that came the realization that he can't consistently perform at the level he has always believed is required to be successful."

"It's just so . . . not right."

Margaret took her grandson's hand. "We have to deal with where we are—not where we think we should be."

"You think he's okay with this?"

"No, but he believes this is what is best, at least for now. Barbara and I have set up a system to keep him connected to the business, but also to make sure he's not being overloaded."

"Is stress what seems to be one of the triggers?"

"Yes, but I would not say the *only* one," Margaret continued. "He has his good days, or good moments. Sometimes it's frustrating because one minute he's there . . . the next . . . he's not."

"Granny, I'm so sorry you're having to go through this."

Margaret looked directly at her grandson. "Ethan, we are *all* going through this. I manage. It's a difficult situation, for sure. But it has affected every one of us."

Ethan subconsciously rubbed his left hand. "Yes, you're right. Sometimes I feel bad about leaving."

"Don't talk like that," Margaret scolded. "You *must* get your education. If Grandy heard you say that—well, you know what he would say."

✳ ✳ ✳ ✳

249

The seat of power at Park Enterprises was William's office on the top floor. The seat of power for the Park family was this upstairs office that Ethan had just entered. Due to his illness, William had begrudgingly relinquished his office at Park Enterprises and much of the authority that came with it.

As Ethan saw his grandfather seated behind his desk, he wondered how long it would be before Grandy would be forced to relinquish this office as well and the authority it represented. In fact, Ethan thought, maybe that transition had already begun with subtle changes to save his grandfather's pride.

"Hi, Grandy."

"Ethan." William stood and rounded the desk. "I thought you'd be on the road by now." He winked. "But I'm sure glad that road brought you here first."

"I just couldn't leave without seeing you and Granny one last time."

"That's touching, Ethan. You know you've always had a special place in my heart." William looked down at the desk blotter and then back up at Ethan with a puzzled look. "Where have you decided to go to college?"

Ethan's mood immediately shifted. He, his father, and his grandfather had had many conversations, and even arguments about this topic. The long-standing tug-of-war between William and Bill about the kids, specifically Ethan, was still ongoing. Bill had wanted Ethan to attend his alma mater. William believed that if Ethan would take the reins of Park Enterprises, he would be best served going to *his* alma mater. The day Ethan announced he had decided to attend the alma mater of his grandfather, William had been ecstatic.

With that one question, it appeared Grandy had vanished . . . once again.

"I'm going to NGU, your alma mater, Grandy," Ethan said gently.

Blinking, William returned to his chair with shuffling steps. "Ah, that's right! In fact, I have something for you."

And, just like that . . . Grandy reappeared.

Ethan sighed. "Grandy, you've already given me *so* much."

"Oh," William scoffed, "this is nothing big. It's just something my dad gave me. Now I'm passing it on to you."

William opened the desk drawer and withdrew a small wooden rectangular box with "Park" embossed in gold on the lid. He opened the box and looked at the contents. Ethan could tell by the expression on his grandfather's face that he was no longer in the room with him. But this look didn't carry the traits of Grandy vanishing. Rather, this demeanor was the quiet, reflective stare of nostalgia.

After several moments, William broke away from his thoughts and extended the box in his grandson's direction. "Ethan, this is for you. It's a pen and pencil set given to me by my father when I left for college."

Ethan reached out and accepted the box offered by his grandfather. The pen and pencil were sterling silver with a grid-like pattern and trimmed in gold. Each writing instrument had a gold medallion attached to the pocket clip with an engraved letter "P."

Ethan choked back tears. "Thank you, Grandy. This is beautiful."

"Realistically, you probably won't use the pen since it's a fountain pen. Too hard to get ink and too slow to write with. But I thought you could at least keep them in your desk."

"Grandy," Ethan exclaimed, "these are priceless."

William sat back in his chair, looking up at the ceiling, still reminiscent, but this time he gave voice to his thoughts. "You know, I created a ton of To Do lists with that set. In fact, that is the very pen I used when I wrote my overall 'Life' To Do list."

"Well then, I'm going to find some ink for the pen. From now on, I will use *this* for *my* 'Life' To Do List."

Ethan quietly walked around the side of his grandfather's desk. William stood and the two embraced. Ethan whispered into his grandfather's ear, "I love you, Grandy."

"I know you do. I love you, too," William said, his voice thick with emotion.

Ethan stepped away from his grandfather, and the two faced each other. William gazed upon a young man with intelligence, potential, and the desire to succeed. Ethan lovingly studied his grandfather, the man who had helped shape his ethos and put him on the path to success.

He cleared his throat. "I should go."

"I know," William said. "Goodbye, Ethan. Work hard and take care of yourself."

Ethan turned and headed toward the door leading to the hallway. As he reached the door, he heard his grandfather call out, "Son, when do you leave for college? Where are you going again? Oh, it doesn't matter . . . . Remember to *say what you are going to do. Then do it.*"

252

✳ ✳ ✳ ✳

Ethan's first term flew by quickly, and then he was home for a semester break. The drive to his parents' house that previous evening had seemed long, though uneventful. It had been Ethan's first drive home from college since the start of school back in September. He had arrived later than he expected and thus found the house dark. Ethan had not lost his familiarity with the house in the three months he'd been away. Without turning on any lights, he deftly made his way up to his bedroom.

There, on his pillow, lay a note handwritten by his mother. In the note, she stated how excited she was that he was home for the Christmas holiday, and how she looked forward to again cooking breakfast for him. She ended with how he had been missed and how much he was loved.

Ethan woke the next morning to the aromatic enticement of the breakfast being prepared by his mother. He sat up in bed and surveyed the room in which he had grown up. He looked at the desk where he had spent countless hours reading, completing homework assignments, and adding and marking off many items on his To Do list, which had kept him focused and guided him on his way to becoming valedictorian of his class.

The shelves were still lined with many of his favorite books. Interspersed with his literary collection were several photos commemorating some of his life's milestones, holiday gatherings, and random fun times spent with his family. Ethan's gaze rested upon one of his favorite photos in the collection. It was a picture Ethan had not been a part of since he had not been born when it was taken. It was a picture of his grandparents, Grandy and Granny. The photograph depicted his grandfather seated at their dining room table, with Margaret standing beside him. She was looking at William with a subtle smile on her face. William, with one hand holding a piece of paper and the other hand on an adding machine, peered directly into the camera.

Ethan arose from the bed, walked to the shelves, and retrieved the frame containing the photo of his grandparents. He stared at the image. William and Margaret had given Bill a camera for Christmas that year. For weeks following that Christmas, no one had been safe from one of Bill's "pop-up" pictures. He would surprise his parents so that he could take candid shots. He preferred to catch them as they naturally were rather than posed.

Ethan had heard that story many times over the years. William had not been fond of being the subject of those spontaneous photographic excursions. Ethan had to hand it to his dad, though. This photograph captured his grandparents perfectly—Margaret always at William's side, and William facing the camera as he did life—head-on, looking directly into the lens.

As Ethan put the frame back on the shelf, he wondered if he would see his grandfather's steely eyes of determination on this visit home. He recalled the last time he had seen Grandy right before he left for college. Grandy had called him "Son." Grandy had never called him by anything other than his name.

Ethan had come to the realization during the drive to school three months ago that a little more of his grandfather had vanished. The news Ethan had received from his phone calls home had not been encouraging, either. He was aware Grandy was slipping away more and more each day, but he had continued to hope for the best. Distance had given him a certain latitude in his optimism. But now the time had come for a full dose of reality. Ethan was eager to see his grandfather, yet at the same time, he dreaded it.

✳ ✳ ✳ ✳

"There's that college man," Constance said as Ethan entered the kitchen.

"Good morning, Mom." Ethan hugged his mother and kissed her on the cheek.

"I waited up until my eyes betrayed my heart," Constance confessed. "It must have been really late when you got home."

"I'm sorry, Mom. I offered to drop off one of the guys at the airport so he could catch his flight home. The traffic at the airport was hectic."

"Well, you were doing your good deed for the day and you're home safe now."

Ethan went to the cupboard containing the plates to begin setting the table. "Mom, I am *so* ready for some of your cooking."

"Ah, you don't like that institutional food?" Trip inquired as he walked into the kitchen.

"I know. You warned me." Ethan laughed. "And you were right on the mark. I've learned not to eat for taste, because it all tastes the same. I eat for shape—square, circle, or triangle."

Constance took mugs from a different cupboard. "I thought you were going to cook most of your own meals?"

"I do," Ethan replied, "but my class schedule meant having lunch on campus four days a week."

"Freshman scheduling error." Trip shook his head.

"When did you get home?" Ethan asked his brother.

"I came in day before yesterday. Three semesters to go."

"It's hard to believe that time has gone by so quickly," Constance reflected. "You guys in college and Claire in middle school."

Trip kissed his mother's cheek. "Come on, Mom. Don't go getting all sentimental. By the way, I'm out for breakfast. I'm meeting the guys for an early game of flag football."

"I have the right to be sentimental. I'm a mom!" Constance returned one mug to the cupboard. "And this mom here says you should at least take a bagel to get something in your stomach. Have fun and don't get hurt."

"Love you, Mom," Trip said as he snagged a bagel from the basket on the counter and started for the door. "Ethan, let's catch up this afternoon," he called over his shoulder.

"Wow," Constance stared at the closing door with a whimsical grin. "He was like a whirling dervish."

Ethan poured coffee into the two mugs she held and took the one she offered him. "How's Grandy doing?"

Constance motioned for Ethan to take a seat at the table where she joined him. She reached out and took his hand in hers. "Ethan," she started, "you have been away for three months. This disease is incremental, and continually progressing. So, you need to be aware that when you see your grandfather, the change in his demeanor may be dramatic."

"What do you mean?" His voice sounded like boots on gravel. He cleared his throat. "You've been telling me in your letters, and Granny writes to me, too."

"Ethan," she said as she moved her hand to his shoulder. "You've seen words on a page, and now you will be seeing the embodiment of those words. It can be a shock. I've tried to keep you informed, but a picture—or the actual being there—is worth a thousand words."

Constance sighed. "It's been tough. Your grandmother has been through a lot recently." She took a sip of coffee and shook her head. "But she's a trooper and insists on trying to keep things as normal for your grandfather as possible."

"Tough in what way, Mom?"

Constance pushed the basket of bacon toward Ethan. He took a piece and set it on his plate. "Ethan, your grandfather isn't able to work anymore. He just doesn't have the focus . . . or the ability . . . ." Constance's voice trailed off. She tore the corner from a piece of toast and put it in her mouth, chewing slowly as if she wanted to put off this conversation as long as she could.

"So, what does that mean?" Ethan stared at his lone strip of bacon. "What does he do all day?"

"That's part of the challenge for your grandmother. He follows her in and out of every room she goes into. He has some good moments when he is present. He will reminisce with Granny and tell her how much he loves her. The next minute, it's as if he's playing 'Twenty Questions.' But it's the same twenty questions all day, every day—no matter how many times she answers.

"Granny gives him chores to try to occupy his time—taking out the trash, folding clothes, marking the day off on the calendar. Some days he's really good at them . . . others . . . not so much."

Ethan looked at Constance, panic in his eyes. "Mom, is he going to know who I am? Has it gone that far already? Is it *that* bad?"

"Ethan, I just don't know. It's hard to say."

"Do you think it will be all right if I go over after breakfast?"

"Absolutely," Constance said. "As I mentioned, your grandmother is trying to keep things as normal as possible. Visiting him while you're in town can be a big part of that process."

She gazed at him with sadness, seeing the changes a few months had wrought, hearing emotional growth in his voice. Yet she knew these changes were not enough to save Ethan's heart from breaking, and there was nothing she could do to protect him.

✳ ✳ ✳ ✳

After a breakfast that had been more about delightful tastes than shapes, Ethan finished unpacking, showered, dressed, and then jumped into his car to head over to his grandparents' house. Though the morning sun was shining brightly and dancing on the poppy red finish, the top on the Mustang was in the up position. Lennon and McCartney were not imploring anyone to hold their hands. This was a somber drive. The talk this morning at breakfast with his mother had made Ethan more apprehensive than he'd already felt on the drive home from school last night.

Ethan was having a difficult time settling in his mind that his grandfather, the patriarch of the Park family, the founder and leader of Park Enterprises, his mentor, was having trouble completing the most menial of household chores. *Surely Mom must have overstated Grandy's condition as a way to manage my expectations.*

Margaret met Ethan in the driveway. Smiling, she hugged him tightly. "It's *so* good to see you."

"It's great to see you, too, Granny. I've missed you."

"I have missed you as well," Margaret said with a tearful sniff.

"How's Grandy?"

"He seems to be having a good morning." Margaret led Ethan to the house. "Let's go inside so we can talk."

Ethan followed his grandmother into the house that he knew as well as his own. He felt he had done as much growing up here as he had at his own home. Yet, this time his walk through the door to the kitchen felt like a walk into the unknown. Ethan was having trouble organizing his feelings and expectations into anything cohesive.

Margaret immediately picked up on Ethan's anxiety. "Ethan," she said calmly, "you're going to be okay. Grandy loves you dearly and wants to see you. At times, he acts so different than the man you knew growing up, but he is also the man who is looking forward to spending time with you."

She reached up and straightened his collar. "Try to relax. Grandy can sense when there is tension around. When that happens, it destabilizes him. Just be yourself and go with the flow. Don't patronize him, though. He can, and will, pick up on that. Be patient and treasure when he's *with* you."

"I'm trying, Granny," Ethan rasped.

"Are you sure you want to see him right now?" Margaret questioned. "Or do you need a few more minutes to gather your bearings?"

"No, I need to see him. Where is he?"

"I understand. Would you like some coffee now, or would you rather see Grandy first?" Margaret asked.

"I'd rather see Grandy," Ethan said firmly. "Mom and I talked this morning, so I'm prepared." He stepped forward, determined.

"He'll be happy to see you. He's upstairs. Why don't you go see if he needs a hand? Sometimes he does."

※ ※ ※ ※

Ethan headed toward the back of the house to access the stairs leading to the second floor. He recalled when, as young boys, he and his older brother had played Lewis and Clark and used these same stairs as a place to build a fort where they staged their own exploring adventures, surveying every nook and cranny throughout their grandparents' house. Ethan smiled to himself as he thought back to how, in his young mind, the staircase landing served as the precipice upon which they peered over their version of the Continental Divide.

He paused on the landing situated halfway up the stairs. It had provided the perfect location for two little boys to create a tent using blankets and pillows.

Ethan's smile widened as he remembered the countless nights he and his brother spent sleeping in their makeshift fort pretending to be explorers of new lands. During one of their "expeditions," he and Trip discovered that if they twisted the top of the newel post at the landing, it could be removed, revealing a small space in the post, the perfect spot to hide the treasures they collected while exploring the frontier—aka the downstairs of Grandy and Granny's house. What they didn't realize at the time was that one day Grandy observed them removing the top of the newel post, and he teamed up with Granny to surprise the boys by leaving little presents in that "secret" place.

Although both boys grew out of their Lewis and Clark phase, Ethan continued to check the secret space whenever he visited Grandy on Saturdays. To his delight, he continued to find treasures. Over the years, Ethan discovered extra spending money, tickets to sporting events, and gift certificates to the local bookstore among the spoils. Over the years, he also came to realize that his grandfather was responsible for this mother lode.

Nostalgically, Ethan turned the cap on the top of the newel post until he could easily remove it. Considering his grandfather's current condition, Ethan expected to find the post empty. To his surprise, he found a single key at the bottom of the post's cavity. The key was affixed to a gold key ring with the Park Enterprises logo engraved on one side and "EP" on the other side. The key appeared to be for a door lock, not a car or a padlock. Ethan wondered what the key would open. He grasped the key in one hand, replaced the cap on the newel post with his other hand, and continued in the direction of his grandfather's bedroom.

As Ethan entered the room, he saw light from the bathroom pouring through the open door onto the bedroom floor. "Grandy, where are you?"

"Ethan, I'm in the bathroom. Come on in. I'm just getting ready to shave."

Ethan walked in and saw William standing in front of the large mirror that completely covered the wall behind the sinks.

William gave his grandson a huge hug. "It's so good to see you, Ethan."

Relief washed over Ethan. Grandy knew him. Despite the conversations with his mother and Granny, he really didn't know what to expect. His imagination had been in overdrive for no good reason. "It's great seeing you, too, Grandy. How are you?"

Stepping back, William appraised Ethan. "Hmm . . . . Let me take a look at what college has done to you."

"Well, one thing's for sure, it's made me hungry for home cooking," Ethan said with a laugh.

William spied the key and key ring Ethan held in his hand. "I see you're still checking our hiding place."

"Of course. So, what does this key open?"

Ethan noticed a sparkle in his grandfather's eye, the same sparkle that had been a predominant feature of his in those pre-Alzheimer days. "That, Ethan, is the key to your future. The key to Park Enterprises' future."

Bewildered, Ethan cocked his head. "Okay, what are you getting at?"

William thought for a moment and then began slowly, as if choosing his words very carefully. "Ethan, I can't effectively run Park Enterprises anymore due to some . . . um . . . health issues. I've made plans for you to take over the running of the business . . . when the time comes. Right now, Dan Stokes is helping me with the day-to-day things. But eventually he will be there to help *you*."

"Grandy." Emotion caught in Ethan's throat. "We have a long time before I will need to use this key."

William smiled. "Of course we do. You know we should have a plan in place to make sure things run smoothly when the time comes, though."

"I see, Grandy," he said, dumbfounded. *It sounds like Grandy is giving up, like maybe he expects me to take over before I'm even finished with college. Why else would he give me this key now? I'm only a freshman.*

"Now, I need to shave," William said. "Would you mind running downstairs and grabbing me a hand towel? It looks like Granny forgot to bring them up after she finished the laundry."

✳ ✳ ✳ ✳

Ethan returned to the bedroom with several hand towels supplied by his grandmother. He heard a harried call. "Is someone there? Anyone? I need help."

Ethan's fear spiked with his grandfather's troubled request. He hadn't been out of the room for more than five minutes. What possibly could have happened?

"I'm here, Grandy," Ethan replied, trying to bolster his own confidence. With trepidation, he entered the bathroom. When he saw his grandfather's image in the mirror, Ethan's heart broke. On the bathroom counter rested a completely empty tube of toothpaste.

"Son, can you help me? Something's not right," William said.

Ethan reached over, turned on the water, and moistened a washcloth. "First," Ethan pointed out, "let's rinse this off your face."

William touched the paste on his face and held his finger to his nose. "Ew—it smells like toothpaste. How did that get there?"

"I'm not sure," Ethan soothed, "but we'll take care of it."

Now I see the "picture" Mom was talking about. It's worse than I imagined.

With the warm washcloth, Ethan apprehensively wiped the toothpaste from his grandfather's face and hands. He opened the cabinet on William's side of the bathroom, located the bottle of shaving cream, and began applying it to Grandy's face.

He searched for a razor, which he found tucked away in a drawer on his grandmother's side of the bathroom. He turned the faucet to "hot" and held the razor under the water. *Okay, Grandy, I have barely done this to myself, much less to anyone else.* Then, shaking the excess water from the razor, he turned to his grandfather.

To keep the situation from escalating, Ethan calmly asked, "You ready? Here we go . . . ." The last words stalled in his throat.

William sat silent and still while Ethan carefully and patiently ran the razor across his grandfather's face. As Ethan prepared another washcloth to wipe the excess shaving cream from William's face and neck, he looked up in the mirror and saw his grandfather looking back at him. The two held each other's gaze for what seemed to Ethan to be both a lifetime and a second that passed too quickly. Ethan could not remember the last time he had seen such clarity in Grandy's eyes. This was the canny look of the man who had been his best friend as far back as Ethan could remember. He soaked up every second, suddenly understanding these moments could disappear altogether at any time.

He noticed tears streaming down his grandfather's cheeks, washing away remnants of shaving cream. For reasons unknown to Ethan, tears also began to stream down his own cheeks.

"What is it, Grandy?" Ethan asked quietly.

"Ethan, what did I ever do to deserve all of this?"

NINETEEN

TO

TWENTY-TWO YEARS OLD

E.P.

Chapter 14
TAKING CONTROL

Ethan walked deliberately to the front of the room and placed his Park Enterprises folio on the podium. Just as his grandfather had taught him, Ethan paused and surveyed his audience. He looked out to the far reaches of the gallery. He noted a room filled with friends, co-workers, and relatives of his grandparents. He recognized friends from school and his neighborhood.

Ethan knew that seated in the front row to his left, he would find his family there. His gaze fell first upon Trip on the far left. Trip gave Ethan a slight nod. Claire occupied the seat next to Trip and tightly held on to her mother's hand. Next to Constance, his dad stoically sat. Last on the row, and closest to the center aisle, was his grandmother. Grandy would not be a part of the audience as Ethan delivered this speech.

Contrary to what he had been taught, Ethan had not rehearsed this speech. He did not have the opportunity, or as he had come to think of it—the luxury of having first practiced this presentation in front of his family. As a result, some hesitancy on his part lay in his worry that he lacked confidence in his ability to deliver the words in a befitting manner. He did feel confident that he possessed an in-depth knowledge of the subject matter and his writing throughout the speech was strong.

The room reminded Ethan of his father's recording studio. There was complete silence. It was *too* quiet. There was not a murmur to be heard from those assembled. All eyes and ears were focused center stage, on Ethan. There was no doubt in Ethan's mind that he had the full attention of his audience. The time to begin had arrived.

"William Park I. My grandfather . . . . "

"He was a husband." Ethan nodded to Granny. "A father." He looked to his dad. "A grandfather." Ethan looked over to his brother and sister. "He was a friend." He moved his gaze over the mourners.

"William Park I," he repeated.

"That title said more about my grandfather than just his name. If you examine that title, William Park I, you will see that it implies there is, at the very least, a second—his son, my father, William Park II. If we go further, there is a William Park the Third—his grandson and my brother, Trip.

"My grandfather, Grandy, was proud to be identified as William Park I. Not because he wanted to be a first, but because a second and a third actually followed. And hopefully, there will be a fourth. That title signified that he had a family. To my grandfather it meant... *family.*

"If you are seated here today, it's because you knew William Park I. And, if you knew him, then you know how much his family meant to him.

"You also know that he worked hard. To the outsider, it may have seemed that my grandfather was more dedicated to Park Enterprises than he was to his family. But as his family, we knew he worked so hard to ensure we would be provided for—and the provision he supplied wasn't strictly monetary. My grandfather recognized that by working relentlessly, honoring his commitments, and doing the right thing, he was setting an example to those of us who followed him—the second, the third, myself, and my sister Claire.

"Grandy taught us in a subtle manner. Don't get me wrong, he also taught us in some not-so-subtle ways."

A slight murmur of laughter rippled through the room. Those who had first-hand experience with some of William's teaching techniques adjusted themselves in their chairs as they recalled with subdued affection his sometimes very direct methods of delivering guidance.

"That was William Park I, though. He believed the greatest gift he could give his family, other than love, had nothing to do with money. Rather, he believed the priceless treasure he could provide was the gift of knowledge. He wanted and needed to teach us about life, business, and commitment from lessons he learned from his own parents and life experiences—both the successes and the failures.

"Despite the enormous legacy Grandy is leaving, he would be the first to admit he had failures along the way. He was human, but he strove to be superhuman in everything he took on. If I could talk with Grandy right now—and I believe we all wish we could—I think he would say he is most disappointed not in his failures, but that he hadn't met all of his commitments. He didn't finish all the items on his To Do list.

"You see, as I mentioned, he was big on commitment. He always told me and drilled it into my head, probably as early as my time in the nursery at Highland Hospital . . ."

Constance squeezed Bill's hand as they glanced at each other knowingly.

"*Say what you are going to do. Then do it!* Following through and standing by his word was important to William Park I. He accomplished this by creating his famous—and infamous—To Do lists."

Ethan looked up from the podium and noticed many of the attendees subtly nodding in agreement.

He continued, "William Park I was a traditionalist. He believed in family. He believed in *his* family most of all." Ethan paused, looked toward his grandmother, and whispered, "I love you, Granny."

"My grandfather committed his life to his entire family as, over the years, it grew. He believed the only things that should infringe upon his time with his family were things that would ultimately improve his family's situation—spiritually, financially, and educationally.

"For almost as long as I can remember, I spent Saturday mornings in the woodshop at Grandy's. It wasn't necessarily about the items we crafted. It was more about spending time together, being in the presence of each other, sharing thoughts and feelings—sharing what was in our hearts.

"Looking back on those Saturday mornings, I believe I learned more about history, math, English—and life than I ever could have dreamed to learn in school. This went unrecognized by my young mind. I thought I was there to simply learn how to take a raw piece of wood and shape it into a family heirloom. Little did I know that I was the one being shaped. He was passing on his knowledge, wisdom, and love. He held dear, as did I, our Saturday morning woodworking sessions. I miss those Saturday mornings . . . ." Ethan's voice cracked.

Composing himself, he started again. "Yes, Grandy loved one-on-one time with each of us. Whether at the beach searching for seashells or shopping for the latest fashions," Ethan said, smiling at his sister, "it really didn't matter much to him so long as a strong connection was made with each family member. He always placed high value on getting together as a family. Any reason or no reason at all was good enough for him.

"My grandfather had another family he valued dearly. That family was created the day he and my grandmother opened the doors to Park Enterprises. I have been fortunate enough to be a part of both of my grandfather's families.

"I have seen firsthand how much his Park Enterprises family meant to him. I'm confident that those who had the opportunity to work with William Park I would attest that he was more than just their boss. He was genuinely interested in their lives away from the job as well.

"I learned a lot from my grandfather. I believe we are all better people for having William Park I in our lives. And I believe the world is a better place because of him.

"William Park I was a man of his word. He was a man of integrity.

"As friends and family of William Park I, may we take the lessons we have learned from him and live them, teach them, and pass them on.

"I say this to you, Grandy, 'Don't worry,'" Ethan stated boldly and firmly, "'I will see your list, and mine, through to their completion.'"

Ethan stood still as his last words echoed throughout the room. Up to this point, he had managed to keep the depth of his sorrow in check. He solemnly closed the folio that had been given to him by his grandfather back in sixth grade.

He turned to leave the podium, paused, and turned back. "It just occurred to me that perhaps I said 'my grandfather' a lot of times today. I did, and that's because I am very blessed that he was *my* grandfather."

A single tear fell upon the Park Enterprises logo.

Ethan turned and left the podium.

✳ ✳ ✳ ✳

Margaret placed the cookie sheet on the table. Four slices of bread with cinnamon floating in melted butter were centered on the sheet. Ethan turned with the carafe in his hand. As he walked to the table, he inhaled deeply the sugary cinnamon mixture. "Granny, that smells so good and brings back some wonderful memories."

"For me as well. My grandmother used to make toast for my sisters and me all the time." Margaret smiled as she sat at the table. "It reminds me of chilly winter mornings."

Ethan set two coffee cups and the carafe on the table, and then sat across from his grandmother. "It definitely reminds me of sleepovers here with Trip and playing games with you and Grandy."

Margaret took the cup of coffee offered by Ethan. "Grandy would get so excited with anticipation when he knew you kids were going to spend the night. It was such fun having all of you here." She winked at her grandson. "You know, it still is."

"I sure do miss Grandy." Ethan spun the coffee cup by the handle, avoiding eye contact with his grandmother.

Margaret shifted in her chair and looked at her grandson. "It's hard to believe it's been almost a month since . . . he left us."

"Granny, I feel like he left us way before then."

"Ethan, I know what you mean. It's the toughest thing I've ever experienced." She twirled the wedding band on her ring finger.

The two sat silently for several moments, caught up in their own memories.

Ethan reached for his grandmother's hand and placed his fingers on her ring. "Granny, how are you doing? There were so many times when I thought we were losing you, too. It looked like you had the weight of the universe on your shoulders."

"Ethan, to be honest, I struggled through many days." Margaret placed her right hand on top of Ethan's, a wistful smile touching the corners of her mouth. "But I loved your grandfather. Still do. And we promised . . . in sickness and in health."

"But who would've thought that a sickness could be so dreadful?"

"Yes, it was a challenge to live with all the unpredictability . . . so much uncertainty . . . never getting enough sleep. I was always in fear that he would wake up and leave the house without my knowing. That happened once. Thankfully, you guys were there to—"

"I remember that night. It *was* horrifying! The whole time I was driving around searching for him, my mind leaped to the worst possible endings."

"Yet there he was, sitting in the woodshop," Margaret said, shaking her head.

"Granny, how were you able to hang in there?"

"It's what you do for those you love, for family."

Ethan massaged his temples as his grandmother continued. "I fed your father when he was a baby, changed his diapers, and made sure he wasn't getting into something that could cause him harm. Why wouldn't I do those things for your grandfather? It was no different—he just happened to be an adult."

"I don't know, Granny. I would feel horrible if I put my wife through that. I'm supposed to be the one to take care of her."

Margaret firmly set her cup back down on its saucer. "Ethan, get off your high horse. Not everything in life can be controlled by us."

Ethan dropped his gaze, startled by his grandmother's stern response.

Margaret softened her tone. "A couple looks after each other. Always, twenty-four hours a day, seven days a week. I know your mom has told you multiple times, not to mention you're a smart guy—we don't get to choose these things. Sometimes life . . . things happen."

"I do know what you and my mom are saying." Ethan sat forward in his chair. "That's why I think it's best that I never get married. I don't want to chance that. Suppose I have the gene. It seems it would be unfair."

Margaret shook her head and wagged her finger at her grandson. "Ethan, you just don't get it. If the tables had been turned, your grandfather would have done the same for me. He would have been the one feeding me, telling me when to chew and swallow. He would have been the one bathing me."

Ethan pushed back in his chair, chagrined.

"Your grandfather would have left Park Enterprises to care for me. He would have done that because he loved me. As much as he loved Park Enterprises, he loved me, your dad, you . . . the whole family . . . more.

He would have gladly done all those things for me, or anyone in the family. With no regrets."

Margaret got up from the table, walked into the kitchen, and stared out the window toward the woodshop. Ethan followed her and put his hand on her shoulder.

"Granny, I am so sorry for all you suffered."

Margaret grabbed a tissue from the box on the counter. "Thank you, Ethan. There was suffering, but also so many good times. Don't shut down your heart and miss out on the joys of love and family because you fear a future that won't fall into place according to your plans. The way you deal with life's upsets is where you do have control. Your grandfather chose to live life. Alzheimer's decided otherwise."

Grandy was a genius, until he wasn't.

※ ※ ※ ※

As Ethan situated himself in the driver's seat, he placed the bag containing his most recent purchase on the floor behind the passenger seat. Leaning across the car, he unlocked the passenger side door and Roger hopped in.

"Mission accomplished," Roger declared.

"Definitely! I think we toured the entire city."

"No, there are three streets we missed," Roger joked. "Do you want to hit those so we can complete the circuit?"

"Ha! I don't think so," Ethan replied. "But there is one more stop on our journey. Are you up for lunch at Melba's? It's my treat for you standing in as such a great Sancho Panza."

"Absolutely." Roger poked fun at Ethan, "I guess that would make you Don Quixote. You know, it did appear for a bit there that we were searching for windmills—not ink."

"I guess fountain pens *are* a thing of the past, so there's not much demand for the ink that goes in them," Ethan pondered aloud.

The engine roared to life as Ethan turned the key in the Mustang's ignition. Roger adjusted the volume knob on the radio, and music filled the car.

"You know, Ethan," Roger began, "we really need to get Available Light going again during the summer."

Ethan grew pensive. "That would be great, except my hand is still not back to a hundred percent. I brought one of my guitars back to college, but it's just not quite there yet. I'm not sure it ever will be."

"Okay, so you can't hit an A minor-ninth chord. Who can?"

"It's not that," Ethan grumbled. "I'm having trouble with even the easiest of chords."

"You'll get there," Roger assured him.

The music continued to permeate the car's interior as the boys fell into a meditative silence while Ethan drove to Melba's. The mission that began early in the morning had taken Ethan and Roger on a cross-city trek that included visits to three different stationery stores. The two young men were, by their standards, starving. They both also had an insatiable craving for the comfort food they believed only Melba's could provide.

Finishing a long sip of his malt, Roger asked Ethan, "So tell me, Señor Quixote, what's so special about this ink that you get me up early and drag me all over town in search of it? Not to mention, you spring for lunch!"

"On the day I left for college," Ethan explained, "Grandy gave me a pen and pencil set that had been given to him by his father. He used the pen from that set when he first began to work on his life goals. The ink is for that pen."

"That's really cool."

"Yes, it is. You know my grandfather. He was big on tradition, family, and passing things down." Ethan smiled with fondness. "So anyway, I've been thinking about my own life goals quite a bit lately since he passed away."

Ethan paused and swept a fry through a mound of ketchup on his plate. "It's time I begin that process," he continued. "I promised Grandy I would use that pen when creating my goals. So here we are."

Roger noticed Ethan's demeanor shift slightly as his friend appeared to drift into his own world, into his own thoughts. "I've noticed you have been quieter—not yourself—since he passed. How are you doing with his death and all? I mean, it seems to me that you were closer to your grandfather than you are to your father."

"In many ways we were closer," Ethan said. "We had a special connection. And he taught me so much about so many different things."

Ethan stopped eating as he delved deeper into his mind, reflecting on Grandy and the impact the man had on his life, along with the influence he continued to have on Ethan's choices.

"Grandy's death was bad enough in itself. But having the disease that took him . . . I wouldn't wish that on anyone." Ethan pushed his plate aside. "It was extremely difficult for my grandmother. For all of us actually, but especially for Granny since she was with him day in and day out. It was painful to watch as he slowly deteriorated, lost his way...and eventually vanished all together.

"There were so many painful episodes where he acted completely out of character. He said and did things that, under normal circumstances, would have never occurred to him to behave in such a manner." Ethan pushed around stray grains of salt on the table.

"It was hard to watch this vibrant, intelligent, caring human being, *my* grandfather, ravaged by that horrible illness. It took over his mind and body." Ethan's voice caught. "To see him unable to tie his shoes . . . or to shave himself . . . .

"The sad thing is that he brought pain to those closest to him—his family."

Roger reached over and grasped Ethan's shoulder tightly. "It was the disease, not your grandfather. He loved you—the whole family, more than anything."

"I know, but so much about it seems so wrong."

"He was a good man," Roger said, not knowing what else to say.

The two sat in silence.

Ethan noticed his friend's somber mood. "Hey, thanks for helping me search for windmills this morning, Sancho," he quipped.

"Okay, Donnie Q, so that brings us back to ink for the pen, and your goals." He raised his eyebrows questioningly.

Ethan flicked a grain of salt from his fingertip to Roger. "You know Grandy and his To Do lists and his desire—shoot—his *need*, to meet every commitment he made?"

"Ri-i-i-i-ght . . . " Roger interjected, "but what does that have to do with *your* goals?"

"Not a lot," Ethan said, his tone indicating otherwise, "except that one of my goals is to help Grandy finish his To Do list . . . since he couldn't."

He shrugged, a silent admission that he knew heavy work lie ahead.

※ ※ ※ ※

Ethan's grief began, not at the time of William's death, but rather when he saw his grandfather's mind deteriorate due to the onset of dementia. As Ethan witnessed and experienced the effects that process had on him and his family, his grief intensified. He did not appear to travel through the full gamut of stages made well known by noted psychiatrist Elizabeth Kübler-Ross. Instead, Ethan's grief manifested itself in a much different manner.

He placed the bottle of ink on the desktop, pulled out the chair, and sat down. Once he was physically situated, Ethan took a few moments to gather his thoughts to become mentally situated as well.

As he perused the array of photos on the shelves above his desk, Ethan was flooded with fond memories and a yearning for those days of familial bliss. All his photographs remained in their usual positions. As he scanned the shelves, the only photograph he didn't see was the one of Grandy and Granny at their dinner table—the one taken so many years ago when Ethan's father sneaked up on his parents and took an impromptu shot. It was his most prized photo. This picture now had a place of honor on Ethan's desk.

He picked up the frame and clutched it tightly. He studied the image, taking in all of the surroundings captured so long ago—the soft lighting in the dining room, the adding machine with Grandy's hand resting on the keys, Granny standing as a permanent fixture at William's side, and Grandy facing the camera and seemingly looking through the lens directly into Ethan's heart and soul.

The film captured more than the apparent random light rays that had been reflected through the camera's lens. Ethan believed one of the reasons this photo touched him so deeply was that the film had captured the essence of his grandfather.

As he stared into Grandy's eyes, he wondered what his grandfather had been thinking when the shutter snapped open for that split second in time. Had his grandfather known, well before his mom and dad had even met, that when he looked at that camera lens he would be looking through it to his grandson? Ethan imagined this to be so.

As his father had deftly operated the focus ring on his camera so many years ago, Ethan brought his own mind back into focus. He gently returned the picture to its place on the desk. He reached for the bottle of ink he had purchased with Roger a few weeks ago during spring break.

Ethan closed his eyes and thought about the goals, dreams, and successes still housed in this little bottle of ink. A sharp focus did not materialize, for his mind quickly returned to the image of William's eyes in the photograph. Ethan was drawn into the sharpness, the determination, and the confidence that was so intrinsic to Grandy's character. He recalled seeing that same look in his grandfather's eyes when they had connected with each other through the mirror last Christmas. Where had Grandy gone? Why had he gone? There was so much more his grandfather had intended to accomplish.

Memories of Grandy's episodes began to rush to the forefront. Feelings of shock, hurt, anger, and embarrassment flooded through his heart as he visualized scenes throughout his grandfather's illness. Ethan relived the helplessness he had felt watching Grandy slowly vanish from his life. He recalled the sheer terror he had experienced on the Park Enterprises job site at the possibility of having to witness his grandfather plummet from the roof and to his death.

Although his eyes were shut, Ethan felt tears begin to form as he remembered the embarrassment he endured when being admonished by his hero in front of his girlfriend and her parents. Ethan thought back to the profound disappointment he had felt at not seeing his grandfather in the front row during his valedictory speech. The pain and heartache of losing Grandy, his best friend, was coming at Ethan full force. Anger at the disease, which had robbed him of his mentor, resurfaced with a vengeance.

Focus. Ethan knew Grandy would want and insist that he focus on the task at hand.

Ethan had learned that simply taking some kind of action would help in his efforts to move forward through this process. So, he wiped back the tears, opened his eyes, and uncapped the bottle of ink. He carefully pulled back on the lever located on the side of the pen and inserted the nib of the pen into the tiny inkwell just inside the bottle. He released the lever, causing the pen to suction ink into the pen's ink reservoir. The pen was ready. Ethan was ready. Just as he had dug deeply within himself prior to setting the goals for his high school years, he would have to do the same, and more, for this list.

His grandfather had taught him that a To Do list should have a positive connotation. Therefore, it should be a list of things *to do*, not a list of things *not* to do. Still very present at the forefront of Ethan's thoughts were all the emotions he had experienced as his grandfather's illness progressed. Hurt. Anger. Desolation. Embarrassment. Fear.

Ethan struggled articulating in the positive. So, despite Grandy's instructions, Ethan boldly wrote with his grandfather's fountain pen, "Do NOT cause my family to suffer such *prolonged* pain."

※ ※ ※ ※

The last echoes of the backing track trailed off as Roger softly placed his drumsticks on top of the snare drum and Ethan stepped away from the microphone. Roger and Ethan looked across the studio at each other and smiled. Ethan quickly made his way into the control room to stop the recording of their cover of the Rolling Stones' "You Can't Always Get What You Want."

"Well, I guess Mick and Keith were right," Roger laughed.

Looking through the control room window, Ethan pushed the button on the talk-back microphone to answer. "What do you mean?"

With a smirk, Roger replied, "C'mon, I know how badly you're itching to play guitar on that tune."

"You're right about that," Ethan answered. "I used to be able to kill it on that bridge."

"And you will again one day. But since you haven't been playing, your vocals have improved immensely."

"Really?" Ethan asked with astonishment.

"Yeah, no doubt. You can almost sing on key now."

"Very funny," Ethan chuckled. "Get in here so we can listen to the playback and see just how off-beat your drumming was."

Ethan stopped the replay of their work. "Man, I wish my hand would follow my brain so I could play guitar on that track."

"It will. Just give it some more time," Roger consoled Ethan. "Like the song—you may *want* to play guitar, but you're not going to *get* that. At least not right now."

Ethan shook his head in frustration. "It's been two years! It feels like I'm having to learn how to play all over—"

"You'll get there. Be patient. It'll happen."

"Why did that storm have to blow in that day?" bemoaned Ethan with a grimace of disgust.

Roger recalled having similar conversations with Ethan since the injury. He knew he'd have to change the subject; otherwise, they could spend hours reliving the horror Ethan had experienced during the thunderstorm while up on a job site roof.

285

"Hey, Ethan," Roger called. "On to more positive things. How's work been?"

Ethan frowned, looked down, and strummed a low E chord on his guitar.

"My work's been great," Roger chortled sarcastically. "At least your dad thinks so. He assigned me to help with the technology design on the new lighting grid."

"That's really cool. Are you still thinking you want to work in that field once you're finished with school?" Ethan asked.

"I can't imagine doing anything else. What about you?"

"Work is work," Ethan mused. "I mean, it's not the same without Grandy. You know, it's hard to walk through the building . . . all the memories . . . ."

"Ethan, you're there to work, not reminisce. Do you think Grandy would *approve* of that sort of attitude?"

"No, you're right," Ethan agreed. "It's just hard to *not* think about it. His fingerprints are *all* over the place."

"Right, and he wanted, *insisted*, that when it's *your* time, *you* are supposed to put *your* fingerprints all over the place."

"I know," Ethan replied, "but this wasn't part of the plan. He wasn't supposed to be gone so soon. He didn't get to finish . . . ."

The conversation once again began to rumble down the bumpy path of negativity. Once again, Roger attempted to steer toward a smoother, more positive track.

"So, do you have a special someone back on your campus?" Roger inquired.

Ethan gave Roger a raised eyebrow. "Do you think I really have time for that? Not to mention, neither my head nor my heart have been in the right place since—"

"C'mon," Roger pushed, "you have to have fun some time. You'll only be an undergrad in college once."

"I know, I know," Ethan reluctantly agreed, "there's just a ton happening right now, and I've stepped up my class load so I can graduate early."

"What's the rush?"

"Work," Ethan said flatly.

"Ethan, enjoy college. Park Enterprises isn't going anywhere."

Ethan eyed Roger. "No, it's not. That's the problem, or one of them. That's why I need to get moving, to get Park Enterprises going somewhere."

"What do you mean?"

"Dan Stokes is doing a great job with the company," Ethan began. "It's making money and closing contracts. But while working there this past summer, I noticed that it's just not the same. It feels as if everyone is only going through the motions. The passion is gone. I think it left with Grandy."

"And you, as 'Mr. Fresh Out of College,' are going to be the one to steer this company back on a course for success?" Roger asked, his voice filled with incredulity.

Ethan paused and stared at the audio console. After a few moments in deep thought, he turned to Roger. "If not me, then who?"

✳ ✳ ✳ ✳

The lights gently reflected off the fixtures located on the floor of the saltwater pool, creating a multitude of prisms that danced along the surface. The underwater speakers caused the sound of the music to be muffled, almost stymied. Ethan recognized the song, but the tone lacked brightness and definition.

As Ethan pondered the different effects the water had on sound and light, he reflected upon the ways Alzheimer's had distorted Grandy's personality. He recalled the times when his grandfather would speak, but the words came out garbled. Whatever Grandy had been trying to communicate became distorted as it made its way from the depths of his internal being through the hazardous minefields caused by the disease.

Ethan was startled by the sudden clarity and volume of the pool music. It reminded him of the time he had been startled by the sudden realization he had experienced when he looked at his grandfather through the bathroom mirror that day he helped him shave. Ethan realized he was experiencing such sharp clarity now because his mother had just walked outside and turned on the surface sound. Ethan also noticed he incorrectly guessed the name of the song that was playing underwater. He had, in fact, guessed the band correctly by recognizing their trademark characteristics, yet he had missed the nuances of this particular song.

He looked up to see his mother walking toward him with a tray. "Hey," Constance began, "you look deeper in thought than the pool is with water. Am I disturbing you? I saw you out here with only the underwater sound on. Do you want me to turn the surface sound back off?" Constance placed the tray on the poolside table.

Continuing to watch the effect the water had on the lights, Ethan replied, "Hi, Mom. No, I'm just watching the water and thinking about Grandy . . . ."

Constance sat beside Ethan and dangled her legs in the pool, just as Ethan was doing.

"I brought some iced tea and snacks for you," she said. "May I join you, or would you rather be alone with your thoughts?"

Ethan reached up and grabbed one of the glasses of iced tea. He took a sip and smiled. "No one makes sun tea as good as you, Mom. I would like it if you stayed."

Now that Ethan had revealed he was thinking about his grandfather, his mother could tell these were not reminiscent thoughts but ponderous ones, weighing heavily on Ethan's life. She took a sip from the other glass of tea and then followed Ethan's gaze out onto the water, waiting for her son to bare to her what was troubling him so much.

Patience was one of Constance's greatest attributes. She learned that if she waited, her children and her husband would eventually reveal their worries. Constance knew that, typically, the larger the burden her loved one carried, the longer it would take for the discussion to begin. In this instance, it took exactly two glasses of iced tea.

"Mom, I still find it hard to believe that Grandy is gone. I mean . . . it just doesn't seem real . . . ."

Constance waited a couple of beats for her son to continue. As he seemed to fall back into his reverie, she spoke. "I know, dear. He was taken from us way too early."

"Not only that," Ethan said, "but way too violently."

"What do you mean?"

"For me, during the last few years of his life, it felt like his *being*, who he was, was ripped from him. There was no telling what his responses would be to anything. It was scary."

"Alzheimer's is a terrible disease," Constance said.

"It's very destructive," Ethan agreed. "The things that Granny had to go through, that the whole family had to experience . . . the uncertainty about anything . . . everything . . . we never knew."

Ethan continued, "We never knew when we would get to really *see* Grandy. I was looking at the lights in the pool and thought, *That was Grandy with Alzheimer's—sometimes he could break free from the depths of the disease, and the true Grandy would make it to the surface.*

"But just like with these lights, you don't know when a beam will break the surface or where. Most of the time, getting connected with Grandy was like trying to interpret the sound from those underwater speakers. You can hear the song and think you know the tune, but it's not clear and sometimes not even the one you had in mind.

"That's how I felt with Grandy . . . . I never knew when he would surface or how deep down he was."

"Yes," Constance said, "it certainly was so unpredictable—and painful to witness. There is no denying that. That's what's so key about family.

We can lean on each other in hard times. You know as well as anyone how much your grandfather valued family."

Ethan thought for a few moments. "I can't imagine, though, that Grandy would have *ever* wanted his family to go through what we've been through! If he had known—"

"Ethan," Constance chided, "your grandfather didn't choose this. It was something that happened."

"Mom, it's something I don't *ever* want my family to go through on account of me."

Constance rubbed Ethan's shoulder. "Sometimes we don't get to make that choice."

Maybe we do.

Chapter 15
LOVE'S DILEMMA

A small family of ducks waddled to the water's edge for an afternoon swim. Leaves quivered gently as a soft breeze caressed the people and wildlife that were inclined to seek respite in the shade offered by stately oak trees.

Stephanie Havens looked up from her reading to watch the family of ducks. She'd figured out early in her freshman year that the serenity of the park was more conducive to studying than the atmosphere of the main campus library.

Now in her junior year, Stephanie had laid claim to the shade of this particular oak. Almost every Friday, during her three years as a physical therapist major, she toted her copious amounts of reading and study materials to this spot. She had even taken to naming the different ducklings that made their appearance each spring.

Stephanie decided to use the upcoming mid-term exams as an opportunity to shore up her grade point averages in each of her classes. In the case of her exercise physiology class, the mid-term accounted for thirty percent of her overall semester grade, a percentage worthy of intense, dedicated study.

With that reminder she returned to her reading, quickly becoming immersed in the subject. Coarse noises of what sounded like someone attempting to play a guitar suddenly tore through the tranquility of her space. She tried to block out the twanging of strings and the awkward placement of chords. It wasn't working. Someone was destroying nature's soundtrack and the serenity she counted on. Stephanie couldn't take it any longer. She had to go to the origin of the sound and let this individual know that perhaps the guitar wasn't their best choice of instrument.

"I do hope you're not a music major."

Startled, Ethan glanced up. He noticed an attractive co-ed staring down at him, fingers in her ears and an impish grin on her face. "Uh, playing like this, and I use the term 'playing' loosely—that would be a definite no."

"Well, whatever you want to call what you're doing, it's upsetting my study time, not to mention Hunky and Dory, who are trying to take the kids for a quiet swim." Ethan watched the young lady gesture toward the pond as a small family of ducks waddled to the water's edge.

He scrambled to his feet to be on more even footing with this lovely girl standing before him. "Hunky and Dory?"

"Yes, that family—Hunky, Dory, and the ducklings." The young lady continued to direct her attention to the water as the miniature flock paddled with ease toward the center of the pond. "They appreciate the tranquility out here as well."

"Sounds like a band from the fifties," Ethan joked. "Hunky, Dory, and the Ducklings, live from Madison Square Garden."

"Cute." Stephanie giggled. Her gaze shifted to the guitar Ethan held. "Speaking of bands and music, that's an expensive guitar for a beginner."

"You're familiar with Martin guitars?"

"I don't know about that," she said teasingly, "but when I hear a 1955 D-18 squalling, it kind of grabs my attention."

Ethan laughed. "You *do* know your Martins."

"Yes, I play some. Mine isn't quite as fancy." She brushed some loose strands of hair away from her face. "But I have a 1963 Gibson B-25."

"That's a fine guitar." The conversation took a short pause as each absorbed the information they had just exchanged.

"I'm Stephanic Stcphanie Havens," she finally said, her hand extended.

Ethan gently set his guitar against the trunk of a large oak tree and offered his hand. "My apologies. I'm Ethan Park."

"I'm studying for my exercise physiology mid-term," Stephanie said. "And while your 'guitar gently weeps,' my concentration slowly wanes."

Ethan chuckled. "Even on my best days, I could never play like Clapton."

"I'm glad you caught the reference," Stephanie said.

She really knows her music. Maybe I should get to know more about her. "Do you study out here a lot?" he asked.

"It beats the library." Stephanie rolled her eyes. "That place is too antiseptic for studying. And way too quiet. I love this park and found the perfect spot under these oaks."

"A physical therapy major, eh?"

"Yes, how did you know that?"

"After an accident to my hand," Ethan said, "when my doctor told me that I would have to be in physical therapy, I started reading up on PT."

Stephanie's interest was immediately piqued. "What happened to your hand?"

"It's a long story," Ethan said. "But the short version is that I fell on a roof and a piece of slag went into my fretting hand. That was not quite three years ago. My guitar playing hasn't been the same since."

"Ouch."

Ethan paused and looked at the palm of his left hand. "Ouch is right. I played lead in a band before I got hurt."

Stephanie reached out, took Ethan's hand, and traced the scar with the tip of her finger. She looked up at Ethan. The electricity of the physical touch coursed through her. "That looks like it must have been really painful."

Ethan looked down at his hand in hers. "In more ways than one. Well, once you graduate, maybe you can come up with some effective exercises that will really make a difference," Ethan said in a half-joking manner.

"Your therapy isn't working?"

Ethan guffawed, "Didn't you just hear the results—or lack thereof?"

"Point taken." Stephanie said.

Unfortunately, she had a mid-term tomorrow and still had several hours of review before she would feel comfortable with the vast amount of material covered thus far in the semester. As much as she didn't want to, Stephanie let go of Ethan's hand. She didn't want to interrupt the moment and what she felt. Stephanie hoped that this handsome young man had felt as exhilarated as she was with the discovery. What she had discovered, she wasn't quite sure, but it certainly was exciting.

"Seriously, maybe I can help. Do you come to the park to break the serenity with that Martin often?"

Ethan turned toward the guitar and then back at Stephanie. Winking, he said, "It beats getting kicked out of the library."

"Very cute." A broad smile swept across Stephanie's face. "You *were* actually listening."

Ethan allowed a slight grin to emerge and shrugged his shoulders. "I tend to do that when I'm interested in the person speaking to me." He paused for a moment. "Do you have a class after your exam tomorrow morning? Maybe we could get together for coffee, and I can give you the long version of why I am torturing this Martin."

"My exam ends at ten. How about we meet here at ten thirty? I'll bring the coffee. And please," Stephanie joked, "leave the Martin at home."

"Great. I'll see you at ten-thirty, sans the Martin."

The wide smile remained on Stephanie's face. She turned and walked back to her tree. Ethan, with a lightened heart, placed the guitar back in its case.

※ ※ ※ ※

Roger gazed with awe through the floor-to-ceiling windows of the executive dining room at Park Enterprises. The city in which he grew up and called home lay majestically before him. He had gazed on the city from an airplane window seat on several different occasions, but those views were, in Roger's mind, from too great a distance as well as too fleeting.

This vantage point, from the Park Enterprises building—Ethan's building—was perfect. The distance was such that it was easy for Roger to recognize the local landmarks and many of the places he had frequented during his youth, as well as various locations where he and Ethan had created fond memories during their high school years. From this position, Roger was able to see the Frey High School campus and even Melba's Kitchen.

He was surprised to discover he could also identify a part of the woods where, as young grammar school kids, he and Ethan had created forts to wage mock wars and forge trails on which to test their motocross skills. Much of their youth had been spent exploring the vast array of activities and mysteries offered by this untamed area.

Ethan entered the executive dining room and managed to approach the table without Roger becoming aware of his presence. He stopped and observed Roger's gaze.

"You know," Ethan said breaking Roger's concentration, "if you stare any harder through those windows you may burn a hole in them."

Roger's consciousness delayed a beat or two before Ethan's voice registered in his brain. He then turned, smiled, and immediately rose to his feet to shake Ethan's hand and give him a hug.

"You may be right. I was just thinking of all the great memories we possess because of growing up in that panorama. Man, we had some fun."

"Yes, we had an idyllic childhood. I think at the time we didn't even realize what we had," Ethan said as he scanned the cityscape.

"We were kids. We weren't supposed to be buried deep in those thoughts. We were simply carefree and enjoying life."

Laughing, Ethan gestured for Roger to sit down. "And that we did!"

Silence descended on the conversation as they entertained the individual memories they had created within the purview of the world in which they had grown from infants to young men.

"Enough of yesteryear," Ethan said. "Let's talk about what's next in our lives and devour one of Chef Duke's phenomenal lunches."

Roger smirked as he settled into his seat. "You don't have to tell me twice. I still have the appetite of a college kid. You know it's only been two weeks since my graduation."

"How was the ceremony?" Ethan inquired. "You know I'm sorry I couldn't make it, but work has been demanding."

Roger pondered Ethan's question for a moment. "If I had to do it all over again, I think I would have done what you did—graduate early and skip the ceremony."

"Really?" Ethan asked. "Did something go wrong?"

"Oh, no . . . nothing went *wrong*," Roger said. "It's just that it was a long, drawn-out affair. Even with binoculars my parents could barely see me. The speeches lasted forever. It felt anti-climactic after four years of blood, sweat, and tears. I think you did it right: pick up your diploma from your counselor, come home, and have a party with family and friends."

"I'm sure if someone from Park Productions, specifically you, had staged the ceremony, it would have been much better," Ethan joked.

Roger smiled at this comment as he opened his menu.

299

"No need to look at the menu," Ethan stated. "Chef Duke is preparing our lunch."

"You really have slid into this whole *executive* thing," Roger snickered.

Ethan grinned. "Hey, I just go where I'm told."

Olivia, the executive dining room attendant, approached the table. "Good afternoon, Ethan. May I get you and your guest a drink?"

"Good afternoon, Olivia," Ethan replied. "This is Roger Wallace, a family friend and newly minted full-time employee at Park Productions."

"Congratulations, Mr. Wallace," the attendant responded with a smile.

"Thank you, and no need for 'Mister.'" Roger added, "'Roger' will be fine. And I'll have iced tea."

Ethan nodded and opened his napkin over his lap. "Same here, iced tea. Thank you, Olivia."

The two young men sipped their tea. Roger placed his glass back on the table. "How has it been, working full time, no homework, with no . . . ?"

"You were going to ask, 'with no Grandy?'" Ethan answered, "The work part is fine. I have learned more in the last six months working with Dan than I believe I learned in all of my business courses over four years." Ethan smiled his thanks as Olivia placed a plate of appetizers on their table. "No homework. Give me homework. At least I could do that, turn it in, and then forget about it! Here, there are deadlines, but one deadline only leads to another."

"Sounds exciting."

"It is exciting, but we don't get a spring break. It just keeps going," Ethan joked. "And you don't get to put in your four years and then move on."

Ethan paused for a few moments, stared out at the cityscape, and gathered his thoughts. "Not having Grandy here is probably the biggest adjustment. There are many times I would like to be able to walk into his office for advice. And I can't do that . . . ."

Roger nodded with sympathy. "I get it. At least you have Dan to lean on."

"Yes, I don't know where the company would be without Dan, or where I would be without Dan," Ethan lamented. "I don't know what I'm going to do when he eventually retires."

"Maybe he would agree to a consulting role," Roger mused.

"Possibly."

"You'll also have to man up and move into your office. You can't keep working out of the conference room," Roger softly chided his friend.

"I know, and I will. I haven't moved into Grandy's office because I believe I need to prove myself to the staff—but even more importantly, to myself."

Roger put down his fork, took a sip of the milk in the chilled glass in front of him, and grinned.

"Do you have any openings at Park Enterprises?" he joked. "I mean, a lunch finished off with homemade apple pie and ice-cold milk. How could I want to work anywhere else?"

Ethan chuckled as he savored his last bite of pie. Washing it down with a large gulp of milk, he smacked his lips and pretended he was going to wipe his mouth off on his shirt sleeve. Both young men laughed.

"I guess we gotta behave now that we're adults," Roger commented.

"Maybe only when we're at work."

"How's the hand doing?" Roger queried. "Is your 'physical therapist' still taking good care of you?"

Ethan's eyes sparkled at Roger's reference to Stephanie.

"Actually, my hand is functioning much better." Ethan beamed. "I may be able to assume my position as lead guitar when we commence the Available Light reunion tour. My *therapist* has worked wonders."

"I'm sure she has worked wonders—not only on your hand but your heart as well, eh?"

"Your observations are astute," Ethan responded, his expression turning grave. "But I don't think this long-distance relationship thing is going to work—"

"Really? Why? From our conversations over the past six months, I thought you guys were getting along fine. You know, I wasn't really joking all that much. It's been obvious that she has done wonders with your hand, but from my point of view, she's done wonders for your heart as well. You were pretty lost when . . . after Grandy . . . ."

"You're absolutely correct." Ethan then quickly added, "But your observation skills aren't quite as sharp as you believe them to be."

Puzzled, Roger sat quietly and waited for Ethan to continue.

Ethan couldn't keep up the ruse any longer. He had held his friend in this captive state of bewilderment long enough. He started to laugh.

"This long-distance thing isn't going to work," Ethan began again, "and if you had let me finish before jumping to conclusions, you would have heard me say that I'm thinking of asking Stephanie to marry me."

Roger sat stunned. He had gone from feeling sorry for his best friend to now being elated. He grinned. "If you weren't such a good friend, and I didn't think your newly functioning fret hand would get hurt, and we weren't in the executive dining room at Park Enterprises, and we weren't adults, and . . . if I weren't so happy for you, I think I'd have to punch you."

Ethan laughed. "You sure did put a ton of qualifiers in there. One would think that you really *don't* want to punch me."

"You're right," Roger commented. "Seriously, though. Wouldn't you want to get more on your feet with work? Save a little money? I mean, I'm happy for you, but . . . do you think you're ready for marriage?"

Ethan shook his head with amusement. "You know me. I'm a product of 'Grandy U.' I don't do anything without a plan. I have been living with my folks, and will continue to do so until the wedding to save money for a house, cars—you know, the things for a married life. The wedding wouldn't be for at least another year, maybe two. Of course, Stephanie knows nothing of this yet. We'll work together on the timing once she says yes."

"And you're sure she'll say yes?"

"Let's just say I'm feeling confident . . . I think."

"You think? Of course she's going to say yes. How could she not? You're a great guy. You deserve this," Roger chimed in.

303

"There is one possible fly in the ointment," Ethan said. "I want to have a DNA test done."

Half-joking, Roger asked, "Why? What, are you thinking you're not really a Park?"

"Of course not." Ethan laughed and then immediately turned serious. "I want to see if I have the APOE gene."

"What's that?" Roger asked.

"It's the apolipoprotein E gene. A DNA test can verify if there is a genetic variant of the APOE gene in a person. If so, there is a greater chance of that person eventually having Alzheimer's."

Perplexed by the science and Ethan's logic, Roger asked, "What does that have to do with you marrying Stephanie? Are you saying you would *not* marry her if it comes back that you have this variant?"

Ethan folded his napkin and set it down on the table. "It's possible it could change things."

※ ※ ※ ※

The sun poured heat and light onto the shiny poppy red Mustang as it crested the second of the three hills in the neighborhood. With the top down, Ethan appreciated the warmth and glow the sun offered as he made the drive home from Park Enterprises. Ethan also felt an inner zeal as he recalled his younger days when his main mode of transportation had been the Schwinn Scrambler he had received from his parents on his eighth birthday.

He chuckled at the memory of racing up and over these very hills with Roger. Though early on neither of the boys had any knowledge of Isaac Newton, they quickly learned the advantages and disadvantages of Newton's law of gravity. Ethan recalled the burning sensation he and Roger had felt in their legs as they pushed as hard as they could to gain momentum against gravity and the rush of exhilaration as they crested each hill and then began their descent, gaining speed with little to no effort.

Now, with minimal effort, Ethan pressed the Mustang's accelerator to engage more of the engine's available 210 horsepower. The car maintained its speed and crested the hill with no strain on the car or on Ethan. The sensation of apparent speed and the wind rushing through his hair were as exhilarating and fun for Ethan now as it had been while riding his Schwinn with his best friend.

In his mind's ear, Ethan could hear Roger bellowing out, "See you later, alligator!"

As Ethan chuckled at the memory, he mouthed, "I hope your legs grow straighter."

Ethan guided his car down the street and into the Park driveway. Since the death of his grandfather, he had taken to parking in the spot that had been reserved for Grandy. After all, the Mustang had originally belonged to Grandy and Granny. It seemed especially appropriate to park here now.

Constance gave one last twist on the corkscrew and then utilized the lever to remove the cork from the bottle of unoaked Mer Soleil Silver. The door opened, and Ethan entered the kitchen.

"Perfect timing," Constance said. "Were you outside waiting for me to open this bottle?"

Ethan feigned embarrassment. "You got me, Mom. Shall I get a couple of glasses?"

"Certainly. You can keep me company while I finish dinner."

Ethan pulled two glasses from the rack and began wiping them with a dish towel. "Where's everyone else?"

"Your dad is still at work, but he should be home soon. Claire is at cheerleading practice. So, you're stuck with me for the time being."

"Mom, I don't know that I'd call it *stuck*. Instead, I'd call it *luck*." Ethan grinned.

"Always the charmer . . . ."

"I'm serious, Mom," Ethan insisted. "It's nice when we get some time together—just the two of us."

"Thank you," Constance said, beaming. "How was your day? By the way, there's a letter for you on the desk."

"Work is good. I'm learning more every day." Ethan walked to the kitchen desk to retrieve the letter.

"Really? I thought you would have had it mastered by now," Constance quipped. "What are you learning?"

Ethan picked up the envelope bearing his name. "I'm learning that I'm not looking forward to the day Dan Stokes—"

He stopped his answer mid-sentence as he recognized the return address on the letter: EPP Research, LTD.

Constance turned to face Ethan, waiting for him to continue. She observed him staring at the envelope in his hand.

"Hello, Earth to Ethan," Constance waved her hand in front of his face.

"Uh . . . oh . . . I'm sorry," Ethan stammered. "I'm not looking forward to Dan retiring. He's a wealth of information and has helped me tremendously. I don't know how I'm going to do it without him."

"I'm sure it will have its challenges," Constance encouraged, "but with the training you received from Grandy *and* now what you are learning from Dan, you will be extremely capable."

"We'll see. I'm excited, but a little . . . just . . . nervous," Ethan explained.

"Understandably. From the look on your face, I'm wondering, is that letter bad news? Who is EPP Research? What do they do?"

Still holding the letter, Ethan paused, took a sip of wine, and then looked directly at his mother. "Mom, it could be good news . . . or bad."

Constance picked up on the hesitancy and tension in Ethan's demeanor and in his voice. Open communication had always been a mainstay in the Park household. It wasn't like Ethan to withhold anything from her. Whether he was experiencing feelings of joy or sadness, pride or shame, boldness or fear, Ethan seemed to always confide in his mother. But then, as he had matured, Constance learned that Ethan would talk when he was ready.

"You know you have my support at all times," Constance gently reminded him.

The timer on the oven rang. Constance took two oven mitts out of the drawer next to the stove, opened the oven door, and removed a steaming hot pan of homemade lasagna. The aroma of the cheeses, pasta, and red sauce filled the kitchen. Constance turned back to the kitchen island to place the lasagna on the wrought iron trivets. She noticed Ethan had leaned the envelope against the bottle of wine.

Ethan took in the sight of the lasagna as Constance removed the tin foil covering. He inhaled deeply. "That smells *so* incredibly delicious."

"I hope it tastes as good as it smells," Constance mused.

Ethan fidgeted with the envelope. He then picked up the bottle of wine and refilled his glass. Ethan took a deep breath. "Mom, I need to talk to you about the contents of this envelope."

"Yes, dear, I'm listening. It must be something major. It's obvious to me that something's been on your mind."

"This has to do with Grandy," Ethan stated.

"Grandy?" Constance furrowed her brow. "Is there an issue at Park Enterprises?"

"Oh, no, nothing to do with that," Ethan replied. "I took a DNA test. The results of the test are in this envelope."

Now his mother was really confused. "A DNA test? For what?"

"I don't want what happened to Grandy and our family to happen to me and *my* family—*our* family again," Ethan said.

A sadness enveloped Constance as the words her son spoke registered deeply within her. She walked around the kitchen island and embraced Ethan. "Sweetheart, you do realize that there was nothing that could have been done to prevent what happened to your grandfather?"

"I know, Mom," Ethan noted, "but . . . I just need to know if it could happen to me."

Ethan picked up the envelope and opened it with the foil cutter located on the side of the corkscrew. He unfolded the single sheet of paper as he retrieved it from inside the envelope. He quickly scanned down to the information he had been seeking. Quietly he refolded the paper and returned it to the inside of the envelope.

Ethan took another sip of wine and then looked at his mother. This proved to be one of the few times in his life when she could not read the expression on her son's face.

"I have the APOE gene," Ethan said in a monotone. "That means there's a good chance that I'll have Alzheimer's."

"Ethan, you don't know that for sure. How will this knowledge benefit you? Will it change the way you live your life?" Constance gently questioned him.

Ethan glanced at the envelope and then back at his mother. "It may . . . I may decide *not* to get married. Why would I want to put a wife—Stephanie—through something like that? Did you see how hard it was on Granny?"

"Yes, I did. I lived it," Constance replied. "We *all* lived it. But, you know, I'll bet if we called Granny right now, she would say she'd do it all over again, *live* it all over again, for just one more minute with Grandy."

※ ※ ※ ※

Despite the vent whirring at full speed, the steam, due to the lengthy amount of time Ethan had spent in the hot shower, caused the bathroom mirror to be completely covered with fog. Feeling refreshed from his shower, Ethan dried off, walked to his dresser, and retrieved his favorite sweatpants bearing the Frey High School logo. As he began donning the sweatpants, his eyes fell on the small box resting atop the dresser.

To anyone observing the square container covered in dark blue velvet, it was obvious that this small, delicate box contained a piece of jewelry. Specifically, this box contained a diamond ring—an engagement ring Ethan had designed, with Constance's assistance, and had made for Stephanie.

As he finished tying the drawstring on his sweatpants, Ethan laid eyes upon another container atop the dresser. For next to the box holding the engagement ring sat another smaller one with a ring inside. This box, though, had been constructed out of wood. Its construction was not even close to the quality Ethan and his grandfather had achieved on all those Saturday mornings throughout his childhood. Nonetheless, it held a special place in Ethan's heart. On the top of this box, the logo of his high school alma mater was still visible.

Ethan thought it ironic that, by happenstance, when coming home last night from Atwood's Jewelers, he had placed the ring he bought for Stephanie next to his high school class ring. This was the very class ring that he had placed on the pointer finger of Lauren's left hand the night of the Senior Ring Dance, the very class ring that Lauren had worn all through their senior year of high school and the first half of her freshman year of college.

He recalled how during the summer after their high school graduation, he and Lauren had committed to keeping their relationship strong. They intended to continue to don each other's senior rings throughout their college careers. In their young minds, the love they had for each other was strong enough to withstand the three-hour drives and the four years

310

of distance. They believed it would be a test of their love, a test they believed they would pass with ease. Ultimately, it was a test they failed.

The failure, or dissolution of their relationship, occurred toward the end of the winter break during their freshman year of college. Both Lauren and Ethan had been eager for the break—to have almost two full months of no classes or homework assignments and almost two full months of time to spend together.

Ethan smiled as he thought back to that specific period. He and Lauren had been inseparable. They spent many afternoons at Melba's enjoying malts and sundaes and trading first-semester stories with former classmates. They snuggled together as they drove to the beach with the top down, despite the cool temperatures. They walked The Trace with their parents and siblings, traveling among the long golden shadows created by the winter sun. They attended holiday parties and gatherings hosted by friends. He and Lauren had been in love with each other and where they were in life at that time.

Or so he had thought. The smile on Ethan's face slowly vanished as his mind brought him to the next logical place during this trip down memory lane—the holidays with his family that winter season.

Holidays in the Park family were traditionally filled with dinners, parties, and spending as much time together as possible. As a child, Ethan loved this festive time of the year. He liked how his grandparents spent most days and evenings at his house playing games, watching Christmas movies, and sometimes even taking late-night swims in the heated pool. The day-to-day routines were suspended, and everyone appeared to be in a jovial mood.

The holiday season during the middle of his freshman year of college hadn't transpired as Ethan remembered the holidays from his youth.

311

His grandfather's behavior had become more erratic. Ethan dug deep into the recesses of his memory to recall a single event that hadn't been affected by William's illness. To his recollection, tears became prevalent at most of these events.

William's illness during that time had begun to know no boundaries. The disease was mercilessly ravaging his grandfather's mind and body.

A beautiful glazed ham Constance had been preparing was ruined when William walked to the oven to check on the glazing process and proceeded to *season* the ham with dishwasher powder. Dinner that evening had consisted of all the fixings for a glazed ham but without the ham. To salvage that evening, Bill had quickly grilled burgers.

Ethan recalled when his grandfather began opening everyone's presents under the tree a week before Christmas and the time he arrived at the front door of the house, ringing the doorbell, wearing only . . . Ethan stopped his mind from traveling any farther down that road.

As was customary, Lauren was present during many of these family gatherings, so she witnessed most of these erratic episodes. Lauren appeared to take these situations in stride, with the understanding that none of these happenings were malicious on William's part. In fact, she had often comforted Ethan after these episodes.

One evening the entire family sat in a circle around the backyard fire pit. The setting was festive as the flickering flames emitted a fragrant pine scent and the logs snapped and popped. Everyone cradled steaming cups of hot chocolate. The mood had been carefree and light. Until...

Ethan had gone inside to refill the hot chocolate carafe. When he returned to the fire pit, Lauren pulled back her lap blanket and made room for Ethan on the chair. He put his arm around Lauren, snuggling in next to her as she pulled the blanket back over their laps.

Without notice, William began shouting accusingly at Ethan, "You should not put your arm around your grandmother in that manner or snuggle so intimately with her. It's inappropriate and disrespectful to me."

In all the episodes that Lauren had been a witness to, she had been just that—a witness. On this occasion, though, William's confusion centered around her. The memory of this unsettling event grabbed Ethan's mind with a steely grip. Ethan's chest grew tight as he recalled how his grandfather's behavior that evening was especially unpredictable and almost reached the point of violence. Bill and Margaret had to gather William to distract him while Ethan collected a hysterical Lauren and took her home.

In Ethan's mind, this incident was probably the catalyst for Lauren's actions the week before he returned to school after winter break. He thought back to that walk along the beach when Lauren removed his class ring from the pointer finger on her left hand and gave it back to him. Ethan recalled how he held the ring in his hand, rolling it over in his palm as tears filled his eyes. He was both shocked and brokenhearted. Lauren explained that she believed the physical distance between the two of them to be too great, and trying to keep in touch was negatively affecting her studies. She maintained that if their love was as strong as they felt it to be, they would find each other once they finished school.

And during most of that spring semester, they kept in touch to a certain degree and for a time. But as the semester progressed, their relationship dissolved as unanswered phone calls became frequent and letters became infrequent.

Ethan strongly believed that the fire pit incident, as he called it, had been too much for Lauren. She never stated that, but he determined in his mind that this singular event shook Lauren to the core and pushed her beyond her limit.

Ethan aggressively thrust aside the thoughts and memories of the semester break during their freshman year. He forced his mind to shift to a positive place. Tonight could prove to be a happy milestone in his life and Stephanie's as well.

Back in the bathroom, Ethan noticed the fog persisting to cling to the mirror, obliterating any possible view of himself. He reached for a hand towel and began wiping the fog from the mirror. As he wiped, he saw a pair of eyes emerge through the fog. The eyes stared directly back, giving him no quarter.

Bittersweet memories rushed forward. Ethan thought back to the afternoon he helped his grandfather shave. He recalled the fog that was clouding Grandy's eyes and his mind. He remembered how, on that day, the fog seemed to disappear as easily as the condensation he just wiped from the mirror in front of him now. And he and Grandy had *connected*! But in an instant, that connection had vanished.

Ethan reached down to pick up the bottle of shaving cream. He saw his tube of toothpaste next to the bottle, which reminded him of the toothpaste smeared all over his grandfather's face. Ethan reached for his razor and moved the blade toward his chin. Before the razor reached its target, he stopped and stared into his eyes and searched deeply into his own soul.

Could he put his future family through an experience like what happened to his own family due to his grandfather's illness? Would it even be fair for him to have a family of his own—a wife and children? He knew he had the gene, after all. Ethan was confident in his love for

Stephanie and hers for him. Could he put *her* through the horror of what Granny experienced? Should he even risk the possibility?

But as mom said, Granny would give anything for one more minute with Grandy. I can't imagine one more minute of my life without Stephanie.

※ ※ ※ ※

Suspended above the roadway, the large full moon cast a soft blue glow on Ethan and Stephanie as they rode through town with the top down on their way to dinner. Cool, dry air permeated the early evening, creating a light, airy atmosphere.

"Look at that," Ethan exclaimed. "The moon is beautiful tonight."

Stephanie gazed upward and smiled. "It looks as though this road leads right straight to the moon. Is that where you're taking me for dinner?"

"That would be pretty cool," Ethan laughed. "This Mustang can do a lot of things, but I don't believe going to the moon is one of them."

As Ethan made a right-hand turn into Aldo's parking lot, Stephanie glanced back over her shoulder for one last look skyward. "Goodbye, Mr. Moon. Maybe we'll see you for dinner some other time."

"Believe me, you will be on the moon, or at least feel like it, when you taste Mr. Sal's Vitello Parmigiana."

Sal greeted the young couple at the door, vigorously shaking Ethan's hand and giving Stephanie a warm hug. He escorted them to the private dining room where a cozy table for two had been pre-set with Ethan's

315

choice of wine, a basket of warm focaccia bread, and two lighted taper candles. He then introduced the young couple to their waiter, Fredo, who was charged with helping to make their evening extra special.

Stephanie gracefully sat in the chair pulled back and offered to her by Fredo.

"May I pour the lady a glass of wine?" Fredo asked.

"Yes, please."

As he finished pouring wine for both Stephanie and Ethan, Fredo stated, "I'll leave you two alone. Your salads will be out shortly."

"Thank you, Fredo." Ethan commented, "It's good to see you again."

"You as well," Fredo smiled. "Please ring the bell if there's anything else I can get you." He motioned to the silver bell positioned on the table near Ethan's right hand.

Ethan looked at Stephanie and raised his glass of wine. "Here's to *you.*"

"And, here's to you," Stephanie responded with a sparkle in her eye.

The couple tapped their wineglasses together, took a small sip, and then placed them back on the table.

"What do you think so far?" Ethan inquired.

"This is over the top, but in a good way." Stephanie exclaimed, "If dinner is as fine as the service so far, it will be . . . well, I'm not sure I will be able to find the words."

The conversation continued to be light while they enjoyed the wine, focaccia bread, and then their salads. The discussion covered music, plays, and current events. They talked about the differences between attending classes and work meetings. After Stephanie filled Ethan in on her budding career in physical therapy, Ethan began relating the history of Park Enterprises.

"You know, when Grandy, my grandfather, started Park Enterprises," Ethan explained, "it wasn't only for the company to make money to support him and Granny. His ultimate goal had always been to pass the company on to someone in the family."

"And, from what you've told me," Stephanie concluded, "since your father decided to start his own company, and your older brother's interests apparently are focused elsewhere, that someone is—you."

"That's right," Ethan replied. "There were times when I was younger that I felt upset with my father for not working at Park Enterprises. The fact that he didn't work there seemed to create constant friction between him and my grandfather."

Over the course of their relationship, Ethan had given Stephanie bits and pieces of the Park family history, but rarely did Ethan show his emotions or give editorial opinions about the decisions or actions that were made by others, specifically his father or grandfather. Stephanie sensed that this conversation would reveal different facets of the Parks and, more importantly, of the man she loved. She sat back, sipped her wine, and absorbed all that Ethan offered on this peek inside the Park family.

"You see," Ethan continued, "my grandfather was *really* committed to family and the family business. Don't get me wrong, my father is also *extremely* committed to family. It was in the area of my grandfather's business where he and my dad had their major difference of opinion.

317

"Basically, that's how I became involved in Park Enterprises. Trip decided that Park Productions was more to his liking. I couldn't see the hard work, dedication, and mostly my grandfather's commitment go by the wayside. So, when my grandfather became ill and could no longer go on, he could no longer work toward fulfilling all of his goals. I promised him I would continue to build the tradition, fulfill his commitments, and operate Park Enterprises . . . grow the business and keep it in the family. Pass it on . . . ."

Ethan paused as Fredo approached the table to deliver their Vitello Parmigiana. Stephanie's eyes widened as she beheld the enticing platters of cuisine placed in front of her and Ethan.

"Oh my!" Stephanie said after taking in the heavenly flavors. "This is *so* beautiful. And the aromas are *fantastica.*"

Ethan grinned, and with a chuckle added, "If there's one thing that can be said for Mr. Sal, it's that he definitely knows how to put on a show."

"I'll say," Stephanie agreed. "This looks like it belongs on a magazine cover."

"Not to mention, it tastes even more incredible than it looks."

The two leisurely enjoyed the sumptuous meal prepared by Mr. Sal and his team of culinary aficionados.

Ethan finished the last bite of his meal and wiped his mouth with his napkin. He gazed at his wineglass. "What happened to my grandfather was, and actually still is, devastating. Not a day goes by that I don't miss him."

"That's understandable. You were so close to him. What a huge loss."

"Yes, the loss was tremendous," Ethan said. "Still is. But the illness leading up to the loss, that was *extremely* painful. There were so many episodes. So heart-wrenching. We had no idea when it would hit, to what extent it would hit, or what the outcome would be . . . always on edge . . . never knowing what fright might be right around the corner. It's very difficult to live like that."

Stephanie reached over and placed her hand on top of Ethan's. "I'm so sorry. I can't even imagine how hard that must have been."

Ethan looked down at the dessert fork, moved it with his left index finger, and then looked at her. "There's something you need to know, Stephanie." He paused and then slowly continued, "I had a DNA test done to see if I have the gene—the APOE gene."

Stephanie blinked and waited for Ethan go on. He sat still for a moment, collecting his thoughts. The pause lingered almost to the point of being uncomfortable. "And?"

"And, I have it, Stephanie," Ethan croaked. "I have an increased probability of getting Alzheimer's. This means there's an increased probability that my family would have to live through that same kind of hell—"

"But Ethan," Stephanie started, "your family is so close, so tight. They would be there for you, support you, *love* you, no matter what."

"I'm confident of that. But I'm going to ensure they won't have to. I will *never* put my family through suffering like that."

"What do you mean? What are you trying to say?"

Ethan put his hands flat on the table. "I'm saying that I won't put myself in a position where my family would have to take care of me like that."

"Ethan, I love you. I hope you know that. Right now you are dwelling in a world of what ifs. Besides, the way medical science is going, there may be a cure before . . . . Regardless, I would stand by you whether they were good or bad times."

Stephanie's reassurance and dedication touched Ethan's heart. "Stephanie, I *do* love you, too. With you in my corner, I always feel stronger. I feel I can do almost anything. But I don't *ever* want to be a burden."

As Ethan took a sip of wine, he recalled the words he had penned on his To Do list the year Grandy had died: "Do NOT cause my family to suffer such prolonged pain." Ethan thought about those words. He knew he would never want Stephanie to have to endure the suffering brought on by watching him deteriorate as he plummeted through the stages of Alzheimer's.

But Stephanie said I'm dwelling in a world of "what ifs." She's probably right. We'll deal with what comes our way. One way or another . . . .

Fredo once again appeared, this time to remove the dinner plates that had been all but licked clean. Earlier, in a moment of levity, Ethan and Stephanie had giggled when they had discussed licking their plates clean before Fredo would come take them away. They hedged on the side of decorum and decided they would savor the tastes with dignity.

As the couple finished their after-dinner pastry, sfogliatella, Ethan grasped the candlestick closest to his side of the table and moved it next to the one nearest Stephanie, a predetermined signal he had coordinated with Mr. Sal. From seemingly out of nowhere, the soft, soothing sounds of a violin began to fill the room. Stephanie looked up to see that the origin of this melodic music, the violinist, was making his way toward them.

320

She glanced across the table, intending to catch Ethan's reaction. But she discovered he was no longer in his chair. She was caught off guard when she noticed Ethan beside her, and on one knee.

He gently took her hand in his and looked up into Stephanie's eyes. He then presented her with the same blue velvet box that had been on his dresser only a few hours earlier. "Stephanie, you bring such joy and love into my life. Will you marry me?"

Tears of elation glistened in Stephanie's eyes as she nodded and tried to say yes. With overpowering emotion, her vocal cords wouldn't cooperate with her heart's desire to respond verbally.

Ethan opened the box, removed the ring, and placed it on Stephanie's finger.

THIRTY-TWO

TO

FIFTY-THREE YEARS OLD

E.P.

Chapter 16
FORWARD MOVING

The familiar tonal sound created by the elevator indicating to the passengers their ascent to another floor in the Park Enterprises building had a soothing effect on Ethan. He had been a passenger on this elevator many times over the years, as far back as he could recall. His first rides had been in the arms of his grandfather.

As a young boy, he found great delight in pushing the button that would take him and his grandfather to the top floor, to Grandy's spacious office. For young Ethan, being in his grandfather's office and looking out over the city felt more like being on top of the world than just on the top floor of Park Enterprises. He had envisioned his grandfather's influence reaching far past the horizon that was in Ethan's field of vision.

The highly polished brass doors of the elevator created a nearly perfect mirror image of the elevator's occupants. This early in the morning, Ethan was the only occupant. He looked into the image of his own eyes afforded to him by the elevator doors. The eyes that returned Ethan's gaze were no longer those of a young boy full of anticipation about spending the day with his larger-than-life grandfather. Nor were they the eyes of a young adult seeking to spend quality time with his best friend and mentor. No, these were the eyes of a young man deep in thought, carrying sadness and disappointment in his heart.

Ethan thought back to the many times Grandy let him sit behind the big desk pretending to be the boss. Grandy had always told him that someday he would be the one running the company. Grandy's dream, which became Ethan's, had been that they would have several years of operating Park Enterprises together. Then Grandy would retire, and Ethan would occupy the spacious office located on the top of the world.

Grandy's goal did not come to fruition. There was one item on his To Do list that Grandy did not have the opportunity to fulfill. That dreaded disease became an obstacle in his grandfather's plan, an obstacle that he had not been able to overcome. The disease had not only put Ethan and his entire family through several grueling years of anxiety, stress, and uncertainty while simultaneously stealing Grandy's mind, but eventually Alzheimer's had completely taken his grandfather from Ethan and his family. The aftermath produced shattered hearts and oceans of tears. The illness was also responsible for Grandy's unfinished To Do list.

The elevator came to a smooth stop as it reached the top floor. The familiar soft tone indicated to Ethan that he had arrived at his desired destination. It was now time to start the workday. As the elevator doors parted, the image of his troubled eyes vanished, and he put aside thoughts of the terrible disease that had taken his grandfather years ago. Ethan exited the elevator to his right.

His secretary greeted him with a warm smile. "Good morning, Ethan."

"Good morning, Sally. How are you?"

"I'm well," Sally replied.

Ethan continued across the hall to the door of his office, which had once been Grandy's office. He reached into his pocket and retrieved the gold key ring bearing the Park Enterprises logo and his initials. This key ring had a singular key attached. Though he had a key ring containing an array of keys for his home and various other locks and doors, Ethan decided it was more fitting that this key should remain by itself on this particular key ring.

※ ※ ※ ※

Dan Stokes entered as Ethan closed his folio. "Good morning, Ethan."

"Hi, Dan," Ethan said. "It's good to see you."

Dan noticed the Park folio with Ethan's name embossed on the cover and commented, "Is that the folio Barbara made for you when you were in grade school? It looks like it's starting to show its age."

Ethan picked up the folio, looked at it fondly, and caressed the smooth, worn finish. "One and the same. You know us Parks—we find it hard to break from tradition, or things that work."

"Really?" Dan joked. "I hadn't noticed."

"Actually," Ethan said as he gave the worn leather a pat, "this folio is in semi-retirement. I only use for it my To Do list. The days of it attending meetings and going out in the field are in the past. I bring it only to this office and home again. That's it."

Dan smiled. "Your grandfather would be proud of you. You're still using a To Do list, just as he taught you."

Ethan raised an eyebrow. "Although I'm in my thirties, I'd be lost without my To Do list. It truly keeps me focused on my goals."

"It's hard to argue with success," Dan agreed.

The conversation gently came to a standstill. Both men allowed their minds to turn to thoughts of William.

Dan eventually broke the silence. "Speaking of retirement . . . ."

"I know, Dan," Ethan said as he rose from his desk chair indicating for Dan to follow him. "Before we start, let's move to the sitting area where we can be more comfortable."

Located at the opposite end of the office, the sitting area had been positioned in front of the large windows displaying much of the city. Margaret had selected a couple of overstuffed chairs, a leather sofa, and a coffee table to create the atmosphere William had desired. She had set all of this on top of an antique Persian rug. The view, along with the homey furniture, could lead one to believe they were sitting in a penthouse apartment as opposed to the office of the CEO at Park Enterprises.

Visitors fortunate enough to have been invited to sit in these accommodations knew the conversation would not be strictly about the nuts and bolts of business. Yes, the possibility of discussing the logistics of a project existed but were unlikely. The past and current CEOs reserved this space for conversations of a deeper nature.

Ethan and Dan each settled into a chair and then both commented on the spectacular view. Dan began the discussion. "Ethan, as you know, my succession plan has been moving forward. We are a month out from my complete retirement."

"Dan," Ethan replied, "first, thank you for collaborating with me on putting that plan together. It has really been working well. There's only one aspect of it that I don't particularly care for—and you know what it is."

Dan chuckled. "Yes, I understand. But the whole point to the succession plan is that in the end someone has to replace me."

"I know." Ethan said gravely, "I just don't know how we're going to do it without you."

"Ethan, you've been at Park Enterprises for almost ten years now, longer if we count all your visits and days spent here with your grandfather. I've seen you grow from a green college graduate into an amazing businessman and leader.

"Your decision to have Rich Barrington shadow me this past year, to get ready to take my place . . . the only thing I can say about that is—*genius*."

"Rich seemed like a natural selection to me," Ethan said. "He has tenure at Park Enterprises, knows the business, and most importantly, he's a good man."

"That he is," Dan concurred. "You and Rich will do great. You, Mr. Ethan Park, have been practically running Park Enterprises for several years anyway. I have just been your training wheels."

"As usual, Dan, you're right. Time for the training wheels to come off, whether I'm ready or not."

Ethan paused as a soft knock on the door heralded Sally's entrance with a coffee service and cups. She set down the tray, poured two cups of coffee, and left as silently as she'd arrived.

"Thank you, Sally," he said with a shake of his head as the door closed behind her. "I can never get my thanks said before she's already gone again."

"Your grandfather had the same issue with Barbara."

Knowing he liked it black, Ethan handed Dan a cup of coffee. "Things will be different around here without you, Dan. You did so much for my grandfather. He relied heavily on you, your expertise, and your counsel, as do I. He respected you immensely, as do I."

Ethan took a sip of his coffee and set his cup back on the table. "You guided Park Enterprises while I was finishing school. Shoot, guided? No, actually you *grew* the business, when it could have all fallen apart. There was a time early on, right after my grandfather's death, when I didn't think the business was going in the right direction. Now, I realize how wrong I was."

Ethan sat forward and pointed at Dan. "You also took this green college graduate and showed me the ropes. You taught me how to tie certain knots and untie others. I learned more about business from you and my grandfather than I could from reading a library full of business books."

"Ethan," Dan responded with depth in his voice, "thank you. You are exceedingly generous in your assessment of my contributions and skills. However, I believe your perspective to be slightly—actually, heavily—skewed.

"This is about Park Enterprises. This is about *you* and the future of both. I'm confident—in fact, I wouldn't even entertain the idea of retirement if I weren't—that Park Enterprises, with you at the helm, is in good hands."

Ethan stayed silent, so Dan continued. "William, your grandfather, would be truly proud of the leader you have become and, most especially, the *man* that you are." Dan choked up with emotion. "As am I."

Ethan glanced down and then met Dan's gaze. "I will do everything in my power to live up to that, Dan."

※ ※ ※ ※

The sun dipped below the horizon, marking the end to another day. Though the sun's light no longer trickled through the branches of the trees, creating variegated light patterns upon the walking path, the path remained well lit nevertheless. Artificial lighting had been strategically placed to provide safe passage as well as to accentuate the beauty of the fauna. The contrasting use of light, shadows, and vegetation generated an atmosphere conducive to the many moods visitors carried with them as they contemplated the circumstances that put them on the path through the arboretum at Highland Hospital.

The circumstance that led the two brothers to be on the path this particular evening was joyous and marked the beginning of the next generation of the Park family. Ethan and Trip remained silent and deep in their own thoughts as they strolled. With no spoken word or physical indication, the two simultaneously paused in front of the small stand of trees that had been planted by their grandfather, commemorating the birth of their father.

"Astounding," Ethan observed as he read the dedication plaque. "Grandy's ideal of family continuity is coming to fruition."

Trip snickered. "Did you *ever* know Grandy to not get what he wanted?"

"Once or twice," Ethan mused, thinking of their father and then Trip going in a different direction than Grandy envisioned. "I guess for the most part you're right. But it wasn't so much about what *he* wanted. I

331

think, for him, it was more about what he thought best for the family—
for us . . . ."

Ethan's voice trailed off, and the brothers once again fell silent.
After waiting several moments for Ethan to continue, Trip inquired, "It
sounded like you didn't finish that thought. And . . .?"

Ethan reached out to touch the trunk of the tree nearest him. He felt
the coarseness of the bark, the cracks and crevices, and the sturdiness of
the tree. Ethan pondered the structure of the tree and realized that even
though the outer surface of the tree wasn't perfect, it was perfect for the
survival of the tree. It provided the interior of the tree with the right
amount of moisture, air, and flexibility to withstand the elements, no
matter how hot, dry, cold, or windy it was.

"Well," Ethan began again, "he didn't *really* get what he wanted, or
planned. That illness caused him to fail at accomplishing all his goals.
He became the one thing he never wanted to be—dependent upon others
for life's basic needs."

Trip reasoned with his brother, "Ethan, Grandy lived an extraordinary
life. He accomplished more of his goals than most people can ever dream
of." Trip bent to pick up a fallen leaf.

"And look how close the two of you were able to become. That was
something he valued greatly. His life may not have ended the way he
planned or wanted. Whose life does? But he lived on *his* terms and stayed
true to *his* standards."

Trip noticed a faraway look in Ethan's eyes. He reached over and
touched his brother on the shoulder and smiled at him. "I think what he
would *want* right now is for you to not be in a funk, brooding over him
on the day your first child, a son, is about to be born."

Ethan responded to his brother's touch and brought his consciousness to the forefront. "Wow! I went away for a moment there. You sounded just like Grandy. It felt like he was the one talking to me." He took a deep breath and shook his head. "And, just like Grandy always was, you're right. Thanks, Trip."

The two young men continued walking through the arboretum in silence. As they neared the end of the path, Trip stopped. Ethan continued on for several steps before realizing Trip was no longer next to him. He glanced back toward his brother and raised an eyebrow. "Too tired to make it to the end of the path? Should I use the fireman's carry and help you along?"

Trip laughed. "No, little brother, you know I can still outrun you."

Ethan smiled. "Well? Stephanie is preparing to give birth to my first son at any moment. They said it would take about twenty minutes to get her situated in the labor room and that I could go in then. Let's get moving. I want to be there for her."

"Okay, one second, though," Trip said. "I have something serious to discuss with you."

"Really?" Ethan asked teasingly. "I thought you and Grandy said this should be a joyous occasion."

Trip smiled. "It *is* a joyous occasion. Listen, Angela and I talked. Traditionally, since I am the first-born son, it would be me who names a son after myself, Dad, and Grandy. But you were closer to Grandy than anyone. Although Angela and I have not begun our family yet, if you would like to, we both agree that it would be right for you to name your son after him."

333

Ethan blinked, paused, put his hands in his pockets, and blinked again, deeply moved by Trip's thoughtfulness.

"William Park the Fourth," he said softly. "But—"

"It sounds right, Ethan. Go with it. Be gracious, say thank you, then shut up."

Ethan cleared his throat and met Trip's amused gaze with a somber one of his own. "Thank you. If it's okay with Stephanie, I'll take you up on that."

※ ※ ※ ※

The key Ethan held felt foreign and awkward in his hand. It wasn't so much the key itself that induced these feelings; rather, it was the fact that he needed the key at all to open this specific door. During his entire thirty-eight years of life, a key had never been required to open the door to Grandy and Granny's house.

Ethan could not conjure up a memory when he had come to this house and didn't find at least one of his grandparents welcoming him at the family door. This would happen no longer. Margaret—Granny— had passed away. Fortunately, Granny's passing did not bring with it a lengthy illness or the amount of trauma that had been present during Grandy's battle with Alzheimer's. One day Granny was here, the next day she passed peacefully while asleep.

Although to a degree it was a blessing, it had a downside as well. The abruptness of the loss was immensely shocking for everyone. She appeared to be in great health with no debilitating or ambulatory issues. Granny's passing provided no one with the time for emotional or psychological preparedness.

On the other hand, the passing of Grandy had been a slow, arduous trek. For some, the remnants of that trauma remained. The realization that Grandy's condition would cause him to slowly deteriorate was extremely painful. In addition, the pain endured caring for a loved one afflicted with Alzheimer's can run deep and cut sharply to the depth of one's soul. No one, especially Ethan, would acknowledge the thought at the time that Grandy's passing in some ways was almost a relief. But the physical death of Grandy did not remove all the painful memories nor thoughts of dreams unattained

"Daddy," Will inquired, "aren't you going to unlock the door?"

Inserting the key into the door handle, Ethan responded to his six-year-old son, "Yes, I was just thinking about all the times I've walked through this door and never had to use a key."

"It's sort of strange," Will added, "Great-Granny not being here. I'm going to miss her."

"She loved you and your sister very much!" Ethan assured his son. "I'm grateful you and Marianne got to have her in your lives—even if it was only for a little while."

Ethan turned the key in the lock and pushed open the door. The kitchen lights were off. There was no welcoming aroma of fresh coffee or baked goods. The house felt asleep, or more accurately, dead. Yet the memories were vibrantly alive and hit Ethan immediately. As he managed to break through his melancholy, fond recollections lifted the heaviness in his heart and brought a smile to his face.

Will flipped the light switch to the up position. Ethan's memories took on an even more vibrant and realistic presence.

"We had a lot of great times in this kitchen," Ethan reminisced. "It seems like only yesterday your uncle Trip and I were running down the stairs for breakfast after spending the night with Grandy and Granny."

"I like sleepovers at *my* granny's. She always plays games with me and Marianne," Will declared. "I wish I could have played games with Great-Granny and Great-Grandy . . . ."

"Me too —" Ethan sighed, "me too."

The latter part of Will's statement caught Ethan off guard and gave him pause. His children rarely broached the topic of Grandy—not due to any underlying issues, but because they had never known him. Admittedly, he had told his children many stories about their great-grandfather. He had, in fact, built William up as a legend. It seemed obvious to Ethan that the effect of William's disease reached even those yet to be born. The great-grandchildren never had the opportunity to experience Grandy's love and guidance. The early passing of his grandfather had robbed not only those who had lived through the ordeal, but also Ethan's own children.

"Let's get upstairs and grab that paperwork so we can get going to meet your mom and sister for lunch," Ethan said.

As they mounted the stairs, Ethan was reminded of the times he and his brother had played the parts of Lewis and Clark. He decided to take pity on Will by not recounting the stories of "explorations" and sleeping on the landing in a makeshift tent. The sound of Ethan and Will's feet on the stairs echoed up and down the stairwell.

Ethan reached the top of the staircase only to realize that the footstep echoes had diminished by half. He turned around to see Will down below twisting the top of the newel post. Just as Will was giving the top its final turn, Ethan was back at the landing. Both father and son peered into the space, only to find it empty.

"I didn't really think I'd find anything," Will muttered, "but I wanted to check anyway."

Ethan and Will entered William's office. Though Margaret had run the household and estate affairs out of William's office after his passing, she had insisted that the office remain as William had left it. Just because the files for managing these matters had been housed in this office and continued as such didn't mean she shouldn't honor the memory of her husband by keeping his office in order.

Ethan quickly located the drawer containing the estate documents he had come to retrieve. He slid the drawer open, noticing his grandfather's precise handwriting on each of the folder tabs. Ethan removed the files for which he had come and slowly closed the drawer. He turned to Will, "Okay, just one more stop."

As he stood, Ethan caught sight of a line of books on the shelf directly above the file cabinet. Granny's flowery cursive adorned the spines on a row of journals, the Park Family Journals. Ethan pulled one from the shelf.

He opened it and began reading. A lump formed in his throat as his eyes perused Granny's handwriting describing how proud and happy she and Grandy had been when they handed him the keys to the Mustang on his sixteenth birthday. He held the book in his hands, and the memories in his heart.

"What's that, Dad?"

"These books, Will, contain our family story—how I came to be and how you came to be."

Ethan began pulling all of the journals from the shelf. "Give me a hand. We need to put these in the car. These books will introduce you and your sister to what a great man Grandy was."

After locking up the house and placing the journals in the backseat of the car, Ethan and Will walked to the backyard and entered the woodshop. Ethan turned on the overhead lights. He briefly scanned the area. Once again, emotion overtook him. It saddened him to see the woodshop covered in dust. Ethan turned around, reached above the door, and firmly took hold of the object of this mission.

Back outside, Will pushed the button opening the rear hatch on the SUV, Ethan then folded the back seats into their flat position, providing space for the Walt Durbahn's sign he carried. Ethan had postponed taking the sign after William's passing, for in his mind the time to hang the sign in *his* woodshop had come too soon. But, now . . . Ethan gently slid the sign into the back of the vehicle. He reached up and closed the hatch.

Ethan walked to the driver's side of the vehicle. He glanced toward the front of the house. His gaze rested upon the "For Sale" sign in the yard.

A tear fell from the corner of his eye.

※ ※ ※ ※

The second-floor window provided an incredible view of the yard. The property gently rolled downward toward a grove of trees and the small creek, which indicated the farthest boundary of the Park's backyard. Ethan looked out the window and observed the landscape below. Yes, the wooded area, the lush grass, and the bubbling creek together created a breathtaking scene. The aspect of this panorama that most captivated and pleased Ethan's heart had nothing to do with nature. To Ethan, the best part of this scene was the sight of his family enjoying one another's company in a setting he and Stephanie had thoughtfully and lovingly designed.

His parents, wife, and children were all gathered around the pool area. Smoke spiraled from the grill as Bill lifted the lid to check the progress of this afternoon's lunch. Constance and Stephanie laughed and smiled while applauding as Will and Marianne displayed their diving skills. Ethan felt a warm glow as he recalled the Park family gatherings when he, Trip, and Claire had been the ones in the pool showing off for Bill, Constance, Granny, and Grandy.

Ethan brought his attention back to the task at hand so he could get downstairs to join his family, sooner rather than later. He wanted to create family memories with his loved ones—memories that would bring a warm sense of love to Will and Marianne when they recalled the days of their youth. Ethan walked over to his desk and carefully sat down. He reached across the desk, took hold of the Park Enterprises folio, and pulled it forward so it was positioned directly in front of him.

He gazed at the gold Park Enterprises logo along with his name, both forever embossed into the leather. Permanent—the same as his commitment to his grandfather as well as his to Park Enterprises. Just as the company logo and his name had been embossed, so were William's wishes and goals forever embossed into Ethan's psyche.

He methodically opened the folio and removed the most current version of his To Do list from the left-hand pocket. With his prized sterling silver fountain pen, Ethan checked off another item that he had just completed. As his grandfather had instructed him, Ethan reviewed the list as both a reminder of what lay in front of him and a reaffirmation of his commitment to these written goals. He closed the folio and placed it back in its usual position on the desk, just in front of the picture his dad had shot of William and Margaret in their dining room. Ethan smiled with admiration at the determination and drive he saw in his grandfather's eyes.

I'm doing it, Grandy . . . . I'm going to complete your list . . . and mine.

⁂ ⁂ ⁂ ⁂

"Hey." Will bellowed. "Here comes Dad."

Constance, Bill, and Stephanie turned in time to see Ethan, sporting his favorite swimming trunks, race down the back steps of the deck, onto the lower section of the yard, and across the pool apron. He mounted the diving board and performed a perfect belly flop into the pool.

Will and Marianne laughed as their dad sank to the bottom of the pool.

Constance commented, "Someone is going to have a very red belly!"

"Oh, Constance," Stephanie laughed, "you should see when he and Will start competing on who can do the best belly flop."

Ethan climbed out of the pool, wrapped a towel around his waist, and hugged Stephanie. "What did you think, Babe? Do you think I'll make the Olympic diving team?"

"I don't know, Ethan. I think you needed a little more height. I'd give that one a 9 out of 10," Bill interjected.

"Yeah, you're probably right, Dad," Ethan said as he appraised the redness of his belly. "Not enough red in here to take the gold medal."

"Okay, okay, gentlemen." Stephanie said jokingly, "I think you should concentrate on making sure the steaks have the proper amount of redness."

As instructed, Bill and Ethan made their way to the grill to check the progress of the steaks. The moment Ethan raised the lid on the grill, the spicy aroma filled the air. Both men took deep breaths and smiled.

"It doesn't get much better than this," Ethan said.

"You're right about that," Bill agreed. "You have the perfect setup out here."

Ethan smiled. "You know, Dad, I took all of those great memories from the cookouts we had in yours and Mom's backyard. I thought about them and tried to figure out what ways the physical surroundings helped to make those times even more special. I incorporated those elements as part of this design and then added some of mine and Stephanie's own enhancements."

"Again, not to get your head too big," Bill joked, "because I'm sure it was mostly Stephanie's design, but it's still an incredible setting."

Ethan laughed. "You won't find me taking Stephanie's credit. She's the brains behind our operation."

"What's this about the brains of what operation?" Stephanie inquired as she approached father and son.

341

"Ethan was just telling me how he had to design this whole layout on his own with no help from anyone," Bill teased.

"You know better than *that*," Ethan countered.

Bill threw his hands up in surrender. "Now that I have the fire going well, I think it's time for some pool time with my grandkids. Get ready for some old-school belly flops," Bill declared as he trotted toward the pool.

Stephanie shook her head as she watched her father-in-law perform a near-perfect belly flop, to the amusement of her children.

"Dad sure seems to be enjoying retirement." Ethan closed the lid on the grill.

"Yes, and I can tell the kids really love having their grandfather around more," Stephanie replied.

"Time sure flies. I remember when these cookouts were at his and Mom's house," Ethan reminisced. "Now Will is thirteen. And me? I'm just old."

Stephanie laughed. "You, mister, are not old. Because, if you are old, then so am I. And I refuse." Stephanie spread towels out to dry. "You will get old, though, if you keep holing up in your office on the weekends."

Ethan hugged Stephanie. He tilted his head back so he could look directly at his wife. "You know the drill, though. When I complete something on my To Do list, I have to check it off immediately."

"You and that To Do list," Stephanie declared. "Don't you feel a little like Sisyphus, endlessly pushing that rock up the hill, only to have it roll down the other side?"

"No. Even in my forties, I still achieve a great sense of accomplishment when working on my To Do list. It keeps me focused. And, more importantly, I'm fulfilling my commitment to Grandy. I'm stating what I'm going to do—"

Before Ethan could complete his thought, Stephanie finished it for him, "—and then you do it. But when will *it*, whatever *it* is, ever be finished?"

Thinking about the final goal on his To Do list, Ethan confessed, "I'm almost hoping I will *never* be finished."

Chapter 11
ON SHAKY GROUND

W hat's your goal?" Roger quizzed Ethan.

"Let's see, it's four hundred to the center, going left. I'd like a slight draw landing about two hundred fifty down, just on the other side of that little knoll," Ethan explained confidently.

"Okay, you said it." Roger taunted him, "Let's see you do it." He stepped back, arms folded. "And to think, I'm just trying to hit the ball somewhere on the fairway."

Ethan laughed as he pulled his driver from the bag and deftly teed up a ball. He stepped back, placing the ball between himself and the fairway. He stood erect with the driver in his right hand as he stared downrange in a trance-like state.

After several seconds, his body relaxed. He approached the ball from the side, placing the face of his club immediately behind the ball. Ethan looked over his left shoulder down the lush fairway one final time, adjusted his grip, inhaled deeply, and began his backswing. The club and Ethan's arms became one as he brought the head of the club behind

345

his body with his arms fully extended. He initiated the forward motion, causing the clubhead to crash squarely into the ball.

The ball took flight. As it gained altitude, it gently arced away from and to the right of the tee box. The initial flight of the ball gave the impression it would continue its airborne journey forever. The ball did eventually begin its descent, drawing left toward the middle of the fairway and the small grassy knoll for which Ethan had aimed.

The two middle-aged men were transfixed as they scrutinized the flight of the ball. Ethan, remaining in his post-swing position, gazed down the fairway with his hands high over his left shoulder. Roger, holding his driver, a ball, and a tee, stood behind Ethan. They watched as Ethan's ball softly landed in the grassy fairway and rolled just beyond the small hill, the point of his aim.

"That was textbook perfect," Roger commented, amazed at his best friend's skill.

"That, my man," Ethan said, "is what happens when you set a goal, create a plan, and then execute."

Ethan and Roger traded places on the tee box. Roger placed his ball on the tee he had just pushed into the ground. He looked toward Ethan. "Now you are sounding just like your grandfather . . . . *Say what you are going to do and then do it!*"

"I must admit, Grandy's philosophy has served me very well over the years," Ethan affirmed, "even when playing golf."

Roger moved back from the ball in the same manner Ethan did prior to executing his drive. Roger stood erect and peered down the fairway. As he moved to address his ball, he turned to Ethan and joked, "Let's see if this works. I'm just going to hit the ball as hard as I can and then hope it lands somewhere on the fairway near yours."

Ethan laughed. "I guess that's some sort of a plan. Let's see how well you execute it."

Ethan and Roger continued plying their way through the first nine holes of the course. They both managed to hit the ninth green in regulation with shots that would make any club-level golfer proud.

The golf ball falling into the cup created a distinctive sound, which put a smile on Roger's face. He leaned over, reached into the cup, and retrieved his ball. "That's a par for me and a birdie for you. Right?"

Ethan nodded in agreement. "Yes, that front nine was fun. Now we're off to the turn."

"I'm going to match you stroke for stroke on the back nine. That front nine was my best in quite some time. Let's stop at the clubhouse for something to drink and a snack before we hit the back nine."

"Now that sounds like a great plan we should be able to execute successfully," Ethan agreed.

Roger pulled the large golf club-shaped brass door handle and allowed his friend to enter the clubhouse before him.

The atmosphere in the clubhouse had been designed to create the illusion that one had been transported to nineteenth-century Scotland. The multi-leveled ceilings, floors, and walls were crafted of dark wood paneling accented with brass fixtures. Seating consisted of the traditional barstools near the bar as well as plush leather club chairs and couches situated throughout the lodge.

The two longtime friends found seats with a view of the eighteenth green. As they watched a foursome hit their shots toward this green, Tiffany, the clubhouse attendant, approached. "Mr. Park and Mr. Wallace, what can I get for you today?"

Ethan looked at Roger. "What's your pleasure today, Roger? My treat."

"I'll have an iced tea, no lemon," Roger replied.

"And you, Mr. Park?"

"I'll have an Arnold Palmer, please."

"Great," the attendant said with a smile. "I'll have those drinks and some snacks out to you shortly."

"Thank you, Tiffany," Ethan said.

As the attendant left to retrieve the drinks and snacks, the golfers on the eighteenth hole completed their approach shots and were now walking toward the green to finish their round on one of the finest golf courses in the region.

Ethan and Roger watched as the foursome lined up their individual putts. Each player was carefully assessing the undulations of the green's surface, the grain of the grass, and the distance between their ball and the hole.

"Which do you think is harder," Ethan inquired of Roger, "lining up a ten-foot putt on that green, or four years of college?"

Roger smirked. "That's one of the toughest greens you and I have played. I believe the question is, 'Which is harder, watching your eighteen-year-old son leave for college, or sinking a ten-foot putt on that green?'"

Tiffany returned with their drinks and several bowls filled with chips, nuts, and pretzels. After she placed the drinks and bowls of various treats for the men to nosh on before beginning the back nine, the conversation continued.

"Touché," Ethan admitted. "It's hard to believe Will is leaving for college in just a couple of months. It feels like only yesterday I was—"

"Yes, it does seem like yesterday," Roger cut in.

"I'm glad my dad's in good health. It was unbelievably hard being away when I went off to college . . . you know . . . with Grandy's condition. At least Will won't have that bearing on his heart and mind."

Roger placed his glass of iced tea on the table and looked at his best friend. "Your son is going to do great, Ethan. He's a Park, so how could he *not*?"

"I want his experience to be just that—great. He shouldn't . . . *no one* should experience what my family lived through during Grandy's illness, watching him slowly fade from our lives like that. I'm going to make sure I *never* let something like that happen to *my* family due to me."

Roger watched the next group of golfers on the course make their approach shots onto the eighteenth green. He turned to Ethan. "That was such a long time ago. Your grandfather provided you with the tools and knowledge to live a successful life. He would want you to focus on creating a positive attitude and living life to its fullest with your family."

Ethan nodded in agreement. "Of course, you're right. And just like Grandy taught me, I do have a plan—a plan for my family."

Roger tilted his head as if trying to capture an elusive sound. Though he couldn't put his finger on it, something about Ethan's statement filled him with dread.

349

✳ ✳ ✳ ✳

Ethan made it a practice to not bring work home on Saturdays. This morning, though, he sat in his upstairs home office reviewing and finalizing a contract that had been dropped off late Friday by the client's attorney. Time was of the essence. He wanted to have the contract ready for the client first thing Monday.

He signed his name to the documents, placed them back in the folder, and set it on the right-hand corner of his desk. He recalled the many meetings that had taken place with the executives from the client company, Formidable Solutions, to get this project to the contract stage. During the negotiations he had reminded his team to be as fair as possible and offer the client the best solution.

He also insisted that his team, as well as the client's, agree to definite goals and a mapped-out plan to accomplish them. Over the years, Ethan felt Park Enterprises had grown not only in size but in prestige because he had continued to deeply embed Grandy's life philosophy into every project: *Say what you're going to do. Then do it!*

The morning sun glinted through the plantation blinds and onto the corner of his desk. Ethan rose from his chair and walked to the window overlooking the backyard. He reached up and fully opened the blinds. He tilted his head closer to the blinds to take in the spectacular view. The pool water rippled in the light breeze, playing with the reflections of the sun off its surface. Ethan recalled the many family gatherings and parties that had been held in that space—Will's and Marianne's birthday parties, graduations, and holidays.

A nostalgic smile inched its way across his face. He cast his eyes beyond the pool, observing the slow roll the lush St. Augustine grass took into the woods. It reminded Ethan of the final fairway where he and Roger played not long ago. Ethan began replaying that round of golf in reverse.

The slight smile became compressed by the straight line of Ethan's lips, and his brow furrowed. *That turned out to be a decent round of golf . . . a great day with Roger. But it sure could have started better . . . leaving the house without my golf clubs, turning around to go home, and then forgetting why I was even back here at the house.*

Ethan shook his head as if to chase away the memory. *It's a good thing Stephanie met me in the driveway with my clubs and another cup of coffee. This forgetfulness seems to be happening a lot. I wonder if she's noticing? I wonder if . . . .*

A tap on the door brought Ethan back to the present. "Come in."

Marianne bounced in and cheerfully said, "Hi, Dad!"

"Good morning, Marianne. Are you ready?"

"Yep, just checking to see if you are."

"Just about. I'll be down in a minute."

Marianne was back out the door as quickly as she entered.

Ethan glanced out the window, then turned and walked back toward his desk. He picked up his pen and opened the folder. *Oops! I already signed this.*

I could never forget outings with my children. Could I?

✳ ✳ ✳ ✳

The light from the full moon seeped brightly through the branches of the weeping willow trees that were aligned like sentinels along the banks of the creek that bordered the backyard. These soldiers of nature are charged with ensuring that those occupying this space are immersed in an atmosphere rich with the sounds of forest and creek. The long, wispy branches muffle any noise that may try to intrude upon the tranquility of the setting.

Ethan and Stephanie had gone through an extensive search to locate the perfect piece of property upon which to build their home, family, and lives. Once the location was selected, the design process began in earnest. As anxious as they were, this was a process neither Ethan nor Stephanie wished to complete hurriedly.

The young couple were methodical in creating the plan. Ethan employed the skills and experience he acquired through his work at Park Enterprises. Stephanie utilized her impeccable good taste and sense of design. Together, in the early years of their marriage, they set up an outside environment that would embrace their fledgling family as well as their extended family and friends. Their goal had been to have a home that would host many holiday gatherings, special parties, and family events—a home they would fill with loving memories. Ethan and Stephanie had decided, if fate should favor their lives, that this would be the only home in which they would ever live.

Stephanie recalled how during the design process, Ethan, with the help of the architects and contractors, kept a secret from her, something neither one of them rarely did. The only secrets throughout their marriage involved some type of a joyful surprise for the other. Ethan's desire, when drawing the plans for the backyard, was to dazzle Stephanie with a small, secluded area where they would be able to share private, quiet time together. Ethan intended it to be a place where their hearts and minds

352

might meld into one. So, he designed a small brick patio near the back of the property, totally detached from the main backyard. For those who weren't observant, it would be easy to overlook this little niche.

Ethan constructed a low wall of brick planters filled with ivies, Asian jasmine, and an array of small rose bushes to define the edges of the patio. At each of the corners he placed columns adorned with gas lanterns to provide just enough light to enhance this tranquil setting. Not one to overlook even the smallest of details, Ethan equipped the bases on each of these columns with small gas space heaters for those chilly winter evenings so he and Stephanie would be able to relax with a glass of wine and watch the snow gently fall into the woods across the creek. To complete the scene, Ethan furnished the patio with wrought iron furniture painted French Quarter Green and made comfortable with linen-covered cushions.

Stephanie determined that lighting the heaters tonight would not be necessary. A bit of a nip was in the air, but not enough to warrant added heat. A light sweater and the love she felt for Ethan, her family, and her life brought her plenty of warmth. Stephanie turned the flame down on each of the lanterns, enhancing the cozy atmosphere. She relaxed as she leisurely scanned the woods and absorbed the sound of the bubbling water softly caressing the rocks as it made its way downstream.

As Stephanie took a sip of wine, she contemplated how in some instances and places, water had the ability to move rocks and mountains, carve gorges . . . even destroy homes and change lives. The same could be said of fate. Greek mythology said when the Sisters of Fate decide to move a life in a particular direction, one has no choice but to acquiesce and accept the decision of the Greek ladies.

Ethan recounted the stories of William's fate, his illness, and all that it brought with it to Stephanie over the years. The frequency of the retelling diminished over time, but it seemed the effects of the distressing experience had not, especially not for Ethan.

During the first few years after meeting Ethan, Stephanie observed that he was holding onto his grief with an iron fist. She recalled how he often used his grief as a mechanism to vent his anger at his grandfather being taken from him, and then his family, in such a painful manner. This anger fueled his drive to not let William's ideals and values vanish along with him. So, Ethan attacked his work at Park Enterprises with vigor and determination.

The anger eventually subsided, though Stephanie noted that it never went away completely. As the anger waned, it appeared Ethan's drive to succeed at Park Enterprises and fulfill his grandfather's vision increased exponentially.

Stephanie, like everyone in the Park family, heard the mantra many times over the years: *Say what you are going to do. Then do it!* Ethan committed himself to adhering to that motto religiously, but Stephanie had to wonder . . . at what cost? Would it be worth it if everything and everyone else around you suffered?

"There is the *most* beautiful woman in the world," Ethan crooned.

The darkness that had begun to creep into Stephanie's psyche quickly dissipated as she heard her husband's voice. "Ah, you are so sweet."

"You're only saying that because I just gave you a compliment," Ethan joked, "and came bearing a bottle of wine."

"Well, there *is* that."

Ethan placed the bottle of wine on the table and sat in the chair next to Stephanie. A calmness permeated the setting as the two relaxed, absorbing the surrounding sights and sounds of nature. The willows delicately danced in the evening breeze. The soft light from the lanterns threw shadows that moved to the symphony created by the gently flowing creek.

Placing his glass on the table, Ethan interrupted the tranquility with a troubled sigh. "Steph," he began, "when Marianne and I were in the car earlier today, I snapped at her. It really upset her."

"Yes, she came to me and told me about it. She was quite hurt." Stephanie met his gaze. "What happened?"

Ethan shifted his gaze from his wife back out to the creek. He pondered what had transpired at the end of what had been an otherwise wonderful father-daughter day out on the town.

"We had a good time shopping, laughing, and simply spending some time together. We ended the afternoon by stopping for ice cream sundaes before heading home." Ethan continued in a droning manner, "On the drive to the house, we were listening to the radio. Marianne was educating me on today's music trends. I guess my mind drifted because the next thing I knew . . . we were in the parking lot at Park Enterprises.

"When Marianne pointed this out to me . . . I was oblivious as to how we got there . . . almost disoriented. I guess that I got frustrated and . . . well . . . I . . . I took it out on her. It troubled me because I knew I was supposed to be driving home, *not* to work."

Once again, the couple fell into silence. But this was not the silence of tranquility or contentment. For Ethan, this was a silence of angst. Racing through his head were thoughts of a drive long ago that he had taken with his grandfather.

Ethan remembered how Grandy snapped at him in the same way and pretty much for the same reason. The gruffness and abruptness

Ethan received from his grandfather concerning that incident still stung him today. Even more disconcerting, and what Ethan often wondered over the years, was the possibility that Grandy losing his whereabouts while driving that day was one of the early indicators of the onset of his dementia.

Am I more like Grandy than everyone realizes? After all, I do have the gene. "You know," Ethan reflected aloud, "almost the same thing happened to me with Grandy. I wonder—"

Stephanie turned to her husband. "Ethan, just because you have the gene doesn't mean you have Alzheimer's. Yes, we are both well into midlife, but I don't think this one incident is any cause for alarm. Like we usually do, you were probably running on autopilot."

"It's just . . . it was a very hard time . . . not something I would ever want to relive," Ethan halfway mumbled.

"I don't think that's the issue. And, if it were, I still signed on 'for better or worse.' I will be here for you, our children, our family— regardless of what happens."

She slowly shook her head, then lay it on his shoulder. "What I think is really at play here is that you are *so* focused on accomplishing these goals that you have set. It's as if you live governed by your To Do list. It seems to consume you. I know you want to accomplish *so* much for our family. That is one of the many, many things I love about you, Ethan—your commitment and dedication to family. But part of that means enjoying our lives today, as well as storing up the memories to treasure always."

Ethan shut his eyes as she spoke softly and soothingly. He listened to her, soaking up the moment, wanting what she said to be true. He hoped to never be a burden to her.

Stephanie continued, "We already have so much to be thankful for—a supportive family, loving children, a beautiful home, a thriving business."

Ethan took a deep breath, then gently sighed. "Thank you, Stephanie. We do live a charmed life and I am incredibly grateful for that. But the realization that I treated Marianne in such a harsh manner is a dagger through my heart."

He drew his wife closer, his hand behind her neck as he stroked her hair. "My job as your husband, their father, has been *not* to hurt you or our kids but to alleviate any pain that could come your way. And I intend to do just that."

SIXTY YEARS OLD

E.P.

Chapter 18
B REAKING F REE

D uring Ethan's sixtieth year of life, he thought back to all the times over the years he was reminded that Grandy turned sixty years old on the very day that he himself had been born. Throughout his life, Ethan always felt incredibly connected to his grandfather. When Grandy began his descent into Alzheimer's, Ethan also felt a downward pull from within.

Even beyond Grandy's death, Ethan stayed connected to his grandfather by clinging tightly to the To Do list. He was looking at it now. Ethan persevered through life's ups and downs by persistent dedication and commitment to creating goals, achieving those goals, and then marking them off the list. Today, only one item remained unchecked. "Do NOT cause my family to suffer such prolonged pain!"—the final item on his To Do list. Ethan had reached the end of the line.

The metal of the Colt 1911a felt cool to the touch. In Ethan's hand, the weapon was weighty. He extended his thumb and released the gun's safety. With the gun tightly in his grasp, Ethan stared intently at the image of his grandfather in the photo on his desk. Racing thoughts swirled about in his head. *Say what you are going to do. Then do it! Set a goal, create a plan, execute.* Ethan took pride in the way he had lived his life—following through on goals set.

The sound of laughter coming through the open window of his office startled Ethan. He expected to be home alone today. Peering out the window, he was stunned to see Stephanie on the lawn below. Gathered with her was the entire Park clan—his parents, along with his brother and sister, joined by their spouses and children. Then he spotted his own children, Will and Marianne, with their spouses. Clinging tightly to Marianne's leg was two-year old Katherine. Every Park in Ethan's bloodline was present in his backyard.

He noticed a large sign attached to the awning above the outdoor kitchen. "Congratulations, Ethan. You did IT!"

Park family gatherings rarely occurred spontaneously. Normally there was a discussion beforehand when something was in the works. Had he been too focused on . . . or, had it slipped his mind?

The color left Ethan's face. He turned, stepped away from the window, and dropped to his knees. So much pain—and what to do with it? His body started trembling. Tears fell across his cheeks as a mixture of emotion overcame him.

The faint sound of Stephanie's voice lilted its way from the backyard and through the window. His stoic resolve began to dissolve. *No, I have to do what I said I would do!*

※ ※ ※ ※

Bill grabbed the ice bucket from the table. "Stephanie, it looks like we could use more ice. I'll get it. Do you need anything else while I'm inside the house?"

"Yes." Stephanie's eyes sparkled. "Would you please let Ethan know he has a surprise waiting in the backyard?"

Bill entered the kitchen and made his way to the butler's pantry. He knelt down, opened the ice machine door, and began scooping. The ice bucket full, Bill replaced the scoop in its cubby, pulled the door by the handle, and let it fall. The ice machine door closed, followed by a loud bang. Stunned by the unexpected blast, Bill dropped the bucket. It tipped sideways and spewed ice across the ceramic tile floor.

He realized the noise he heard had not emanated from the ice machine door but from something much more powerful. Bill stood and tried to find the source of the sound. He headed to the stairway in the back of the house. Halfway up the stairs, the smell of gunpowder assailed his olfactory senses. Dread of what may have occurred flooded over him.

He grabbed the newel post at the top of the second-floor landing, used his momentum to round the corner, and raced down the hall. An ominous aura filled the hallway as a sliver of light from the last door on the left wafted through a smoky haze.

Bill knew that was the door to Ethan's office. He crashed through the office door, afraid of what he might find. Bill panted heavily, and drops of sweat popped out on his forehead. He found Ethan down on the floor . . . on his knees, with a gun in his hand.

He rushed to his son. "What's going on? What happened? Are you okay?"

"Yes. I was . . . uh . . . Grandy's gun accidentally went off."

"Are you sure you're all right?" Bill's heart pounded out rapid-fire beats.

"It scared me more than anything. Luckily, my library of books caught the bullet."

Bill looked at Ethan and noticed his eyes were puffy and red. He slowly reached for the pistol, took it from his son's clutched fist, and carefully placed it on the desk. He then helped Ethan to his feet and ushered him to the couch. Both men dropped into the sofa.

"I was getting ice . . . " Bill gulped in air between words, " . . . when I heard a round go off. What were you doing with the gun?"

Ethan looked toward the folio on his desk. "I was about to check off the final item on my To Do list—

"What does that have to do with a gun?"

Ethan lowered his eyes. There was no way he could ever tell his father how close he had come to making a deadly decision. "For some reason, the thought of Grandy's gun popped into my mind. I took it out and looked at it, wondering about its history and all. Foolishly, I chambered a round—"

"How did the gun end up discharging?" Bill turned his head, pinning Ethan with his gaze.

"When I set the gun down on the desk, I must have placed it too close to the edge because it fell to the floor. When the gun hit the hardwood, it went off."

The sound of laughter and kids splashing in the pool diverted the conversation. Bill cleared his throat. "You know, Stephanie invited all of us over to surprise you." He stopped and locked eyes with his son. "Are you sure you're all right?"

Ethan reached over and placed his hand on his father's shoulder. "Yes, I'm fine, Dad. A bit shaken. I'm sorry I alarmed you."

Bill let out a sigh. "Stephanie thought it would be special to have everyone here today to help you celebrate Park Enterprises going public. That's no easy task in today's world. Grandy would be proud of you. *I'm* proud of you."

Ethan was deeply moved by his father's words. He got up from the sofa and walked over to the open window. He looked down at his wife, his mother, his children, his nieces, his nephews—alive with activity. He turned back to his father. "Just so you know, today is my last day of working that To Do list."

"Really? That's great. And what was that final item you were about to check off?"

"You know, Dad," Ethan began slowly and thoughtfully, "it no longer matters because I'm shredding the list."

Ethan turned and looked out the window. He was quiet. Bill entered into the silence, still unsure of what just transpired.

Finally, Ethan spoke.

"When I saw everyone outside . . . you and Mom, Trip and his family, Claire with hers . . .Will and Marianne . . . and especially sweet, little Katherine, I realized Grandy never intended for me to live my life driven by a list. A list can only lead you to a place. And although following a list might bring you to a successful place of completion, arriving at that place is not what we should live for."

Ethan stopped, turned, and faced his father. "No, we live for family. That's the goal. We live *because* of family."

Upon hearing those words, Bill felt a sense of relief.

He stood and joined Ethan at the window. In quietude, father and son watched the gathering below.

After several minutes, Bill broke the stillness. "You know, Grandy was a remarkable man. Probably one of the smartest men I've ever known—and dedicated."

Ethan smiled warmly. "Yes, he was indeed that."

Bill continued, "And while I'm sure he would have preferred the end of his life to be more on his terms, I believe he would have been proud of the way his family rallied around him in his final years."

Ethan's throat grew tight. "Dad, did his illness seem like a burden to you?"

"I'm not going to lie, Ethan. It was stressful. But life isn't wrapped in a neat package. Love for family oftentimes calls us to transcend who we think ourselves to be . . . to reconsider our fixed thoughts and behaviors." Bill shook his head as if to snap out of going too far down a tender path.

Ethan wrapped his arms tightly around his father. "I love you, Dad. Thank you for being there for me."

"I love you, too." Bill wiped his eyes, gave Ethan a fatherly slap on the shoulder, and headed toward the door. "Come on down and join everyone at the pool. Your whole family is here to celebrate you."

"All right. I'll only be a minute," Ethan replied.

"Don't be too long," his father called from the hallway.

Ethan walked to the desk, picked up the list, and turned on the paper shredder located in the corner behind his desk. He fed the pages into the shredder, watching closely as the last page vanished, and then turned off the shredder.

After retrieving the Colt from the top of his desk and removing the clip, Ethan placed the gun back in the box handcrafted by his grandfather. Instead of opening the drawer, he walked over to a bookshelf on the other side of the room, taking the box with him. Tucked away behind some books on the bottom shelf was a safe. Ethan knelt down and turned the dial on the outside of the safe, gaining entrance. He placed the box inside, walked back to his desk, and looked down at the Park Enterprises folio laying open. Carefully and deliberately, he closed the weathered folio. Returning to the safe, he placed the folio next to the box holding the gun, shut the safe, and headed for the door.

Just as he was about to cross the threshold, Ethan abruptly stopped, noticing the spent shell casing on the floor near the couch. He bent over and picked up the cartridge.

Ethan returned to his desk, opened the top drawer, and placed the cartridge inside. He closed the drawer and then paused. After looking at the photograph of Grandy and repositioning it slightly, he pressed two fingers to his lips and then tenderly touched the picture on the desk.

Ethan was ready to go downstairs. There was a granddaughter waiting for him . . . .

Epilogue

The lights shone brightly on the stage located in the Frey High School auditorium. Once again, the lights and program design had been provided by Park Productions, which had been the tradition since Bill created the company many years ago.

Once again, these lights were shining down upon the valedictorian of the current graduating class as the recipient delivered her graduation speech. Once again, it was a Park who earned this honor.

"It has a been a great privilege to attend Frey High School with my fellow classmates. We have learned together, grown up together, and now we will graduate together." Katherine paused. She fixed her gaze at those assembled as the audience, along with her classmates, erupted in applause.

Katherine then directed her eyes toward the front row of the audience where she observed her father and mother enthusiastically clapping. Immediately to their left sat her grandmother, Stephanie. Katherine slowly shifted her focus farther down the row. In the final seat sat her beloved grandfather, Ethan. Tears of joy were streaming down her grandfather's face as he proudly made his way to his feet to give his granddaughter a standing ovation. The rest of the audience, as well as Katherine's classmates, followed Ethan's lead. The din of applause increased exponentially.

Just as with Ethan's graduation many years ago, the families, friends, and loved ones gathered backstage to offer congratulations to the newly minted graduates. Ethan and Stephanie walked excitedly among the frivolity. While he eagerly searched for Katherine, Ethan reminisced about his own graduation so long ago. He smiled as he recalled the joy he felt then by accomplishing the goal he had set—to be valedictorian. Ethan also remembered all the hard work and dedication it had taken to accomplish that goal. The energy emanating from the graduates, friends, and families in the room also brought to mind thoughts of the overwhelming disappointment Ethan had felt immediately after his own graduation in this very building. The man who had done so much to help him accomplish his goal, his grandfather, had not been present at the celebration of the accomplishment. Ethan winced.

He quickly brushed the thoughts aside and let the joy of the occasion wrap warmly around his heart.

Stephanie spotted Katherine first and picked up the pace to reach her. "Hold on, sweetheart, I'm still figuring out how to get this new knee up to speed," Ethan said with a laugh.

"I'm sorry, dear," Stephanie stated as she slowed her pace and wrapped her arm more tightly around Ethan's waist.

Katherine enveloped her grandparents in a firm group hug. "Gram and GeeToo—" as Ethan was known to his family "—I'm so glad you made it!"

As they released their embrace, Ethan wiped tears from his cheeks. He grinned at his granddaughter. "There is nothing that would have kept me away from seeing you on that stage giving your valedictory speech today. I would have crawled on my hands and my new titanium alloy knee to be here."

Katherine chuckled.

As Ethan was finishing his boast, Marianne, her husband Paul, and Uncle Trip arrived to commend the beaming graduate. "GeeToo, we had you covered. You're not crawling anywhere as long as Trip and I are around," Paul said with a clap on his father-in-law's back.

Ethan looked at Paul and then Trip. "Thank you both for everything you've done since my knee surgery. I've never felt more helpless. You guys have literally shouldered the load of me and for me."

Trip smiled and hugged his brother tightly. "Ethan, that's what family is for. We're here to help."

Ethan replied, "I know, but I've been a big burden recently."

Trip released his grip and locked eyes with his brother. "It's not a burden when it's family. It's a privilege. When someone in our family is in need, it's a greater opportunity to show them how much we love them."

The brothers held their gaze for several seconds. "Trip, you're right," Ethan said. "It took me too long to figure that out. But I'm grateful I finally did."

My Parker Fountain Pen

The pen on the cover of this book originated with my Grandmother, Teresa Blasi Rojas, who gave it to her daughter (my mother), Maria del Pilar Rojas Blasi Parrie, when I was born. She wanted my mother to use it to write in my baby book.

When my father was in the U.S. Navy, he was stationed in Spain which is where my mother was born and raised. In 1960, my mother and father married and moved to the U.S. I have many memories as a young boy of my mom sitting at our dining room table writing letters home to Spain on those super thin pieces of onion paper with this pen. As a side note, my mother also typed letters to home on an old Smith Corona manual typewriter, which I still have.

In her early thirties, Mom contracted cancer. When the effects of cancer caught up to her later in life and she knew her time was short, she called me into her room. She opened her dresser drawer, pulled out an old jewelry box, and retrieved the pen. She wanted to give it to me before she passed.

My mother was very particular about the type of ink that went into the pen. When it was time to add ink, she called me over to watch because she knew I was fascinated with the process. It was something, the way in which the ink would draw into the pen via the little pump handle on the side. Over time, I visited quite a few different stationary stores, etc., looking for the special ink. Eventually, I found a place to purchase the proper ink – the bottle "must" have the little reservoir just inside. I used the pen at work, strictly for signing documents, for several months but became concerned I might lose it, so I decided to retire it. Now, it has a place of honor on my desk and will be handed down to one of my children.

Several years ago, I was in Calgary for my daughter's wedding. I had a day to explore the city, where I stumbled upon a little stationary store. Inside I found a modern version (ball point) of the same pen. I bought it, and that is the pen I use on a daily basis and the one that I will use at book signings for *Ethan Park*.

Acknowledgements

I would like, first and foremost, to thank my parents, who encouraged me to pursue this creative endeavor. One of the last things my father told me before passing away in 2020 was "Write your book!"

Well, Dad, I did it! Here it is.

Of course, there are many friends and other family members who encouraged, prodded, cajoled, and helped me throughout my life. They patiently listened to my many story ideas as I often spoke about *what would make a great book or movie*. Thank you for humoring me in all those discussions! I realize I must have hijacked numerous conversations over the years. But through all of those story-tirades, you all patiently listened. At last, there are tangible results.

A few people need to be singled out. First, there is Granny. She introduced me to reading as a toddler. As a result of sitting with her in the green rocker over many hours, I learned how to read *Stop That Ball*. Through her tutelage, I discovered that reading books is fun.

Rich and Margie, my "reading cousins," introduced me to books that challenged the mind and soul. On those long summer days when it was too hot and sticky to do anything other than read, we explored new worlds and expanded our horizons and minds.

There is also a deep indebtedness I feel toward my close friends who heard me talking about Ethan, William, and the entire Park family as if they were people who exist in the real world. To me they are real. The writing of this book has brought them to life both in my mind and heart. Thank you, Frank, Karen, Dan, Kelli, and Cathy N. for reading the very first, incredibly rough draft. The fact you took time to read something of this length means the world to me. Your feedback and support have been invaluable.

Thank you, also, to my family who agreed to read and provide comment on that early iteration into Ethan's journey: Jim, Sheila, Uncle, Lizzie, Eric, Courtney, Mike, Will and Yakira. I promise you all, I won't put you through such a rough first draft again.

I wish to give a tip of the hat to Candy at Fruitbearer Publishing, LLC. From our first phone conversation I knew she would be the person to get this book to print. Candy, thank you for sharing your story *I've Never Loved Him More*. Your journey with Drew inspired me to forge ahead with *Ethan Park*.

A huge thank you to Connie (also at Fruitbearer Publishing, LLC), the "editor." And edit she did. Through the many iterations of Ethan's trials and tribulations, Connie imparted to me vast amounts of knowledge and technique that helped make *Ethan Park* a better story. She was extremely patient with me as I tried to get what was in my head onto paper. Thank you for your perseverance and dedication to this project. It's no wonder you've had success in this field!

I'm not sure when Candy asked Elizabeth to take on the role of author liaison, representing Fruitbearer Publishing, LLC, that Elizabeth realized it would require so many lengthy phone calls and too many emails to be counted to get this book to print. Elizabeth displayed an amazing amount of patience and tact in dealing with the plethora of "rookie" questions I posed; not to mention my most persistent question, "When will this part be finished? What's the next step? When will it be done?" On top of all of that, Elizabeth attacked this project with an incredible amount of enthusiasm. She went the extra mile(s) by bringing new ideas, thoughts, and creativity to the project to make the book even more special.

It's one thing to write a book, it's another for it to be visually appealing. Helen (from Fruitbearer Publishing, LLC) took the raw words of *Ethan Park* and created something for the eye to behold. She managed to take my rough visual ideas, fine tune them into something coherent, and create a visually stunning presentation.

It has been a joy and a Blessing to work with everyone at Fruitbearer. Thank you for your knowledge, support, and great care.

Lastly, and definitely not least, Ethan would not exist, would not have come to life, without the help of Buscia. She and I spent countless hours on the phone and through video calls discussing my verbosity. She listened to many of my creative idiosyncrasies and humored me even when they veered too far off the path. We exchanged hundreds of emails as Ethan's life unfolded on the pages before us. The hours we spent poring over text and discussing the next scene seem a blur.

Buscia, you stuck with me through it all and helped me realize a dream. Thank you!!!

Peter P.

About the Author

Peter grew up along the shores of Lake Ponchartrain. He has been fortunate enough to have lived in several different areas throughout the U.S. His extended family hails from southwestern Louisiana and across the Atlantic to Barcelona, Spain.

It was during summer stays with cousins who lived amid the rice farms of southwestern Louisiana when Peter developed a passion for reading and knowledge. From those early years of curling up with a book under the oaks to escape the summer sun along the bayous, to evenings nestled next to a warm fire during frigid winters in the Rockies, Peter always sought out a place and time to read.

A thirty-year career in broadcasting provided Peter with opportunities to travel extensively throughout both the U.S. and abroad. These travels immersed him in a multitude of different cultures—from the U.S., and Europe to Asia and Central America. During these sojourns, he amassed story ideas, plot lines and anecdotes for use in his own novels.

Peter was raised in a culture of family-owned businesses from restaurants to auto-repair shops, and technology-based companies to art galleries. At an early age he began watching and learning as his grandparents, parents, and other relatives built businesses through hard work, perseverance, and the relationships they developed with their employees and their customers.

When he is not writing, Peter spends time playing golf, riding motorcycles with his lifelong friends, and traveling the U.S. exploring its various cultures, traditions, and people.

To Order

For autographed copies or speaking engagements,
contact the author:
Peter Parrie
peter@parriebooks.com

Also available from your
favorite bookstore